SoulBound

SoulBound

Greg Pappas

Library of Congress Control Number: 2009906361
ISBN: Hardcover   978-1-4415-4937-2
                Softcover   978-1-4415-4936-5

The cover art, entitled "Strangely Familiar," is by renowned artist Rein Nomm.

To contact Greg, send e-mails to: SoulBoundTheNovel@gmail.com

This book was printed in the United States of America.

To order additional copies of this book, contact:
Xlibris Corporation
1-888-795-4274
www.Xlibris.com
Orders@Xlibris.com

61914

A word from the author—

First and *foremost,* I'd like to thank my nephew, Tommy Duncan, for challenging me to write a book and for his encouragement and collaboration in the trying process of getting it done. I'd also like to thank my family for their tremendous support, my friends from OriolesHangout.com, as well as my many tax clients for their support and encouragement.

I'd also like to thank Harford County Sheriff's Office, Sergeant Dave Betz and his wife Julie, FBI relations man, Neal Schiff, and the local Baltimore FBI Office's Rich Wolf, for their kind words and important technical assistance.

Last but not least, a very special thank-you to Barbara Hall and Hank Scudder for their lengthy efforts in polishing the final product.

Thank you all.

—Greg Pappas

Chapter 1
Three Seconds

April 6, 1994

The cool wind blew softly through the open bedroom window, and the ceiling fan whispered rhythmically in the heart of the spring night. Jimmy always liked it a bit chilly. He lay upon his bed trying to write a poem with only moonlight to see by, as his little brother, Alex, slept peacefully across the room.

They lived in Annapolis, Maryland, but were on a mini-vacation, along with their parents, at their Aunt Bonnie's home in South Baltimore. Aunt Bonnie was their dad's sister. She lived alone with her three cats: Samurai, Mocha, and Nino.

His family went there a lot, and, as always, Jimmy's father had taken them to visit the many tourist sites in the area. Among them was Alex's favorite, Fort McHenry, the historical site where American troops courageously withstood the British naval bombardment in the War of 1812, which inspired Francis Scott Key to write "The Star-Spangled Banner."

Jimmy shifted on his bed, trying to find the words to express his deepest love for Danielle Fuentes, but was lost as usual. Words did not come easily to him, as his poor grade in English class would attest. He hated his English class and felt stupid with each venture into Mrs. Williams's room. He was embarrassed to be there, as being twelve in the fifth grade (the result of being held back in the third grade) made him a year or so older than the other kids. The advantage was that he was bigger than the other kids, which curbed any open mocking. Being the only boy in school with a faintly developing mustache didn't hurt either.

Jimmy thought Dani was the most beautiful girl in the world. They were classmates in English, and he remembered her mentioning her love of romantic poetry during a lesson earlier that year. This was his big chance to impress her and he wasn't going to blow it. Then . . . it happened fast; in three seconds, his life changed forever (. . . 3). A shimmering glow radiated through the window into the room (. . . 2), and by the time he realized something strange was happening (. . . 1), he felt a surge of . . . something . . . fill him . . . and then darkness.

Alex's cry of "Breakfast!" the following morning startled Jimmy awake. He opened his eyes and noticed something odd; he was sweating still, and more importantly, had wet the bed. *Oh boy* . . . He hadn't wet the bed in years, and he needed to hide the evidence. Jimmy hastily removed the sheets and blanket and flipped the mattress onto its other side. After remaking the bed and tidying up, he quickly showered before making his way downstairs.

"James Carson Kassakatis!" his mother hollered, just as he came into her view. She then continued,

"Oh, there you are, sorry sweetheart, I thought you were still in bed." She playfully messed up his already messy dark hair.

Jimmy's parents were avid antique collectors; his father, Chris, had completed his ninth year as a history teacher at the nearby Bryan Preparatory School, and his mother, Cheri, was a local Annapolis historian. Jimmy and Alex grew up in a home full of genuine respect for other cultures and peoples, although neither shared their parent's affinity for the past . . . as yet.

The smell of pancakes and sausage caught Jimmy's attention as he made his way into the kitchen. His redheaded little brother, who was two years his junior, was halfway through his plate as Jimmy sat down to eat. Their father had just finished his plate and said he would be back soon, mentioning that he needed to go to the store.

Chris grabbed his keys and waved to his sister and wife as he headed out the door. The women were sitting in the living room chatting.

Jimmy sat quietly as he ate. It was strange that he ate pancakes *with* sausage, because he hated sausage. His head was spinning with what to tell his parents, or whether he should even mention the previous night's event. He noticed Alex picking his toenails at the table, so he threw a patty of sausage, hit Alex right upside his head, and watched as Alex's face turned a shade that nearly matched his hair color.

Alex screamed bloody murder, and upon locating the now-broken patty, he stood threatening Jimmy, as if he was going to throw it back—or worse.

The older knew the younger wouldn't dare.

Their mother soon appeared and started asking what was going on.

Jimmy said he was sorry that he threw the sausage at Alex, but that he had warned him to stop doing *that* at the table . . . it was disgusting.

Alex said he wasn't doing *that* but merely attempting to pull a splinter from his foot . . . whereupon he showed the still-stuck splinter.

Jimmy was shocked that his brother was telling the truth, being it was such a rarity.

Their mother demanded an apology, and Jimmy did so, begrudgingly.

The younger boy said nothing, and still in a huff, walked upstairs a few moments before he headed outside. Jimmy finished eating while his mother muttered disapprovingly to herself at the sink.

All he heard was ". . . and your uncle would never have . . ." as he went back upstairs to think. His mom stopped muttering as her son had gone too far off to hear her . . . and she had a tear running down her cheek as she remembered her brother.

Jimmy had been named after her brother Jim (James Carson), who supposedly overdosed when he was a teenager, many years before. Now, her brother's memory lived only within the mind . . . of a still-saddened sister.

Chapter 2

Days of Future Past

Jimmy Kassakatis (Kas-ah-cat-iss, Greek) had a vivid imagination, so he figured he must have dreamt the weird sensation he'd had the night before. Then again, *it didn't feel like a dream. And it wasn't anything like . . .* he paused to consider an appropriate term *. . . the visions.*

His imagination was, truth be told, a bit unimaginative, until he suffered a seizure when he was seven, falling from his top bunk bed onto the hardwood floor below. It happened in November of 1989 . . . Alex had screamed as his brother thrashed upon the floor.

Only moments later, their parents rushed into the room in an understandably panicked state. Jimmy bit his father's fingers hard before Chris managed to secure his leather wallet into his son's mouth, pressing his tongue down, thinking in line with the misconception that the wallet would prevent the boy from swallowing his tongue. Jimmy was taken to the emergency room and, hours later, was found to have suffered a seizure. A brain scan had revealed a high level of epileptic activity, so the doctors prescribed Phenobarbital.

He took the medicine for a few years, but somehow, remarkably, during these years, he had developed an uncanny ability to predict the future—whether it was a natural phenomena or a drug-induced one—remained a mystery.

It began on January 4, 1990 . . . when Jimmy interrupted his mother's telephone conversation and told his mom that a train was going to crash that day and many people were going to die. Sure enough, it happened; a passenger train in Ghotki, Pakistan, crashed, killing 307. Jimmy's accuracy and matter-of-fact demeanor shook his mom considerably.

That same year in mid-July, Jimmy received another strange vision and immediately drew what he saw. He hung the drawing up on the refrigerator, then forgot about it and went on with his day. His mom noticed the drawing soon afterward. She was concerned as she held the disturbing drawing in her hands, depicting death and destruction . . . but then she overheard the television reporting that an earthquake had struck the Philippines. Cheri immediately rushed to see. There on the screen was a photo taken after the quake struck . . . it looked exactly as Jimmy had drawn it!

A couple of years of periodic predictions and spooky-good accuracy came and went, and then Jimmy's parents began weaning him off his medication. Slowly, but surely, his "visions" decreased, until they ended almost entirely.

The last thing Jimstrodomus predicted came at a softball field. It was September 1993, just seven months before the incident with the strange light at Aunt Bonnie's. He had joined his brother and mom to watch his dad play softball. His mother introduced him to Miss Connie, the wife of "Sarge" Grimm, a teammate of Chris's. Miss Connie was obviously pregnant.

Cheri asked her son, "Jimmy, can you tell Miss Connie what she'll have, a boy or girl?"

Without hesitation he said, "Both. One boy and a girl, both with blond hair and blue eyes . . . just like their mother."

Miss Connie laughed a bit and said that she was only having one, but two months later, she had twins, a boy and a girl, both with blond hair and blue eyes . . . just like their mother.

Chapter 3
Second Soul

Jimmy knew that vacation would end in two days, and with the visit to Fort McHenry over, he could relax for a day before packing and returning home to Annapolis.

Samurai or "Sam," as Aunt Bonnie called him, purred his way into the room and curled up beside Jimmy. Sam was a cool, sleek, gray cat, and the youngest of Aunt Bonnie's three cats. Sam took a liking to Jimmy after not being seen for the first three days here. Stroking the cat's back, Jimmy noticed that a small patch of hair was missing. Then, as the cat turned to look at Jimmy, he noticed something else wrong. He immediately, yet gently, grabbed Sam's head and turned his face so that he could see into the cat's mouth. *Hmmmm . . .* , he thought, noticing the redness and swelling . . . *could be Eosinophilic Granuloma.*

In danger from this gum and skin disease, Sam needed immediate care. Jimmy gently picked him up and brought him downstairs to bring this to Aunt Bonnie's attention.

Minutes after his aunt rushed the cat to the vet, Jimmy's mother asked him the obvious question: "How did you know?"

He looked at her strangely, seemingly in a daze, and shrugged his shoulders before commenting that he must have read about it in a magazine or something. That answer seemed to satisfy her curiosity, and she kissed him on the cheek and told him he was a good boy.

Jimmy barely heard her as he thought to himself—*What . . . what's wrong with me?*

Alex had returned about this time and looked hopelessly bored. He asked Jimmy to take a walk down to Lynnwood's music store, as Alex played the violin in his school's music class. His little brother seemed gifted in music and schoolwork, whereas "gifted" was a word Jimmy had never heard associated with his name. Jimmy didn't like the violin or have any interest in musical instruments, but at this moment, he thought if he would ever want to learn one, then it would be the guitar. It seemed the coolest, but Jimmy knew he was just too lazy to learn.

For some reason, his expected response of "No thanks" was a resounding "Sure!" and the pair began to run off. The boys got one step outside before nearly knocking their dad over.

Chris stumbled a bit before securing his balance and the bag of groceries he carried.

"Sorry, Dad," the brothers echoed, as Chris eyed them curiously.

He then asked, "So, where's the fire?"

The dumbfounded look upon his sons' faces caused Chris to laugh heartily and ask the boys what they were up to in such a hurry.

Alex explained they were off to Lynnwood's to check out the latest instruments.

"Well, will you be passing by Tremont's (Candy Shop)?" he asked the pair.

Jimmy spoke up and said that they would, and then asked his father if either he or their mom wanted anything.

Chris was pleased with Jimmy's answer and pulled a twenty from his pocket and handed it to him. "Take this and get yourselves whatever you like, and I'll be sure to swing by there myself later to get your mother a little something."

The boys were ecstatic and thanked their father repeatedly. Just as they were rushing off, they could hear their dad yelling to them, "Take care . . . and beware the reluctant dragon!"

It was something Chris said often, but they had no idea what he meant. Though they had asked him to explain it on many occasions, Chris simply said. "There are some things in life you need to figure out on your own"—one of many lessons he instilled in them.

As they would be heading home in the morning, they were determined not to waste their last day of vacation. Leaving Tremont's with a Halloween-like bounty, they walked a few blocks farther to Lynnwood's. It was a nice South Baltimore neighborhood where most of the older women called the boys "hon," which was short for honey, but sounded like "hawn."

The marble steps that rested in front of most of the row of homes shone brightly in the sunlight. The sun felt warm, giving slight reprieve from the cool breezy day. Alex informed Jimmy that Mr. Goralski, the storekeeper, was a nice man, but they needed to speak up a bit because he wore a hearing aid. The youngest Kassakatis had frequented this shop and had gotten to be a familiar visitor.

The boys arrived with two rather large candy bags and sat them down just inside the shop door. An elderly man with horn-rimmed glasses and a gray cardigan sweater was in the shop as the two boys entered.

"Good morning, boys," said Mr. Goralski.

The boys returned his greeting and proceeded to look around . . . checking out the latest instruments. Naturally, Alex walked over to the violins and asked Mr. Goralski in a loud voice if it was okay to play one.

Mr. Goralski agreed and the boy set right to it. For a ten-year-old, he sure could play.

Jimmy's mind seemed in two places at once, and he felt . . . odd. There was no other way to describe it. That's when he saw the acoustic guitar. He walked over to it and picked it up. Yup, it was a top-of-the-line "Ovation" model. He felt a surge of something within, an excitement of sorts. Jimmy sat down on a nearby chair and, amazingly, began to play. This foreign instrument, one he had never even touched before, resounded in James Taylor's melodic "Fire and Rain."

"I've seen fire and I've seen rain. I've seen sunny days that I thought would never end . . ." Jimmy sung aloud in a sweet soulful voice.

Mr. Goralski and Alex stopped what they were doing, their eyes focused on the boy with the guitar. Although he struggled slightly, it was obvious he had played before . . . and very well indeed. He finished "Fire and Rain" and continued on playing Jim Croce, Joan Baez, and Simon & Garfunkel tunes, with his eyes shut tight.

"Jimmy?!" yelled Alex, who was astonished yet somewhat concerned.

Mr. Goralski yelled for Jimmy at the end of Croce's "Time in a Bottle," but the boy seemed in another world, never flinching as his brother and Mr. Goralski continued to try to get his attention.

When he stopped playing, a half hour or so had passed. He opened his eyes to looks of shock. His parents were there now, and had been shaking him, as their hands were still gripping his shoulders.

My parents?

Alex had used the phone to call them and had stammered through an explanation of the situation at the shop.

Jimmy went to bed upon arriving home and was thankful that his parents did not go too overboard with their questions.

"I don't know." "I'm not sure," was all he could offer them in explanation.

Chris and Cheri gave each other a look that meant they might need to seek professional help.

As worried about him as they were, their concern was nothing compared to his. He felt odd inside . . . as if he had somehow changed. He was quite terrified. He felt things he had never felt, knew things he had no reason to know and—as one might expect—his twelve-year-old mind couldn't quite wrap his head around what was happening.

That was a long time ago, a lifetime it seems, but almost yesterday, all at the same time. Professor Jimmy Kassakatis was thinking about the beginning of his fateful journey into madness and wonderment, fourteen years prior, but it always came to this: "All we are . . . are years in the sun."

That's what Marie says. Marie Anne Beale . . . Jimmy's pet veterinarian and guitar-playing poet.

The first of twelve.

His oldest friend.

And besides his own, his second soul.

Chapter 4
Marie Anne Beale

Marie was the first of twelve souls that Jimmy had "absorbed," "collected," or, even better yet, "bonded with." It was her soul—that shimmering light—that had collided into Jimmy the night he was writing the poem . . . that April night in 1994 . . . the night that changed everything. She was the first of the SoulBound, just thirty-one when she drowned in Baltimore's Inner Harbor in 1981.

· · · · · · · · · · · · · · · · · · ·

Marie Anne Beale was born in Niagara Falls, New York, on February 22, 1950. She had moved to New York City at eighteen and studied to be a veterinarian. It was 1968, and her world was just soooo groovy. She played guitar, sang her favorite tunes of the times to help pay for school, and was a true human being. She protested against the Vietnam War and marched with thousands on numerous occasions. She loved animals and despised anyone who mistreated them. She became a vet as she had always dreamed, and was among the best young vets in New York.

She had moved to Baltimore in 1978 to be close to her mother. Her mother, Ashley, wasn't much of a mother when Marie was little, as Ashley left Marie's father and abandoned Marie and her two older brothers when Marie was just eleven. Ashley wandered through life drunk for nearly fourteen years until being "saved."

Wendy Peters did indeed save her, as she was Ashley's Alcoholics Anonymous Sponsor. It was she who set Ashley on the 12-Steps and saw her through. While there, Ashley got to know a regular named Wilson Purdy, a devout Christian who had lost faith and was court-ordered to attend the meetings after a DUI.

Through their struggles together, their friendship bloomed, and eventually the two got married in the spring of '75. They both began attending church again, and each made their peace with God and their pasts. In the fall of '77, Ashley found the courage to contact and ask forgiveness of Marie and her siblings. Ashley was a very different woman now. She was loving, caring, and a real sweet woman. It was easy to see where Marie got her disposition.

Wilson made very good money as the owner of a construction business, and Ashley convinced him to entice Marie to come to Baltimore to open her own veterinary hospital. He would cover all the costs and have her staffed with two employees as well. He only asked that he be allowed to name the place.

Marie was completely giddy. She moved and opened "Our Savior's Animal Hospital" in September 1979, and ran a successful and rewarding business.

During an off day in July 1981, she was on a first date with a man named Alan Howard. She rarely treated herself and decided to take a chance. He seemed nice enough, opening the doors for her and doing other gentlemanly deeds. They had walked about the Inner Harbor one bright sunny day, when Alan suggested they ride a water taxi. A water taxi is a twenty-foot-long, shallow boat with bench seats meant for carrying passengers about the harbor. These taxis were safe and pleasant experiences on most rides; however, this one ride would be anything but.

Distracted by a pretty girl, who was yelling to him from the shore, the taxi pilot had bumped excessively hard into the drop-off/ pick-up spot. Marie and Alan were knocked overboard, and Marie's head struck the hard wall. She disappeared beneath the water.

After twenty minutes, authorities had to force Alan out of the water; he had repeatedly searched in vain for his date. Divers found Marie's body an hour later.

Over the weeks and months since Marie's spirit had entered into him, Jimmy learned about her . . . and she about him.

It started slowly, with her saying *"Hello"* to him as he lay in bed to go to sleep, about ten days after they had become SoulBound. Her "voice" had not been audible, but rather internal. The surprise was that Jimmy hadn't reacted as expected, but almost felt at ease with this revelation.

Their new "life" together was certainly extraordinary, but there was an understanding, something unsaid, something that just seemed right. Marie had indeed died, and in her fear of the moments following, decided against going into The Light that formed before her. She became what most people often referred to as a ghost . . . a lost spirit. She was only nominally aware of her surroundings and had not felt right in her mind until after merging into Jimmy.

Marie was generally quiet, yet she would occasionally mind-speak to Jimmy when she felt he needed a voice of reason.

One night while he lay in bed, he made the decision to ask Marie why she came into him. It was an awkward moment, and he was afraid that he had overstepped his bounds. But she, in her sweet voice, told him that she was merely a lost soul trying to find The Light and that *his* "light" drew her to him, sort of like a moth to a flame. She went on to explain that she had tried on a number of occasions to move back out of him, but seemed stuck within him. She also explained that she had very few answers for him. She had no idea why this happened.

He was still a bit confused, but merely closed his eyes and wondered about the "light" he had within him; the one that had drawn her to him.

Days later, he finished the poem he had been writing for Danielle . . . the poem he was working out on the night Marie's merge shocked him unconscious. He seemed to have a much better knack for words since then. It went like this:

"You do not see me, as I seem gray . . .
Blending into a too gray world
But there are colors beneath the veil you see . . .
A boy whose heart beats for thee . . .
A rhythm meant for a special girl
Open your eyes my darling and smile . . .
I await you with arms open wide
Come talk with me?
—Jimmy"

He had given the poem to Danielle in the hallway by her locker as she was grabbing some books. Danielle took the page and read it. Then, as Jimmy's hopes were peaking, she laughed aloud after reading it, showed it to her girlfriends in the hall, and again to other girls in the classroom before the class began. She looked at him and mouthed "No way."

The sounds of laughter humiliated him. He was crushed—like a bug-on-a-windshield crushed. That took quite a while to get over, but at least Marie was there for him, as always, a light in his darkness.

Author's Note: Life is funny sometimes, as Danielle and Jimmy became good friends during Jimmy's last year in high school. She had apologized for being so inconsiderate when they were younger, and said that what he wrote had been very sweet. She had become a very cool person. They fell out of touch after graduation, but Jimmy learned a couple of years later that she had been killed in a car accident.

People *can* change, and life, well . . . it's just too short for grudges.

Chapter 5
Mongolia

June 1996.

In the summer of '96, Jimmy's father, Chris, successfully organized a trip to Mongolia. Many of his students and a few colleagues from nearby colleges were off to see the sites of such legendary figures as Attila the Hun and Chingiz (Genghis) Khan. (Chris refused to call Chingiz "Genghis" in the traditional way, basing his pronunciation on research he and other colleagues labored on.)

Jimmy had absolutely no interest in going, so naturally, Chris took him along. Alex had been "spared," because his mother felt he was a bit *too* young.

Jimmy was miserable the whole way there. Airports *and* passports *and* body searches *and* luggage foul-ups, *and, and, and . . .*

Jimmy was fourteen now and had actually done very well the past school year, earning top honors for the seventh grade. He felt strongly that he had earned a real summer vacation, not an exile/punishment.

Mongolia was bleak. It wasn't nearly as cold as one might expect, but compared with Annapolis in June, it felt like the Ice Age. With two local guides, the group set out for the steppes where

Chingiz Khan's empire had roots. The rocky terrain was difficult to travel, but their guides seemed unfazed. The mountains stood like stone sentinels, guarding some unseen treasure. They visited a temple that was, well . . . powerful. It was weird, but Jimmy felt a sense of honor and peace there. Bill Kitt, Chris's closest friend and co-leader of the trip, remarked that they were standing at a place of great significance. He explained that the spirit of Chingiz Khan was said to reside at the temple, and it was Mongolia's holiest shrine.

The researchers soon set off for the site of Chingiz Khan's final ascension to becoming Mongolia's greatest leader, and, to some, a living God. He had been born Temujin, the son of a Kiyat-Borjigid chieftain named Yisugei. Temujin, though born as a son of a chieftain, suffered many hardships. His father was poisoned by a rival clan and died, scattering the Kiyat-Borjigid to the four winds. Years later, his wife was kidnapped by another rival clan.

Temujin wisely sought the aid of a mighty clan leader, and with his help, he cunningly and savagely destroyed those who had taken his wife. His wife was saved and his reputation as a warlord grew.

Temujin's military skill earned him notice by the most powerful lord in the Mongol tribes. Through sheer military genius and ferocity, Temujin earned his way into a final showdown for control of the largest Mongol tribe. Temujin's armies defeated Senggum on the battlefield, and Temujin was anointed Chingiz Khan, meaning Strong Ruler. The ceremony took place at a Khuriltai (a meeting of the chieftains) in 1206 AD.

Chris's tour party drove a few 100 miles to the northwest to the ancient battlefield and set up camp that night near the Khuriltai. Jimmy, quite weary from the long ride, fell fast asleep.

During the night, he awoke restlessly. He rose from his warm bed and, after getting dressed, quietly walked out of the tent. The night air was chilly . . . it was like opening the freezer door and holding your head inside for too long.

Jimmy felt something was out of place. He didn't understand what that was, but Marie seemed to be trying to tell him something. He felt strange, like an antenna was down in his head, "hearing" only interference. That's when it began . . . from out of the ebon in front of him, a shimmering light moved gracefully toward him. He stood transfixed as it approached from some fifty feet away.

He was scared silly, yet he could not move. The closer the "light" got, the less fear he felt, until it washed over him . . . a natural, easy feeling.

That's when Shen Koketai bathed Jimmy with a new soul . . . one nearly 800 years old.

Chapter 6
Blue Boy

Jimmy didn't pass out from the shock as he did the first time, but rather he embraced the SoulBound. Visions of a world much different from his own flooded through him. Shen Koketai was a Mongol warrior fighting under the command of Temujin, the soon-to-be Chingiz Khan. Koketai, pronounced Kō-kuh-tī (first and last names are switched in Asian cultures), died, when he was merely seventeen years old, during Chingiz Khan's decisive victory over Senggum to claim the reign of the Mongol tribes. Koketai had been killed with a volley of arrows as he and others charged in during an offensive.

Jimmy felt multiple sharp pains in his chest at that moment and cried out in understanding. Tears streamed to collect in brown puddles beneath his drawn face. A sadness he had never experienced with Marie enveloped him. Koketai never knew love or felt the touch of a woman. He was never . . . Koketai's visions and emotions paused for a few moments before he continued. Jimmy had sensed an internal conflict and a moment of shame from Koketai. He knew that the young man had not intended to share certain privacies.

Although Koketai had died, he still witnessed his people's victory and the coronation of the new Khan, Chingiz. Glorious pride filled Jimmy at that thought, until a sense of loss overcame him. He felt Koketai's loss . . . of life, and at fourteen, he now understood the feeling of death. It was a feeling that could not be put into words, only felt, and Jimmy felt it now as strongly as he felt his own life, before the sensation faded.

Jimmy then began to sense many other things, as he encountered a multitude of new memories and information. Koketai was so named because when he was born, the umbilical cord had been wrapped around his neck and he had turned blue before they unraveled it. Koketai meant "My blue boy." His mother was a good woman, loving, yet hard. He had three older brothers and two older sisters, each of whom helped to raise him from the outset on the path to becoming a warrior.

Koketai had thirsted for the opportunity to distinguish himself. He was riding horses at age four and taking care of his own at ten. His father, Jsun, had instructed him in the finer points of riding and weaponry, and Koketai could ride and shoot his bow with great accuracy by the time he was Jimmy's age. He was less skilled with his sword, but could do well enough if needed. He had proudly joined Temujin's armies barely a week before his death.

The new soul's walk-down-memory-lane had taken a physical toll on Jimmy and he needed to rest. He returned to his tent, exhausted. When he awakened in the morning, he had a splitting headache.

His father gathered the group for one last venture before making their way back to the States. Their guides took them to meet a tribe of modern Mongols who still did things pretty much as they had 800 years ago. Clan Chris traveled east for about sixty miles before stopping near the camp of the Mongols. They got out of their truck and trekked about two miles southeast before seeing the camp ahead. Leather tents dotted an area roughly the size of a football field, forming the camp. Many horses tethered to posts, eating and drinking, as a few people milled about.

The guides asked Chris's group to wait there, allowing the guides the chance to approach first. A few Mongol women and children could be seen peering from the tents, as a dozen or so Mongol men appeared on horseback from the far side of the camp and rode to meet the guides.

Within minutes, the outsiders found themselves sitting in a large tent, being offered small bowls of food. The Mongol men laughed aloud at some private joke as the children happily examined the expedition's clothes and equipment.

Bill wondered if they were laughing at his expense, surmising that he may be the only "black" person they had ever seen, coupled with the fact that the children spent as much time touching his skin as they did the other things.

Jimmy felt a bit at home *and* a bit foreign. He understood their language to a degree, as modern-day Mongol language had changed somewhat since Koketai's time. He rose, moving quietly away from the group in the tent, to walk outside.

A few Mongol men watched him carefully as he approached the horses.

Jimmy looked at one and said in the ancient Mongol tongue, "Brother, may I ride?"

The man looked a bit surprised and spoke softly to the other two men beside him. He responded that it would please them all to see him ride.

Jimmy then asked if he might borrow a bow and quiver to shoot a bit as well.

The men agreed.

Jimmy quickly saddled the largest horse and patted it softly upon its head while whispering to it in the ancient tongue.

Chris and Bill, along with a few others from the expedition, walked outside at that moment to watch Jimmy step up onto the horse, armed with bow and arrows. Chris began to yell something, but Jimmy took off before he could do so.

James Carson Kassakatis broke free . . . he felt a rush unlike any he had ever known before. He struggled atop the dark brown horse a bit before growing quite comfortable and at ease. He then maneuvered the horse in war-tactic ways, unseen in eight centuries. He was a blur upon the quick beast; they were as one as he pulled his bow out and notched an arrow. An old tree that had other arrows in it suffered four more shafts as Jimmy unleashed them rapid fire, and with great precision. He was alive.

Jimmy came to understand more about his gift each passing moment. He not only felt their memories, he gained their abilities, like playing guitar at the music store. Jimmy was now three souls in one.

He felt joy unbound and made his way back into camp to the obvious shock of his witnesses. He thanked the men for honoring him as he returned the bow and quiver and re-tethered the horse.

The Mongol men said something to the effect that Jimmy showed the skill of their ancestors.

Jimmy smiled and again thanked the men for their generosity.

Chris was astounded, seeing his son perform for a second time in an uncanny way.

Bill asked Jimmy where he learned to speak Mongolian, as well as how he could ride and shoot so well.

Jimmy paused for a moment before explaining that he learned Mongolian by reading a translation guide on the trip, and he had taken archery in school. Riding, Jimmy surmised deceitfully, must have been a natural ability.

He was spared further scrutiny as some members of his party began occupying themselves with filming and documenting the daily activities of the Mongols.

Jimmy gathered around a fire within one of the tents when asked to do so by an elder Mongol woman. She and other women and men among the clan sat and smoked some form of packed tobacco. She spoke to him in her tongue and said she sensed in him the spirit of her ancestors.

Jimmy wasn't sure what to say to this, but felt that Koketai was eager to respond. Therefore, Jimmy let Koketai speak through him. It was a strange sensation and the first time Jimmy had really figured out how to allow a soul to speak through him. It just seemed natural.

Koketai said that he was Shen Koketai of the Kiyat-Borjigid tribe. Against Senggum he rode, with the armies of the living God, Chingiz Khan, and was killed honorably in battle. He spoke proudly of the greatness of his lord, the great Chingiz Khan. Koketai went on to speak of days past and the sadness he felt of the state of his people today. He finished by telling them that he was honored to know them and that he was proud that they have continued with the old traditions.

The oldest woman was teary-eyed and tilting her head slightly, gazed deep into Jimmy/Koketai's eyes. She whispered a prayer and dropped a pinch of some powder into the fire, sending a puff of smoke into the air. She reached for Jimmy and motioned for him to bow his head.

He did as requested, and she gave him a handcrafted ornate stone necklace, a symbol of the "Oneness" between her people and their ancestors.

Jimmy rose afterward as Koketai faded back within him. He again bowed deeply with his hands together in a sign of prayer and peace, and thanked her and the others who sat about the fire.

His father entered the tent and told him it was time to go.

Upon returning to the truck, Jimmy again felt beset with exhaustion and curled up on his seat to sleep.

As he faded into black, Marie's soothing voice mind-whispered, *"Well done . . . both of you."*

Chapter 7
The List

Tuesday, May 20, 2008.

Jimmy awakened from his Mongolian recollection to a very hectic voice.

"Professor Kassakatis, you're up next!"

Gertie Ruud had just celebrated her sixtieth birthday and was now thirty-four years his senior. She was secretary of the History Department at Russell College, where Jimmy had worked as Professor of Historical Studies the past three years. Jimmy had no idea what he would do without her.

He was a shining light in the college and was about to lecture the assembled students, as well as many high school and elementary school history teachers, about the historical significance of Chingiz Khan and the Mongolian people. Also in attendance were the deans of certain stellar prep schools and many of the more prominent universities in the Mid-Atlantic region. Jimmy was hot, a two-time Pennington Award winner as the best collegiate teacher in his field for the Mid-Atlantic region.

Having the combined intellect of many people within him garnered Jimmy a quick trip through high school and college, and he graduated from this very college at the age of twenty. Jimmy had been through lectures like this before and figured today would follow the usual pattern . . . When he stepped away from the podium to a round of loud applause (he hoped), the recruiters would descend on him like a pride of hungry lions.

Sure enough, after a mesmerizing lecture that enthralled his onlookers, Jimmy heard a thunderous roar of approval as he stepped off the stage. He had taken the opportunity to speak, at times, in all the six languages that he knew. Universities like Maryland, Penn, Virginia, North Carolina State, and others bombarded him, as expected, with a new suitor being the prestigious Northwestern University. He was a rock star in the teaching profession and he was a good-looking fellow to boot.

The ladies clamored for him, from eighteen-year-old freshman to colleagues in their fifties. He was now twenty-six, six feet one, and well built. He had slightly messy and amply gelled dark hair, cropped in the popular "George Clooney" fashion. While not quite on par with his academic accomplishments, he had gained a bit of a following in the writing world, as his collection of poetry entitled, *Whispers, Shadows, & Dreams,* had recently been published. These poems and shorts were a foray into the wondrous and romantic, yet touched upon a darker side that spoke of true depression and inner pain.

"Sissy shit," that's what Dragon called it. Frank "Dragon" Jackson was Jimmy's toughest soul and had been Jimmy's fourth bonding. Dragon, after all these years, still held the award for "hardest to get along with."

Jimmy was intriguing and would be quite a catch if not snared nearly two years before. He had not asked Dee to marry him just yet, but his courage was at an all-time high. He thought that their two-year first-date anniversary in eleven days would be the right time.

Jimmy first noticed her when she, as a student of his at Russell College, first entered his classroom. There were many attractive young women who had come through his classrooms, but only the dark-haired beauty he knew as Denise Conway could make his heart race. He found himself smitten, but being professional, kept his feelings to himself during her two years there. Destiny smiled on him though, when he was introduced to her at his friend's pool party just after she graduated. Dee was friends with Rae Brando, who was the little sister of the party host and Jimmy's longtime best friend, Tommy Brando.

Within a minute of Jimmy's arrival at the party, Rae had grabbed his hand and led him across the deck to meet her best friend; the one Rae had been telling him about. Jimmy was nervous, feeling as if Rae was setting him up for disaster. But that was a lost thought when the young woman, who had been facing away from them, turned around as Rae called her name.

"Dee!"

The next few moments were frozen in time . . . the moment he met *The One*. He just wished it had gone more smoothly.

How beautiful . . .

Jimmy was overcome with a familiar and strong attraction for the cute twenty-four-year-old brunette and was awestruck as Rae introduced them. So much so that as he reached out to shake her hand, he tripped over someone's cooler and crashed into her.

She laughed and asked if he was all right. He said he was fine and apologized for being clumsy, and she said, "No problem, professor, something tells me you meet all the girls this way."

Being a professor at such a young age still took getting used to. Rae and Jimmy laughed along with Dee, and her sweet demeanor stoked his already fiery heart. Gorgeous *and* sweet . . . could it get any better?

Rae moved away, and Dee asked Jimmy to follow her, leading him past the built-in pool and to the end of the yard. Dee leaned on the wooden fence that bordered Tommy's yard, and Jimmy stood beside her. They talked a bit about her time at the college and his class in particular, and he surprised himself by admitting to her that he had been quite taken by her.

She smiled after he said that, but remained quiet.

After a few moments, Jimmy began to feel as if he needed to change the subject, but she said, "I used to dream about you . . ."

She did not finish the thought . . . and he just smiled wide along with her, as they shared a few quiet moments in contemplation. It was the start of something beautiful.

Dee was exactly his type. She was ladylike at the "right" times, but funny and down-to-earth. She was very sexy (in a girl-next-door way), with full, dark, wavy hair and a smile so bright it put a lighthouse to shame. She was driven to be successful in the business world as well and was currently the assistant manager at a local branch of the Sebastian Federal Bank.

Jimmy fell hard for her. She was the piece to his puzzling life that he had sought for many years. So, in eleven days, their two-year first-date anniversary, he was going to ask her to marry him. He was more than a bit terrified that she would reject him. However, as terrified as he was at the possibility of rejection, he was petrified of telling her the truth about himself . . . about being spiritually, emotionally, and physically connected to twelve other souls.

Jimmy realized that he would have to be a real jerk to wait until after he asked her to marry him to confide his strange truth to her. He decided to get together with her as usual that night and break it to her then. He went over his approach repeatedly in his mind and "felt" the approval of the adult female souls within. Jimmy had seven female and five male SoulBound, with the last being a little girl he had merged with just a few months before. This most recent SoulBound had been the most unusual, in that he couldn't get a decent "reading" or feel for her, knowing her name as Carrie Ann and her age (six), but nothing more.

Jimmy decided to provide a list of the SoulBound to help Dee become as familiar as possible with each of them. He listed them in order of when he had bonded with them.

1) Marie Anne Beale: Veterinarian, drowned, 1981 (thirty-one years old)
2) Shen Koketai: Mongol warrior, died in battle, 1205 (seventeen years old)
3) Su Yi: Chinese launderer, strangled, 1871 (twenty-two years old)

4) Frank "Dragon" Jackson: Biker, motorcycle accident, 1995 (thirty-eight years old)

5) Nan: Slave, Smallpox, 1845 (thirty-four years old)

6) John Jaden: US Navy sailor, drowned, 1960 (nineteen years old)

7) Brennan Payton: Network tech trainer, car accident, 2003 (twenty-seven years old)

8) Millie Liddell: Retired housewife, stroke, 1946 (seventy-one years old)

9) Karen Two Storms: Financial advisor, heart attack, 1992 (fifty-eight years old)

10) Jean-Paul Lalande: French sailor, cannonball, 1827 (twenty-five years old)

11) Gina Imbragulio: Italian pianist, plane crash, 1953 (thirty-two years old)

12) Carrie Ann: (six years old)

He knew the details about all of them, but not about Carrie Ann, the exception; he assumed the details would eventually be revealed to him, at least he hoped they would. He knew each of them on different levels. They were part of him, all of them, bound to him as he to them. They were one . . . yet separate entities. Jimmy had struggled for years with the realization that he walked around with dead people within him, dead . . . yet quite aware, quite alive.

He wanted to answer any questions Dee had about them, and he was prepared to explain the circumstances as best he could. He fully expected her to freak over this, but he cared so deeply for her that it was breaking his heart, even as he prepared for her that evening.

Millie then mind-spoke to Jimmy, giving him some good old-fashioned advice.

"Either she loves you for who you are or it just isn't meant to be. You just move on if not."

He had grown to love the well-meaning Millie, but she sure seemed to make a habit of saying things that somehow always made him feel worse for hearing them.

· · · · · · · · · · · · · · · · · · · ·

Camilla (Millie) Avent was born in the spring of 1875, in the shadow of the Appalachian Mountains in West "By God" Virginia. She was a good Christian girl, raised to be so by her God-fearing mother, Nadine, and Nadine-fearing father, Roscoe. She had two brothers and two sisters, Millie being the eldest. When her mother passed away of natural causes (if poison can be called such), Millie was left to tend to her brothers and sisters. Her dad had disappeared the day her mom died and, as far as she could tell, he'd never been caught.

Millie had to quit school. To make ends meet, she married a twenty-six-year-old carpenter named Earl "Leebird" Liddell, two days after her fourteenth birthday. Times were hard, and she did what she had to . . . not necessarily what she wanted. While there was an obvious age discrepancy, Earl was always good to her and her siblings. He was the hardest worker she ever knew, and was seemingly the first one up and awake in the whole county, hence his nickname. He worked as a carpenter when work was available, and made due as a handyman when not. Neither Millie, her siblings, nor her children ever went hungry.

She gave birth to her first child, Earl Jr., when she was seventeen, and subsequently had four more sons over the next six years. When she passed of a stroke at the age of seventy-one, she had been blessed with five children, eleven grandchildren, and twenty-one great-grandchildren, although she had lost one son (Delvin) in WWI and two grandsons in WWII.

She had been the matriarch of the Liddell clan, the pillar of strength and virtue throughout their collective tree. She was an avid reader and loved the old stories about cowboys and the Wild West and was involved heavily in church activities . . . most notably running the church's charity drive each winter.

Though she lived what one might call a "fairly normal" life, for her, even now, it was one she missed with every fiber of her being. It was why she hadn't gone into The Light on the day she died. Her stubbornness wore off and the understanding that her time had come had been too late . . . until she was given a second chance . . . namely Jimmy.

Chapter 8
Dee Day

As he entered his home, Jimmy spotted Dee in the dining room. She was wearing a soft white turtleneck with faded jeans and her favorite socks, SpongeBob SquarePants footies, which Jimmy had given her, among other gifts this past Christmas. She had a key to his colonial home, which sat overlooking the bay, and she had let herself in as usual. She had ordered his favorite food (deep-dish pizza) and had lit candles on the dining room table to set a romantic tone.

Ahhh . . . how he loved sausage and pepperoni, deep-dish pizza from Momma Asonte's. It was a favorite stop many nights on his way home, as it was only five minutes from his front door. "Momma's" had been on Illinois Avenue since Jimmy could remember. *Ironic*, he had thought often, *Chicago deep dish on Illinois Avenue.*

He kissed Dee warmly, gently holding her to him. Tonight was going to be among the most important of their lives.

"Je vous aime," he whispered as he continued to hug her.

He released her to a typical Dee retort, "You mean you love my pizza."

They both laughed as Jimmy went to the closet to hang up his long black coat. He was dressed as he was when he left the lecture earlier that day; except his tie was so loose, it barely hung on.

"You wanna eat first or shower first?" Dee asked as she opened the box of pizza to peek inside.

"All depends. Will you be joining me in the shower?" he responded half joking.

At that, Dee launched herself at Jimmy and loudly responded, "Oh, baby, take me, take me in the shower. You beast, you shower stud, ohhhh ohhhh . . ."

Her laughter echoed about the apartment, as she had tripped in her zeal for play and tumbled them both to the ground. They were laughing hysterically as they grappled playfully on the living room floor.

Jimmy accidentally banged his head on the table, and after only a brief pause to be sure he was okay, they both erupted again into laughter.

He began to undress and said, "If you insist on the living room floor, then by all means . . ."

"Uhhhhhh, I prefer the shower, my lord, as thou art quite stinky in thy current state."

Again, laughter rained as Jimmy stood up, his pants around his ankles, "As you wish."

He bowed and kissed her hand and motioned for his "lady" to follow him to the shower.

After "showering" and eating the pizza, Dee put in *their* movie, "The Princess Bride." Dee would often jokingly refer to Jimmy as Wesley and Jimmy would naturally call her Buttercup (the romantic characters in the movie). He asked her to wait until later, as he had something to discuss with her.

She hit the remote and the television went dark and silent.

This was it, the moment he had feared for some time. And in this wondrous mood they shared, it pained him even more so. He began wringing his hands together, which was something he did unconsciously whenever he got nervous.

"Everyone keeps secrets, some dark, some silly, but I have to share one that borders on . . . well . . . bizarre. I assure you that I am not joking," began Jimmy as he started to shake slightly.

His heart rate had jumped to where he could feel it through his shirt.

"The only place to start is from the beginning I guess. Bear with me, sweetheart."

He paused to collect himself.

"When I was twelve years old, I experienced something that changed not only my life, but my . . . essence." Jimmy paused again and closed his eyes briefly while Dee sat holding his hand with a look of deepest concern etched on her face.

He continued, "I was visiting my Aunt—along with my family, staying a couple of nights one weekend. I was tired naturally, but still awake lying in my bed, when a . . . 'light' entered my bedroom window and within seconds, somehow . . . entered me. I passed out and awoke the following morning. Over time, I began to realize that something had happened to me that night, something far crazier than a light colliding with me. I began to discover abilities that were not my own, like playing guitar and having the ability to diagnose pet diseases and conditions. I started recalling memories that were *not* my own."

He became transfixed now, getting that *I'm away* look about him.

Dee cautiously spoke between sentences and asked, "You mean you had been possessed?"

Jimmy turned to her now, as his gaze had rather drifted off.

"No, no. Not possessed, bonded. A thirty-one-year-old woman named Marie became 'SoulBound' with me that night in my room. She drowned in 1981 at the Inner Harbor and had been a veterinarian and humanitarian among other things. She was the reason I discovered newfound abilities. We had melded together, like connecting souls."

Dee just sat there staring in disbelief, as her world seemed to shudder a bit around her. Her eyes welled with tears as she had figured that Jimmy was having a nervous breakdown. She stood up and moved away from the sofa they sat on and walked to the glass doors that opened onto the balcony and said, "So, you have a ghost inside you . . ."

It sounded a bit sarcastic and a bit fearful. She peered outside and stared off into the serenity of the Chesapeake Bay.

"Baby, I know this seems crazy, and I can only imagine what's going through your head right now, but . . . I'm not nuts. You know me. No one has ever gotten to know me as much as you have."

Jimmy had stood as he spoke, but did not approach her.

"There is so much more to tell . . ." he didn't move a muscle, as he contemplated what course of action to take.

Dee opened the glass doors and stepped out onto the balcony, as the wind casually blew her wavy dark-brown hair about. The Annapolis night-lights sparkled to kiss the incoming tides, which touched lightly upon the shore. There was a sense of calm about her as she gathered herself to respond. The bay had always called to her soul, and the inner peace it brought was a welcome friend amid the chaos she was feeling. She turned to Jimmy and extended an arm toward him, an invite to come to her.

"Let's take a walk," she said warmly, as she took his hand in hers.

After dressing for a chilly stroll, the pair set out to walk along the shoreline. Neither spoke until Dee asked Jimmy to continue, after a good five minutes of silence.

Jimmy's heart leapt with joy, though his dreams of a future with Dee still flickered perilously in the bay breeze.

"Thank you," he said warmly.

He proceeded to tell her everything. He explained to her that besides Marie, he had eleven other souls within him. He told her that as far as he could tell, they were stuck within him, unable to carry on as ghosts in the outside world, but lived now only within him. Then he explained to her as best he could about each of them, and gave her the list he created to help her understand better. Jimmy told her that if he were in her shoes, he would immediately think about Multiple Personality Disorder.

He continued to explain . . . he had been to numerous doctors and psychologists to no avail when he was a teenager.

His parents were sure something mental was at fault, although he never confided the truth to them. They had seen too many strange things to imagine he was "normal." After the fifth professional could find nothing to suggest a disorder, he was free from further scrutiny.

"It took me a long time to understand that what was happening to me was unique. It seems that I'm the only person to ever have such a thing happen to them, or at least I am the only one that I know of. I researched my 'condition' online many times, to no avail." He paused before continuing.

"Only two other people know the truth, besides you, that is, my shrink, Dr. Lena Vaccaro, . . . and as you might guess, Tommy."

Dee knew that Tommy Brando was Jimmy's best friend and that they had known each other for many years, but didn't know that Jimmy was under the care of a psychiatrist.

"I haven't seen Dr. Vaccaro for a while now, I don't know, maybe a couple of years. She'd 'tested' me in every professional way and got frustrated with me a bit when I refused to allow her to share my situation with others who may have been more qualified than she was. I haven't been back since, though she has tried calling me a few times. I didn't want a freak show . . ."

As Jimmy finished speaking, he realized they had just arrived back at his home and they went back inside. He had a lump the size of a tennis ball in his throat, as he was stressing so bad.

After gathering her keys from the kitchen, Dee paused, and in a somber tone, said that she needed to be alone for a while, that she needed time. She walked slowly out the front door.

As he watched her go, Jimmy hoped she hadn't just walked out of his life.

Chapter 9

Dio Santo...

Jimmy awakened the following morning and knew he hadn't a prayer to function in his duties at school, so he called Gertie and explained that he had taken ill and would be off for a few days. Gertie told him she would get Michelle Channing to handle his duties while he was out and not to worry.

The students are going to freak, Jimmy imagined, as Channing's teaching style was vastly more "old school" than his. However, Jimmy's real concern was Dee. He wasn't sure what was going to happen. His whole world seemed on hold while she decided what to say or do about Jimmy plus twelve.

The next few days passed excruciatingly slow. Jimmy hadn't showered since that night with Dee, and he had grown an unaccustomed five o'clock shadow. He passed a good bit of the time by playing his grand piano, which rested in the sunken living room. Yes, with Soul #11—Gina Imbragulio—being a concert pianist . . . well, you get the point. He played the piano every so often . . . a beautiful and sweeping sound resonated about as he did so. Gina was remarkably gifted, so Jimmy was now too.

. . . .

Regina Imbragulio was born among political turmoil in Italy, in the town of Trieste, on September 2, 1920. Times were difficult for everyone, and the labor force, the men working the factories, warehouses, and shipping yards, 600,000 strong, seized control of their facilities in a display of solidarity and with the intent to increase pay, among other goals. Times were indeed tough, but fortunately for Gina, her father had been a teacher and not subjected to the labor dispute. She admired him greatly, eventually following him into the profession, becoming a schoolteacher herself. Her passion, however, was the piano, which her mother had taught her to play. Her mother was very good, but Gina was remarkable. She felt alive while seated at the keys. She had fallen in love with playing in her teens, after years of playing in a thoroughly bored state, due to her mother making her do so since the age of five. Gina loved the piano second only to the man she was engaged to marry. However, fate intervened.

Gina never married, nor had children, a sorrow that stays with her still. It wasn't because she was homely; on the contrary, she was strikingly pretty. Gina was well-proportioned, five feet seven, with long, wavy blonde hair and emerald green eyes—the envy of most women and the living dream of most men. Ahhh, but the men would have to keep dreaming . . . all but one that was—Rafaele Romano. It was because of her love for Rafaele that she never married . . . nor knew the joy of motherhood. They met when she was twenty and had dated for eight months, until the fateful day he asked her to marry him. She happily agreed, but her happiness faded quickly as Rafaele was rounded up among other young men and forced into the army just that night. Fascist Italy . . . Mussolini . . . WWII.

He wrote to her nearly every week and continued to encourage her to try to follow her dreams of playing piano professionally, but she felt it best to stay where she could ensure a decent future and make an honest living . . . teaching. Gina fretted for Rafaele's fate and justly so. On March 19, 1941, after failing to receive a letter in months, Gina received a visitor to her home . . . Rafaele's mother, Flora. Her heart sank at the look in the eyes of the distraught woman.

Flora was mumbling "Dio Santo (Oh my God)" over and over and slumped down to the floor, a river of tears pouring forth as she handed Gina a photo of her son.

She had wrapped the frame in black fabric . . . for her Rafaele was dead.

Gina never loved again. It took years before she was able to gather up the courage needed to strike out and try to become a professional pianist; a dream her parents and Rafaele had always wanted for her. She succeeded in the spring of 1952, being invited and accepting an invitation to join the prestigious Trieste concert group, Molto Bello. Her dream of making it was short-lived however, as she was aboard a flight to Rome to meet the group for the first time when the plane crashed upon takeoff. Among 126 passengers, 119 survived . . . she was not among the fortunate.

• • • • • • • • • • • • • • • • • • •

Jimmy spent time playing guitar as well, but did so virtually alone. None of the SoulBound had spoke to Jimmy, as even Marie was taking a hiatus. All sensed Jimmy's desire for solace. He was miserable and sat half-heartedly watching television, wondering about Dee.

"It'll be okay, Mr. Jimmy," mind-spoke a voice Jimmy had heard only once before.

It was Carrie Ann, Soul #12, the reclusive six-year-old that Jimmy had become SoulBound with four months ago.

"Miss Dee loves you very, very much. And love . . . is stronger than anything," she continued, as Jimmy became nearly overcome with emotion.

He barely avoided tears while telling Carrie Ann that he appreciated her kind words and that she was such a good girl. Within Jimmy's mind raged a battleground of shame and pain, and love and hope. He had sensed that this little girl died horribly, and despite her tribulations, she still had enough love in her heart to try to comfort a depressed grown man. Jimmy knew that as blessed as he was, he shouldn't get too emotional, but it was difficult to manage so much in his mind. This is when Nan, Soul #5, became Jimmy's "soother."

He called her that because she gave him the wonderful gift of relaxing his mind, by singing softly to him, tunes from her days slaving in the fields. He never asked for it . . . it was just a lovely surprise . . . each and every time.

With Nan's help, Jimmy eventually fell asleep for a couple of hours on the sofa, before being wakened by a knock at the front door. In his haste to answer, he nearly knocked over the green vase Dee had helped him pick out to decorate the living room.

Still not quite awake, he yelled, "Uno momento."

That had been Karen Two Storms, his Spanish-speaking Soul #9, lending him a helping thought. Jimmy opened the door and saw immediately that it was dark outside. Standing in the darkness on his front porch was a man. Jimmy flipped the light switch just inside the door and saw that it was his brother, Alex.

"Hey, Bro . . . come in," he said, as he smiled warmly at Alex.

He always enjoyed Alex's company, as Jimmy thought his brother was the funniest person he ever knew. As Alex passed him, Jimmy noticed a somber expression. He had been crying. Alex walked down into the living room before sitting without taking his coat off. Jimmy closed the door and immediately moved to sit beside him.

". . . What's wrong?" Jimmy asked as he rubbed his hands together.

Alex began weeping "Jimmy . . . ," he had trouble finishing.

Jimmy's mind flashed *Dio Santo!*

"C-car accident. Mom and Dad . . . they're gone Jimmy, they're gone."

Jimmy began to sob . . .

"G—Gone? What? . . . No! Noooooooooooooooooooo!"

Alex hugged him closer, and with more love than at any other time in their lives. And the two grown men, these brothers, clung to each other in sorrow . . . in pain . . . and deepest loss.

As the brothers cried, twelve souls cried with them . . . yeah, even Dragon.

Chapter 10
Spirits to the Winds...

Tuesday, May 27, 2008

The morning was overcast and threatening as Jimmy and Alex made their way to the Church of Our Lord. A strong wind blew, and there was concern that a storm could ruin the day, but the local weather report showed it should miss them. Jimmy had picked up his brother and they were moments from the church when he heard it . . . Carrie Ann had started to sing sweetly . . .

"When you look up to the sky, and the clouds darken your day,
They're happy shades of silver, not sad shades of gray,
The weather sure gets rough sometimes,
But there are rainbows in the rain . . .
And please remember always . . . it never hurts to pray."

It was a rare moment indeed that Carrie Ann spoke, but here she was, singing an uplifting song for Jimmy on the day of his greatest sorrow. Jimmy was so touched, all were all the souls within him, and he said, *"I adore you, Carrie Ann. That was quite beautiful . . . thank you, sweetheart."*

The other souls responded as well, expressing how wonderfully she sang.

Carrie Ann smiled the faintest of smiles, before retreating into her solace.

The church rested just off the Chesapeake Bay and was the place their parents frequented most Sundays. It was only minutes from Jimmy's home, and he and Alex arrived forty-five minutes early to meet with Pastor Stonesifer and Funeral Director Emma Henley. The brothers were wearing all-white suits, the opposite of tradition, just as requested in Chris and Cheri's wills. Their wills expressed quite clearly that all in attendance should wear white to celebrate life, rather than black, to mourn death. In addition, the boys were requested to have the parents cremated and have their ashes spread over the bay waters outside the church.

The church was adorned in a variety of beautiful flowers, as the attendees, numbering in the hundreds, filtered into the pews. Emma Henley had been a Godsend, working almost miraculously to put together wonderful ceremonies with very little time. She was a little thing, less than five feet tall, with striking features, red hair, and green eyes . . . looking as if she had walked out of an old Humphrey Bogart movie. For a woman in her seventies, she moved about with the grace and energy of a much-younger woman.

The ceremonies were not completely traditional, in that, after a brief traditional prayer and a few words from the pastor, the attendees who wished to, came before the gathered and spoke of their memories of the departed. Many humorous stories and words of deep affection carried over the mass. Laughter and tears were prominent as about a dozen friends and family members took turns.

When the last speaker finished, which had been Tommy Brando, Alex stood up and made his way to the podium. He hugged Tommy before moving to the microphone.

"I have nothing prepared . . . but I just wanted to say that I think this has been a beautiful show of love and admiration for two extraordinary people . . . ." He began to cry openly, not attempting to wipe away the tears. "Mom and Dad were wonderful parents. They raised me, in more ways than one. They gave me . . . life . . . both theirs and mine." Tears fell unabashed.

"My many special moments with them belong to me alone . . . and I will keep them sacred within me. I hope you all understand. Mom, Dad . . . I miss you, dearly . . . and my heart will always be open to you, wherever you may go. All my love . . ."

Alex put both hands to his heart and looked heavenward. He stepped away from the podium as Jimmy walked slowly to take his place. The two embraced briefly before Jimmy stepped up to the mic.

"I am . . . overwhelmed, by the outpour of love displayed here today," he said shaking his head slightly, tears welling up.

"In keeping with my parents' wishes to celebrate life, I see before me a sea of white . . . except for Jeffrey there in the back, who must've missed the memo."

Jimmy pointed at his black-dressed cousin and laughed as the gathered burst into laughter with him.

Jeffrey feigned undressing, but was rebuffed when his mother hit him playfully with her purse, to more rounds of laughter.

"Fitting, for those who know Jeffrey, he's always been a little pepper in the salt of life." Again . . . rounds of laughter.

"This . . ." Jimmy again pointed to Jeffrey and around to the attendees. ". . . this is what my parents meant . . . when they said that '*We should all rejoice in these moments because they will never come again.*'"

Jimmy continued, "Life happens . . . in small moments, in everyday things, it blesses us all, at least those of us with eyes to see."

He paused a moment before continuing.

"These last few days, I came to realize just how much I had taken my parents for granted."

Jimmy could not deny his watering eyes and began to cry.

"Mom, Dad . . . I'm s-sorry that I didn't tell you often enough h-how much . . . you meant to me. So, I'm telling you now . . . that I love you . . . I miss you terribly . . . ," he was barely audible over his weeping.

". . . and I will live my life . . . honoring yours. I wrote this for you a few hours ago . . . and I will try to get through it."

He looked heavenward and began.

"We brave a smile as tears rain down,
Pouring from heavy hearts.
For though we lost you here on Earth,
You're found where heaven starts.
And with wings, you fly to touch the sky,
So high to breathe the blue.
You dance the wind with feathers white . . .

For that's what Angels do.
You'll ride the clouds and hug the sun,
And play with the silver moon.
Then paint the rays of the coming dawn . . .
For our eyes to share the view.
Now, we know you . . . Souls of Gold,
Aglow in Peace and Light,
You'll lift our spirits
To soar with yours . . .
So we, as well . . . can fly."

There wasn't a dry eye in the place as Alex approached Jimmy, and again they embraced.

Alex moved closer to the mic and asked the gathered to follow them outside to complete the ceremonies. It was still overcast, but rain was not called for.

The attendees made their way outside to the area set up for the spreading of the ashes. Mrs. Henley was quite calm and collected as she deftly, and almost unnoticed, directed her people about to where they needed to be. She was using hand signals and was always on the move.

The brothers stepped out onto a specially made cross-shaped pier that had just been set out into the bay. The pier had been donated to the church from a previous "Ashes" ceremony.

Mom? Dad? Are you smiling? Jimmy considered briefly as the podium and wireless mic were set up just as the final few folks gathered to watch.

Mrs. Henley and her helpers moved off the pier and stood by with the rest of the attendees, as Jimmy began.

"This ceremony is often referred to as the 'Spreading of the Ashes,' but today, I know Dad would've preferred something else. It was about three or four years ago when he had spoken to me after the funeral of a colleague. The colleague's family conducted this ceremony and it was indeed called the 'Spreading of the Ashes.' Dad spoke of the beautiful service, but in Dad's own humorous way, he said it sounded like making a dirty sandwich."

Jimmy laughed and everyone laughed with him.

"Dad said 'Spirit to the Winds' would be better. Therefore, Alex and I will now release our parents' 'Spirits to the Winds.'"

As the brothers let the ashes spill over the head of the cross, the wind indeed swept the "spirits" up into overcast skies. As all gathered watched, the sun, unseen all day, broke through the veil above and showered them all with a touch of warmth and light. It was an unforgettable moment . . . of life.

Yeah, Jimmy knew, *Mom and Dad were smiling . . .*

Chapter 11

...All of You

"I'm so proud of you boys," Grandma Mary said, as she kissed her grandsons and hugged them tightly. She was their mother's mother and their only living grandparent. The crowd was breaking up and heading to the reception at the local VFW, as the brothers shook hands with, and hugged, family and friends.

Aunt Bonnie, along with her older brother Chuck (the brothers' rarely seen uncle), approached Jimmy to commend him for such a beautiful poem and for the wonderful words he shared. It wouldn't be the last time that day he was showered with adoration.

As Emma Henley was walking past Jimmy to make arrangements to reclaim the microphone, and for the cross pier to be pulled to shore, Jimmy stopped her.

"Mrs. Henley . . ." He gave her a huge hug and said privately to her that he held a special place in his heart for her. He then kissed her on her cheek and cupped her hands in his. He mouthed, "Thank you," and smiled at her as she, with tears in her eyes, mouthed, "You're welcome."

Jimmy sought out his brother and spotted him, grouped with his wife of five years, Kathy, and their ten-month-old baby girl,

Melissa. Alex picked Lissy up high and began to play with her. The baby laughed in that adorable baby way.

Such a good father, Jimmy thought proudly.

Uncle Jimmy walked over to play with her and to greet Kathy, playfully attempting to avoid her dirty-blonde "big hair," which had a habit of getting in his eyes, his mouth, and whatever else was open.

She laughed as always with him and noticed that Jimmy had gone still for a moment. Sure enough, her brother-in-law *had* gone still, for he saw Dee standing and staring at him in the distance. She was clad in a white-buttoned sweater and white slacks. She had obviously attended the ceremonies and had stayed out of sight. She motioned as she had at his home, with arms outstretched for him.

Jimmy paused briefly to kiss the baby and asked the couple to excuse him a moment as he walked toward Dee, who waited by the shore.

As he approached her, he noticed she had been crying, and her cheeks were still wet. Dee spoke first.

"I'm so sorry, Jimmy. I can't imagine . . ." she began but cupped her hands over her mouth and began to cry again.

Jimmy said nothing, but gently pulled her to him and held her head to his chest to comfort her.

Dee looked up at him after a few moments and said, "Jimmy, forgive my timing, but I couldn't wait." Dee paused and brushed her windswept dark brown hair out of her eyes. "I love you . . . dearly. And I want to be with you—all of you."

She laughed at the inside joke as he laughed with her.

A great weight lifted from him in his time of greatest need, and the emotions of the day overcame him, dropping him to his knees.

She fell to her knees upon the cool sand as well and held Jimmy to her as he wept uncontrollably.

"I've got you, Jimmy. I'm holding you now . . ." She gently stroked his hair as she wept with him, ". . . and it's gonna be okay."

Chapter 12
Colors

The reception went as well as the funeral had, and Dee watched the man she loved, in all his splendor. Jimmy could be very outgoing and personable, while at other times, more reserved and quiet, but here he was quite sweet, funny, and comforting . . . and Jimmy even got the rare opportunity to do the five magic tricks he had mastered years before. Not borrowed from any of his souls, this skill was his alone.

The kids and many of the adults were blown away . . . Jimmy adding an entertaining flair to the magic for effect. The SoulBound, each alone within Jimmy, were enjoying the good times, but Karen Two Storms preemptively warned Dragon about making a comment . . . as she just knew he was going to say something rude. She was right, as he *was* about to "strike," but appropriately held his tongue.

Unbeknownst to all, Carrie Ann watched the reception from her own little corner of Jimmy . . . and even cracked a smile.

Jimmy and Dee were the last to leave, besides Bill Kitt, that was. He was quite drunk and partially lying across two metal folding chairs, holding a bottle of wine in one hand and a diaper in the other.

I can only imagine, Jimmy thought as he made the decision to avoid a cab and take Bill home himself.

With Dee's help, they got Bill to his feet and eased him into the back of Jimmy's silver Sebring convertible. The car wasn't really much of a multiple-passenger car, but it did well enough for getting Bill home.

Bill muttered to himself in the backseat as he lay down in the curled-up fetal position.

Dee asked Jimmy to turn the heat up a bit and then raised her voice a few decibels.

"Remind me to slap Alex the next time we see him. Did you hear what he said to Jeffrey about my knees being dirty?"

Jimmy laughed, and Dee protested only for a few seconds before joining him.

Upon arriving at Bill's home, Pookie (yes, Pookie), who was Bill's much-younger live-in girlfriend, gathered him out of the car with Jimmy's help, and took him inside their home.

Jimmy had called her moments before pulling into the driveway.

Once Bill was put to bed, Jimmy bid Pookie good-bye and he and Dee began the short ride back to Jimmy's place. As they drove the fifteen minutes back, Jimmy relayed a story he heard his sister-in-law Kathy tell about a cookout at his parent's home the summer before.

"Pookie had been drinking, and she, being an attractive twenty-three-year-old, white woman, said that Bill, being a fairly attractive, fifty-eight-year-old, black man, was the best lover a woman could ask for. Pookie started in with the intimate descriptions, and the other women who were gathered about listened in shocked silence. Aunt Bonnie, who had been passing by, overheard a few words and got a piece of chicken stuck in her throat as she gasped.

"Pookie, who we later discovered was in medical school, immediately leapt up and Heimlich-maneuvered Aunt Bonnie to safety, before sitting back down to continue her story. Most of us had no idea what had just happened, as it happened so fast."

Jimmy was snickering nearly every other word . . . barely containing the laughter.

"So, my aunt, crooked glasses and all, wearily thanked Pookie before heading into the house to lie down. Pookie kept blabbering on as if nothing happened. She went on to explain that her given name was Laurie Jo Magaha, but that Bill called her his Pookie, so it stuck."

Jimmy laughed a bit more about that and Dee just shook her head and smiled.

Those were the last words spoken that night as the couple undressed quietly and went straight to bed. Dee fell fast asleep as Jimmy lay with memories of the day's events running through his weary mind. The SoulBound took this brief opportunity to express their condolences to Jimmy. He loved them all, as it was typically sweet of them and he replied with appreciation. For now, he was exhausted, but the recollection of the sun bursting through the clouds was repeating, engraving itself in his mind. Soon enough though, with the comforting call of the bay as a backdrop and the sweet and soft voice of Nan sounding a lullaby, Jimmy, too, succumbed to sleep.

• • • • • • • • • • • • • • • • • • •

Nan became the fifth SoulBound in November of 1998, as Jimmy was touring a few colleges throughout Georgia. Nan was so easygoing, and her SoulBound went pretty well, as well as these things could go. It didn't take long for Jimmy to come to realize that he was going to enjoy her company and friendship an awful lot. Jimmy held a special place in his heart for her. He felt blessed to have known her all these years and he told her that every so often, as if she'd forget his deep admiration, love, and respect for his most sweet and gentle soul.

Nan was born on May 2, 1814 . . . straight into slavery, just as her parents before her. Her parents worked together in the cotton fields of Stafford's Grove, a plantation near Savannah, Georgia. She began the fourth generation of slaves on her father's side and the fifth on her mother's. Trying to explain to Jimmy what slavery was like, well, was a difficult proposition for Nan, but she tried her best to give him an understanding.

Imagine . . . just close your eyes and imagine you are stuck in a sea of quicksand and the nearest solid ground is hundreds of miles away.

This quicksand is slow . . . it will take years and years to take you under. You have no hope, not truly, and only the small comfort of others like you who are sinking around you, offering you the slightest comfort, the slightest joy.

Life is a ritual . . . a daily foray into pain, hard work, and hopelessness.

Jimmy had heard Nan daydreaming at times and glimpsed one of the more sad memories in her life . . .

Rain comes again, it comes and comes hard.
We get together in hopes to not be washed away.
The fields be covered in rivers of mud.
'Cause the sun not smiling for days.
Noooo . . . not smiling at all . . .

Despite the hardships she could not overcome, Nan was at peace with her fate and was a beacon of all that was good in the heart of the human spirit. Jimmy planted and kept up with a flower garden, which beautified the entire north side of his home, because Nan had maintained a tiny flower garden of her own. Ohhh . . . how she loved flowers, loved the bright colors. She was a hard worker, picking cotton with the best of the adults as she grew. They respected her for her quiet yet sweet demeanor. Many complained about their fate, but not Nan. She kept a peaceful appearance nearly all the time. In her late teens, her parents were moved from the fields and into the servant's quarters. They were in much-better living conditions, spending time serving the personal needs of their "masters." They had no choice, but still became unwelcome to some of their former companions in the fields. Unwelcome to some, but certainly not to

Nan. She was overjoyed when able to see them, which was every few months or so.

The one event in her life that deeply troubled her . . . the one thing that stung her heart forever, was the discovery that her parents had been killed after they had attempted an escape one cool autumn night. A neighbor caught them as he was making his nightly rounds about his property. When he brought them back to Stafford's Grove, the master, Anson Stafford, decided to make an example of the maroons (escapees). I'll skip the awful details. What had hurt Nan was the feeling of abandonment . . . the knowledge that her mom and dad were going to leave her without so much as a "good-bye." Her sense of abandonment was overwhelming.

Nan wasn't fancied by most of the male slaves as she was not regarded as a pretty girl, but rather a bit of an ugly duckling. However, her sweet nature and kind ways endeared her to all, but more so to Hank, a gangly yet hardy field slave, two years her junior. They were married as slaves married in those days—secretly—and eventually had four children, two boys and two girls. Nan made the terrible conditions less terrible as her children grew up with her attitude, with smiles touching the corners of their little mouths . . . the harsh world in their futures a distant dream. Nan was so sweet that sugar would be jealous, and she painted the hearts of those who knew her with colors *so wondrous* that they'd put a rainbow to shame.

Nan caught the smallpox when she was thirty-four; her four children were teens by then. With smallpox being contagious, she was kept separate from her family, in a small shack at the farthest end of the property. Master Anson made it known that all were to stay away from her and that he would have a doctor check in on her every few days to try to help her get better. Despite this, she did not get better, but rather regressed considerably, and after two weeks in bed, she knew her time was running out.

Her back pain, the awful mouth and face sores, and the fever were getting too hard on her. So . . . she painfully asked the slave who attended to her, a woman named Ebby, to summon Hank and her children. They arrived minutes later and stood on the other side of the room, a sheet hanging between them. Hank was crying, a hard, strong man and not one to well up . . . bawling uncontrollably for his sweet Nan. All of the children were crying too, and the youngest, her daughter Keezie, had to be restrained from tearing down the sheet and rushing to her mother.

Nan's pain forced a cry off from her ravaged body, and they stopped the fussing and listened closely, ears to the white sheet, straining for her words. This sweet and gentle soul was now but a whisper, her voice faint . . .

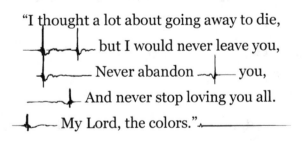

"I thought a lot about going away to die,
—— but I would never leave you,
—— Never abandon —— you,
—— And never stop loving you all.
—— My Lord, the colors.".——

Chapter 13

One to Go

The cute brunette awakened early Saturday while Jimmy still lay sleeping. It was 7:00 a.m., and Dee had trouble remaining asleep as her inner clock was used to getting up at seven each morning. She slid gently from the bed, as to not wake Jimmy, and barefooted her way into the kitchen to start her required coffee. She needed only to make enough for herself as Jimmy never drank coffee, preferring the odd orange assortment—juice, drink, or soda.

All that and he hates oranges, Dee humored herself.

During the week, Jimmy, still naturally distraught and in mourning, had been much more resigned than usual. Dee had just *been there* for him, lending an ear or a shoulder as needed. Today was the second anniversary of their first date, and she thought that it would be asking too much to expect him to remember, much less to hope that they could somehow celebrate.

As the coffee brewed, Dee strode into the hall, grabbed a towel from the cupboard, and went into the bathroom to shower. The large bathroom, featuring a kick-ass Jacuzzi, as with the rest of the home, was "George'ous." Dee, Tommy Brando, and Jimmy playfully called everything in the home "George'ous" because Jimmy's gay friend, George Young, had built the home for Jimmy and helped decorate to boot, muttering "gorgeous" to himself as he went. Karen

Two Storms, Soul #9, being a lesbian herself, had a good sense of humor and just shook her head, laughing playfully.

After Dee showered, she put one of Jimmy's long T-shirts on to walk around in. Jimmy always told her that she was adorable in his shirts. So, she thought he'd appreciate waking up to that. She sat at the kitchen table and was reading the morning newspaper when Jimmy walked slowly into view.

"The Lord of the Manor awakens," she said playfully.

"G'morning," Jimmy mustered as he wiped the sleepies from his eyes.

"You want me to make you something for breakfast?" she asked thoughtfully.

He seemed to ponder this question momentarily before answering. "Yes . . . I'd like to order six slices of buttered French toast, each with a side of half-burnt bacon, and Karo Syrup . . . not that maple stuff."

Dee's eyebrows raised as Jimmy continued. "Also, I'd like a pitcher of freshly squeezed orange juice and lastly, as always, one beautiful maiden to shower with the Lord before he eats."

Jimmy smiled and walked over to hug his sweetheart. She returned his hug before feigning offense.

"Well, his Lord will have to shower alone as I've showered already."

Jimmy replied alertly, "I said '*beautiful*' maiden, sorry, you must've misheard me."

Dee pushed Jimmy and began to chase him about the house as he repeatedly apologized for his obviously mirthful remark. He had made his way back into his bedroom and stood bouncing on his bed as Dee entered the room.

"If you think I'm just going to jump into bed with you after those comments . . ." she began, as Jimmy cut her short.

"Well, how about jumping *on* the bed then?"

His smile was infectious, and she managed a kind of "Mona Lisa" as she approached him. He extended a hand and helped her onto the bed. He began to bounce and she rolled her eyes uttering, "Jimmy . . ." in that *I-don't-know-if-this-is-a-good-idea* kind of way.

Jimmy continued smiling at her as he helped her up to bounce. Dee began to laugh with him as they bounded ceiling-ward.

"Your bounce is quite George'ous by the way."

She then stuck her foot out and tripped him, and he crashed down upon the bed. They always knew how to enjoy each other and were as playful a couple as anyone could imagine. Jimmy grabbed out and pulled Dee down atop him as she again feigned a protest.

"That 'beautiful' comment in the kitchen, you know I owe you one, Jimmy," she said, with a wicked grin etched upon her face.

Jimmy then kissed her.

Dee immediately pushed away, cupped her hand over her mouth and nose and said, "Morning breath!"

Jimmy sat up and with resignation said, "*That* didn't take long."

Jimmy showered and shaved before reentering the kitchen.

"Did you use mouthwash?" Dee queried jokingly.

"Naturally," he responded with a wry smile.

Jimmy approached her and hugged her from behind while she read the paper.

He spoke softly. "I thought we should go out tonight, you know, to celebrate our two years together."

She lit up like a Christmas tree.

She whirled around and kissed him before replying, "I wasn't sure that you would remember . . . with everything that's happened."

Upon saying those last few words, Dee's doe-like brown eyes watered a bit.

He then said, "I'd like you to know something . . . I remember things about you that I don't about other people—little things, big things, all things you. So let's celebrate our time together and do it in style. I've made reservations for Momma Asonte's . . ."

Dee hurled the newspaper at him telling him he had better not.

Jimmy laughed and said, ". . . just kidding, just kidding. The reservations are for seven o'clock at Simone's."

Dee seemed pleased by this choice, but chastised him for always messing with her head.

"You're right, sweetheart, I'll try to work on that," Jimmy responded with a devilish grin.

Simone's by the Bay was the first restaurant Jimmy had taken Dee to when they had begun dating, and it had an indoor-outdoor setting, just the way they preferred. Simone's was not a formal restaurant, but rather—as Dee called it—"high-end casual." Neither Jimmy nor Dee were fancy in their tastes, so Simone's was just enough down-to-earth to suit them. It was a fine-looking restaurant and was decked out in Parisian décor and featured a live pianist, but it was not a "true" French restaurant, it was more French-Lite. The menu was chockfull of everything. They featured a variety of meat and fish dishes, and—as Dee often remarked "... a Chef salad to die for." Jean-Paul Lalande was especially pleased to hear that they were going there, as it was a reminder of home.

. . . .

Jean-Paul was the tenth soul Jimmy became bound to. Jimmy melded with Jean-Paul when visiting, of all places, Greece. It had been among many stops on a European/Mediterranean historical venture. Jean-Paul had died off the west coast of Greece in the "Battle of Navarino" on October 20, 1827.

Naturally, it had been there that Jimmy "found" Jean-Paul. Jimmy had been traveling via tour ship, when the ship fatefully anchored within the Bay of Pylos, formerly known as Navarino. En route to shore and to the town of Pylos, Jimmy felt the by-then familiar "surge" from beneath the boat. As was usually the case, Jimmy had been thrust into an unfamiliar world. Yet, as the initial shock wore off, he eased together with his newfound soul.

Jean-Paul was a merry soul, a friendly sort that saw a silver lining in all things. He was born in Paris, 1802, and had been an only child. His father was a laborer, and his mother worked doing the neighborhood laundry. Jean-Paul was often teased by the neighborhood children for having the most beautiful naturally curly, blond hair that anyone had ever seen. He was quite handsome, but not the toughest kid about. Upon turning sixteen and determined to be a real man, he set out to toughen up in the

French Navy. He got his wish, and then some, taking a variety of beatings by the officers and crew, among other unspoken deeds. He became among the heartiest fellows on the ship by his twenty-first year and was well respected among his mates. Despite what was done to him, he never complained . . . not once, not ever.

Jean-Paul had never married, nor had children, but was very respectful and proper with the ladies and quite good and uncle-ish with children, and truly loved to mingle with the locals wherever they put to port. He died instantly when struck by a cannonball to the chest, knocking his crushed corpse well overboard. In all the years he has been SoulBound to Jimmy, he had never complained . . . not once, not ever.

. . . .

Jimmy said he needed to run an errand, and Dee thought it would be nice to visit her parents, whom she felt she had been neglecting recently, so the two split up for a few hours. Jimmy returned in the early afternoon and decided to wash his car as it was to be the chariot of the evening. It was a very hot day out, typically unpredictable, as the weatherman had thought it would be "Sunny and seventy-four degrees." He got the sunny part right, but it had to be ninety this day.

Jimmy had a lot on his mind as he soaped down the car. He was attempting to memorize what he had written for Dee later that evening. He reviewed the lines repeatedly until he felt sure he had it right. The odd thing was that he never had much difficulty remembering anything as it seemed that Marie and the others helped his recollection of things when he forgot. He needed all the help he could get; this was more than an anniversary . . . it was to be the night Jimmy proposed to Dee.

His errand had been to pick up Tommy and try to pick out the engagement ring. They searched three stores before Gina Imbragulio directed Jimmy to the right one. It was she, the Italian pianist and the eleventh soul, who reminded Jimmy of the ring that Dee had admired when Jimmy had taken her shopping for her birthday in December. Dee had mentioned that "this ring" was nice and jokingly said that Jimmy shouldn't mind a mere two thousand dollars. As Jimmy paid the two grand, Tommy laughed before saying playfully, "Thank God you made up your minds."

Jimmy laughed at the inside joke before he thanked Gina for the assist and thought, *One big thing down, one to go.*

Chapter 14

Silent as the Sun

Dee returned hours later and told Jimmy it was great that she was able to visit her parents. She said they were both doing well and had hoped that she would bring Jimmy with her the next time.

He replied, "Sounds cool," as he finished hand-toweling the car while "The Riddle" by *Five for Fighting* played on the car stereo.

His ability to wash and wax his car had been fairly pathetic until Brennan Payton came along. Brennan was a car enthusiast and former street racer, as well as the head network-tech trainer at a rising company called T-Royce. He made nearly 200,000 dollars annually before the accident took his life. He was young, a bachelor, had money, looks, and charisma to spare, giving him "mad game." Brennan was driving a modified Supra and was out at night showing it off to his latest girl, Miranda, when he lost control speeding around a hairpin turn. Snuffed out in a heartbeat . . . game over.

Jimmy was happy to learn from the SoulBound, picking and choosing their best qualities and skills, but when it came to Dee, it was all just Jimmy.

"I went out with Tommy to the mall. He needed to spend his self-imposed quota of $100 per week on movie DVDs, you know, the 'special collector's edition' ones or the 'special director's cut.'"

Dee snickered at that known truth about Tommy. Everyone knew that Brando had an amazing collection of movies, set up in specific order of his "Top 200" favorites. Tommy had constantly egged on "Jimmy Bucks" to buy a "1,000-inch" giant screen to watch movies on, as Tommy's 60-inch was just "too small."

Jimmy and Dee showered and got ready for their night out as the afternoon waned. They left a little after 6:30, with the temperature still in the mid-eighties, and arrived a few minutes early for their reservation. After giving fair advance to the proprietor as to the evening's importance to him, Jimmy was pleased to have the host wink knowingly as they were seated. The waitress came out after a minute and introduced herself as Wanda, before realizing that Jimmy knew that already.

"Well I'll be . . . Hi, Professor!"

Jimmy smiled and said hello before he looked to Dee.

"Dee, this is Wanda Krichsky, a student of mine at Russell."

Dee smiled as Jimmy continued.

". . . and Wanda, this is my girlfriend, Dee Conway."

The women exchanged pleasantries and the giddy student, getting back to her job at hand, asked them to look over the menus, telling them she would return to take their order shortly.

Jimmy was nervous and seemed to have difficulty selecting something from the menu. Dee noticed, but kept her curiosity to herself. They eventually ordered, with Dee getting a cod fillet on a bed of white beans and Jimmy a one-pound rib steak with smoked mashed potatoes. A few patrons were eating at the outdoor tables, and Jimmy could see the sun moving closer to the horizon beyond them. *It's getting close.*

Jimmy fidgeted about the table and eventually excused himself from the table and made his way to the men's room. He washed his face in cool water and dried off as he stared in the mirror.

"Calm down, it's gonna go great," Marie mind-spoke in her naturally soothing "voice."

"Yeah . . ." was Jimmy's only response, as he again reviewed the lines he would speak to Dee in less than an hour's time.

Jimmy, slightly more confident, walked back to the table and arrived just as their food did. He muttered something about impeccable timing and sat down to eat.

Dee's curiosity/concern could no longer be contained and she asked him what was wrong. She said he seemed uneasy and nervous.

He feigned ignorance before laughing a bit and telling her that he couldn't believe his good fortune. He was a little nervous because he had wanted to make a good impression on her, this night above all others, to prove how much she meant to him.

Dee seemed satisfied and rather pleased with Jimmy's seemingly honest and rather sweet answer. They chatted about many things, mostly about Dee's childhood memories, and laughed quite a few times at her misadventures.

After eating, Jimmy took Dee's hand and went to the piano, which was without a pianist, who had taken a break merely moments earlier. Jimmy sat at the piano, Dee sat beside him, and he looked into her eyes as his fingers brushed the keys. Dee sat in amazement at the skill that Gina Imbragulio had passed to Jimmy, painting the keys in strokes that awed those in earshot. The music was utterly beautiful. Every note was perfect . . . as Jimmy continued to stare deep into the eyes of his beloved.

The patrons were stunned at how wonderfully Jimmy played and applauded happily as he finished.

He then rose and nodded to the "audience." Dee just hugged him and whispered, "I loved that."

It was ten minutes after eight as Jimmy completed paying for the meal, leaving a rather generous tip. He held Dee's hand and walked outside, not toward the car but rather the shore.

It was time . . . *The sun is setting.*

///////// The curtain rises /////////

Silhouette seagulls cried overhead as the couple walked slowly along the beach, holding hands. The wind's warm and soft breeze enveloped them as the waves crashed lightly upon the shore. The sun faded slowly over the horizon, casting beautiful colors across the seascape, spreading about the ocean like the wings of a giant bird. Neither spoke, but took it all in, enchanted in the moment. Until . . . Jimmy stopped and spun about to stare deeply into Dee's eyes . . . went down on one knee . . . and said,

"You've kissed me softly, Sweetheart, held me close and whispered your dreams to me. You've taken my heart, and I'd fall apart, if our love wasn't meant to be. I believe so strongly in us, in our trust, in all of what we do. I know it's real, for I easily feel, the love that flows from you. Time cannot steal away our love, for it's a thief without a prayer. And no one or nothing can take away, the hopes and dreams we share. Open your heart and let me in, then open your soul to me. For our time has come, two become one, and our love shines for all to see. And now, I kneel before you . . . a happy man, who knows what he wants in life. So hear my plea . . . on bended knee, I ask . . . Will you be my wife?"

As he was finishing the last few words, he took out a little black box and opened it as he knelt.

Dee stood, transfixed, with tears trickling to the sand beneath her. She then attempted a smile as she sobbed, "Y-Yes, Jimmy . . . yes."

Overjoyed, Jimmy led Dee to a more secluded part of the beach . . . where . . .

Outlined clouds move with ease, across an indigo sky.
Shadows and wind shift on cue as the baton rises high.
The Orchestra begins to set the rhythm, the ocean tides in time . . .
As the couple, now awash in the silver of the Night Sun,
lay naked to the stars.
Their eyes shimmer to reflect their desires,

Their passion growing as they kiss . . .
The Conductor quickens his delicate pace as they continue this.
The couple swims in each other's souls,
smiling in sweet surrender . . .
Then gently, they collide . . . inside
Warmth envelopes them . . . and they cry in pleasure.
"Yes . . ." she moans again, as they blend,
Fingers entwined, a rhythmic glide . . . two souls beating in tune
Like Cupid's arrow, felt . . . not heard . . . silent as the sun.

///////// The curtain falls /////////

Chapter 15

Fortunate Souls All

The couple made their way back home after the night of their lives. Moments from home, Dee screamed out, nearly giving Jimmy a heart attack. Dee held her hand out toward him as if to better showcase her ring and proceeded to tell him that she had been so much in shock earlier that she hadn't really noticed the ring was the one she had joked about wanting. Jimmy smiled contently and then replied, "I'm happy you like it."

Their joy knew no bounds . . . flooding Jimmy's home with laughter as they entered. It was 11:00 p.m. as they kicked their shoes off and made their way into the shower. The sand fell from them as they washed. As they neared being done, Jimmy pushed the showerhead to point straight down. He turned to Dee after wiping water from his eyes and took her hands in his.

"Didn't we just do this?" she asked as she giggled.

Jimmy retorted sarcastically, "Yes, but I want to do it again."

He then laughed before continuing. "I thought that, maybe, you'd like to move in with me."

Dee raised her eyebrows for a moment, and it was apparent that she was considering it. She stared at him a few more moments and cracked a smile before replying, "I do spend a lot of time here as it is, so making it official would be cool. I love it here with you, Jimmy, so . . . yes, I'd love to."

She kissed her man warmly as Jimmy beamed inside.

After the shower, the pair stepped down into the living room. Dee was chattering aloud at what seemed to be a thousand words per minute, considering arrangements she would need to make to bring her things over and where she would put them. She also worried aloud about her parents' reaction. Dee was a grown woman and had been on her own for two years, but she still knew that her parents' beliefs in living arrangements were old-fashioned.

"I can hear Dad now, 'You live together *after* you get married, not before. You're a good Catholic girl for Christ's sake.'"

Dee shook her head at the hypocritical commentary, then continued. "You know I love them, but they can get almost medieval on me about things. Plus, we need to pick a date and, oh my God, there's so much to do. I like outdoor weddings, but indoor has its charms too . . ."

Jimmy nodded his head in agreement at the end of every sentence, as he had learned not to interrupt Denise Conway when she rambled like this.

Jimmy returned to work on Monday morning and had a lot of catching up to do after missing so much time. He joyously greeted Gertie and made his rounds to say hello to the other faculty. He eventually made his way to his classroom and spotted Michelle Channing, where he thanked her warmly for filling in. She hadn't been told that Jimmy was expected back, so she had again prepared to teach in his stead.

Michelle was in her seventies, where exactly, Jimmy wouldn't guess. She had her short and obviously colored, dark hair up in a bun, and wore a traditional, classy flowered dress. Michelle had been the professor Jimmy replaced three years prior. She was retired, but helped out when needed. After filling him in on where the students were in their studies, the elderly woman shuffled off. As she walked out, Jimmy nodded to her approvingly.

It took mere moments before Jimmy got into his rhythm, educating his students on the history of the arms race between the United States and the former Soviet Union. These were the sort of lessons Jimmy loved to educate his students on . . . delving into the heart of the stupidity of nations and the few occasions that the entire world's future hung in the balance. He then followed the discussion up with a viewing of the music video from singer Dan Reed called "The Dictator." The song/video shared Jimmy's views on greed and power and the most important of all lessons, the power of love and self-awareness. When Jimmy spoke to his students, they truly listened. He had an almost supernatural way (no pun intended) of getting their attention. He moved and spoke as if life itself evolved around what he was saying. He was in his element, showing why the teaching community had honored him, and it sure felt good to be back.

Sometimes he wondered where his gifts came from. He wasn't always sure if the things he did were natural, or unnatural, given his unique spiritual state. However, Jimmy decided that it didn't matter where he began and they ended . . . they were family now . . . a collective of lives . . . fortunate souls all.

Chapter 16

Two Storms

It was an overdue exercise . . . introducing Dee to the SoulBound. Jimmy had been giving this a lot of thought in recent days and realized that this needed to happen from both Dee's and the SoulBound's point of interest. Jimmy announced to the SoulBound that he was planning to introduce everyone to Dee that evening after dinner. It was Friday, the 2nd of June to be exact, and Jimmy stopped by Momma Asonte's after work and picked up a pizza and Dee's favorite munch-ons, mozzarella sticks. They seemed to do this ritually on Fridays, although it was rarely mentioned or planned.

As they ate, Jimmy brought up the subject about her meeting the individual SoulBound, much to Dee's surprise . . . pleasant surprise that is. She seemed excited about the idea and was happy with Jimmy for suggesting it . . . a subject she had considered often and had hoped would be discussed sooner rather than later.

So . . . after dinner was finished and the dishes were cleaned, Jimmy asked Dee to come with him into the living room and to sit upon the love seat, opposite him, himself seated on the couch.

"Wow . . . I'm way more nervous than I figured I'd be," Jimmy uttered.

He paused and closed his eyes for a few moments before opening them and saying . . . "Dee, I'd like you to meet my very good friend and the first of the SoulBound . . . Marie Anne Beale."

Jimmy seemed to go into a trance before he moved slightly uncomfortably in his seat and opened "his" eyes; his eyes were his, but it was Marie who looked out from behind them. She then spoke to Dee.

"Very pleased to meet you, however oddly."

Marie had Jimmy's voice, but laughed embarrassedly and differently than Jimmy did. It was obviously a warm and friendly greeting, to which Dee replied, "Odd . . . certainly, but overdue as well. It's awfully nice to meet you, Marie."

Dee stood, as did Marie, and they moved toward each other and gave each other a gentle hug. They both laughed a bit and sat back down, upon which the "girls" chatted for about ten minutes or so before they realized there were others awaiting their turn.

As each SoulBound was given the chance to meet Dee, they did so in the order they became bound to Jimmy. It was an eerie experience for most, as they had never done the "back-in-body" thing with Jimmy before, yet they all managed to get through the experience quite well.

John Jaden, Soul #6, had hugged her a bit too long, but winked at Dee knowingly, to which she joked that he was the one to keep an eye on. As they each came and went, Dee was nearly overwhelmed with joy and emotion . . . as she had been speaking with and hugging the dead . . . those who had passed on . . . yet she stayed strong throughout the bizarreness of their circumstances.

The night ended as Jimmy asked Carrie Ann if she'd like to meet Ms. Dee, to which the child simply said, "Yes."

There were no words to describe it . . . Dee's heart . . . her very soul . . . was touched forever by the experience.

As Dee lay in bed that evening, her mind raced. It would take a great deal of time to familiarize herself with all twelve SoulBound, to remember them as individuals, as Jimmy did. She knew she would never know them anywhere near as well as he did, but she wanted to try to be on good terms with them all. In addition to her encounter with Carrie Ann, the person she was struck by and found the most interesting was Karen Two Storms. Karen had been in a similar field as Dee—Dee was the assistant manager at a bank, whereas Karen had been a financial advisor for various companies and had been quite the entrepreneur in her day.

· · · · · · · · · · · · · · · · · · ·

Karen Two Storms was born in Dallas, Texas, on August 14, 1933, to Juanita Maria Ramirez and Two Storms. Her mother was Mexican and her father Native American. Two Storms was Navajo-born, and he was named thus because he had been born during the collision of two storm fronts on the plateau near his home in Arizona. He never referred to himself as Navajo, but rather Dine', meaning simply "The People."

The baby was given an American name, "Karen," to help her get through her soon-to-be-hard life. Karen grew up as a fierce and proud person and wouldn't back down from a fight, outnumbered as she often was. She was taught her mother's language of Spanish and she learned English at school and throughout the community, but her father never taught her Navajo. He said that she could be overwhelmed with learning two languages as it was. He was a kind soul, but rarely said a word, whereas her mother was a real talker. Juanita spoke in Spanish the majority of the time, throwing out the occasional English word or phrase, and even the rare Navajo. Karen was an only child until her brother Mark came along shortly after her fifteenth birthday. She adored him and was a wonderful big sister.

Karen knew that she was different than the other girls, and although there were many Spanish-speaking girls around, she felt that there was more to it than that. She was seventeen and had still not shown any inclination for boys, as most of the girls swooned over Trevor Quale, the football star at the school, or Devin Taylor, the gorgeous Glee Club leader.

No, she sensed something was "wrong" as her affections, which were rare, were for female companions. She admired Shannon VanOrsdale's beautiful hair and sweet demeanor, and although there were many pretty girls about, Shannon seemed the only one who wasn't put off by Karen's attention.

"What's wrong with me?" Karen would often wonder.

Karen never acted on her feelings for she knew that she would be beaten and ostracized from the community. Her parents would disown her . . . or at least she expected as much. It was time for her to leave, as school was over and she knew that she needed to start a new life . . . anywhere but Dallas.

She told her parents that the wind was calling her East. She was smart and knew that speaking of such things would make it easier to sway her parents' understanding a bit more her way. Sure enough, her father stood up from the sofa and paused before telling her that his love for her was stronger than the mountain, but that if the wind beckoned you, you must heed its call. He hugged her with a determined strength, as if he would never hold her again, and then brushed her long jet-black hair out of her face. He cupped her face in his large hands, to stare into her deep brown eyes, and told her to never forget who she was and from where she came . . . she was Karen Two Storms . . . daughter of the Dine' and Mexican people, and now, Child of the Wind.

She cried at the sight of her proud father's tears and moved quickly to embrace her momma and baby brother and continued to weep openly. She was given money to take the bus east . . . and to follow the path of the wind.

Karen worked hard cleaning homes for the wealthy in and around Washington, DC, and as always, had to overcome the prejudices associated with a person of her cultural background and cinnamon skin color. She saved every penny she could until venturing out on her own, starting her own cleaning service. It was called Eastern Wind Cleaning Services. She eventually paid her way through college in her mid-thirties, and it was there she met her special someone—twenty-two-year-old college senior Jaime Donovan. Jaime was the cutest and most shy girl Karen had ever met, yet she opened up to Karen without a word. They became lovers, and best friends, and remained so until Karen's untimely death by heart attack at age fifty-eight. The two women had been planning to start a new business together—Two Storms Financial Services—that never came to be.

Karen ignored The Light that beckoned her in 1992. She was fiercely determined to stay where she was . . . near her love and best friend, forever.

Jaime had been devastated by Karen's death, but got on with her own life, eventually contracting and succumbing to AIDS in 1997. Karen had been truly lost . . . a pain that stained her deeply within . . . where even the wind couldn't reach her.

Chapter 17
Lullaby-Bye

The next morning was Saturday, and after a beautiful and insightful evening, Jimmy felt refreshed . . . and decided to stop by the local Donut Shoppe to pick out "The Dozen Deal" before he went to visit his brother, Alex. He was hopeful that Kathy and Lissy were there as well. He hadn't spoken to Alex since the reception six days previous, and he wanted to make sure Alex was doing okay. In addition, getting to see his niece was always a thrill. Jimmy adored her and was known as a baby freak, meaning he loved babies, regardless of whose child it was. Naturally, he was far more attached and extra affectionate toward Lissy.

Jimmy arrived at Alex's home within ten minutes. That was another wonderful thing about living in Annapolis—everyone was close. Kathy, still plump after having the baby, answered the door and was pleasantly surprised to see her brother-in-law. She gave Jimmy a hug and invited him inside, telling him that Alex had not returned home yet but was expected soon. Baby Melissa was wide awake and smiled excitedly as Jimmy entered the living room. She was grabbing the edge of the sofa and pulling herself up to stand. It was a "looky-at-what-I-can-do" moment.

Jimmy immediately clapped and smiled happily in return.

"Good job, Lissy!"

Jimmy was in a special place with his niece . . . life was pure in these moments, and it gave him respite from the outside world. He played with the baby for a while as Kathy straightened up the house. She had been an accountant before having Melissa, but having such a beautiful bond with her daughter had Kathy considering giving up her career, or at least putting it on an extended hold.

While playing with the baby, Jimmy could feel the joy of many of his souls, with the women-souls in particular being giddy. After a bit, Lissy got tired and Kathy said it was her nap time.

Jimmy asked if it would be okay for him to rock the baby to sleep and she hesitated before agreeing. With the combined abilities of three mothers and a couple big sisters, Jimmy held her like a pro, cradling her as she fussed in vain, fighting the coming sleep.

Kathy watched him as she finished tidying up the place, listening as Jimmy began to sing. He sang old lullabies, some that she had not heard before. The first few were from Nan, who had raised four children of her own. These were the songs she sang to her babies. He then sang a few in languages that Kathy was unfamiliar with, but she knew that Jimmy spoke six languages, so she was not that surprised.

Thanks to Su Yi, Soul #3, Jimmy was indeed singing in Chinese to the little one. He sang in soft tones as Lissy rested comfortably, seemingly entranced as her blue eyes began to close. Jimmy finished with a beautiful lullaby in Italian; Gina had no children of her own but had sung this to her little brother when she was in her early teens. He was enjoying the songs and felt at peace as the women—and even a couple of the guys—cooed within him. He even heard faintly, in the recesses of his unconscious mind, Carrie Ann humming her own little lullaby.

As the baby fell silent and quite asleep, Jimmy stopped singing and whispered simply, "Lullaby-bye."

It was what his mother used to say after singing her boys to sleep.

Jimmy was about to get his sister-in-law's attention, but at that moment he heard Alex come in through the front door.

Kathy greeted him with a finger to her mouth in the "shhhhh" symbol and proceeded to hug and kiss him.

Alex waved quietly to his older brother, who was still seated in the rocker, cradling the baby.

Kathy walked over to Jimmy and deftly picked the tot up to take her to bed.

Alex then greeted Jimmy as they happily shook hands. Little brother was a bit shorter than big brother, but heavier, and had short chestnut-colored hair.

Before Alex could ask, Jimmy said, "I'm just being a big brother, checking in on you."

Alex smiled and responded, "We're doing fine, it's been a bit tough, naturally, but we'll be okay. What about you, you all right?"

"Yeah, like you said, it's been a bit rough, but I've had some wonderful things happen."

Jimmy waved for Kathy, who was just returning from settling Lissy into her cradle, to come into the room and asked the couple to sit down for a spell.

She did as asked, and she and Alex sat upon the sofa, with Jimmy returning to the rocker.

"Dee and I are getting married," Jimmy said with a big smile lighting his face.

"Oh my God!" the couple said simultaneously.

"That's great, Jimmy!" Alex said happily as he got up to hug his brother.

He then offered, "Grats, Bro, I am really happy for you."

Kathy was obviously pleased and said, "Ditto," as the three laughed a bit.

"She is also moving in with me, although the details are still being worked out."

Alex then responded, "Wooooow, my big bro is growing up and everything."

Alex laughed and Jimmy snickered back. Kathy was getting excited and asked Jimmy to give her the details about how he proposed.

The professor then heard Dragon muttering, *"Sissy shit,"* again. Jimmy fought the instinct to roll his eyes before telling Kathy that she would have to talk with Dee to get the details.

"Jimmy, Jimmy, Jimmy . . ." began Jimmy's most charismatic soul, John Ezekiel Jaden.

". . . When are you gonna learn? Forget what Francis says, be your own man."

"Screw you, you sea-faring faggot!" Frank "Dragon" Jackson replied.

"Hey! Not cool!" Karen chastised Dragon for his "faggot" reference, as he rolled his eyes. John was a brash young man, albeit with his heart in the right place.

Growing up in Kenosha, Wisconsin, with strict parents and more specifically a belt-wielding daddy, the class clown in John Ezekiel Jaden secured many a red mark upon his rear end over the length of his schooling. He also spent numerous days punished in his room and confined to his bed. But typically, John risked lying beneath the covers playing with his plastic green toy soldiers against direct orders not to have fun while being reprimanded. He carried one in his pocket at all times . . . a reminder to always have fun.

He had three sisters and a brother, Christine, Janet, Estelle, and Zachariah—all older than he. Little brother couldn't help being funny, humoring his siblings and friends all the time. However, he tended to be a bit reckless in how he did it. He would often tempt fate at the family dinner table . . . a "no-fun" zone. As his parents and siblings said grace, John would flick a pea or other small veggie at one of his sisters or brother, testing their care for him. He knew one word from any of them and a good butt-whooping was soon to follow, but most often they watched out for him, annoying or not. For a small boy, he could sure take a whipping with the best of them.

He was a huge Red Skelton fan and admired Milton Burle a great deal as well. He watched them and felt that he could do what they did, but he had no clue how to go about becoming a comedian. It was 1958, and Jaden wanted to get away from Kenosha, away from the American Motors job that awaited him after he graduated. No way was he working there though, because that meant working at the company his father, Noah, had worked at quite miserably for many years. Noah had to call in a favor to get his son the work, but always knew that his youngest child was likely to leave Kenosha. He was right.

So, when John graduated, he did what all aspiring comedians did in those days . . . he joined the Navy. Jaden was a "deck ape" aboard a US Amphibious Fleet Flagship—the *USS Mount McKinley*. Deck apes were the crewmen who swabbed the decks of the ship and kept the outside of the ship clean and tidy. Despite the "crap job," the truth of the matter was that he really was having the time of his life, seeing places many most others could only dream of, such as the Sistine Chapel, the Parthenon, and running with the girls on the beaches of Rio de Janeiro.

However, in 1960, just two years into his duty, his fun-loving ways and great adventures came to an abrupt halt during a night at sea in the North Atlantic. During a particularly nasty storm, he had been ordered by the Boson's Mate to take out a few trash containers and dump them overboard. The order was not only foolish, as it was very dangerous to be on deck in the rough seas and high swells. For John, it turned out to be deadly. John, with a mate named Lenny helping him, was bitching furiously about the "horseshit job . . ." John then joked that perhaps his toy soldier should handle this one. He pulled the tiny plastic man out and pretended it was doing the trash run when a wave swept him over to the side rails. John was holding on to the rails as his feet hung over the edge of the ship. He screamed for Lenny's help, but as Lenny reached him and grabbed his arms to pull him back onto the deck, a swell about thirty-five feet high smashed into them both. Lenny survived by holding on to the rail. John was lost forever to the sea.

Left, right, left . . .

We all fall down . . .

· · · · · · · · · · · · · · · · · · · ·

"C'mon, Franky, you know I'm just playing with ya. You and me are a lot alike, just you're a bit rough around the edges and uneducated is all."

John just didn't know when to quit his messing around.

"If I ever get the chance, I'm gonna . . ."

A third voice interrupted the banter.

"Chill you two; can't you see this was a special moment for Jimmy?"

That voice belonged to Brennan Payton, Soul #7, having followed John in the order of bonds.

Karen chimed in with *"Exactly."*

A four-soul war of words ensued as Jimmy shook his head and cracked a smile as he made his way out the door.

Chapter 18

Engage

Upon arriving home after visiting his brother, Jimmy saw Dee unloading a few boxes from her car. He immediately went to help her.

Dee said, "Good timing, sweetie. How was your first day back?"

"Smooth actually, no glitches."

"Good, good," Dee responded, before continuing. "I stopped at the new Kimberly Michaels store at the mall and got some new shoes . . . since it was on the way here."

She smiled at Jimmy as she did when she knew what he was thinking.

He returned her smile with an "Uh-huh," raising his eyebrows in that knowing way.

She then went into the house and set the box she was carrying atop another one she had brought in before Jimmy arrived home. Jimmy walked in right behind her with the last box and Dee said, "I was thinking that I could set up my things in the spare bedroom, that way you wouldn't need to move any of your things around. That okay?"

"Uhhhh . . ."

Jimmy paused as he thought about that. Finally, after about five seconds he said, "Yeah, good idea. No problem here."

"Are you sure? I mean, I could just find a few drawers . . ."

"No, no, I'm sure." Jimmy cut her off and smiled. "Honestly, it's a good idea. I was just thinking it over a bit." He then kissed her as he took a box into the spare, errrr, Dee's room.

She had brought some necessities, including a few knick-knacks, some pictures and some clothes as well. Jimmy let Dee set up the room as she saw fit and, as she walked about setting things in place, he asked her what she wanted to eat for dinner. She replied that she had already eaten and that he should get whatever he wanted.

Jimmy went into the living room and was about to turn the TV on when it hit him, hard . . . a flash in his mind . . . of a terrible darkness. He winced and closed his eyes, trying to figure out what it was, and then it hit him again, even harder. He cried out, as the pain he felt was simply horrific. He had fallen back onto the sofa and had sat up to figure out what it was that just happened. He immediately connected with each of his souls to determine what they might know. In a mere few seconds, he knew. Carrie Ann was sobbing and it crossed his mind that she could be having—as strange as it sounded—a nightmare.

"Carrie Ann? Are you okay, sweetie?"

There was a pause . . . until Jimmy felt a deep . . . darkness envelop him. He was feeling cold and began shaking. He was reliving her last moments alive. He knew that Carrie Ann was "projecting" this incredible fear onto him. Jimmy focused, melding minds into one singular train of thought. He now saw and felt what she had. It seemed real, seeing and hearing through the little girl's memories. But the nearly pitch-dark room he was in provided barely enough light to see anything . . . anything that is but a dark form in the dark room. Him.

Fear beyond anything Jimmy had ever experienced washed over him, paralyzing him. Something . . . this Shadow Man . . . was coming . . . for him. It was just then that a distant voice within his mind called to him, *"Jimmy. Jimmy!"*

In moments, Jimmy was ripped back into his well-lit living room. Dee was calling his name as she stood over him.

"Jimmy! Oh my God, are you okay?"

"Dee . . ."

Jimmy was still shaken from his meld and wanted to question the child while it was all still fresh in his mind.

". . . I'm okay, but . . . Carrie Ann . . . something happened to her, something terrible."

"I don't understand. What happened?" Dee replied as she walked quickly into the kitchen and brought back a glass of water.

"Dee, I need you to allow me some time to deal with this. I have to reconnect with her."

Dee handed him the glass of water and, obviously concerned, she moved away from him and walked slowly back into her new room.

He again focused and sought to meld with Carrie Ann, ignoring the questions among the other souls who were aware that something was wrong. When Jimmy sought to "speak" to a specific soul privately, he would often create a place for them to go, usually beneath a great old oak tree among lush fields of green. He found serenity there and found it was perfect for settling down unsettled souls.

Carrie Ann was crouched in a corner of a square "room" for lack of a better term. It was empty and incomplete, kind of a reflection of the girl before him, he guessed.

He said hello. She was sobbing and didn't respond right away. *"Let me take you to a beautiful place, where we can talk. It's safe there, I promise."*

Jimmy extended a hand to the child, but she wouldn't move. Jimmy wanted to help her, desperately, but didn't want to push too hard, too quickly. He then decided to allow her time and he told her he hoped she would talk to him soon, before fading back to his normal self.

Jimmy was twisted into knots before hearing a voice that untied him.

"Hello Captain."

It was Marie, extending her friendship.

"Hi #1."

Jimmy had been a big "Star Trek" and "Star Wars" fan. Yes, you can be both. However, Marie, who liked the original Star Trek show, had grown very fond of the *Star Trek: The Next Generation* series and liked to occasionally refer to Jimmy as "Captain," to which he most often replied to her by calling her "#1," as in the show. He knew the situation with Carrie Ann was very disconcerting, but Marie always calmed him down. Marie could not see anything that happened between Jimmy and Carrie Ann, but could always see what Jimmy was doing in his regular life. Each soul was connected directly to Jimmy, but not each other.

They could not communicate directly unless Jimmy specifically allowed it, although each knew through Jimmy who everyone else was. At times, Jimmy would create opportunities for chat between them, such as when the four souls argued earlier. When he did this, they could hear, but not see each other.

With Jimmy acting scared and having told Dee that something terrible happened to the little girl, Marie knew he was hurting over this.

"Can I help in any way?"

Jimmy paused a moment to consider.

"Not unless you could meet with Carrie Ann directly. She sure could use a motherly figure." Just as Jimmy spoke those words, it hit him.

"Marie, we could try you know. I've never attempted it before because I never saw how, but maybe we could meld together, deeply, like when we are at the oak. Then (he walked excitedly about) *with us connected, and me in a sort-of trance, you could use my abilities to not just speak with, but really meet with Carrie Ann . . . just the two of you."*

When he heard no immediate response, he asked her playfully, *"You there, #1?"*

A few tense moments of mind silence were broken with, *"Aye Captain. Whenever you're ready."*

Captain Kassakatis anxiously lay on the sofa, propped his head up on a throw pillow, breathed deeply, and gave the command . . . *"Engage."*

Chapter 19
So Cries the Child

A beautiful blue sky held sway over the fields, green as the fields in Irish lore. There were billowy white clouds and the wind blew softly, whispering through Marie's curly brown hair. Jimmy sat beside her beneath the old oak as they had many times before. It had become almost second nature to them, their meld, or bonding if you prefer, was easier in comparison with the others. Jimmy always thought it was because Marie was so easygoing. Marie was sitting with her legs crossed, as Jimmy, now facing her, did the same.

"This may get," he paused, *". . . weird."*

Marie closed her eyes . . . *"She needs me Jimmy . . . she needs us."*

The two of them began to focus completely, attempting to connect to each other on a level never attempted before. Jimmy knew that this could go badly, and neither knew what would happen. All they had was hope and, fortunately, each other's strength. Jimmy's mind was complete serenity as Marie faded from his world. All he knew was peace and he seemed without a care in the world. He opened his eyes under the old oak tree and stared off into the deep blue skies.

Meanwhile, Marie opened her eyes and stared off into the gray recesses about her. She felt very strange, as she was now in complete control of Jimmy's mind. She felt more alive now than at any time since that day at the harbor. She could feel the gift of Life, its very essence permeating about her. But she knew that she was here for the child, not for her own selfish reasons. Just ahead, in an empty room, with just enough light to see by, was a child crouched in a corner. Marie approached the sandy-haired little girl, but didn't wish to frighten her. So, standing where she imagined the door would be, she said, *"Hi, Carrie Ann, I'm Marie, a friend of Mr. Jimmy's."*

The six-year-old, clutching a stuffed animal of some sort, slowly turned to look at Marie. The girl's tear-stained face was drawn and had that terrible look of desperation.

Marie smiled at her and said, *"I know how lonely it is here, and I sure could use a new friend."*

As Jimmy expected, Carrie Ann couldn't help but see that Marie was someone she could not only trust but also get close to. Carrie Ann finally spoke, albeit between sobs.

"I'm scared, Mrs. Marie . . . please . . . ," the little girl stopped and began to cry much stronger, a look of total fear imprinted on her face.

Although Marie had not had children of her own, all who knew her felt that she would have been a great mother. She reached for the girl and gently pulled her close. What shocked her was that she had taken on a physical form . . . she could actually feel the frightened child, and both seemed as real as they were in life; a remarkable turn of events.

Carrie Ann wept and rocked within the sweet woman's arms. Marie spoke in hushed tones as she patted the child's back, whispering that everything would be okay. Marie's voice was soft, gentle . . . and as the little one listened, she imagined Mrs. Marie as a dandelion in the wind. It was one beautiful thought . . . amid a sea of sadness.

The dandelion became more certain that it would be okay to go further.

"Jimmy said he thought you may be too scared to talk about something . . . bad . . . that happened."

Marie was very uncomfortable in prying, but realized it was necessary to help.

"If something bad happened to me, I would feel better if I were somewhere pretty. We can go to a beautiful place and talk there, if it's okay with you. It's a bit dark and chilly here, and I bet that if you came with me, you'd feel a little better. Mr. Jimmy is waiting there now."

The child did not respond immediately as she continued to sob rhythmically into Marie's blouse.

Marie didn't say more for fear of pushing too hard, as Jimmy had feared earlier. She continued to hold the girl and waited her out. Minutes passed.

Worry, however, turned to relief as Carrie Ann looked up at Marie with a tinge of hope in her teary hazel eyes and asked, *"Are there pr-pretty flowers there?"*

Chapter 20

Asunder

The "girls" appeared a few feet from where Jimmy lay relaxing beneath the oak. He seemed entranced, until Marie feigned a cough to get his attention. Jimmy looked up to see his old friend and the little girl he had been so desperate to talk with. He rose to greet them, and as he stood, Carrie Ann recoiled a bit.

Marie smiled at the child and introduced her formally to Jimmy.

"It's very nice to meet you, Carrie Ann, very nice."

Jimmy noticed that the child was a bit reserved toward him and realized that strange men must be low on her list of favorite people. He also noticed the pair appeared as real as any living person . . . the ghostly visages gone. He was pleasantly surprised.

Carrie Ann gave Jimmy a brief little smile before she turned to look around them. Beautiful flowers *were* there, amid rolling green hills and blue skies. They were in the shade of a great big tree, and as the adults had hoped, the child felt very comfortable here.

"I like it here, it's very pretty. Um . . ." Carrie Ann continued, yet seemed hesitant before asking, *". . . are we in Heaven?"*

Marie and Jimmy gave each other a "that's-a-biggie" look, and Jimmy realized that he would have to explain as best he could their situation.

"Carrie Ann, remember when you and I first found each other? I tried to talk with you then to explain, but all I could get from you was your age and also that your name was Carrie Ann. Do you remember that?"

The little girl gripped Marie's hand with purpose and just nodded at Jimmy. He was pleased to see that she had begun to become attached to Marie.

"You were scared, and rightfully so. I'm so sorry that you've been scared and didn't understand what was happening to you."

Jimmy paused and knew that what he was about to explain to her would be . . . very, very hard.

"You are not in Heaven, not just yet. A bad person took away your life, but for some reason you never went into The Light. Apparently, you were too scared to do anything. Carrie Ann, sweetie, I am a man, a real man, still alive and living as you did, on Earth. It seems that I have a gift, a light that you saw and walked into, and this light that comes from me, well . . ." Jimmy went fishing for the best words to use.

"Well . . . instead of having you go to Heaven, it brought your soul and mine together. You and Marie are the same. She, along with eleven others, live within me. We are like a community of lost souls. It's a hard thing to explain, Carrie Ann, but do you understand any of what I said?"

The little girl seemed a bit confused and looked over at Marie, as the trio had decided to sit during Jimmy's explanation.

Marie then added, *"Mr. Jimmy is telling the truth . . . you and me and some other people have passed away, but came here*

*instead of Heaven. We will go to Heaven someday, but we're not
sure when. All of our souls have come together here. I was the
first one here and I have known him now for over fourteen years.
You can trust him, he is a wonderful man."*

Marie smiled at the little girl in her comforting way.

"So . . . I am dead," the thin child said resolutely.

She then began to cry again and asked repeatedly for her
Mommy.

Marie's heart was breaking, as she knew there was nothing she
could do. But, as always, she tried. Marie again cradled the girl in
her arms and attempted to soothe her in soft whispers.

Jimmy sat by and realized that he may be able to help if he could
connect with the frightened little girl. Perhaps he could get her full
name and find out where she had lived. Perhaps . . . he could find
out what happened to her. How she died.

When Carrie Ann had calmed down a bit, Jimmy took a risk and
asked, *"Carrie Ann, what's your last name? Mine is Kassakatis.
That's a funny name, huh? What's yours?"*

She sobbed slightly, but answered, *"W-Weaver, Carrie Ann
W-Weaver."*

"That's a pretty name, isn't it, Marie?"

Marie answered matter-of-factly, *"It sure is . . . it's very
pretty."*

Marie looked at Jimmy and knew what he was up to and
followed his question up with one of her own.

*"I was born and lived in a place called Niagara Falls, in New
York State. That's pretty far away from here in Maryland. Where
did you live? Do you remember?"*

Marie smiled at the child as she asked. Carrie Ann then seemed to consider the question before answering.

"I lived in Arbutus and went to Arbutus Elementary School. Miss Susie was my teacher." The girl seemed to open up as she continued, *"We lived on Maiden Choice Lane: Me, my mom, and my brother Robby. He is two years older than me. My dad sees me on weekends sometimes . . . I mean . . . he used to."*

She had brought her stuffed animal and squeezed it close to her as she said those last words.

Jimmy looked at Marie and nodded at her as if to say "So far, so good."

What Jimmy was about to do, well . . . it may have been wrong, but he saw no alternative.

"Carrie Ann, earlier when you were remembering what happened to you . . . there was a cold, dark room, and a voice in the darkness."

The child went dead silent and stared at Jimmy; rather she seemed to look past him, her green eyes far away. The green rolling hills began to sway slightly and the blue skies darkened about them.

Marie looked around with the strongest sense of "wrong" saturating her every fiber.

Jimmy realized his time was fleeting and he continued to talk to Carrie Ann.

"Sweetheart, can you still hear me? I need you to tell me whatever you can about the bad man. Do you remember where he took . . . ?"

"Noooooooooooooooooooooooooo!"

Carrie Ann's horrid screams ripped the very foundation of the imaginary world about them.

"Noooooooooooooooooooooooo!"

Her screams then tore asunder the darkening skies, to reveal the advancing black beyond. The ground beneath them was in upheaval as Jimmy and Marie both reached the child. As they did, the hills became a wave of deepest darkness, and it was closing fast. The Oak was dripping something . . . red . . . blood!

"Carrie Ann!" Jimmy screamed to get the attention of the small girl, whose hands were clutched over her face.

"We gotta go, now!" Marie yelled franticly as the darkness closed in on them.

Jimmy screamed at Marie, *"You have to get out of here, take Carrie Ann with you. I'll be right along."*

Marie sensed something amiss in the way Jimmy said those words and screamed at him, *"No, Jimmy, it's too dangerous!"*

Jimmy smiled at her and lay back down at the base of the tree.

"Jimmy!" Marie screamed with every ounce of her being.

There was no time, so the blood-splattered heroine held Carrie Ann close as the black began to swallow them. And then, in a heartbeat, through Marie's will, they vanished.

Chapter 21
The Shadow That Speaks

Jimmy's mind was adrift . . . upon an ocean of darkness, he floats. He is cold . . . brutally cold. Jimmy comes to and finds that he is unable to move and can barely see, as the light in the room is very slight. There is movement. That's when he knows, that's when he remembers. He was with Marie and Carrie Ann, but . . . the darkness enveloped him. He had to know. He had to. He got his wish . . . but is tied to a chair, bound and gagged. A baritone voice riffs the pitch about him . . .

"One by one the chosen will fall, 666 in all. A procession of caskets across the land . . . a black and crimson caravan. You will be number 126."

Jimmy feels his hair being pulled hard and it feels as if it's being torn from his scalp. He yells out from the pain and is silenced as a pair of hands clamp around his throat. *Wait . . . those are not hands!* He cannot fight back as his hands are bound, he cannot breathe.

"Are you scared? I wonder what it feels like to die . . . ," the voice whispered as *something* squeezed Jimmy / Carrie Ann's windpipe.

Jimmy / Carrie Ann, in eternal fear, were frozen in fright as the dark man released them. Through the terror and tears, he/she notices the darkness is alive, moving about a poorly lit room.

It shifts as if it were a thousand black ribbons in the wind . . . and the wind is angry.

"May your last memory be of staring into the eyes of The Shadow That Speaks! May Mother Dark embrace your soul!"

Those eyes! A muffled scream . . . he/she cannot move, they cannot escape . . . they can only die.

A hard slap to Jimmy's face and then another, brought him back to where he lay on the sofa. Dee was straddling him, screaming his name, and as Jimmy came to, he realized where he was, but still couldn't breathe. He was clutching at his throat, and with his eyes bulging to burst, he pointed at his throat to Dee.

Dee quickly pulled Jimmy off the sofa to the floor, maneuvered behind him, and attempted to give him the Heimlich maneuver. The problem wasn't a stuck piece of whatever; it was in Jimmy's mind. When she realized her efforts weren't working, Dee began to panic. She screamed at Jimmy for help, asking what was wrong.

He was turning blue and slowly stopped thrashing about.

Dee reached for the phone on the end table and dialed 911.

The operator answered in moments and Dee immediately said, "Send an ambulance to 406 Secluded Circle in Annapolis. My fiancé is dying! He can't breathe, he isn't moving!"

She dropped the phone and decided to try mouth-to-mouth resuscitation. She pinched his nose, tilted his head back, and began to blow into his mouth . . . three long breaths.

Nothing, and no pulse either.

She shook him a few times and yelled his name in desperation, "Jimmy!"

At that moment, a brilliant flash of light blinded her, and it took her a few seconds to get her bearings.

What the hell was that? She thought before continuing.

Dee again tried three long breaths before she realized . . . he was dead. Jimmy was dead. That is when the panicked young woman got angry.

"No! It's not your time, Jimmy, not now! Breathe, damn it!"

Again, she began to press upon his chest, trying to remember the proper placement of her hands, learned when she was in high school.

"Breathe!"

She continued to switch back and forth from chest presses to mouth-to-mouth until . . . Jimmy coughed aloud and spit up a bit before he caught his breath. He rubbed about his throat and continued to take deep breaths, with focused intent. Tears streamed from his bloodshot eyes, but his color was returning.

Dee was overcome with emotion and cried uncontrollably for the lover she had lost and miraculously regained. She had brought Jimmy back from the black, and she kissed him gently as he sat up against the base of the sofa.

Jimmy sat with a dazed expression as Dee stood up and ran to the kitchen to retrieve a glass of water. He could hear the running water, and a part of him longed to drink, but his mind felt uneasy, something was . . . missing. Something was wrong.

Marie's voice was heard then, and she was crying, *"Thank God . . . we're all so thankful you're okay. But . . . Jimmy, the light . . . she made it . . . into The Light."*

In moments it hit him, Nan, Soul #5, once a slave in life, was free at last. She had gone in the moments Jimmy had died. The realization that he had died hit him like a thunderhead, yet his joy for her was a more powerful emotion.

Jimmy was terribly weak and his body felt beaten down, torn asunder. Yet even with an ambulance siren wailing that painful reminder, Jimmy raised his teary eyes heavenward, to Nan, put his trembling hands upon his heart . . . and smiled.

Chapter 22

Ain't No Sunshine

"Good morning, James, or should I call you Jim?" the doctor asked as he walked into the hospital room.

He was a middle-aged white man, mostly bald, with the twenty hairs remaining combed over across his shiny head. He was moving about in that "I'm in a hurry" mode.

"Jimmy, actually. Jim never seemed right, so . . . ," the patient responded in a raspy voice. The doctor, obviously not paying attention, said, "Very good, Jim. I'm Doctor Townsend. How are you feeling?"

The physician's "rushy" demeanor and obvious lack of attention to detail aggravated Jimmy, never a fan of doctors.

"Jimmy feels good. Jimmy's throat still hurts, but Jimmy feels he can go home at any time."

The doc raised his eyes from the chart he was holding and smugly retorted, "Fine, Mr. *Kakakakkis*, you appear to be well on the way to a complete recovery. I'll have a nurse finish up with you before you are released."

Jimmy was pissed, as he knew the doctor had deliberately mispronounced his last name. Therefore, as the doctor was leaving, Jimmy fired one last shot across his bow.

"Thanks a lot, *Mr.* Townsend, you take care."

Jimmy smiled as big as he could as the doctor shook his head before the door closed behind him.

He's no Patch Adams, Jimmy concluded.

"Talk about male bonding . . ." Dee blurted out while shaking her head, having witnessed the juvenile display from her chair next to Jimmy's bed.

"So, Mr. Kakakakkis is it? You wanna brush your teeth before the unsuspecting nurse arrives?"

Dee was smiling as Jimmy feigned being appalled at the insinuation that his breath was less than minty fresh. Jimmy had been awake for about an hour and knew that she was right, as usual.

"As you wish."

Jimmy, still sore from his brush with death, ambled toward the bathroom a few feet from his bed before pausing to look back at her,

"Baby . . . thanks, for everything."

After his release just after 4:00 p.m., Dee drove him home. During the ride, he used his cell phone to call both Alex and Tommy to let them know he was on his way home. They had visited him briefly the night before, but he had been sleeping.

Dee couldn't help but overhear Jimmy talking with Tommy.

"It hurts to talk, so I'll chat with you in a few days. That cool? All right, bro."

Jimmy hung up moments later.

Dee had to know exactly what happened to Jimmy. *Exactly.* This was not an option.

"Tomorrow morning, we talk, okay?"

Jimmy was resigned and shifted in his seat as they pulled into his driveway, but answered moments later, "Yeah."

Once home and snuggled into his king-size bed with a warm cup of herbal tea, Jimmy turned on the *Bose* radio and appropriately heard "Ain't No Sunshine" by Bill Withers, circa 1971. He loved this sad song and quietly listened to Withers's heavy lyrics . . .

• • • • • • • • • • • • • • • • • • •

Ain't no sunshine when she's gone
It's not warm when she's away
Ain't no sunshine when she's gone
And she's always gone too long, anytime she goes away . . .

• • • • • • • • • • • • • • • • • •

Memories flooded him . . . Nan meant so much to him. Marie and Nan were kindred souls, who should've been sisters, and Nan's ascension hit Marie as hard as it did Jimmy. He lay thinking of Nan moving on . . . into The Light . . . and smiled approvingly as he slowly nodded off.

Chapter 23
The Gathering of Ghosts

Early next morning, Dee had called the college to inform Gertie that Jimmy had a relapse of his illness and that he would be out for some time, and that it might be best to get a permanent substitute during the remainder of summer classes. Jimmy was not happy about missing more work, but work was a distant thought now. He had far greater needs now, far more urgent matters. He needed to formulate a plan, designed to hunt down the man that killed the sweet six-year-old within him. He had slept for fourteen hours the night before, and besides showering and eating breakfast, he had returned to the comfort of his bed.

As he lay in bed, he began to meditate . . . and within minutes, an idea hit him like a ton of bricks. He considered the idea for a few heartbeats before beginning to put his thoughts into motion. He was deliberate yet determined, and slowly began to gather the other souls, minus Carrie Ann, into a "room" within his mind. A room set up like a conference room. Eleven chairs.

Jimmy had never tried to do this before. As he focused, he worked one-by-one to bring them to the meeting. He didn't know if it would work or not, but he had to try. He was beyond angry about what the madman had done to Carrie Ann. He was seething. He hoped that someone at the gathering would help him figure out the best way to help him hunt the demon down . . . hunt it down . . . and kill it. The old Jimmy would not have considered violence, killing . . . but after his experience, he seemed somewhat harder-edged.

One by one, the SoulBound entered the room and stood about the large circular table. Jimmy fancied this table style since his reading about King Arthur and Camelot. The souls were visible to each other as if they were alive and at the ages they were when they passed. They were also dressed in the way they most often did while alive. They were all astonished to see the others about them and the room began teeming with conversation and introductions. They were even more astonished when they realized they were in physical form . . . a feat Jimmy still hadn't yet figured out.

Marie was hugging Su Yi, while Millie and Karen were introducing themselves. Jean-Paul, Brennan and Gina were huddled briefly, saying their hellos before moving about the "room." Shen Koketai sat alone, quite uncomfortable with the whole spectacle.

"Truce, bro, no hard feelings," John Jaden said to Dragon as they shook hands. Dragon smirked, but didn't reply. Gina and the other souls who didn't speak English had been able to grasp it immediately upon being bound with Jimmy, so everyone there was able to participate in the conversation. Call it fringe benefits.

The effort of the gathering had put a great strain on Jimmy. He felt pulled from all sides and had explained to each of them that he may seem unwell and perhaps even somewhat distracted, as he sat at the table.

All knew that further introductions and opportunities to get to know each other better, would come at another time. They were here for a serious matter, and Jimmy—sensing that it was time to get started—asked everyone to sit. A myriad of ethnicity and cultures sat about the round table, and all eyes focused upon the man who was their connection to their current manifestation of life . . . and death.

Jimmy rose from his chair and he looked into the eyes of each soul present and said, *"Welcome, my friends, and thank you for this. This is the first time we have been brought together as a group, and it is my intention that these gatherings will continue periodically. Each of you has addressed questions and concerns with me privately and I have found that all of you discuss the same matters of importance and curiosity. Today is not the day to go over these matters, because as you all know, we are here to determine the best course of action to hunt and kill the murderer of little Carrie Ann Weaver: The Shadow That Speaks."*

Jimmy's demeanor and matter-of-fact nature in uttering those words was a bit discomforting to most.

"Before we begin, Marie and I determined that she should leave this meeting to attend to Carrie Ann, as the rest of us deal with the dilemma before us."

Marie rose and nodded to the others before she "blinked" away.

"This will be an open forum, one that I will do my best to manage." Jimmy began.

"I am a writer and a teacher of history and generally not one to consider an act of violence and revenge. However . . . as I

have already shared with each of you, my recent venture into the darkness, you now know as I do that this . . ." Jimmy paused as he began to shake with rage. *". . . demon . . . must be stopped . . . must be eliminated for what he has done to Carrie Ann and the others. He must be destroyed before he kills again!"*

All the souls were entranced and torn as Jimmy was obviously seething with hatred. Every word spewed venom. Every glance haunted them. Jimmy seemed a changed man. They had no idea.

"What do we know about this Shadow man?" asked Koketai, as he stood up to walk slowly about the table.

Jimmy and all there were caught off guard, yet sat back down as the warrior continued.

"What clues can we gather to determine who he is and how to find him?"

Koketai was a young man used to speaking to others in a quiet yet analytical way, a way that one could not only not ignore, but also draw out the utmost interest. He continued.

"We know that the child was taken from her neighborhood, in an area fairly local to here. We know that this killer said that she was the 126th victim. Was he lying for effect . . . or bragging about the sickening truth? I for one tend to believe him. So, if he has killed over a hundred, I would assume that it has likely been within a sensible distance of his home, as most predators hunt within their home territory."

"Yes," began Karen Two Storms. *"I recall reading on numerous occasions about serial killers and their tendencies. Koketai is likely correct in his assumptions. Perhaps you could research missing*

people in the Maryland area to see if you can pick up any clues."
Karen was looking at Jimmy as she uttered the last sentence.

"You might wanna be careful where you poke your nose,"
voiced John Jaden, as he now stood to address the gathered.

*"I know . . . errrr, knew some military intelligence guys back
in the Navy. We would shoot the breeze at this little bar just off
the Gulf of Mexico, in Alabama, called . . . ummmm . . . hmmmm,
yeah, well it's been awhile."*

John laughed aloud, but the others seemed a bit impatient for
him to get to it.

*"So . . . where was I, yeah, these guys told me something
interesting. They explained that half the arrests they made were
gifts . . . you know, the bad guys gave themselves up by their
stupidity or just wound up walking in and admitting their dirty
deeds. It eats at their conscience . . . the guilt. My point being that
snooping around at a library or wherever . . . looking into Carrie
Ann's files may get you noticed."*

Jimmy responded almost immediately and made no effort to
hide his anger.

*"What alternative is there, John? You have a better idea? Let's
hear it."*

John seemed unfazed and sat back in his chair and replied,
*"Just trying to help is all. I thought it was you that invited us all
here to do just that."*

Jaden smiled that pirate smile that the ladies always found so
appealing. All grew quiet for a few moments until Jimmy responded
in a much-humbler tone, *"John . . . I'm sorry man. You're right . . .
and thank you. I don't know what's wrong with me lately. My*

apologies to everyone for being out of line. However, time is short, and unless someone has a better idea . . . I feel the need to try to investigate this as best I can, with due awareness of the potential dangers of being noticed."

He winked at Jaden at that last comment before rising to say a few final words.

"There are many inherent issues at work here. On my heart and soul, I swear to you . . . you all . . . I will spend more time with you to help sort out the various personal issues you have. But for now, you must all continue to wait it out. I love you, guys. You're a big part of my life, and I thank you for your help and ideas. Keep them coming, because if I've learned anything in the last fourteen years . . . it's that I, perhaps more than any person who ever lived . . . am not alone."

With that, the gathered shook hands and shared quick good-byes, before they slowly faded away . . .

Chapter 24

3:13 a.m.

It's far too warm for 3:13 a.m.

There was a brief sense of . . . something familiar. Sense of mind was overcome by sense of body, for though the heat was less intense in the basement than upstairs, it was entirely too hot.

Tyler "Jack" Hill had decided to avoid calling Regal's—the heating and air-conditioning company—to fix his air conditioner. Having someone poking around his home was unwise. So he suffered and made those he brought here suffer even more. The sweat beaded his body as he turned the cold knob on at the washing machine basin. Here is where he normally washed up . . . after.

The Latino boy, named Oscar, had been about sixteen years old. He had dark hair and brown eyes . . . eyes with a once-bright future . . . now dimmed to darkness. Jack had taken his hands, or what might pass for hands, and choked the life from the boy, as the shadows ebbed about in wicked display. Oscar was yet another tragic victim . . . bringing the tally to 158. One hundred fifty-eight souls . . . slaughtered—men, women, children . . . as young as six and as old as eighty-eight, unfathomable to all but Jack.

His mind drifted . . . to wonder about how he came to be what he had become. He was entirely cognizant of what he was doing, aware and blissfully proud of who he was . . . a most destructive and powerful being—Godlike, and an angry God at that.

Jack went to take a cool shower, to put his anger to rest for a bit, to wash the heat and hate away. For now, he would relax . . . as he would find his hate again . . . and soon.

· · · · · · · · · · · · · · · · · · · ·

No air to breathe in the darkness, not entirely aware, but knowing that something terrifying was happening . . . cannot breathe . . . . I'm going to die . . . I'm going to . . .

"Jimmy!" screamed Dee from the bed.

"Jimmy, it's me . . . Dee!"

The thrashing form of the professor abruptly sat up, and with fear etched into his face, he opened his mouth to speak to Dee, instead he spit up some water. Fear filled his bloodshot eyes, but Dee couldn't see that, as the room was too dark.

"Sweetie . . . . You okay?" she asked in a concerned tone.

"Yeah . . . . Thanks," he said somberly before he turned the light on.

The room illuminated in a soft glow as Jimmy stood by the light switch, squinting his way into the master bathroom. His naked form was a bit wet from having spat up the water he had consumed before he laid to sleep. This was unfortunately a typical occurrence for the Soul-Collector.

Dee had grown accustomed to these uneasy moments, but it unnerved her nonetheless.

As near as the couple could tell, the SoulBound dreamt just as they did in real life, and the nightmares in particular transferred to Jimmy's unconscious mind while he slept, causing him to be thrust into their nightmares.

"Marie, are you okay?" Jimmy surmised that this dream was hers, based upon her death by drowning.

"Sorry. It's a recurring dream . . . and . . . ," Marie decided to leave it at that, *". . . I'm okay, sweetie, g'night."*

"Good night, Marie."

What Jimmy didn't realize was that it had been John Jaden's nightmare, but Marie knew he was too proud to admit it, so she took the "hit" for him. John gratefully acknowledged her deed with a bow, as the SoulBound had now all figured out how to reach each other without Jimmy's help. This was significant news, but Jimmy was so busy and strained that he had been oblivious.

Jimmy stood at the window in his bedroom that faced the beach and realized as he stared into the dark horizon that there would be time for sleep later. He got dressed and walked outside along a sandy strand . . . and he concluded that he needed a plan. They all needed his plan.

As he pondered his next step, sweat began to bead upon his furrowed brow. He glanced at his illuminated watch, and with a feeling of familiarity thought, *"It's far too warm for 3:13 a.m."*

· · · · · · · · · · · · · · · · · · ·

Somewhere in the night, somewhere close by, a cell phone was being dialed with a quivering hand.

"Yes, of course, I'm sure, it's happening . . . happening right now."

Chapter 25
The Hunt Begins...

Tuesday, June 10, 2008

The local library didn't open until nine o'clock, so Jimmy felt a bit awkward as he waited just outside the front door at five 'til. He could feel the stare of the gray-haired woman who was going about her morning pre-opening duties.

He stood about for a bit, wearing a white *Under Armour* baseball cap, dark sunglasses, light khaki shorts, and a cool, purple, *Tommy Bahama* short-sleeve. The morning was already eighty-two degrees, and being recognized was the last thing he wanted. His silver-and-black Kenneth Cole watch read 9:03 a.m., so his eyes bounded between the library clock, which matched his watch, and the gray-haired lady at the front desk. By this time, he could see in the door's reflection, a young, pregnant woman and an older woman, who was holding her hand, approaching the door. It seemed they were going to join him in line.

To his surprise, they went past him, opened the door and proceeded to enter the library. He immediately followed them in and walked up to the front desk, where the gray-haired woman, now shoving a couple pieces of gum into her mouth, stood waiting.

"The door is on a time lock, it opens automatically at nine," she mustered between chews. "You're not the first, won't be the last," came the almost disinterested follow-up.

Jimmy was about to chastise her a bit for her attitude but thought better of it.

He walked into the main area of the library, then continued to a side room that was chockfull of newspapers and monitors. He came here when he needed to research specific historical events or if he needed to brush up on some subject material before presenting it at school. He began to wonder where to start, before deciding to try the Web, so he used a localized search engine and keyed in "Carrie Ann Weaver." The results started to come in quickly, and soon enough Jimmy was immersed in articles, mainly local, about Carrie Ann. He had asked Marie to keep Carrie Ann busy while he was doing this, so the child could avoid recalling it all . . . as she was apt to do.

Jimmy focused on the paper most local to Carrie Ann's home—the *Southwest Gazette*—as it seemed to have the most details. The date was March 4, 2004. It was written two days after the child vanished while walking home from school. As he read, he noticed that the woman who wrote the featured article, who went by the name Maegan Lee, wrote from a deeply personal level. She went on to explain that she was the child's aunt, Carrie Ann's mother was Maegan's sister. The depth of despair was evident, as the reader was awash in the loss of innocence and the horror of the unknown. Family members and local authorities had searched everywhere in a ten-mile radius, with some even going farther out to comb the enormous Patapsco State Park for any hint of the girl.

There were no witnesses, no clues—just the certainty that Carrie Ann was alive and well as she left the safety of the school at 2:30 p.m. She was seen walking her normal five-block walk toward home by two of her classmates, but after she went around the first bend, the sweet girl was never seen again . . . whisked away to pay a tragic toll.

Jimmy spent hours combing through the child's articles, which grew fewer and fewer as time marched on. Nothing new came to light, and being an amateur at this, he felt rather helpless.

"Boss . . . maybe my boys could get some answers," Frank "Dragon" Jackson said in a matter-of-fact way.

His boys . . . meaning his biker gang, the "Road Dogs."

"How so?" queried Jimmy, noticing Dragon's recent affinity for calling him "Boss."

"They ain't exactly choir boys; they might be willing to offer a hand or a fist to help hunt down this pussy."

Jimmy responded sincerely, *"If I get nowhere . . . yeah, maybe I'll get with you about that . . . thanks, man."*

Having Dragon around sometimes had its advantages . . . though the women SoulBound were often offended with his affinity for profanity. Dragon was a surly man, no different in death than he was in life. Surly, yes, but a good guy deep down.

· · · · · · · · · · · · · · · · · ·

Frank Jackson was born and raised in Baltimore, beginning in 1957, so he was a local guy, a comfort to Jimmy. Frank was anointed "Frank," not Francis, nor Franklin, simply Frank. His mother was a blunt woman, never pulling her punches. She was a chain-smoker, but looked after her only child as best she could. Frank's father died before he was born, but had two other kids he never took care of, so . . . . Frank didn't miss out in that regard.

Frank grew up dirt poor, living only a mile from what was now Harbor Place, a beautifully renovated tourist attraction. But in the '60s and '70s, it was, well, a dump. Regardless, he didn't care either way, as his love was the road and being on it. The movie *Easy Rider* was in his heart; it drove him to get his first Harley. He knew nothing since but the road, his gang, his drink, and his women.

His gang brother and leader, named "Certified," anointed him "Dragon." Dragon had become a Road Dog when he was twenty-two, and life was heaven on earth. Now, Frank was no angel, far from it, but he never . . . **never** hurt an innocent. While his gang was among the more casual around, they got into their share of brouhahas, battling on occasion with other local biker gangs when they happened upon the same bar.

Dragon earned his name in the most bizarre way . . . he was a tag-along for a year before being accepted into the fold. He had been with the guys at The Bare All, a "titty bar," as it was often referred to, when a fight broke out between his crew and the "Sinisters" from nearby Pigtown. Frank, during this bar fight, reacted instinctively as he was smoking a cigarette at the bar. He took a big gulp of Jack Daniels, fired up his lighter . . . , and blew out the whiskey at a rival biker that was running at him . . . you can imagine the rest.

After his acceptance became official, Dragon wasn't idle. He was the one that organized the charity drive each Thanksgiving and Christmas, as he had a deep affection for poor children. He wouldn't ever admit it, but he was really just a big ol' teddy bear beneath the surly manner and the unshaven hulk of a man he was. He lived life with a love for the road and died doing what he loved, veering off a rain-soaked turn on Route 1 and hitting a telephone pole. He died after a three-day fight in the hospital, but should have died instantly . . . the doctors and nurses admired him . . . tough bastard.

· · · · · · · · · · · · · · · · · · · ·

Jimmy felt he had done enough for the day and decided to return to the library the next morning and try to see if he could piece together some sort of database of missing victims in a fifty-mile radius from where Carrie Ann was taken. He returned the research materials and left the library, down, but not out.

As Jimmy exited the library, the local Baltimore office of the Federal Bureau of Investigation received an automated alert. The FBI had flagged the area's library computers for certain keyword combinations to aid them in their current investigation of "The Shadow That Speaks." Prominent among them: *"Carrie Ann Weaver."*

Chapter 26
Alpha & Omega...

Federal Bureau of Investigation,
Baltimore Field Office,
Woodlawn, MD.

Case Agent Carol Kennedy hated that her partner tried without fail to get her to begin drinking coffee. She hated coffee. No, she despised it. Yet, here again, fresh from Dunkin' Donuts and steaming through the poked plastic hole came the horrific aroma that haunted her every morning.

"Asshole," she muttered as she spotted him through the glass window of her office.

Him . . . Agent Tony Omega merely smiled his boyish smile before feigning ignorance, his Dunkin' Donuts cup, held in his right hand, a bit incriminating. Their relationship was an interesting one.

She was forty-eight, his senior by sixteen years, and had served in the bureau for nearly twenty-five years, ranking among their most tenured agents. She wasn't well-liked, nicknamed "Alpha-bitch" by those who privately dared, but she was thorough and among the best in the field. Though she was old enough to be a grandmother, she had very little maternal instincts. She never married and had no children, but she was strong and not someone to be trifled with. Her short-styled red hair was iconic at the department, as she hadn't changed it since she started there, but it perfectly matched her fiery green eyes.

She was used to younger partners, nearly always men, who took her alpha-dog ways as a challenge to their manhood . . . except this new one, Agent Omega. He was . . . different. Antonio Jorge Omega was a smooth operator, not one prone to mistakes. He was brash at times, but not cocky; a confident thirty-two-year-old Latino. Tony changed his last name the very day he turned 18, from Alves to Omega. He had a rebellious and troubled childhood, and wanted to start his life anew. So, he took the name Omega from a comic book he had once read about a group of superheroes called the Omega Men. He never regretted that decision . . . as it seemed to add an air of mystery to him. Fortunately his relationship with his parents (Tony was an only child) had improved a great deal, and he realized they were the only two people in the world he could honestly say that he truly loved.

Omega was a looker, or so it was whispered among the women in the bureau, and being single without children made him even more desirable. As much as he loved the ladies, he loved being an agent even more. He was assigned to "The Shadow That Speaks" case over a year ago, becoming the second partner to Agent Kennedy on this case.

Her first partner had gone "missing" days before Omega was brought aboard. Agent Justin Sykes had been on the case with Kennedy for two years before he simply disappeared after leaving work late one night. Neither his car nor his body had ever been found. His wife, Jen, and their two teen girls hadn't given up hope. Agent Kennedy knew better.

"You see the library alert?" Agent Omega asked his partner as he came around to her open door.

She eyeballed his coffee cup before responding.

"Reading it . . . call the library right now and have them keep today's video recordings safe and sound until Gotti arrives to secure them."

Gotti was in reference to their gopher, first-year agent Steve Gottranelli.

"Somebody's interested in Carrie Ann . . . so we're now interested in them, yes?"

Agent Kennedy spoke almost to herself, a "faraway" look in her eyes.

Agent Omega was already headed off to make his call.

Agent Kennedy had a keen intuition and felt that there was something about this library alert . . . something that was going to blow this case wide open.

Chapter 27
Mind Games

Jimmy arrived home ten minutes after leaving the library, disappointment etched into his weary face. Dee had phoned him moments before he pulled into the driveway and had informed him that she had taken off work a bit early and would be home soon. He brushed it off as nothing unusual and went about doing what he often did when frustrated—he took a shower.

The hot water cascaded over him on all sides as he positioned himself directly beneath the showerhead. He felt at peace here, relaxed. He kept telling himself that all would be fine and that everything would work out. The Shadow would be caught . . . soon. It was then he heard the front door open and close . . . the rattling of keys being dropped on the kitchen table.

"I'm in here, Dee!" he yelled. "In the shower . . . be out shortly!"

Jimmy finished up and towel dried before he walked out toward his bedroom.

Dee's voice was raised as she said, "We have company. You may want to hustle up with getting dressed."

Company? I wonder who she means?

"Right, I'll be right out!" he replied.

A refreshed and dressed Jimmy walked curiously out into the living room only to stop dead in his tracks. Dee was sitting with a middle-aged woman, who was tall and thin, her shoulder-length, dark hair framing a taut face. More importantly, she was someone Jimmy wanted nothing to do with . . . his former shrink, Dr. Lena Vaccaro!

"Hello again, Jimmy," Dr. Vaccaro offered with a wry smile.

He stood with a furrowed brow and though he said nothing, his obviously annoyed look implied *"What are you doing here?!"*

"We've been in touch for some time now . . ." Dee sounded off—worry and fear etched across her face.

". . . So, please sit down with me, and let me explain." Dee's voice was shuddering.

Jimmy stood transfixed. Anger at Dee . . . anger at his former psychiatrist welled up within him.

"How could you do this?" he asked Dee, as memories of past discussions with the shrink crept through his mind.

"Please . . ." Dee motioned him to sit next to her, gently patting the soft cushion to her left.

Jimmy begrudgingly began to move toward Dee, as Marie's voice whispered in his mind, *"Remember, Jimmy, you can't trust her. Remember what I told you . . . what she said when you were unconscious at her office."*

He remembered all right . . . He had gone to see Dr. Vaccaro a few years back, on a regular visit, when she asked him if it was okay if he underwent a new hypnosis technique. She inferred that it might be very useful in helping him deal with the anxiety of his SoulBound. The doctor was aware of his bonds with the ten souls (at that time) that were such a major part of his life. He was struggling with the demands of handling their many needs while trying to live his own life. He eventually succumbed to her desire to try to help him and allowed her to inject him with a new drug, which would bring him to near unconsciousness, but would allow him to respond to her without recollection of anything that happened. Hypnosis had failed thrice before. Although Jimmy was unaware of the events about him during the procedure, the SoulBound were—that was the doc's first mistake.

Dr. Vaccaro had asked her patient, during previous sessions, for detailed information about every soul, but he always denied her that, simply sticking to mundane information. He would give her their first names, what time period they were from, and what country. Therefore, with Jimmy unaware, she attempted to take advantage and gather this same information from him while he was under—that was the doc's second mistake.

As Jimmy attempted to answer her, his words became a jumble of various languages. The SoulBound couldn't prevent Jimmy from responding, but they could, and did, take over his voice. All she got was a mismatched collection of six languages, and unfortunately for her, she only spoke one. She did not understand what was happening and was unaware that the SoulBound could hear her every word.

Without further thought, she picked up the phone, dialed out and said, "The session was a failure, unknown reason. I'll try another way."

Dr. Vaccaro paused while someone responded before finishing the talk by saying, "Don't worry, he has no idea"—that was her third and final mistake.

Jimmy had been sent home with instructions to call the doctor the next day. But after being told everything by Marie and the others, he broke off all contact with Dr. Vaccaro and had not spoke to her or seen her again . . . until now.

Jimmy's mind was a whirlwind. He figured that the shrink had no idea that he was on to her. However, he couldn't be sure, figuring that she may have put it together after he left her office. He should have told Dee what had happened at the doctor's office, but with so much happening, it had slipped his mind. He would play along . . . for now.

"Fine, but only for a minute, I have somewhere to be," Jimmy lied, as he sat beside Dee.

Dee spoke then. "Sweetheart, I've obviously upset you by doing this, but you need to look at this from my standpoint."

She shifted in her seat and continued . . . "As your friend . . . as your soul mate, no one loves you more than I do."

Her voice was shaky, her eyes welling with tears.

"With all we've been through, the thought of losing you to these traumatic episodes, waking up drowning . . . it scares the hell out of me. I can't take it, Jimmy. I'm a wreck."

Jimmy sat in silence, but with a sense of shame overcoming his anger.

"So . . . when Dr. Vaccaro contacted me—yes, behind your back—because she knew you'd react this way, I decided to hear her out. She was the one you were working with, trying to work out how to deal with your amazing gift. And sorry to say so, but in typical male fashion, you decided you wanted to end your treatment. Perhaps you figured you would be able to handle it on your own, but as your future wife, and as a woman with plans to have children . . . eventually, I knew that I could never consider that unless I was sure that you were, well . . . stable."

"Ah, so this is how *you* 'handle things'?" Jimmy had regained his angered state. "I would NEVER go behind your back, under any circumstance!"

Dr. Vaccaro cut in.

"Jimmy, please, there's something that needs to be known before this gets any further out of hand."

She stood up, pulled out a photo, and handed it to Jimmy. He took it as Dr. Vaccaro continued.

"This is under the strictest confidence that I'm doing this. What I'm about to tell you . . . were it to get out . . . it would end my career."

Jimmy lowered his eyebrows slightly, certifiably suspicious.

"His name is Randolph, a retired factory worker from New Mexico. Jimmy . . . you are not the only one."

Those words hit Jimmy like a thunderbolt. He stared at the photo . . . a bald-headed black man, perhaps in his fifties . . . strange eyes that reminded Jimmy of a lizard of some sort. He kept looking . . . part wonder, part denial.

"You can't believe her, Jimmy, you know better." Marie tried to talk reason.

"Jimmy . . . he's agreed to meet with you. I've already made arrangements. For privacy, errrr legal reasons, neither of you could meet at the other's home, but . . . a neutral site, my office, was agreeable. He'll be here tomorrow at my office at noon. He was hesitant at first . . ." she began to walk the room, staring out the bay window as she continued. ". . . like you are now, and had a hard time believing that you existed."

Dr. Vaccaro paused and spun to face Jimmy.

"I won't lie to you. I have professional reasons to study this phenomenon. But more importantly, *you* will get to sit down and speak to someone *like you*. One who has mastered the ability to control what we're terming—thanks to you—SoulBound. And while you have ten (Vaccaro wasn't aware of the latest souls), he has fifty-eight."

Again, a thunderbolt.

"Lies are most believed when the liar gives great detail," Su Yi spoke words of wisdom. Words that hammered into Jimmy's brain as he knew that Yi rarely said anything, unless she knew it was worth the effort.

"Why should I believe you?" Jimmy asked the doctor, "This could all be a lie."

Dr. Vaccaro walked toward the front door and grabbed her keys from her purse. As she turned the knob to leave, she answered as she faced the door, "If he is not there, then you caught me, Jimmy; I've lied. You will never see me again. But just think . . . what possible reason would I risk alienating you?"

She turned this time to face him.

"Meet Randolph tomorrow at noon, at my office, and get the help you deserve. You are on the verge of answers . . . ones you've been seeking for over fourteen years."

With that, she turned and left, leaving Jimmy's mouth opened, but stunned to silence.

Chapter 28
The Fork in the Road

To believe or not to believe . . . *that* is the question. Jimmy continued to stand and stare at the front door, the floor in front of him, and just about anything in his peripheral vision, contemplating what had just happened. The SoulBound remained quiet as Jimmy's mind took it all in.

Dee waited anxiously on the couch, having remained still as she watched him.

In some ways, this was one of those moments . . . the kind that helped define relationships. Jimmy turned and walked slowly back to the living room, and he sat again, but this time away from Dee. He spoke to her as he shuffled his hands together, staring off toward the front door.

"I'm trying to resolve things . . . it's a bit confusing."

He looked at her now, and Dee's trembling was noticeable.

"You didn't know . . . what she did to me. I never got around to telling you about it. I'm sorry for getting mad at you, but for future reference, I'd prefer you come to me first about anything that has you concerned."

Dee nodded as she wiped away a few tears. She was relieved to hear him speak this way, as he had never been angry with her before, but was now concerned about what he had not told her.

"I appreciate you trying to understand my reasons . . . If it's okay, can you tell me what happened? What did she do to you?"

Jimmy proceeded to tell Dee everything that the SoulBound had told him about what had happened at Vaccaro's office a couple years ago. He stood up afterward and asked Dee if she'd like a drink.

She responded that she would . . . an iced tea, if any was left.

After returning with her iced tea, he asked her to replay how she and Vaccaro first communicated. Dee replied that Vaccaro had called her out of the blue about a month ago and had wanted Dee's help with setting up a meeting with Jimmy about Randolph. Vaccaro didn't have a chance to explain who Randolph was because Dee immediately began to tell the psychiatrist about her fears for Jimmy's life. Dee knew that Dr. Vaccaro was aware of Jimmy's SoulBound, and let Vaccaro know that she was also aware and how Jimmy had confided everything to her.

Dee continued to explain how Vaccaro warned her of the dangers that Jimmy faced and how important it was that Dee keep in touch whenever Jimmy had an episode. On more than one occasion, Dee had contacted Vaccaro, even early in the morning, to explain what was happening, including the latest incident while Jimmy was out on the beach.

Vaccaro then told Dee that this was why this meeting with Randolph was so important . . . and that she needed Dee's trust.

Dee agreed to set up today's meeting, but was unaware who Randolph was or why he was important . . . as she had just learned this—along with Jimmy—moments prior.

Jimmy sat there, comprehension washing over him. The pieces were falling into a clearer picture.

What possible reason would she have for lying? He thought again.

"She has no power over me, Dee. If this is some elaborate plan to get me to open up to this stranger and tell him everything, they are sadly mistaken. Who knows . . . that may be what they are up to. But I don't see the downside of going . . . because worse come to worse, I'll leave . . . never talking to any of them again."

Dee weighed in, "Knowing what I know now, I don't trust her either . . . I mean she has had a lot of time to scheme on ways to get you back in the fold . . . so to speak. Don't go, Jimmy . . . just don't go."

"You know she's right, Jimmy, we are all in agreement . . . if we may say so?" Marie interjected cautiously.

"Of course, Marie . . . I value everyone's views, always. However, what if what she says is true? Just think about that . . . what if?"

As Jimmy mind-spoke, his eyes closed and his lips moved slightly, as if he was talking to a small bug.

Dee recognized the signs that Jimmy was mind-speaking. He didn't always close his eyes that way, but when he went "under," it became a matter of waiting him out.

The debate within lasted a few minutes, and when Jimmy emerged from the discussion, he looked at Dee, smiled and said, "Sorry, hon, the Souls were a little upset that I'm considering going tomorrow."

Dee replied that it was okay, but her face had turned a slighter shade of anxious. She came right out and asked, "Are you going tomorrow or not?"

He had a shifty grin and remarked, "Yogi Berra once said that when you come to a fork in the road . . . take it."

Dee didn't appreciate his play at humor and Jimmy's smile quickly faded.

"Sorry . . . yeah, I'm go . . . ."

"I'm calling Lou (her boss)."

Dee had cut him off mid-sentence, knowing Jimmy's answer before he gave it. She grabbed her cell phone from her purse and, as she dialed a number, she said,

"I'm taking a personal day tomorrow. I'm going with you."

She spoke in a matter-of-fact manner, and Jimmy could do nothing but nod his head before finishing, ". . . ing to go."

He stood bemused, as he hadn't counted on Dee's plan. But as he walked away, the optimist in him thought, *Things could be worse*. Yeah.

Jimmy realized that he had disappointed everyone, Dee, the SoulBound, and Yi, in particular. It took great effort and reason for her to make her "voice" heard. Jimmy tried to mind-speak with her, but she was not making herself readily available. He sighed and spoke to her anyway, simply thanking her and saying that he was grateful for her wisdom and sorry that he was not going to heed her advice.

Yi was a proud Chinese woman and quite stubborn when she wanted to be. As Chinese names are the reverse of Western culture-based names, Su was her husband's family name, such as

Smith or Jones. Yi, meaning "high spirits" was her given name (first name).

. . . .

Guan Yi was born in the outskirts of Shanghai, on December 12, 1850. Her parents were launderers in the great city, situated on the eastern edge of China. During this time, there was political and cultural turmoil, culminating in the Taiping Rebellion. Yi's father, Kang, knew that he would soon have to take his family away. Finally, in the spring of 1852, Kang, his wife, Huiliang, their son, Ru, and baby daughter, Yi, boarded the "Golden Whale" passenger ship . . . destination: San Francisco.

Just a few years prior, the great gold rush of 1849 had caused an urgent need for laborers, and while tens of thousands of poor Chinese immigrants came to get in on the action, Kang took his savings and opened a laundry in the heart of San Francisco. Yi and her family stayed in San Francisco and ran a profitable business.

Yi loved dolls, and her mother had tinkered around a bit, making cheap versions of the store-bought ones. Yi admired her mother's even temperament and quiet confidence, but she was more like her dad, strong-willed and stubborn, more often than necessary. Yet, for the majority of the time, she was a sweet girl, loving and very compassionate. She would feed the stray dogs behind her house, against her father's strict orders.

Yi was married at age sixteen to a man named Su Yaozu, who was the son of a rival launderer. It was an arranged marriage, but one that both she and Yaozu were pleased about. They were both attractive and had secretly had a crush on one another whenever they spotted each other in public. Yaozu was twenty-one, married to a beautiful bride, and was going to be given enough money by both fathers to open his own shop. He gratefully agreed, and after speaking to many friends and relatives, had a decision to make between two promising towns. The decision was vital; he had come to a fork in the road.

After thinking on it for days, he decided to head south to a growing town in need of a shop such as his . . . Los Angeles. The choice seemed cursed from the outset, as Yaozu broke his leg in a wagon accident during the trip. The town was dirty and not the friendliest place toward immigrants, especially Chinese ones. The couple opened shop after considerable delay in the winter of '67.

It took over a year before the couple's business started to turn a profit, and times had been very tough. In the autumn of 1871, Yi and her husband decided that it was perhaps the right time to raise a family. Yi, in particular, was giddy as she always wanted to be a mother; she realized her passion for dolls stemmed from this desire. She wrote to her parents often and happily began a new letter to inform them of this wonderful development. They would never get it.

On the October night, as Yi was writing and Yaozu was preparing for bed, an angry anti-Chinese mob ripped through the tiny Chinese area of town—ransacking, robbing, and killing many of its residents—including the innocent couple. Yaozu was shot twice, once each in the gut and chest, and died instantly. Yi was strangled while being violated by two men, a Latino and a White.

They lost their lives because of the hatred of men and the ignorance that so many had about those who are different.

So unnecessary . . .

so, tragic.

Chapter 29
The Cover of Night

As evening came upon him, Jimmy decided he should call Tommy, as he hadn't spoken with him in some time, and that was quite unusual. Tommy was his best friend, confidant, and all-around go-to guy.

The pair was somewhat like two school-age girlfriends or BFFs (best friends forever). They were around each other so much that rumors spread that they were gay. Nope . . . just a couple of guys who couldn't care less who knew how much they enjoyed each other's company. Therefore, Jimmy was happy to dial Tommy's cell and catch him up on the happenings.

Tommy answered in his typical *"attempting to fool the caller with a fake answering service message"* voice. Jimmy laughed literally every time. "Waaaasssuuupppp?" Jimmy cheerfully asked.

"Nada . . . just checking out some of the latest movie trailers. It's been awhile, but there are some definite 'first night it's out-ers.' How you been?" Tommy replied.

"Well, I have a lot to tell you. You have a few hours?" Jimmy snickered, but followed up, "Seriously, you'll need to turn your monitor off for this."

"All right, shoot."

That was Tommy's reply meaning "go for it."

By Brando's account, it seemed as if the professor had started one of his lectures, as Tommy could barely get a word in. When Jimmy told him about the lizardy black man, Tommy couldn't help himself and laughed aloud. At the conclusion, Jimmy metaphorically stepped away from the mic and sighed—awaiting Tommy's never-ending barrage of questions and insightful advice—but Tommy unexpectedly replied, "I'm going too."

Before Jimmy could argue the point, Tommy cut him off with one of his favorite juvenile antics . . . he said, "Jimmy, you just need to understand . . . this . . ." Brando then intentionally hung up the phone. It was his way of saying "period."

Jimmy growled, but knew Tommy would do that.

Jimmy informed Dee that Tommy would be attending the meeting with them, and she could tell that there was no use bothering about it.

They watched television for a while and went to bed around 10:30, a bit earlier than normal. They had a big day ahead of them, especially Jimmy.

He lay in bed with Dee asleep next to him, his mind bouncing from one subject to another. He felt uneasy now and wasn't quite sure why.

"*Retiring for the night, Captain?*" Marie queried.

"*Yeah, #1 . . . you have the helm.*"

"*Awwwww . . . she always gets the helm. When do I get the helm?*" John feigned being bothered by Jimmy playing favorites.

He then laughed along with Jimmy and Marie, as Jimmy replied, *"I tell you what, since I'm getting better at creating places within me, perhaps we'll visit the bridge of the Enterprise . . . soon."*

"I was only joshing ya, but cooooool!" Jaden happily replied, excited about the chance to pretend to be in space.

Marie chimed in *"All right, Johnny Rocket, let Jimmy get some sleep."*

"Aye-Aye . . . good night, Captain. You too . . . #1."

Jaden just never stopped amusing himself . . . of course he was only barely more than a kid when he died. So he fit right in, watching Star Trek along with Jimmy over the years and loving it as much as Marie and Jimmy did. Nineteen; that's how old John was when he died that night aboard his ship.

It was hurtful to Jimmy when he considered the depths of loss suffered by the friends and families of the souls within him, but Jimmy felt an even greater sorrow regarding his youngest souls . . . Carrie Ann, Koketai, and John. The expression "Life just isn't fair" was unfortunately a painful truth.

Jimmy lay on his right side as a large circular fan blew on high. Even with the air conditioner on, he liked a good breeze. Dee was that rare woman who didn't mind the cool air each night. That was just another sweet reward for having her in his life.

Jimmy was exhausted and ready to sleep. However, as he tried, he started feeling uncomfortable. He sensed . . . something. Something familiar to him, but . . . he could not place it . . . and eventually yielded to a much-needed sleep.

• • • • • • • • • • • • • • • • • • •

Outside of Jimmy's home, under the cover of night, a black van lurked. Agent Gottranelli, working on orders from Case Agent Kennedy, had been recording Jimmy's phone conversation with Tommy and was keeping an eye out for anything unusual.

Gotti had been there for about two hours, and while not the brightest agent, he was a hard worker. Gotti was known as a man who got the job done; however, he generally took a bit longer than most of his contemporaries to get there. He had barely scored high enough to make it as a special agent, scoring the second lowest among the trainees at Quantico. "Observation" was his one true strongpoint; yet, had he a keener eye, he might've spotted the shadowy figure that stood mere inches from Jimmy's bedroom window.

Looking in . . . sensing . . . learning . . . waiting . . .

Chapter 30

A Dreaming Darkly

A dreaming darkly . . . ongoing . . . pitiful. This night was one for the ages . . . as the darkest poetry amid his book, *Whispers, Shadows & Dreams,* seemed to come alive within Jimmy and trap him in a bizarre web of nightmares . . . *something was wrong . . . something was . . .*

The shadows shifted between real and otherworldly. Jimmy's visions were full of sorrow . . . deepening . . . desperate. A black Egyptian jackal, like the ones seen painted on the tomb walls of the great Pharaohs, stalked about a twisted fantasy world, one without color, only shades of black, white, and gray. Jimmy bounded about in fear, a solitary figure with one purpose—survival. He seemed without hope, adrift . . . as a tumbleweed in an old ghost town. The visions shifted to just that . . . an old ghost town like back in the old Wild West. The sky flashed as if storms were ongoing, but without sound . . . merely hushed whispers of a fearful wind and the creak of something metal, something left abandoned to the elements. The object of the creaking came into view as his mind's eye changed camera angles, bringing into sight the roundabout. The metal structure, like a disk with rails to hold on, was spinning ever slowly in the diseased breeze. The creaking was reminiscent of whale songs, the strangely sad ones. The roundabout was not alone in its misery, as a seesaw, merry-go-round, and other old-fashioned playground and carnival equipment seemed to merge into . . . wait . . . he knew this . . . he felt the answer . . . ah yes . . .

Something is just a bit . . . off-center, at 11:36 p.m.
It happens so often that . . . it's just
. . . I guess it's in my head . . . I guess
Time seems to move . . . awkwardly
A draft blows so cool, that ghosts can feel it
And my body shakes in sudden quakes
. . . Awakening The Beast
Yes, the Strange-Time comes
An escape, or rather sentence, to Outer Reality
Crooked moments of thought cascade for me
I catch glimpses, like short films, real short
But vivid shards of bizarre remind me where I am
Hold me where I am
And I see the Dark Carnival,
Where the Mad are at play
Until . . . they notice me,
And point at me screaming "Forbidden! . . ."
Then . . .
The carousel creaks slowly . . . to a halt
The wicked games cease . . . for playtime's over
The Mad retreat into the shadows . . .
For The Beast has come for me . . . .
Claws extended, reaching . . . . !!!

// . . . SWITCH . . . //

. . . And fell the skies
Blood-colored clouds and black rain
Pained breath scolded throats and lungs
And our eyes felt as flames
The cries of the living drowned the cries for the dead
For death's merciful touch had fallen upon them
And there was no noise but desperation . . .
No silence for the suffering
We were living a nightmare,
For dead became our dreams
And hope had become a four-letter word,
Spoken in whispered tones . . .
In The End-Time . . .
Our world lay shattered
A wasteland of rubble, fire, and sorrow
Our homes, every building, destroyed in haste
Laid low by hellish winds
And trees and brush wept smoke tears
In their final throes of agony
And the bodies . . . the children . . .
My memories shutter me still
And I am become but dust . . .

On and on the nightmares tortured him. The madness was nearly unbearable as he began another nightmare, only to have it end as suddenly as it all began . . . with the appearance of the ominous black jackal. However, this time it just bared its teeth before it faded into the distance . . . both in Jimmy's weary mind and outside his bedroom window.

Chapter 31
God I Love Her

Jimmy awoke at 8:30 and could smell breakfast cooking, with the aroma of sizzling bacon and sausage wafting through the home. He knew Dee was "at it" in the kitchen, as usual. He sat up in bed and noticed he was damp and where he laid in bed was too. The nightmare of the previous night came back to him, as did the visions of the jackal. It was troubling, he knew, but not sure why.

He rose off the bed to hop into the shower and decided to ask the SoulBound if anyone had any idea what happened last night . . . and was surprised to hear them all describe terrible visions from their worst nightmares. Jimmy was not alone in this after all.

Everyone was concerned and Marie, who had been with Carrie Ann, told Jimmy she would need to speak with him privately regarding last night. Marie had been spending a great deal of time with the child, becoming for all intents and purposes—a surrogate mother. Marie had become quite fond of Carrie Ann and looked upon her with the eyes of a protective parent. Since the SoulBound had learned how to visit with each other, the "community" within Jimmy was more active than ever, with many of them spending time developing friendships and sharing stories from when they were "alive." Subconsciously, Jimmy was aware of the recent transformation within him but had other pressing matters that distracted him from fully exploring it.

The SoulBound always had the courtesy to avert their attention whenever Jimmy was in need of privacy, so while Jimmy was showering, he had to coerce Marie to keep talking.

She closed her ghostly eyes and embarrassingly continued. She told Jimmy that her visions/nightmares or whatever they were reminded her specifically of the day Jimmy, Carrie Ann, and she had that dreadful episode beneath the old oak tree.

Jimmy paused as she finished and he suddenly began to get a strange feeling about what Marie said, but was interrupted by Dee's yell of, "Breakfast is ready, sweetie!"

Jimmy yelled back that he was halfway through his shower and would be right there.

Marie continued. *"Tonight, Jimmy, let's get together tonight, maybe 9'ish?"*

Jimmy said that would be fine. He then tried to get Marie to continue a bit, but she replied by telling him that Carrie Ann needed her anyway. Somewhat embarrassed, he replied, *"Of course, see you then."*

Jimmy finished his shower and his mind was a whirl, thinking about what Marie Anne Beale had to tell him, about what he and the others experienced last night, about the big meeting with Randolph, about The Shadow That Speaks, about, about, about . . . it was truly overwhelming.

Jimmy just sat at the edge of the bed, aimlessly strumming his guitar. He was dead silent. He was trying hard to stay calm, to relax, but he couldn't. He could hear Dee's voice getting a bit louder, and he could tell she was on the phone with Rae, Tommy's sister.

As she entered the bedroom to remind him that breakfast was ready, she began to speak, but paused, noticing a defeated and weary aura about him, as he sat slouched . . . halting his empty playing.

"Rae, I'll get back to you, sweetie," she said, and hung the phone up.

Compassion, a strong suit in her, welled up . . . for she knew her man; she could feel his angst, his fear, his madness. She simply walked up to him and stood in front of him, barefoot, with a pair of flimsy shorts and partially see-through white sleeveless top. He saw that she was there, and as he raised his head to say he would be in to eat shortly, she gently bent down and kissed him, full on the mouth . . . warmly, softly.

There was nothing to compare to this . . . no moment shared more intimate. Dee stared deeply into the eyes of her beloved and stealing a line from his poetry, said quite romantically, "When I'm with you, my heart flutters like a butterfly . . . dancing in the wind."

Jimmy's smile lit the room, as he yet again kissed his love deeply. They merged their lives and then delved further into each other to find that their love ran deeper still . . . This love that they shared was unbridled and bare . . . and the world had no meaning here.

When they finally surfaced, their bodies glistening in passion's wake; they would kiss again . . . and venture back from whence they came . . . . into the deep.

Afterward, as they lay cuddled in serenity and contentment, he had only one thought in his now cleared mind . . .

God I love her.

Chapter 32

Intuition

Agent Steve "Gotti" Gottranelli reported back to her lead investigator, otherwise referred to as Case Agent Carol Kennedy, and her second, Agent Tony Omega, filling them in on Jimmy's activities over the past couple of days. Kennedy's team consisted of twenty or more agency specialists, forensic and otherwise, as well as upward of thirty or so agents. When a serial killer admits to well over a hundred killed, the case takes on a completely new level of importance . . . especially because they believed him. He seemed brutally honest, gloating by leaving his calling card at the scene of his crimes: a black jackal business card with the victim's blood spelling out a message or a number. The last card they had showed victim #141—an unprecedented body count.

Gotti briefed the pair on Dee and Tommy and explained that a woman, a shrink to be exact, by the name of Lena Vaccaro, had arrived the day before and had spent about twenty minutes inside Jimmy's home before leaving. Gotti went on to add that she had beamed as she walked out the front door, like a kid in a candy shop.

A shrink? Both Kennedy and Omega thought at the same time.

An interesting turn of events . . . thought Agent Kennedy . . . *interesting indeed.*

She thanked Agent Gottranelli and told him to look into this Dr. Vaccaro . . . find out what he could about Jimmy's association with her and report back to her. Gotti left and Agent Omega closed the door behind him and stood there with his hands in his pockets, looking at Kennedy with that "Jackpot!" look about him.

She had that faraway look in her green eyes before replying aloud in a poor British accent, "Instincts, my dear Watson . . . instincts indeed."

Agent Omega was certain she was boasting, albeit in an odd way. They were onto something . . . she was running her pencil through her short cropped red hair, something she did often . . . a sign that her gift, her uncanny intuition, was functioning full force.

She just smiled wryly and told Omega to accompany her to Trent Prison.

"Trent? Why Trent?" he asked.

She replied that she wanted to see a "colleague" of hers, a man she'd had the unfortunate duty to do business with in the past . . . a dirty dog, a scumbag, a fly on the wall named Richard Dinkins, but better known as Ricky Dinks. He was just the sort that could help out in this investigation. A man without morals, without remorse, without . . . hope.

Dinks was in trouble, to put it mildly . . . a rat, a bean-spiller in an inescapable community of criminals who hated his kind. He was to be in Trent for only five years, getting forty years reduced despite the first-degree murder charge facing him.

Dinks was smart and knew how to work the system: plea-bargaining and informing on the "L-Train," noted D.C. drug czar Lionel Simms. Ah, but therein lay the rub. The L-Train would snuff him out despite the D.A.'s assurances that the guards would pay special attention to him . . . a plan designed to protect him—laughable.

His sentence had him in Trent for merely two days, and he feared for his life . . . and rightfully so. So . . . imagine the glee in his heart at the sight of Agent Kennedy and her companion as they sat comfortably in the offices of Warden Joe Dan Herzog. Herzog, the state's senior warden, asked Dinks to come in.

The guards escorted the short, skinny man into the enclosed room, leaving him cuffed but otherwise free to move about. Herzog told Dinks that he had special visitors and that he would be best served to pay heed to them and be respectful. Dinks nodded, and the warden left the Agents to chat with his inmate, with a word of appreciation from Agent Kennedy to take with him as he went.

Herzog closed the door behind him, and Omega got his first good look at the criminal, thinking that for a man that was supposedly twenty-eight, Dinks looked more like forty.

The convict sat, flipping his greasy, dirty-blond hair out of his face and started to speak, but Agent Kennedy cut him off by saying quite clearly, "So Dinks . . . you want to get out of here . . . permanently?"

. . . .

"Not cool . . . ," Jimmy said while laughing. Dee was getting dressed as Jimmy sat at the edge of the bed, decked out for the day's events. She asked him what was "Not cool," and what was so funny. He knew this was coming.

Jimmy pulled a semi-fib, telling Dee that Brennan was admiring him for having "game."

Dee's intuition was too good; she responded doubtfully, "Hmmm, I bet . . . tell Brennan that he's got an ass-whooping coming to him one of these days."

She shook her head, managing to smile where the "guys" couldn't see. She was right, as Brennan had been joking about Jimmy "getting some" amid other "guy-only" commentary.

Jimmy knew Brennan was messing around, and the other guys laughed along, even the time-period-challenged pair of Koketai and Jean-Paul, who were learning a great deal about the "modern" world not only from observing Jimmy and the outside environment, but also through numerous chats with their fellow souls. All of the SoulBound took the time to get to know one another . . . but some were better at it than the others. Dragon, while quite approachable, intimidated most of the others, intentionally or not. Some were reluctant to spend time with him. Regardless . . . time was something they all had plenty of.

An hour later . . .

The Hummer's sound system was blaring so loud that it seemed to bounce every house in the "cul de sac" up and down. Jimmy rolled his eyes but was reminiscent of a Monty Python sketch—the one in which the Sun was jumping up and down on the ground, shaking a home and its owner to their foundations.

Tommy Brando.

Tommy was indeed pulling into the driveway with his newly discovered affinity for Linkin Park quite evident. Tommy would go into musical phases, where whatever artist he was into at that time seemed to envelop him. Jimmy knew that Brando would spend as much time discussing the merits of his latest and greatest muse as he would discussing the impending meeting at the psych's office. There was no way around it without "blocking" the nearly juvenile exuberance Tommy oozed. So . . . being a great friend meant a few sacrifices.

"Awesome sound system . . . as always. Man, Linkin Park . . . it's mind-blowing!" Jimmy boisterously welcomed his best bud.

Tommy smiled as he turned the system off. Then it happened . . . surprise, surprise . . . Brando didn't discuss Linkin Park, but rather asked Jimmy how he was feeling.

Well I'll be . . . Life is *like a box of choc—*

"Mr. Casadias!" . . . came the nerve-racking noise bursting forth from Jimmy's least favorite neighbor, Vernice Lumbutter.

John Jaden opined quite humorously that *"She put the nay in neighbor."*

"Sir, clearly the homeowner's association forbids this sort of ghetto-ish disruption! I mean, are you attempting to harass me? Should I make a call to Mrs. Surtain at the HOA? I mean, seriously!"

Jimmy's initial reaction was one of apology; however . . . a quick word from Brennan Payton shifted Jimmy into a retaliatory response. It was one of only a few instances where Jimmy allowed one of the SoulBound to take over.

"Ghetto-ish? Pardon me, ma'am, are you inferring something about inner-city music? Are you spewing a racially motivated perpetration upon this man's right to freedom of choice? His mother is black, is that what this is about?"

The look upon the nosy neighbor's face was priceless. Brando, wise to what was happening, followed up with, "What? She said something about black people? What kind of racist bull . . . someone call Channel 3 news, I want a camera crew out here immediately!"

Jimmy was laughing hysterically inside. The other Souls were astonished and were enjoying the episode wholeheartedly . . . phantom popcorn for everyone.

"Oh Lord, no! That is not what I meant at al . . ."

Brennan/Jimmy cut her off . . . "Calm down now, everyone, calm down. I'm sure that the local news needn't be contacted, as this was surely a misunderstanding."

"Yes, yes!" A flustered Lumbutter agreed. "I apologize for appearing insensiti . . ."

"As you well should!" Brando finished for her.

"I'm not so sure I can forget this . . . my uncle down at the NAACP would gladly investigate this situ . . ."

It was Vernice's turn to cut Tommy off . . .

"Not necessary . . . not at all. The music was a bit loud and I ju . . ."

Obviously, to everyone but the neighbor, Brando again feigned a vicious retort, which promptly spun a shaken Lumbutter away for good . . .

". . . uust was leaving. Be well . . . best wishes to your families."

She couldn't have scampered off any quicker. A virtual applause echoed throughout the vessel that was James Carson Kassakatis . . . and Brennan, back inside, bent at the waist for his adoring fans . . . twice . . . three times for good measure.

Jimmy and Tommy went back toward the house giggling and huddling like two middle-school girls when they spotted the non-approving and almost parental presence of Denise Conway. Was this a punishable offense?

"Okay, boys, you really should be ashamed."

Dee index-finger-waved at them as they made the front steps. "Brennan, was that you? You three ought to be . . ."

They all waited for the berating to begin. ". . . proud of that classic ass-whipping!"

She hugged the "boys" and laughed along with them, as she pulled off the anger, feigning quite well herself. Hugs and laughs seemed a mere precursor; nervousness venting . . . the proverbial calm before the storm.

Dee followed the guys back inside as they would be leaving shortly. But as she entered the home behind them, she paused . . . getting *that* feeling . . . just *knowing* that the meeting wasn't a good idea. Her intuition rarely failed her, but her coming along was supposed to buffer the worry over it. Supposed to.

Chapter 33

Beyond the Distant Door

The Hummer was a sweet ride and one neither Jimmy nor Dee had the pleasure of experiencing before. It felt like they were about to attack something. Linkin Park began to blare moments into the ride until Dee screamed at Tommy to be more considerate, to which he animated that "Ooooppss-sorry" reaction and turned the system off. Jimmy would need time to relax and prepare for the big meeting. The ride would take an hour to an hour and a half, depending on traffic. They headed out of Annapolis north toward Bel Air, twenty or so minutes north of Baltimore.

Jimmy looked out his window at the vehicles they passed, and some that passed them, but he felt a particular excitement as three Harley-mounted bikers passed them. Dragon naturally was checking out which models they were on, muttering approval, yearning for Jimmy to ride again, and soon. Jimmy had never liked bikes, but Dragon convinced him to get his license and give it a try. Jimmy got a Harley, to Dragon's delight, rode a few times a year and did indeed love it. Jimmy could feel Dragon's yearning and made a mental note to ride when this was all over.

After a nearly silent ride, they arrived at the Graydon Center, an upscale office for many of Greater Baltimore's finest psychiatrists, including one Dr. Lena Vaccaro. As they walked through the beautifully designed garden entrance, Jimmy's memories of his last visit struck him as they passed through into the building. He couldn't help but recall the times he had spent there, or his attempts to help Dr. Vaccaro understand what he was going through. It took about three months of "therapy" before she had seemed to get a glint in her eyes, an awareness of truth . . . a glimmer of his special potential. Now, he was returning to her after she had attempted to circumvent his wishes for the SoulBound's privacy and attempted to drug him into a state of revealing . . . well, everything. Now again, here he was . . . because she had appeared to offer him a peace pipe, an appeasement of sorts . . . the semi-mysterious Randolph.

Tommy had moved ahead of Dee and Jimmy, and approached the front desk guard. He explained that the three of them were together and that Mr. Kassakatis was there to be seen by Dr. Vaccaro.

Jimmy smiled a bit as Tommy was keeping a few fingers to his right ear, pretending to be Secret Service, a silly game they often played when they were about. The guard seemed unamused and told them to go ahead to the third floor, suite #301. They took the elevator up and got off on floor three, with Tommy stepping out and seemingly giving the "clear" sign for the others to venture out of the elevator, as it seemed safe.

Dee just rolled her eyes at the immaturity, while Jimmy just couldn't bring himself to *not* laugh, so he did a bit.

There it was . . . the jokes were done with . . . for at the end of the hall to their left was Vaccaro's office. Dee smiled at Jimmy as he slowly walked toward suite #301. The double wooden doors were shut and a large gold-framed sign clearly read "Dr. Lena Vaccaro."

They entered the office and approached the receptionist, a rather large fellow; and an obviously different person than the petite sparrow of a woman who had occupied the desk in years past. He greeted them and asked politely in a rather deep voice, if Jimmy was Mr. Kassakatis? Jimmy responded yes and the man said his name was Carl and that Dr. Vaccaro would be with him momentarily.

As the three of them sat down, Vaccaro's personal office door opened at the end of the long hallway and she smiled at Jimmy and waved for him to come in.

This was it . . . he kissed Dee, who held his hand tightly and whispered that all was going to be okay.

Tommy shook his hand and said that he had Jimmy's back.

However, as Jimmy turned toward Vaccaro . . . all he could wonder about, all he could think about, was what lay waiting for him . . . beyond the distant door.

Chapter 34

All the King's Horses

Jimmy had not returned Dr. Vaccaro's smile. He simply idled past her and stood transfixed in her doorway . . . looking at the back of a brown, baldhead, of whom he could only assume would be the man he had come to see . . . Randolph. Jimmy stepped back a moment to acknowledge Dee and Tommy, giving them that "I'm going in" look. And with that, he did.

Dr. Vaccaro closed the door behind him.

Back in the waiting area, the receptionist/bodybuilder, Carl, asked Dee and Tommy if they'd like a glass of water or soda. They replied that they would, but as Carl stood up to get the drinks, the double doors of the office opened, and all hell broke loose. A Caucasian man wearing a baseball cap, with a crazed look about him, burst into the office screaming for Dr. Vaccaro, all the while having two guards draped over him, attempting to bring him down.

A slim, young woman (girlfriend or wife perhaps) was frantically yelling for "Marvin" to "Stop it" . . . to "Calm down."

Carl was quick to ask Dee and Tommy to go back downstairs to the first floor and that he'd come for them shortly.

Without hesitation, the pair moved hurriedly past the scrum that ensued and caught a glimpse of Carl assisting the guards as the doors shut behind them.

They took the stairs, as the excitement was too heavy for a wait for the elevators. Dee and Tommy were just about down to the first floor when they raised eyebrows at each other with that "That was strange" look.

Dee then said, "Okay . . . I'm not real comfortable leaving Jimmy alone up there."

Tommy responded quickly with, "Me neither."

With that summation, the pair proceeded back up the stairs and spoke of their prepared excuse, of how they were concerned for Jimmy's safety. As they breached the door to the third floor, they noticed at the opposite end of the hall, two guards supporting/carrying away the man who had freaked out in Vaccaro's office, accompanied by the woman who was with him and another older, bald-headed, black man.

With that, Vaccaro rushed from her office with Carl at her side and upon spotting Dee and Tommy, said in a rather excited tone, "Did you see him? Jimmy, he just went into a rage and fled the office!"

Dee and Tommy's bewildered expressions of concern had not a moment to be voiced as Vaccaro added, "Surely you had to have spotted him? No? . . . Carl with me . . ."

The confused pair began to mutter a response, but Vaccaro and Carl pushed past them and ran down the flight; Dee and Tommy were right behind them.

"Carl, call security and have them close all doors to the building . . . no one in or out until Mr. Kassakatis is found!"

"Everyone focus and calm down!" Marie yelled out to the other SoulBound . . . each attempting to get Jimmy to awaken, to resist the drugs coursing through his veins.

"Dragon! Pay attention to where we are and where we're going. You know this area well, right?"

"Shit yeah!" Dragon said excitedly.

"Karen, the guards are speaking in Spanish, try to catch what they are saying and remember what they say, word for word."

"You got it," Soul #9 replied.

Marie was taking charge, and for the first time in her life, she was the center of everyone's attention. She continued to get everyone to focus on not only understanding what was happening, but also why . . . as well as where they were currently, and where they were headed.

Jimmy was in utter unconsciousness, after some shady maneuvers from Dr. Vaccaro, the man called Randolph, and the other role players in the acting job that just unfolded merely minutes earlier.

I'll fill you in on what happened . . .

As Jimmy had entered Vaccaro's office, he was stuck with a needle from behind by Dr. Vaccaro and fell unconscious into the arms of the figure known only as Randolph. Moments later, there was a loud commotion from the waiting room with yelling and some obvious physical confrontation ensuing.

As Randolph gently lay Jimmy down, the noise outside Vaccaro's office waned and the office door opened. Carl, followed by "Marvin"—the man of similar build to Jimmy who had caused the commotion moments earlier—the two guards, and "Marvin's" apparent girlfriend came into the office with smiles upon their faces.

"Bravo to all . . . but there is work to do," uttered Vaccaro. "We haven't much time."

The Jimmy look-alike quickly undressed as "the crew" got to work, helping to swap out Jimmy's clothes. In less than sixty seconds, Jimmy had been dressed as the other man had been. The guards quickly lifted Jimmy up, putting a cap upon his head, pulling the brim low to better obscure his face. With Randolph and the young woman accompanying them, they moved quickly out of the office toward the other end of the hall (spotted by Dee and Tommy), down the stairs, out through a back door, and into a waiting ambulance.

Meanwhile, Vaccaro and Carl gathered themselves and moved out of the office ready to win the Academy Award for "Best Villainous Duo."

During the craziness that ensued, which grabbed the full attention of the rest of the SoulBound, little Carrie Ann was singing/sobbing Humpty Dumpty . . . ". . . *and all the King's horses and (sniff) all the King's men . . .*"

She never finished, but continued to cry for some time and remained for the time being in a most unfortunate and familiar place . . . all alone.

Chapter 35

Into the Nether

Dee dialed 911 on her cell phone, while Tommy stood . . . a panicked portrait. Dr. Vaccaro and Carl had brushed past the confused and alarmed pair, as Vaccaro barked orders over her walkie-talkie. It seemed that Jimmy had no way out, but *why would Jimmy freak like this?* wondered the good guys.

"911, what's your emergency?" came a strong male voice on Dee's cell.

"My name is Dee and my fiancé Jimmy apparently just went a bit nuts at the Graydon Center in Bel Air, off of Bel Air Road," voiced a concerned yet remarkably calm Denise Conway.

"Explain what you mean by 'nuts,' ma'am. Has your fiancé hurt himself, anyone else, or caused a disturbance?"

"Well . . . it's disturbing to know that he bolted from his psychiatrist's office and possibly fled the building, which immediately went on lockdown."

"Can you describe your fiancé Jimmy to us?"

"He's a Caucasian male, a bit over six feet tall, with dark hair and blue eyes."

"And what is or was he wearing?"

"A pair of khaki slacks and a silky white Armani shirt."

"Ma'am, we'll send an officer to you. Can you meet with the officer out front of the building?"

"I guess so . . . I hope that they'll allow me out," Dee replied hesitantly.

"Remain calm. Help is on the way."

"Thank you," Dee replied and flipped the phone off.

Tommy was being escorted back toward Dee, as she had only lost sight of him for a few moments. Two guards had him in the traditional carry-forward position, each wrapping Tommy's underarms within their arms. Brando was obviously pissed as they released him back to Dee and announced that he was to remain there until the building was cleared for visitors to leave.

Brando responded, "Sirs, yes sirs!" giving an obviously sarcastic salute.

The guards shook their heads, muttering to themselves as they moved away to their previous positions.

"What was that about?" Dee asked.

Tommy replied, "I had an idea . . . I thought that if I could get to the rooftop, I could have a clear view of the . . ."

A loud alarm sounded at that moment, startling them both to silence. After the third siren sounded, there was an audible clicking resonating about the building and the quickly moving Dr. Vaccaro and hench-receptionist Carl came around a corner toward Dee and Tommy.

An out-of-breath Vaccaro said, "The building has been cleared, so there is no danger within the building. If you'll be so kind, allow us to escort you back to your vehicle . . ."

Dee wasn't having any of what Vaccaro was serving . . .

"Escort us? Are you saying Jimmy is not inside the building?"

"As I was saying . . . he is not inside the building, and although our guards have searched the parking lot and the building grounds, Jimmy is nowhere to be found."

Dee became just a bit irate.

"What the hell did you do to him? What did you say that made him freak like that?"

"Doctor-patient confidentiality . . . I can't say what . . ."

"Can't . . . or won't?" Dee took a step toward the taller woman . . .

"Jimmy better turn up safe soon, Lena . . ."

Dee stared a fierce stare into the eyes of the shrink, a clearly threatening look. Dee knew she had to go . . . so she and Tommy left the building, just as two squad cars from the Sheriff's Office arrived.

· · · · · · · · · · · · · · · · · · ·

The man called Randolph spoke quietly into his cell phone, so as not to be overheard, as his cohorts moved an unconscious Jimmy along the narrow path on a gurney. They had arrived at their destination, a long-abandoned psych ward known as Haven's Gate, well . . . formerly abandoned. Randolph remained outside, continuing his cell chat, as the two guards, Vasquez and Galaraga, along with Randolph's girlfriend and assistant, and former model/ actress, Erin Adams, continued inside and up to the fifth floor.

"I know where we are, no problem," Dragon said to the others and to Marie in particular. *"Haven's Gate (he shuddered) . . . now this is not good."*

He went on to explain that this was a former hell-hole for the mentally disturbed and that a friend of a friend had the unfortunate occurrence to have stayed and died there back in the '80s. Haven's Gate was shut down by the Health Department after a nasty truth-piece about what really went on there aired on local 'Channel 12 News' . . . Geraldo style. It was a chamber of horrors, with human experiments at the heart of it.

"This is going to get ugly," Marie said sadly, but pointedly.

Karen added, *"Everyone, think, we gotta act quickly. Jimmy is out of it."*

At that moment, the captors wheeled Jimmy off the elevator and turned left down the hall. As they went down the dilapidated and foul-smelling hallway, they passed under an archway, where written were three large words . . . all scrawled in blood . . .

INTO THE NETHER

Chapter 36

What Lies Waiting

Agent Kennedy couldn't believe what she was hearing . . . her secured phone drifted away from her ear momentarily as she took it all in. Her spy dog, Dinks, was informing her of the most amazing set of circumstances. Unbeknownst to Dr. Vaccaro and companions, Dinks had inserted his skinny self through the ceiling of her Graydon Center office early in the morning, with the help of Agent Omega, and was privy to the remarkable events that unfolded; a virtual fly on the wall. The ex-con had slipped out the building after the lockdown ended and used his cell to call Agent Kennedy. Agent Kennedy was impressed, but Ricky was the sort of man that was savvy enough and motivated enough to do what was needed. He continued the story and then told her that he had contacted Agent Omega to tell him what was happening, and Omega subsequently spotted and tailed Randolph and crew.

Agent Kennedy told Dinks to meet her at the Exxon station, a quarter of a mile south of the Graydon Center, and then she called her partner to find out what was happening. The timing was perfect . . . he had just arrived a block from Haven's Gate and told her that the kidnappers had unlocked the outside gate and had driven through to the building ahead, after relocking the gate. Agent Kennedy knew things were getting perilously close to unraveling . . . she didn't want anyone to know that she was investigating Kassakatis, but also realized that he was in serious danger. She told Omega to sit tight and to let her know if anything happened . . . she was on her way to him after picking up Dinks. With Kennedy's head already spinning, Agent Gottranelli walked into her office and grabbed her car keys. He could see she was in a rush and asked if he could ride along. He had been ordered to investigate Vaccaro and was returning with some info . . .

. . . .

Dread permeated . . . the SoulBound sensed it and all grew silent as the gurney came to rest in an open room deep within the wing of the ward. They had passed guard centers with once-locked electric gates, rolled past now-empty rooms on either side of the hall, filled with rotting but still visible padded walls. Rats were evident, as were recently evicted vagrants.

Carrie Ann was very unhappy here, and her once-solo despair was now shared by many of her fellow souls. At least Millie and Su Yi were at her side, comforting her as best they could until Marie could follow up. There was a foreboding, a sense of something . . . wrong . . . something better left to the dark places from which they came. There had been horrid acts committed in this place, mind-boggling pain, and hopelessness so thick that you could hang a painting in midair. John Jaden, Soul #6, stood rigidly, his eyes piercing the gloom . . . beside him was Koketai, his eyes as transfixed as John's. They saw something . . .

something that frightened them, but the military men were familiar with fear, and they would not blink in the face of it.

Something moved about the room that Jimmy lay in, not visible to the eyes of the bad people who had brought him there . . . but ohhhh it moved . . . just out of the light.

Marie, Gina, Jean-Paul, Dragon, and Brennan noticed the other two men staring . . . and they moved forward slowly to see what they were looking at . . . irresistibly drawn toward the two.

In mere moments, they all saw it . . . all remained quiet, all became desperately still . . . as they spied . . . The Shadow That Speaks!

A feeling of *doom* washed over them all: both captors and SoulBound alike.

Erin spoke of her fears loud enough that the cockroaches in the sub-basement could make out her words. "Ummm, this place seriously creeps me out . . . seriously!"

Her Spanish-speaking companions laughed a bit to themselves, much to her displeasure.

"You two had better watch yourselves . . . or Randolph will not be happy to hear that you're making fun of me," Erin stated.

Vasquez and Galaraga became quiet at his mention, knowing that Randolph had a special affection for the failed model/actress, and wisely followed Erin's lead in preparing Jimmy for whatever it was they had planned for him.

Back outside, Randolph completed his call and walked briskly into the building. Randolph Gage was the U.S. Government's Director of DEEPER, the **De**part**m**ent for **P**ara-Psych**e**

Research, which was a black sect, secret . . . underground. The general public, senators, high-ranking government officials . . . you name it, they were unaware of its presence . . . or its "work." Gage wanted to be certain . . . to see Jimmy with his own eyes—study him—before moving him to top secret facility in Sterling, Virginia.

Gage had a long and strong arm, indeed, placing some of his own people throughout the mental health and paranormal realms, into positions of power, into position wherein they could hear things . . . to know things.

Lena Vaccaro is one of Gage's people, and Randolph felt they may have hit the jackpot with her most unusual patient: Professor James Kassakatis. She had been worried about approaching Gage with her earlier findings about Jimmy, but eventually realized it was a necessity to push the envelope and reenter Jimmy's world, with Gage's backing. After her failed attempt to coerce Jimmy into voluntarily giving her more information about his SoulBound experiences, she and Gage thought it best to back off for a while . . . to create a plan. They would lure him with the hope of another Soul-Collector and eventually take him to Haven's Gate for a few days to determine the validity of his claims and the reason Jimmy could do what he did.

This . . . was what Gage did. Most of his subjects had turned out to be fakes, or simply crazy. Still, once in a great while, there was the unexplainable, like the time with that Tyler Hill boy and the darkness . . . Gage still quivered at the thought.

As Randolph made his way upstairs via the elevator, turning left down the hallway on the fifth floor, his course was set . . . Into the Nether . . . where the darkness awaited him.

Chapter 37

Nether Enter, Never Leave

Dee and Tommy embarked upon an hour-long search for Jimmy after their chat with the local police. Dee had given the police her cell phone number and Tommy's too, and knew they would let them know if anything came up. The pair went miles away in all directions, asking people if they'd seen Jimmy. No luck. Tommy told Dee to drop him back off at the Graydon Center and for her to head home and see if he'd somehow returned there.

After a quick debate, she agreed and dropped Tommy off out front of Vaccaro's lair, then proceeded to drive home.

Dee arrived back home, hoping beyond hope he would be there, though she couldn't help but feel a bit uneasy about what she and Tommy had witnessed. Had Jimmy gone nuts? All she knew was that he was missing . . . gone, nowhere to be found . . . like ripples in a pond, disappearing in time. She had heard no screams at the office earlier. He just seemed to slip away, quietly, silently . . . Dee stared out of the front window; the light outside was waning . . . "*It's getting dark,*" she thought to herself.

. . . .

"*What the hell . . .*" John Jaden muttered, as the SoulBound stood bunched, quietly watching what human eyes could not see.

"Hell . . . yeah, that describes it," Dragon responded softly.

Some of the SoulBound said a prayer or three as a black . . . thing . . . shifted slowly about the shadows in the room. It was void of light, devoid of empathy, a pitch form seemingly wrought from the farthest depths of hell. It had a human form at its center, yet the phantom moved of its own volition . . . part wave of darkness, part tentacles of shadow . . . all death.

Tyler "Jack" Hill knew he could easily kill them all, but he was too focused, wanting his oncoming adversary to know . . . to *truly know* his power. *"Ahhhh . . . Gage is finally here . . . how perfect."*

Revenge would be so sweet . . . to be able to exact it upon the man who had experimented on him—hell, helped to create him—when he was just a boy . . . it seemed so perfect. Who would have thought that Randolph Gage would reemerge into his life after all these years? Was it coincidence? It didn't matter . . . nothing mattered now.

As Randolph started down the hall, he sensed it . . . felt that horrid presence; he had not felt it in many years. He turned immediately, quickly moved back down the way he'd come, grabbed his walkie-talkie, and yelled for Erin and the guards to "Get the hell out of there! Now!"

Too late. Erin and the guards were suddenly scared so badly, they were frozen with fear.

Gage could tell that the walkie-talkie button was depressed on the other end, but no discernable words were uttered, merely the mumbling, trembling sounds of those about to die.

Jack Hill was *very* displeased. Gage had sensed him, and was now scrambling to get outside, away from him and the little group he held captive. Highly irritated with Gage's failure to join them, Jack effortlessly began to eliminate the guards and Randolph's girlfriend—he saved her for last, savoring the thought that her loss would be a very personal one for Gage.

Gage knew it was too late for them, as he had made it outside to the van. He turned off the walkie-talkie just as he heard his lover and the guards' screams.

Agent Omega heard the bloodcurdling screams from his car and could feel the anguish even a block away. He grabbed his cell and phoned his senior partner as he drove his vehicle toward the building and rammed through the gate. The van that brought the unconscious Kassakatis there went hurtling past him in the opposite direction. Gage was inside.

"Screams coming from the building, God-awful screams . . . the van just pulled off, unsure who was in it! Call for backup, I'm going in!" Omega yelled before hanging up the phone.

Agent Kennedy put the cell down momentarily yelling, "Dammit, Omega, no!" She then hit the gas . . . yelling for Gotti and Dinks to, "Hold on!"

Agent Kennedy then flipped her phone back on and dialed for backup.

Tony Omega drew his weapon as he proceeded to enter the building. The screams were ongoing . . . haunting his every step. He had never in all his years heard pain such as this . . . he made the sign of the cross as he began to climb the stairway. He stopped at each floor to be certain where the screams were originating from, but he knew that he had to keep going up. As he reached the fifth floor, the screams stopped. Memories of his worst nightmares flashed before his eyes, but he had a job to do . . . so he breathed easy for a moment and then slowly opened the fifth floor door. Flashlight out and on. Gun at the ready. He moved out into the hallway, thankful that flickering florescent lights gave decent visibility into the gloomy hallway beyond.

"Into the Nether . . . cute," Omega thought as he passed beneath the archway where the bloody words were set to warn. There was dead silence, yet the agent trudged onward . . . doing his duty. He paused briefly at the former guard's gate and continued past. He checked each room on either side of the hall as he ambled on, finding only emptiness and darkness. He thought he was ready for whatever was ahead, but as he approached the area with the gurney, he could see where the screams had come from—his eyes seeing only black and red. Then the black came for him.

Agents Kennedy and Gottranelli had arrived out front of Haven's Gate just moments after the police. Kennedy told Dinks to stay put and jumped from her vehicle, barking out orders to the officers who had just drawn their weapons, flashing her ID.

"You two around back, you two and Gotti with me!"

She was the Alpha-bitch. She was a veteran of many years. She was hard as iron . . . yet for the first time since she began as an agent, she was scared . . . she could feel the doom of it all. It was her damn instincts . . . her intuition. It was always right, it seemed . . . and would be again.

Within minutes, they found him, Agent Antonio Jorge Omega, her partner . . . her friend. What was left of his body was found slumped against the back wall of a room in the farthest reaches of the wing . . . a gurney lay empty, and three other bodies were strewn about the room, blood and body parts everywhere . . .

James Kassakatis was not among them.

Kennedy approached Omega and welled up inside. She was a warrior . . . and she wouldn't shed a tear . . . not here . . . not now. It was then that she spotted it. A card placed prominently upon Omega's chest—the picture of a black jackal and a message written in blood . . . "Nether Enter . . . Never Leave . . . #'s 159-162."

Chapter 38
Hell Hath No Fury . . .

The SoulBound's screams had been short-lived as all went silent . . . all went dark. The blackout occurred as The Shadow That Speaks finally had come back for Jimmy's limp and unconscious body, and the dark man's terrifying presence caused many of the souls to scream, especially after witnessing what he had just done to the freshly massacred.

Hours later, Jimmy came to . . . slowly . . . the SoulBound as well, and noticed he lay upon the ground, amidst grass and some formed stones. It was very dark out, so eyes began to adjust to the moonlight. The formed stones were headstones . . . grave markers . . . he lay among the dead. A graveyard seemed to pop up all around him as his woozy head gathered more and more visual information.

"Jimmy, are you okay?" Koketai asked.

"You okay, bro?" Brennan asked.

"We've all been rather concerned," Jean-Paul remarked.

"Yes, quite," Gina added, as the professor stood now upon his feet.

"Yeah . . . we appear to be in a graveyard, sweetie . . . that's not good," Millie chimed in, in her usual "means-well-but-Jimmy-would-rather-not-hear-it" way.

186

Jimmy just rolled his eyes.

"I'm fine . . . I guess."

He was thoroughly confused and was just about to ask what was going on when Marie, who had been attempting to console Carrie Ann, said, *"Jimmy, Dr. Vaccaro betrayed you, stuck you with a needle, and you've been unconscious ever since."*

She went on to tell him everything that had happened, pausing and showing the same fear she had felt earlier at the mention of The Shadow That Speaks and what he did. The last thing any of them remembered was the sound of sirens and the specter of death.

Jimmy shook his head sideways, but as he started to move about, wooziness overcame him, relegating him to sit back down on the ground. The gravity of the situation was becoming apparent. His wallet and cell phone were missing. The Dark Man had set him up.

"Guys, I'm in trouble. My wallet . . . ! We've been set up . . . he took us away from the crime scene and left us here, so the police are going to think that I did it!"

Su Yi spoke then. *"Your wallet and cell were on the table next to the gurney in that awful room earlier. I saw it."*

A few others added that she was right, for they remembered that as well. Jimmy tried hard to figure things out, when he suddenly leapt to his feet. He remained still, standing with the look of shell shock . . . Something (he felt a presence) . . . was (he felt it inside him) . . . wrong. There was a sense of something familiar, but somehow different . . .

John Jaden quickly asked, *"Jimmy?! What's wrong? If you're worried about the pol . . ."*

"No . . . shhhhhhhh."

Jimmy was probing within . . . gleaning the source of the sensation.

"There's another presence inside me . . . but it doesn't feel quite like any of yours."

The SoulBound were stunned, and none could recall sensing anything unusual or *new*. Marie spoke up then, *"Jimmy, are you certain?"*

"Yeah . . . I get nothing on it though. No reading . . . male/ female . . . nothing, except that it feels . . . wrong. I think . . . I think I have a thirteenth soul!"

. . . .

Agent Kennedy stared at the card on Agent Omega's chest. Her partner, and the only man she had ever had feelings for, lay dead . . . ripped to shreds. She shook her head in disgust and began to rise when it happened . . . she saw it in her mind . . . the black Jackal. The thought had occurred to the team that she had assembled that the name "Jack" could somehow be involved, based on the picture of the Jackal, but they didn't have a suspect until now . . . and his name? *James Carson Kassakatis. Gotcha!* She turned away from her partner with pain and passion in her voice.

"Gotti, have Kassakatis's house, workplace, and the familiar places he visits, watched. I want to know where he is. I want him found!"

"You got it."

"Tap his phones, as well as Conway's and Brando's. He may be just stupid enough to contact them."

"I'm on it."

"Oh . . . and Gotti . . ."

"Yes, ma'am?"

"Congratulations . . . you're my new partner."

"Right. Good."

Gotti ran off, pleased, yet somewhat disturbed.

There was a blaze in the eyes of the lead agent, venom in her heart, and a growing malice that she knew she needed to control. She needed her wits about her, as well as all her skills and vast experience.

She wasn't about to blow it now.

She'd set right the wrongs.

She'd bring him to justice.

Dead or Alive.

DEAD OR ALIVE!

Chapter 39
Prey Without a Prayer

Tyler "Jack" Hill had a look upon his face as he walked through his front door . . . a look of contentment, a look that said all is well and right in the world. He was pleased with himself. He was so smart, so savvy . . . the stupid FBI will hunt Kassakatis down, and he'd be their Number One suspect. Jack loved being smarter than everyone else, stronger than everyone else, and more powerful than any human being that ever walked the planet. It was great being this . . . great! However, all it took was one errant thought, one miscue that resurfaced amidst the brilliance and sheer destruction . . . he remembered "the one that got away." Randolph Gage . . . so close, so near death.

Gage . . . he'll come for Jimmy again. He always comes for what he wants. And I'll be waiting.

Jack was just one of those kids that seemed downright evil from the beginning. He tortured small animals, birds, and insects as early as two years of age. His parents were good people and were torn by his awful ways. It was odd for a youngster to show no sense of love or goodness—ever. He was nicknamed after his father, as most friends and family saw the toddler as the spitting image of his dad. Little Jack hated going outside and lived most moments sheltered in his room, preferably a dark room. He was deemed too violent, too dangerous, to go to school. His parents had tried to home school him, but eventually gave up and contacted the authorities after they found numerous mutilated cats and dogs in a strange semblance of a circle strew about his room.

At eight years old, wicked little Jack was taken to a facility for disturbed children. He remained at the New Hope Juvenile Center for less than a year before he began having visions. He would draw future things, things not possible to know. The doctors were astounded and subsequently were contacted by a man named Gage, Randolph Gage. Gage took the boy to his secret facility in Sterling, VA, and ran "tests" on the boy. He began conducting experiments, delving into things better left alone. Gage's experts attempted to "capture" the way to glean the future, attempting to isolate the methods that the Hill boy employed . . . to no avail.

What happened next changed the lives of multitudes of people. Gage ordered an experiment on the Hill boy, one dark in nature, deeply immoral, but Gage had a job to do.

The human mind is complicated and not understood well enough to be prodded about, as Jack Hill's was. Nevertheless, Gage had his scientists and doctors use an experimental form of radiation to attempt to stimulate Jack's brain, to help open his mind, to help Gage see into the processes of clairvoyant thought. What he/they didn't know was that little Jack had a darkness within that could not be x-rayed, seen on scans, nor diagnosed by any doctor . . . so when the radiation touched the deepest and truly forbidden areas of the human mind, it all went terribly wrong. Jack became the darkness, it warped about him, it enveloped him, it embraced him, and he it.

Jack was terrified at first, but exhilarated by the essence that filled every fiber of his being, and the blond-haired child rose from the table, wide awake, and quite aware. He killed the lights first, as they were his enemy, and hurt to boot . . . then began to kill the fools that remained. He was a blackened whirlwind . . . tearing, gnashing, shearing, stabbing, and ripping. Body parts flew as if from a wood chipper . . . it was exhilarating.

He escaped the facility, with Gage's people hunting him, but Jack simply slipped into the shadows, as they were everywhere . . . ah yes, the boy would be free, and the world for many would never be the same. "Little Jack" Hill was changed, a monster, an abomination . . . in every sense of the word.

That was so long ago . . .

Jack finally took a shower and went to bed, a man without nightmares, but rather one who became them.

"Yesssss," he thought as he lay, "Gage is like everyone else . . . prey without a prayer!"

Chapter 40
The Altar of All Faiths

The rain began to slowly fall, the typical sporadic drops landing about Jimmy. It was then that Yi noticed the building nestled among the rolling hills, just a few 100 feet north of where Jimmy stood . . . with Jimmy and the other SoulBound too distracted by the apparent discovery of a thirteenth soul to take notice. Technically, Jimmy had only eleven SoulBound remaining after Nan made it into The Light; however, Jimmy held a place for her as the twelfth, regardless of her ascension.

The building had a raised and pointed roof, like a church or temple, but as such was probably closed at this time of night. Yi determined that she should mention her sighting to Jimmy and did so as the others were discussing the potential issues at hand.

"Jimmy? There is a building, perhaps a church or temple—just a bit north of where we are—perhaps you should get out of the rain?"

"Yes . . . good idea, Yi . . . thanks," Jimmy responded as the raindrops began pounding down quite hard.

He easily made his way through the graveyard, as his eyes had adjusted quite well by now. Jimmy noticed an old Chrysler LeBaron parked outside on the gravely driveway as he approached around the left side of the building, to where he expected to see the front entrance. Sure enough, the large double wooden doors faced the currently unoccupied side road that ran north and south alongside the building.

Jimmy spotted a name as he galloped up the steps—The Altar of All Faiths. He knocked upon the great doors hoping that the car was an indication that someone was there. He waited impatiently as the liquid heavens emptied down upon him, all the while nervously pacing in front of the entry. His wait ended in short order as the doors opened wide and an elderly black gentleman ushered him out of the pour.

"Come in, friend, come in! It's raining cats and dogs, eh?"

The drenched professor sidled inside with a grateful, "Thank you kindly!"

The doors closed in behind him and Jimmy could see that he indeed graced the entrance way of a church or temple. Wooden pews lined up in rows in the typical church fashion, and there was a large open area at the front, raised a couple feet up from the floor.

"Welcome to The Altar of All Faiths, young man. I'm Reverend Casey Darcelle. How can I help you?"

Jimmy greeted the elder preacher with hesitation rather than his name . . .

"John Doe, I presume?" laughed the Reverend as he smiled wide. "C'mon and follow me to my quarters."

"Reverend, my name is Jimmy," the younger man replied, feeling bad about what had just happened. He continued.

"My apologies, sir. I just need a place to get out of the rain and collect my thoughts . . . if that's okay?"

"This is a good place to come to when one has storms about . . . we'll have you dry and fed in no time, and perhaps you can collect yourself in the meantime, yes?"

"Ohhhh . . . yes, sir, thank you so much," Jimmy responded as he walked behind the preacher, a bit distracted by the area surrounding a large cross at the back of the church.

He wasn't sure why, but he felt uneasy here . . . while feeling an inner peace simultaneously.

How was that possible?

He then asked, "Sir, what time do you have? My watch is broken."

"11:36 p.m.," came the unpopular reply.

Ohhh boy.

Jimmy had always had a weird feeling about that time, ever since his mother had told him that he was born at 11:36 p.m. He would awaken to see that it was 11:36 p.m. or happen to glance at his watch if he were out . . . again, almost in a paranormal state, it seemed to draw him to notice it . . . 11:36 p.m. The odd recognition of that time became so much of an annoyance that he wrote a poem about it and added it to his poetry book. Ironically, it was the first nightmare that terrorized him last night.

"Thank you," Jimmy replied, albeit uneasily.

The professor continued behind Reverend Darcelle through a door on the back left wall to the side of the altar. The door led to a hallway that ran only about twenty feet and came abruptly to an end at the foot of a flight of stairs, of which the elder man trekked up.

"They built this church in '57 and just updated the bathroom and few appliances here in the past year . . . lucky for you that you weren't here previously. It was outdated, dilapidated, and nearly closed down. Thank the Lord, my prayers—and the budget—got it done."

He laughed a bit.

Jimmy enjoyed the Reverend's easygoing nature . . . he made good company. The pair arrived at the top of the stairs and through the door that led to the preacher's apartment.

"You called it a church just then . . ." Jimmy partially asked and stated.

Darcelle replied, "It was originally built as the Church of the Redemption, a Baptist faith venue . . . but back about three years ago, with not enough money to keep the church open, a coalition of sorts was formed. A local Jewish temple, a mosque, and a few other spiritual centers decided to pool their money and use this facility for everyone. They got the idea from some movie. So now, Muslims, Jews, various Christian-based faiths, Buddhists, and other faiths come here on a schedule to practice their beliefs. There is something beautiful in it, I tell you."

"That's truly . . . amazing," Jimmy surmised.

"Yes, sir . . ." the Reverend replied as he smiled and then pointed ". . . bathroom's down the hall there on the right. Go get yourself dried off and if you need to use the phone, it's right here on the wall in the kitchen."

"Again, thank you for everything."

Jimmy took the Reverend's advice, and dried off with one of the bathroom's hand towels. Luckily, he wasn't completely drenched.

He stood in front of the old mirror, certain that it was the same one that had been there for over fifty years, and stared into his reflection. The SoulBound had become so familiar with Jimmy; they had a knack for knowing when it was okay to "speak" up and when to just let the man be. Jimmy appreciated the silence . . . for he didn't get it nearly enough. His eyes were bloodshot and he appeared haggard and pale. He couldn't help but think that the Reverend would have likely suspected him of doing drugs.

"Yeah," Jimmy thought sarcastically, *"that's just what I need."*

Chapter 41

The Harmonica

Jimmy made his way back into the main area of the small apartment, situated in between the kitchen and living room. Reverend Darcelle appeared to be making coffee and reaching into the fridge when he spoke.

"You want something to drink? Coffee, tea . . . orange juice, perhaps?"

"Just plain water would be great."

"I don't have any 'plain' water, but good old-fashioned Harford County tap is freshly squeezed."

Jimmy again laughed at the Reverend's attempt at humor.

"Yes, I'll take the old-fashioned stuff . . . just fine, thanks."

"Have a seat here at the table . . . I've got plenty of lunch meats and cheese . . . you can help yourself to a sandwich or we can have some soup if that suits you."

Jimmy was starving and said that he'd make a sandwich, which would be great. He helped himself to a ham and cheese sandwich on a fresh Kaiser roll. The Reverend had good taste in food, Jimmy thought appreciatively. After returning the remaining foodstuffs to their place, and washing his knife, Jimmy sat to eat. He ate quickly . . . as if it were prison food.

The Reverend noticed the ravished young man eat like there was no tomorrow, but held his tongue, fearing his playful nature might be a bit overbearing. Instead, he simply asked, "Will you be needing a ride home?"

Jimmy had been caught off guard and wasn't sure how to respond to that. He mustered "I'm not sure . . . yet. If I could stay for just a bit, Reverend Darcelle, it would be a gr . . ."

"Casey . . . call me Casey. It's my middle name, only my mother called me Paul."

"His mother was a great woman," Jean-"Paul" added, to a round of snickering from many of the SoulBound.

Jimmy simply nodded as the preacher continued.

"I've been here for twenty-four years. All these years, I've been here and not once have I been awakened to a stranger at my door. Well, rather the Lord's door. This *is* the Lord's House, not mine."

"Sir, I am truly sorry about th . . ."

"No no . . . I wasn't complaining, young man, just getting to a point."

He sat across from Jimmy at the table, eyes wide, and a cup of decaf coffee steaming in front of him as he continued.

"Just because I'm an old-fashioned man of the Lord doesn't mean I'm normally the Motel 6 type."

The Reverend was referring to the "We'll leave the light on for ya" commercials . . . and Jimmy got it.

"However . . ." the man took a sip of the dark brew, ". . . I have a rather strong sense of character . . . and with you, I sensed a lot of that."

Jimmy raised his eyebrows as the Reverend chuckled a bit, laughing at the astute observation.

"You have no idea."

"Well, that is certainly true . . . certainly true. If you need a ride home or if you have a need to stay the night, you're welcome."

Jimmy knew that Dee and Tommy would be worried sick, but Dragon had worried him when he suggested that calling them might be bad all around. He agreed. He needed time . . . and this nice old man was offering it.

"Yes, sir, staying just this one night would be a blessing."

With that, the Reverend stood and shook Jimmy's hand, and an accord was reached. "You can stay in the guest room . . . if one can call it that. Ain't more than an eight-by-eight room . . . a walk-in closet is more like it."

Again, he chuckled in that grandfatherly way. He showed Jimmy to his room. Jimmy peered in and remarked, "It'll hold me then, I'm six-by-two."

They both laughed again . . . as the Reverend nodded to him and walked back into the kitchen to turn off the lights.

Jimmy closed the door, undressed, and got into bed. He lay in bed with visions of another crazy day ransacking their way throughout his overused mind. Barely visible in the moonlight was a cross on the opposite wall from where he lay. He stared through the gloom at the holy symbol . . . a joy coupled with uneasiness washed over him. It was the same sensation as before when he had passed the altar area. He wasn't happy with what was going on and lay for an hour or more with no Nan to lull him to sleep.

He missed her deeply. He missed Dee as well, but there was much at stake and he needed to be sharp.

The thunderstorm that raged outside had abated, and as Jimmy lay waiting to nod off, he heard it . . . a sound outside his window. He rose from bed to look outside . . . the moon affording little light. A freight train had stopped nearby and was passing through . . . but the sound wasn't the train, it was a harmonica. He could see that there was an old man playing it, dressed as a vagrant, moving slowly along the road. The professor closed the curtains and returned to bed. Quietly, he listened . . . they all did, and Jimmy began a poetic free-styling to the SoulBound—a rare event indeed—despite the call to slumber . . .

"The harmonica greets the night. Like an old locomotive, it careens the trees and streets . . . a soulful cry. It speaks to me as I lay to sleep, for the old man plays without care of time, a voice to the winds, a plea to be heard, if not seen. It's a song unlike any other, as it falls upon me heavy; a hand held to my heart in chords that so touch me. I hear a sadness in this song, it tries not to hide its sorrow. No filtering the pain . . . on this train.

"Notes begin again to call out of a life filled with regret, and yet there is much more to hear . . . a tune that beckons a deeper ear. Hopeful that within the din of the track, we may see the good in him . . . see the wonder of his dreams, though broken, he believes them still, and wrote this song to say out loud that it's okay . . . Life has taken, but he is given this harmonica to play.

"Memories whistle along with him and go where the music takes them . . . to lay their sounds upon me, a lost dream found, on this night to lay and remember . . . that there is more to life than me."

"Beautifully deep," Marie offered . . .

"Oui, magnifique," Jean-Paul agreed.

"Very good, my friend," these words came from Jimmy's most reserved and ancient soul, Koketai.

Others replied just as appreciatively, to which Jimmy simply smiled. With that, they nodded off for the night, the harmonica fading into the distance . . .

As he drifted further into slumber, there was movement within him . . . there stirred in darkness. While the thunderstorm earlier had been dangerous, the storm within Jimmy was a killer.

Chapter 42
The Ultimate Question

Thursday, June 12, 2008

Jimmy sat up in bed, wiped the sleep from his eyes, and then glanced at the clock on the wall beside the window. It showed 6:32 amid the dawn that filtered through the drawn curtains. He caught the aroma of bacon and happily made his way into the kitchen. Sure enough, the Reverend was hovering over the stove, eggs and bacon on the menu. Jimmy knew that the Reverend was the sort of man who would be making enough for them both, and cleared his throat to get Darcelle's attention.

"You look like a bacon-and-egg man. I figured you'd be out here once the bacon wafted through the apartment."

"You're on to me," Jimmy answered agreeably, a grin cracking his non-morning-person face. Jimmy sat at the table and realized as he stared at the back of the friendly man, that he had never, not that he recalled anyway, spoken with a "man of God" about anything more than casual chit-chat, and *that* was most often when a religion-based college official was attempting to recruit him.

Religion was a subject discussed very rarely in Jimmy's personal life and rarely referred to by the SoulBound. It was apparent through comments over the years that each of the SoulBound had their own belief system when they were alive, and some were thrown a bit by becoming ghosts. Dragon never believed in God or any form of afterlife, so when The Light appeared to him the first time, he panicked. He didn't know exactly what to believe now, but he believed in an afterlife.

Jimmy sat and pondered . . . it occurred to him that he may now have an opportunity to discuss his "situation" with a man that seemed not only trustworthy, but also to have a wisdom that emanated from him.

"Reverend . . . errr, Casey rather . . . Do you have time to talk with me? It's rather important."

Reverend Darcelle was just sitting down to eat, setting out the food on the table so they both could help themselves.

"Yes, I have a couple hours or so before I need to prepare for my day."

Jimmy smiled sheepishly as he uttered, "I may just need most of that time."

"Well then, let's eat as we talk . . . that okay with you?"

"Oh yes, of course," Jimmy said as he fixed his plate, but he was too busy preparing his thoughts to start eating.

Jimmy had experience revealing the truth about himself, as he had recently told Dee everything and had told Tommy many years prior. He began at the beginning . . . telling the Reverend about his visions as a child . . . about the night the light entered his room and how he had passed out in shock. He continued with the entire story as the Reverend quietly and quite intently listened . . . eating and drinking non-decaf coffee as he did.

Casey had asked questions as Jimmy told his story, making sure he hadn't misunderstood, and Jimmy appreciated that.

Jimmy continued on through to Carrie Ann, The Shadow That Speaks, his death for thirty seconds, the previous day's events that led to his awakening in the graveyard, the potential discovery of the still-as-yet-unknown thirteenth soul . . . and finally his arrival here at the "Altar."

The Reverend—who had long since finished eating—asked Jimmy to accompany him downstairs.

Jimmy grabbed a few cold pieces of bacon, as he hadn't taken a bite of his food the entire time, and rose to follow the holy man.

The Reverend spoke very little during the roughly hour-and-a-half it took to get through the talk, again, just asking a few questions, and Jimmy was a bit curious, concerned even, as he went down the stairs behind the older man.

The building was empty as usual at this time of the morning, on a Thursday, as Reverend Darcelle and Jimmy entered the main area of the church. The Reverend headed straight for the altar and came to sit at the edge of the stage upon which the altar and podium rested. A large cross dominated the room on the back wall, rising up near to the ceiling, which was roughly thirty feet high. A giant curtain had been installed for when the non-Christian faiths were in, pulled to cover the cross, as it was not a part of their belief system.

Jimmy settled himself beside the Reverend, anxiously awaiting his reaction, but instead, felt compelled to stare at the cross . . . an uncomfortable sensation twisting within him, but a peace resonated throughout him simultaneously.

Jimmy knew the thirteenth soul had bad intentions . . . he just knew it.

"My new friend isn't pleased to be here."

Reverend Darcelle responded, "I was curious about that . . . I wanted to see how you would feel being here . . . how you would react."

"Whoever, whatever it is, I don't want it in me. Can you help with that?"

"Perhaps so, but I think you have a question inside you, one begging to be asked. One needing an answer to soothe your soul and put your mind at ease," Reverend Darcelle offered, all the while staring deep into the blue eyes of the younger man, who had finally looked away from the cross.

Jimmy was confused for a moment and muttered "aloud" to the SoulBound.

"What's he talking about? What question?"

Jean-Paul Lalande was the first to respond, and Jimmy knew he was right the moment he said it.

"It is the ultimate question for you, Jimmy, unique only to you . . . and not to sound like the Vaccaro witch, but . . . one you've sought an answer to for so long now . . . The question is: Why me?"

There was a hushed agreement among the souls, and Jimmy, who had looked away momentarily, stood and faced the holy man and replied, "Why me?"

"What do you believe the answer is, Jimmy?"

Jimmy was hoping for an answer, not another question, but responded openly and honestly. "I really don't know. One might believe that I'm completely insane and that the souls within me are *seemingly* real, but actually detailed fantasy with a base in historical accuracy. Or perhaps one may determine I have Multiple Personality Disorder. For me, I know that they are real, I am truthful, and everything I've told you is 100 percent true. Why I'm able to do this has been an ongoing question . . . and frankly, one I don't expect to get an answer to until I die."

"I see," said the elder man. "In more ways than one."

He stood, facing Jimmy and spoke strongly and with deep impact.

"During our talk last night, you told me in no uncertain terms that you've had two miraculous things occur in your life. First—you were given the miracle of 'sight,' able to see into the future through this gift from God. Second—Jimmy, at no time in recorded history has anyone carried another's soul within them, but you have not only one other, you have twelve souls 'aware' within you. Whether you believe in God or not, you must be able to see . . . ," Reverend Darcelle paused for dramatic effect. ". . . that you are—a *miracle*. You, Jimmy, *you* . . . have been chosen by God to carry on a mission that *only you* can accomplish. The devil that you seek will be ready . . . will you?"

Jimmy looked away momentarily before looking back to the Reverend and replied, "I'm terrified . . . this thing . . . It is living darkness . . ." A look of almost desperation overcame him. ". . . and I don't know how to destroy it."

The man of God raised his voice to instill, to ingrain into Jimmy's brain- hope, and more importantly- faith.

"You will find the way, Jimmy . . . God wouldn't give you a task that you haven't the means to complete!"

Jimmy was shocked a bit at the power of the man's words, and watched as Reverend Darcelle walked to the steps that led to the altar and up past the podium toward the great cross. Again, the Reverend spoke aloud. "It doesn't take a religious scholar to glean that through God's word that the number three is Holy. If the Lord has granted you two miracles, young man, rest assured that He will send a third."

Jimmy felt uplifted . . . given a spirit to carry on with a fervor . . . though conceded, *"I am going to need it."*

Jimmy's parents had been churchgoers, followers of his father's Methodist church, but they never forced their religion on their son, a rare thing for most parents. Jimmy never spoke aloud of his own beliefs, but he would classify himself as more "spiritual" than "religious."

John Jaden "spoke" up at that moment. *"Jimmy, we've all been listening and I felt it was possibly important to remind you of something . . ."*

Jimmy listened intently and raised his eyebrows as Jaden continued telling him what was so interesting.

"Hmmm . . . that never occurred to me . . . thanks, bro," Jimmy replied and thanked John for the idea.

"Reverend . . . you were mentioning the power of three, that three is a holy number . . . it is a curious thing . . ." Jimmy continued, himself pausing for effect.

". . . John, one of the SoulBound, reminded me that I was born in 1982 . . . March the 3rd . . . 3-3."

With that, the Reverend smiled as if he'd won the lottery, nodded his head at Jimmy, and turned to kneel.

Chapter 43

Diamonds in the Dust

Before the cross, the Reverend prayed, and aloud he thanked the Lord for the miracles that He had bestowed upon such a good young man. As the old man prayed, that very "good young man" again found himself staring into the heart of the cross. He was appreciative of the feelings that washed over him. A comforting sensation, a protective and loving essence . . . it was a beautifully moving moment . . . until—

"Nooooo!" Jimmy screamed . . . as he felt a sharp "force" quake through him, causing a massive headache and a mighty fear and distrust to overcome him.

"Jimmy?! What's wrong, son?"

The Reverend had whirled around and was making his way back toward Jimmy.

"I . . . I want it out of me!" The Professor yelled as a feeling of deepest dread poured over him.

The darkness within him was not happy in the church and had let Jimmy feel its displeasure.

Jimmy rushed from the church and out the front entrance, where the sun was bright, the wind was subtle, and madness etched into the face of a terrified man. He walked back toward the graveyard, where he had found himself just the night before.

He slowed and halted among the first few rows of tombstones. It took only a few moments, but Jimmy felt his body relaxing a bit, the tenseness in his face abating, and the fear draining away. He stood upon the still muddy ground, uncaring about the mess, and put his hands over his face, then through his hair, as the feeling that had ravaged him passed . . . at least for now.

Reverend Darcelle approached Jimmy gingerly, as Jimmy figured that the situation had unnerved the man a bit.

"Are you okay, son?"

First came the truthful reply, "At the moment."

Then came the heartfelt apology—Jimmy was unable to turn and look the preacher in the eye, "I'm so sorry, sir."

"It's okay, Jimmy, it's okay. But . . . . uhhh, we're going to have to do something about that."

The way the Reverend said that made Jimmy laugh, and then Darcelle joined in. What the Reverend didn't know, and never would, was that what resided within Jimmy was not something that an exorcism could rid him of.

Darcelle then asked him, "Why the graveyard, Jimmy . . . is it the comfort of passed souls?"

Jimmy paused to consider for a moment and replied, "Diamonds in the dust . . ." his answer was spoken as if he had more to say, but he said nothing further, looking about quietly.

The Reverend came to stand beside Jimmy, though Jimmy seemed not to notice, his eyes scanning the markers all around them.

Darcelle asked, "Hmmm . . . if I may . . . what does that mean?"

Jimmy continued from where he began earlier. "I wrote something . . . about the beauty of life and death. It's about understanding and respecting those who came before us. My parents initially taught me this, but The SoulBound have brought me an awareness that can barely be explained."

"Care to regale me? I'm a good listener," came the warm reply from the Reverend.

The professor began as he looked away to the graves about him . . .

"I hear them speak, faint and weak.
I hear them laugh and play.
I can watch them all,
Through photographs
Stilled shadows of yesterday,
And I imagine them as they imagined me,
In the twinkling of time, in eyes so wide,
Dreaming of days past and days yet come,
Like so many of us have done.
History was the present moments ago,
And years do ebb and flow,
Carrying memories that ride the winds,
Singing to minds to listen and know,
And to capture these essences . . . So . . .
Look deeply into these photos . . .
The echoes of Father Time.
Telling tales of love and life from old,
Of lives that thrived, alive and bold.

Of dreams attained, of sickness and pain,
And family lost along the way.
Lives . . .
Like you and me . . .
Alive in the time we call history,
But history speaks if you've ears to hear,
So I feel it's our duty and trusts
To remember their songs,
Shining souls long gone . . .
Now lying . . .
Like diamonds in the dust."

The reverend responded with awe and excitement, "Whew! If I could speak that way, my congregation would never leave! You are no devil, but you sure are silver-tongued."

He laughed heartily, amazed in the moment. He then added, "That reminds me of the best thing I ever wrote. It went like this . . . 'Roses are red, and violets are purple, stupid!'"

Laughter erupted between the muddy-bottomed pair, but the laughter was short-lived—as a booming voice yelled, "Don't move! Hands above your head!"

Chapter 44
The Plot Thickens

The Reverend threw his hands up at the same time Jimmy did, but was told immediately to back away from Jimmy. The two Harford County deputies had spotted the wanted man as he ran crazily from the "Altar" a minute before, and pulled in around the side of the building, calling it in before rushing to apprehend him.

Deputy Logan—Jimmy couldn't help but notice that he looked very much like Robert Redford—was putting the cuffs on Jimmy as his female partner kept her gun on him.

The "Natural" clamped the cuffs down and said, "You're under arrest."

"Officer, may I ask what this has to do with?" Jimmy asked as he tried hard to remain calm.

No response.

Dio Santo. "Oh my God" is right.

"Look . . . I was at a meeting with my psychiatrist when I blacked out and awakened near here, lying in the graveyard. Dr. Vaccaro stuck me with a needle and then . . . . Nothing—until late last night."

The female, Deputy Gretchen Charles, spoke then. "We're not the ones you need to explain anything to. We're taking you in and you can explain everything then."

Jimmy looked back at the Reverend who had remained standing nearby. As the deputies led Jimmy away, he spoke up, "Thank you . . . for everything."

"The Sundance Kid" remained in the squad car as his partner went back to get the Reverend's information. After about two minutes, she returned and they pulled away.

Deputy Logan drove off as Deputy Charles called in the arrest—Jimmy handcuffed and securely in the backseat.

. . . .

Agent Kennedy had just returned from the heart-wrenching visit to Omega's parents' home when she got the word that Kassakatis had been holed up at a church a few miles from the crime scene. He was in custody and being brought into the local Sheriff's Department. She had set up an office there as a command post of sorts, expecting a lengthy search. She was putting the puzzle together as best as she could, getting the news from Gotti that Dr. Lena Vaccaro had gone missing.

"The plot thickens," Kennedy thought.

Her wait was nearly over as the deputies were now about fifteen minutes out. She had him now . . . or so she figured.

. . . .

Deputy Charles spotted the white van with the police lights approaching from behind them.

"Odd," she thought.

Her partner spotted the van too and said, "What the hell is that?"

"No idea, but it's coming fast."

The squad car's lights were already on, so they weren't moving off the road . . . but the white van moved up alongside them in the oncoming lane. A gentleman in a black, two-piece suit and glasses rolled his window down and flashed a badge, pointing for them to pull over. So as not to cause an accident, Logan slowed to allow the van to pass them and, as it did, it slowed to a stop.

"What the . . ."

He had no choice but to stop as four men in black, two-piece suits leapt from the van and walked toward the squad car, the same man who earlier flashed a badge, did so again, as he stepped ahead of his companions.

"Let me see what's going on," Deputy Charles said as she got out of the vehicle and approached the oncoming men.

"Redford" watched from within the car and radioed in that they had been stopped by a group of men in a white van with police lights. He had just finished calling it in when he saw that another white van had pulled up behind him, nearly on his bumper. Furious, he got out of the vehicle, while at that moment, four more men jumped out of the vehicle and approached him. While Deputy Charles was talking with the first group of men and "Redford" was just getting to the second group, the call came in on their radios . . .

"Do not stop . . . do not engage!"

That had been Agent Kennedy . . . too late. At the same time, the deputies were overpowered with stun guns, gagged, hog-tied, and left off the side of the road.

Jimmy watched the entire event unfold and was completely confused and alarmed as the men grabbed him from the vehicle. A stun gun, gag, and hog-tie later . . . he was on the road to who-knew-where. His fears would have to wait . . . a needle saw to that.

"Great, another nee . . ."

Marie took control and shouted out as she had before, *"All right, guys, you know the drill!"*

Chapter 45

Truth & Consequences

It was early Thursday afternoon, and the sunlight was protruding through the venetian blinds as Tommy paced about the kitchen. He was making his clockwork-like call to Jimmy's cell phone. It had been roughly twenty-four hours since they last saw Jimmy, and Dee, mimicking Tommy, was pacing the length of the living room, hoping something would turn up. As Brando finished dialing, he anticipated the answering machine and was stunned by, "Hello?" on the other end of the phone . . . a woman's voice! Someone answered!

"Hello! Who's this? Is Jimmy there?" came the frantic reply from Tommy as Dee bounded excitedly toward him, her mouth agape.

"No, Jimmy's unable to come to the phone at this time . . ."

Tommy was about to respond, but there was a loud knock at the door at that moment.

"Hold on just a second . . . please don't hang up! Someone's banging at the door!" he spoke up as he and Dee both ran and opened the door.

"Yeah . . . that would be me."

The voice on the other end of the phone stood at the door, accompanied by a cadre of uniformed police officers and FBI agents wearing their "raid jackets," emblazoned with large FBI letters on the back . . . she wore one as well and held Jimmy's cell in her gloved hand. The red-haired woman, sweat beading her lithe frame on this hot spring day, introduced herself.

"I'm Special Agent Carol Kennedy, and I have a warrant to search this premises."

Agents Kennedy and Gottranelli, along with a good portion of their investigative team, took over the Kassakatis home. Agents rummaged through the house as the officers set up yellow tape around the perimeter of the home.

Jimmy's nosy neighbor, Mrs. Lumbutter, was tickled pink at the drama unfolding, and immediately called the local community association to report the happenings.

Dee's desperate plea of "What's going on here?" went unanswered as she and Tommy were herded to the kitchen, to be seated at the table.

Agents Kennedy and Gottranelli sat opposite them, having shown the warrant to search the home. After introducing themselves, the agents smiled at one another and Gottranelli spoke first, to Tommy.

"Mr. Brando, if you'd be so kind as to come with me . . ."

He stood as he spoke and motioned for Tommy to accompany him.

Brando looked to Dee, who nodded in that "I'm okay" way. Tommy stood and walked behind the big agent, following him out to the balcony.

Dee and Tommy had seen enough shows and movies to know that they were being separated for questioning. Indeed—it *was* time to "discuss" the circumstances with Jimmy's "friends."

Dee and Tommy were asked numerous questions regarding the currently unpopular professor. Basic questions . . . feeler questions meant to gauge nervousness, spot tendencies. Standard practice.

Dee, scared and still in the dark about why the agents were there, asked outright, "Ma'am, please . . . why are you here? Is Jimmy okay?"

Agent Kennedy's intuition, coupled with her expertise in reading body language, told her that Dee was sincere in her concern. Admittedly, Kennedy had mixed feelings over Jimmy's potential guilt as the events of the day had taken a surreal twist. She was not as gung-ho as before, but maintained her normal steady ways . . . knowing all would come to light eventually . . . and soon—if she had anything to say about it.

"It's time," Kennedy surmised.

Agent Kennedy's face went from friendly and inquisitive to serious in a heartbeat, and she asked none-too-kindly, "I'll tell you all you want to know, but first, Miss Conway . . . you tell me, truthfully . . ." she continued snidely, ". . . what was the reason behind Jimmy's visit to Dr. Vaccaro's office?"

Agent Kennedy would occasionally ask to be called Carol when she determined that it gave the desired impression that she was a compassionate woman and not just an agent; this was not one of those times. Her attitude was evident in the way she asked the question as to why Jimmy had gone to Vaccaro's office.

Not one easily intimidated, Dee stared deeply into the emerald eyes of the woman who knew something of Jimmy's fate and/or whereabouts.

Agent Kennedy stared back without blinking.

Two strong-willed women. The sort of women you want in your corner . . . on your side.

Dee contemplated the answer, the truth. *The Truth.* That was a doozie. How could she betray Jimmy's secret after she had gone behind his back with Vaccaro a couple of days before? She decided to try a truthful reply without divulging anything.

"He had an appointment. It was obviously very personal."

"Obviously, Miss Conway, but you and I know both know . . . that's on the surface."

The agent leaned in a bit toward the younger woman. "I want what you know. All of it." Her statement wasn't to be trifled with, she was determined.

Dee saw something in the eyes of her momentary antagonist, something she had to find out about . . . and in her genuinely sweet way, did so.

"Someone . . . died?"

The agent leaned back into her chair, taken by surprise at the question, as she had expected answers instead. Kennedy relinquished her intimidating and forceful demeanor, becoming momentarily what she had hoped not to—Carol.

"My partner . . . Agent Tony Omega," her reply a sad and heartfelt admission.

It was Dee's turn to sit back in her chair, speaking softly as she did.

"I'm sorry . . . sincerely."

The agent returned as swiftly as she left . . .

"We both want the same thing, but I can't help you, or Jimmy, without getting answers. Again . . . Why did Jimmy go to see Vaccaro?"

Dee knew Tommy wouldn't reveal Jimmy to the other agent, she was sure of it. It was all on her, and everything was coming to a head. Jimmy was missing, an FBI agent was dead, and they wanted answers about Jimmy's meetings with his shrink. She had to reply . . . for Agent Kennedy's facial expressions showed her simmering. Her time for weighing the consequences was up. At that moment, she was given a brief reprieve, as a male agent, who seemed to be no more than college age, approached the women and interrupted.

"Agent Kennedy?"

She looked at him frustratingly until a glance back from him indicated that he had found something.

She rose from the table and said, "Stay here, I'll be right back."

Kennedy followed the young agent out the front door and turned left around the side of the house. There was a group of forensic specialists going over an area outside Jimmy's bedroom window, and the young agent told Kennedy they had found a footprint and something else on the ground. As Kennedy approached, a female specialist named O'Meara, her hair in a ponytail and wearing white gloves, stood to fill her in.

"Ma'am . . ." she nodded and began to speak as the Case Agent voiced inquisitively, "Whatcha got?"

"There's a shoe-print, but it's faint. We're working on it, but here . . . ," she paused and crouched down, motioning for Kennedy to do the same and pointed at something.

". . . you need to see this."

The specialist was showing her superior something partially embedded in the dirt, just beneath the window. The Case Agent got down onto her knees and took a good look . . . it was a bent piece of paper, or something. Yes, that something was a business card, and although only half of it showed, it showcased roughly half of a black jackal.

Well, well . . . the noose tightens.

Kennedy stood and directed the team to check for prints not only in this area, but off into the strand of woods nearby. She then told Specialist O'Meara to bag the card and to have it checked for prints. After taking a moment to survey the area, she added that the specialist should attempt to get prints from the window and even to try the siding. She directed the young male agent, who had been standing by, to go and alert Agent Gottranelli to the findings.

He walked briskly around to the front of the home to carry out her orders.

This was big. The evidence against Kassakatis was mounting. She walked back toward the front of the house and stopped just at the corner, pondering. She was trying to put this bizarre puzzle together. It appeared that the professor was her man, although the black jackal card seemed too convenient. Then there were the strange abductions, first by a group at the Graydon Center, then by a sizeable group posing as some arm of law enforcement. The water muddied further when word came from the deputies that had captured Kassakatis earlier . . . they felt that the black-clad abductors were pretty regimented, and likely military or government trained.

She was about to head back in and finish with Dee when Gotti came toward her, exiting the house from the front door. Kennedy decided to update him on the latest findings.

He nodded in a satisfied manner, hands on hips, and after a pause said, "I've got nothing so far from Brando. He's a real smart-ass, that one. Any luck with the girlfriend?"

"Not yet, but I am close."

Gotti nodded and then asked, "I almost forgot to ask you . . . what did you want to do about Dinks?"

Kennedy shrugged her shoulders at the thought of the informant. He was a huge help so far, but she needed to figure out how else to use his services.

"Have one of the veteran agents take Dinks back to the office. I will find a use for him shortly."

"You got it."

With that the agents separated, Gotti going to take care of the orders for Mr. Dinkins, and Kennedy went back into the home to finish up with Dee. As she entered the home, she was detained by yet another agent . . . one she knew pretty well; Faust.

"Ma'am, I found something . . ."

Kennedy looked to Dee as she passed her and said, "Continue sitting, I'll be right with you."

As far as Dee was concerned, the agent could take forever.

As the Case Agent followed Agent Faust, she couldn't help but notice that his features—a strapping man in his thirties, dark hair, brown eyes—were quite similar to Omega's.

They moved into the sunken living room, around the corner, and down the short hallway to the main bedroom. Faust directed her to look at the object that was in a zip-lock bag, lying on the bed. She picked it up and stared at it. It was the spreadsheet that Jimmy had created for Dee when he first broke the news to her about the SoulBound.

1) Marie Anne Beale: Veterinarian, drowned, 1981 (thirty-one years old)

2) Shen Koketai: Mongol warrior, died in battle, 1205 (seventeen years old)

3) Su Yi: Chinese launderer, strangled, 1871 (twenty-two years old)

4) Frank 'Dragon' Jackson: Biker, motorcycle accident, 1995 (thirty-eight years old)

5) Nan: Slave, smallpox, 1845 (thirty-four years old)

6) John Jaden: US Navy sailor, drowned, 1960 (nineteen years old)

7) Brennan Payton: Network tech trainer, car accident, 2003 (twenty-seven years old)

8) Millie Liddell: Retired housewife, Stroke, 1946 (seventy-one years old)

9) Karen Two Storms: Financial advisor, heart attack, 1992 (fifty-eight years old)

10) Jean-Paul Lalande: French sailor, cannonball, 1827
   (twenty-five years old)
11) Gina Imbragulio: Italian pianist, plane crash, 1953
   (thirty-two years old)
12) Carrie Ann: (six years old)

Faust, keeping his voice low, whispered that the list was found among Ms. Conway's things.

Agent Kennedy continued to browse through the list, obviously confused by it. The first eleven were strange, but then she saw it! The final name . . .

Son of a bitch!

Kennedy spun—the fire had returned—and she glared back in the direction of one Denise Conway.

Chapter 46

. . . When You're Dead

Professor Kassakatis awakened after a couple of hours, although he had no idea how long he had been out. He was no longer hog-tied . . . but something was wrong. He couldn't think right . . . couldn't remember . . . his mind a shifting mist. The SoulBound were unable to help him, because he could not hear them . . . he was too medicated . . .

The SoulBound could feel Jimmy's pain, his confusion, his entrapment; and none more so than Brennan Payton.

• • • • • • • • • • • • • • • • • • • •

Brennan was probably the most uncomfortable of all of Jimmy's souls, because Brennan was claustrophobic. He didn't like feeling that he had no way out, and it haunted him daily. For someone who loved cars as much as he did, it would seem curious that his phobia wasn't an issue when sitting within what amounted to a steel cage. The psychiatrist determined that the power of the vehicle, the exhilaration derived from the thrust, overshadowed the sense of entrapment. That seemed to make sense. Brennan was in heaven behind the wheel, and had been since he was three years old . . . since the day his dad, Herman, introduced him to go-carts . . .

Herman Payton was a go-cart enthusiast as far back as his memory would take him, and it was his skill behind the wheel of those makeshift racers that earned him the respectful title of the Go-Cart King. The folks residing in Baltimore's low-income Westside had called him that, or "King" for short, for the better part of six decades . . . even now at the age of 66, he couldn't walk a block to the local grocery store without a complimentary "What's up, King?" or "Here comes the King."

Herman stopped racing in the alleyways and streets of the city in his early twenties, long after most others kept at it . . . his winnings were more respect than cash. Yeah, the "King" was retiring, stepping away from the thing he loved the most, well second most . . . as he was settling down by marrying his girlfriend of two years, A`mana. She loved Herman, and respected his interests, but she was ready to get married, settle in, and have kids . . . so he stayed involved with the young kids in the neighborhood, helping them build their own carts, still having fun in a community that had too little. Yet everyone knew where his allegiances lay.

Brennan was the fifth and last of Herman and A`mana's children. He endured throughout his childhood, having three older sisters and a "typical" older brother named D`Andre—semi-bully/semi-protector. Brennan's least favorite memory to this day was the night his brother locked him in the attic—Brennan was just seven years old.

Neither D`Andre nor his sisters had even the remotest interest in Herman's go-carting, but little Brennan did . . . with a passion that rivaled his daddy's. Though he pretended to drive by sitting in the carts his dad was making for other kids, he had to wait years until he could actually drive one. The day he turned ten, his mother finally allowed the boy to race. He raced just about every weekend from then on, until he turned sixteen.

During those years, he had developed a strong father-son bond and a real love for speed. The community had understandably tried to call Brennan the "Prince," but his dad squashed that quickly, not wanting his son having the same name as a certain flamboyant and hard-edged rock star.

The day after his sixteenth birthday, Brennan got his driver's license, gave up go-carts, and found a new love—cars. His dad was worried that the need for speed would be Brennan's ruin, so he limited the amount of time Brennan could drive. The tough love angered the youngster, who studied hard in high school and eventually earned a scholarship to a local college, Morgan State. Once in college though, Brennan had the freedom to run hard. He raced souped-up street cars for money on weekdays, and "pinks" on weekends. Amazingly, he never got caught, though nearly every other member of his "crew" did.

He graduated on time from Morgan in '98 and eventually settled into his head network—tech trainer job. Brennan was a wiz with computers and networks and made serious dough for such a young man. He had too many "girls" to count, three different sports cars, money well-invested and well-spent (in his eyes anyway), and was a genuinely fun and well-liked guy. He had it all going for him, going to sign the papers on his first home the following day . . . but was snuffed out in an instant, doing what he loved most. If he only would have slowed down a hair . . .

Ah well, regret is a bitch . . . when you're dead.

Chapter 47

Painting in the Rain

Dee was returning to her chair when Kennedy, accompanied by Faust and another agent, approached her in the kitchen. Kennedy then announced, "Denise Conway, you're going to be detained. We'll be taking you in for questioning concerning your knowledge of The Shadow That Speaks case and the death of little Carrie Ann Weaver."

Kennedy had a smug look about her, and nodded to Gotti, who had been informed of what was happening, to do the same to Brando.

Dee was in shock, her mouth agape, and her eyes the size of golf balls.

The detainees were brought to the FBI's Baltimore Field Office. They were understandably frightened, as each was taken to a separate holding room. They weren't under arrest, not yet at least, but would be questioned in regard to their knowledge of the case, Jimmy's involvement, the list, and Carrie Ann Weaver.

Again, Agent Kennedy sat in with Dee, and Gotti did the same with Tommy. Tommy felt that it would be up to Dee to divulge whatever truths she wished as far as Jimmy was concerned.

Agent Gottranelli asked Tommy about the list, about Carrie Ann, about Jimmy, about every and anything . . . and Brando just denied knowing anything. He was going to play hardball.

Kennedy entered the ten-by-ten-foot holding room, which contained Dee. The far wall had an oversized mirror, and Dee knew it was a two-way mirror, as many TV and movie watchers would. A mid-sized and hard plastic table, along with two accompanying chairs furnished the drab room. "George-ous" it was not.

The red-haired agent came to sit across from Jimmy's fiancée, equipped with a recording device and a red attaché case. She came right to it.

"Ms. Conway, your fiancé is a person of interest in an ongoing murder case. A strange series of events has occurred, and the truth of it is that it has left me and the Agency somewhat concerned, as well as feeling somewhat closer to resolving the case for good. Some things don't add up, while others point to clarification."

Carol Kennedy was smart, she had to be to get where she is, and she was going to pull out all the stops to get to the truth. Ms. Conway sat in stunned silence, her world unraveling . . .

Dee spoke up a split second before the agent was going to continue, and this time it was Ms. Conway who spewed venom.

"Jimmy is not a murderer, if that's what you're implying!" Dee scowled at the older woman . . . . rage had her trembling from the adrenaline rush.

Dee continued. "You don't know what he's been through, what he has to deal with every day. It's ridiculous to think he's capable of harming anyone, much less . . ." She couldn't say "murder."

The agent fired back quickly. "What do you mean—what has he been through? And what is he going through now that has you so defensive?"

Dee realized she needed to control herself, for it was "divulge all" or "fly by the seat of your pants" . . . and blurting out things wasn't helping. She decided to avert her eyes from the other woman, and folded her arms in front of her as if she were announcing, as a child often does to a parent, *"I am through listening to you."*

Kennedy, noting the younger woman's behavior, shifted gears. She realized that Dee was the type who'd reply better to softer tactics. After these last couple of years of tracking the bastard, she was close . . . and this talk was vital in unraveling the answers. She switched up on many occasions to get to what was needed. But this time she went off the grid . . .

"Dee—may I call you Dee?"

"Sure," came the barely audible reply.

"I'm Carol . . . call me Carol, if you like. Come, take a walk with me."

Dee was surprised when the agent left the recorder and her attaché behind and moved to the door, which she opened. Carol motioned for Dee to follow and the younger woman finally rose from her chair, unfolded her arms, and complied.

The two agents behind the two-way mirror looked at each other and just shook their heads.

The women walked through the hallways of the office and took the nearest staircase down, reappearing on the concourse that held Carol's car. Carol remained quiet, as did Dee, as the agent continued to her personal vehicle, a "sleek and stylish" black Nissan Murano. Carol asked Dee to take a ride to the harbor with her, and Dee replied with a simple nod of the head.

The sun was settling low in the sky as early evening arrived. It took about twenty minutes to arrive at the Inner Harbor, Baltimore's main tourist attraction area and a very pretty place to walk around. After the agent parked, the women moved toward the water to stroll upon the large brick walkway that bordered the harbor. A soft breeze blew in from the water, a welcome addition, though the heat of the day was thankfully subsiding.

A US Navy destroyer had made a scheduled appearance that day, and was docked in the mouth of the harbor, gathering large crowds, which could almost touch the sides of the big ship.

Walking around the Inner Harbor was always a fun venture, but the precarious pair that stepped onto the bricks at that moment—and moved toward the open bay—weren't there for fun.

The agent started, "There is a great deal we need to discuss, but I wanted to thank you for your appreciation of my loss. Tony was a great guy, only thirty-two years old . . ."

Dee was surprised by the agent's admission.

Carol continued . . . "I'm going to break a few Agency rules, but I feel that I can trust you. I'm going to tell you everything and hope that through my opening up to you, you'll return the favor, getting us both what we want . . . resolution."

Again, Dee was surprised, yet remained silent, the women walking at an easy pace.

Carol continued . . . "I'm the Case Agent, or lead agent if you will, on an ongoing serial killer case. Tony was the second partner of mine to die at the hands of the killer. The killer refers to himself as The Shadow That Speaks . . ."

Dee was getting nervous as the agent went on.

". . . and he's killed well over a hundred souls so far, many of them children."

Dee didn't see *that* coming and uttered, "Oh Jesus."

"You can see the enormous importance of catching the killer, who has taunted us with his calling cards," the agent reached into her pocket, withdrawing a duplicate of the one that had been placed upon Omega's chest.

"This is a replica of the one left behind on my partner's ravaged corpse."

She handed it to Dee and got the reactions she expected . . . shock and curiosity.

Dee asked, "Whoa . . . What do you make of it?"

"The black jackal is on every card he leaves behind or occasionally sends us. The numbers you see represent the most recent four that he's killed so far."

Again, Dee was blown away by the revelation of so many dead—162. Kennedy carried on as Dee continued to stare at the card.

"Okay . . . here's what I know. We have the library system flagged and noticed that Jimmy was looking into the death of a little six-year-old girl named Carrie Ann Weaver, one of the killer's victims . . . #126. Since then, we've been tapping his phones and have had agents monitoring the house. We knew he was going to see Vaccaro."

Dee's mouth was wide open, too stunned to speak . . . *This isn't happening.*

Kennedy continued. "Jimmy was abducted at the Graydon Center by a group of people, lead by the shrink, Vaccaro . . ."

Dee stopped dead in her tracks, as the sun fell over the horizon . . . her temperature rising fast.

Kennedy stopped and looked into the now burning eyes of her detainee. The agent continued, ". . . who had stuck Jimmy with a needle the moment that crazed man entered the office. It was a setup, you all were duped, Dee. The receptionist, Carl, was in on it, directing both you and Brando out of the room. They all pulled a switch of clothes with the man who acted as if he were going crazy in the office. The frantic woman, the crazed man, the 'guards,' Vaccaro, and a black man with a bald head who goes by the name Randolph, pulled it off, taking Jimmy out of the building just as Vaccaro sounded the alarm. It was brilliant, but we bugged her office and one of our people witnessed the ruse."

Dee's brow was furrowed, her mouth open slightly as the shock of the story hit her hard. *Oh Jimmy* . . . The older woman sensed Dee was ready for more, and at this point felt there was no turning back.

"Vaccaro and Carl stayed behind to continue with the act, fooling you and Brando into believing Jimmy went nuts and had fled the building. Meanwhile, my partner was waiting nearby and got word from our guy that Jimmy was being abducted, so he followed the van after noticing the kidnappers had put Jimmy inside and pulled off in a hurry. Tony tailed them to a deserted psyche ward called Haven's Gate—shut down years ago for human rights violations—as I and some other agents were en route to back him up. Then Tony heard the screams of those who became victims 159, 160, 161, and 162 . . . four of the five that had taken Jimmy there. So . . . Tony, being Tony, went in without backup, trying to do his job . . . be a hero."

This time it was Agent Kennedy—Carol—that looked away . . . and she started to walk again to deflect notice of her tearing eyes.

Dee walked beside her, terrified at what she was hearing, fretful of her lover's fate. She couldn't help it, so she spoke up then.

"Carol, what happened to Jimmy . . . is he okay?"

Dee's tears fell unabashed. "As far as we know, yes," The agent replied as she found a bench to sit on, and she did.

Dee joined her and asked, "What's that mean . . . as far as you know?"

"When we arrived at the psyche ward, Tony and the others were dead, but Jimmy was missing, only his wallet and cell phone were left behind."

Dee then asked the obvious question, "Where is Jimmy now?"

"I was just getting to that . . . Dee, Jimmy is a suspect in the case, although there are some very abnormal events unfolding that defy logic. One of the things that we considered about the black jackal cards was that the killer was telling us that his name was Jack, the first four letters of jackal, but no suspects have come under suspicion with that name, so we have put that in the background, until last night . . . I noticed that your fiancé's name had the initials of JCK, the 'A' coming after 'J' in James."

Dee immediately responded, "Carol, I'm telling you, it's not Jimmy."

Kennedy went on, "We put out an APB on Jimmy and two Harford County deputies spotted and arrested Jimmy this morning at a church near Bel Air. He was found standing beside a reverend in the mud of the graveyard there."

Dee was going to interrupt, but the agent continued, "Just minutes after the deputies left the church with Jimmy in the back of the cruiser, the deputies were pulled off the road and assaulted by two groups of people, seemingly government agents or military of some sort, based on the deputy's descriptions of them. We have no idea where they went or who they were, and trust me, I went hard to my superiors about this and they have had nothing to report back . . . not yet at least."

"Jesus . . . ," Dee could only sit and stare at the older woman, shaking her head in disbelief.

Kennedy seized the opportunity to get some answers, asking outright, "Dee, I've told you so much more than you have the legal right to know . . . I am breaking every rule in the book, and I'm doing it because my instincts are telling me that besides the evidence against Jimmy, there is more to the story. I need, no—*we* need, *Jimmy* needs your help. I need answers and I need them quickly. I need you to explain everything you know to me, about Jimmy, about Vaccaro . . . about . . . the list."

The veteran agent pulled out a copy of the spreadsheet that had Carrie Ann and the other SoulBound's information on it.

Dee took the list, looked at Kennedy, and cried uncontrollably. She was shattered about the drama unfolding and seemed on the verge of a breakdown. All her hopes and dreams seemed to fade, and a truly helpless feeling came over her—it triggered a memory long forgotten . . . .

She overheard her Grandpa Conway speaking to her father in the den . . . Grandpa was explaining how he felt over his wife's Alzheimer's . . .

So desperately frustrated . . .

   so utterly helpless . . .

      like painting in the rain.

Chapter 48
Revelations

As Dee and Agent Kennedy sat on the bench at the harbor, Jimmy lay sedated upon his bunk, awaiting more testing. He hurt . . . badly. *They* were not too gentle with his brain, with his body . . . probing, poking, searching, seeking . . .

He lay in a bed in an all-white room, padded all around, and he was grateful that the lights were off. The SoulBound were frantically trying to figure out how to help, to no avail. The darkness that resided within stirred again, and despite Jimmy's condition, he sensed it. His mind: chaos . . . unable to focus, unable to hear his SoulBound, or even remember them; he tapped into multiple realities, memories mixed from people he knew, some he made up, and something lurking inside him . . .

Jimmy sensed his SoulBound, but the professor's mind was fractured by the animals walking/testing/living beyond his room. Jimmy was desperate without understanding desperation . . . confusing reality without realization. He yelled out, "Hello?!?!"

When no one responded, tears leaked from bloodshot eyes to fall upon Linus, Jimmy's new friend, his blanket.

The SoulBound heard him, though he couldn't hear them in return. Brennan, Millie, Su, Koketai, Jean-Paul, John, Karen, Gina, Dragon, and Marie were in constant discussions on ways to get through to Jimmy. Carrie Ann was the lone exception . . . she had become nearly catatonic since the recent encounter with the dark man.

Marie was caught between attempting to help Jimmy and take care of Carrie Ann. Marie spent time consoling, cradling the child, comforting the little one as often as she could. The other ladies, and even John and Koketai, spent time with her. Carrie Ann hadn't spoken and Marie had naturally grown worrisome; she knew that helping the child was important, but getting Jimmy out of his current situation was paramount.

Brennan and Jean-Paul had spent untold hours trying to figure out a way to "leave" Jimmy . . . break free of their virtual prison existence. The feeling was that if they were able to roam again as ghosts, they could get a message to someone to help, perhaps Tommy and Dee . . . or even the police. No luck . . . yet.

· · · · · · · · · · · · · · · · · · · ·

Dee held the copy of the list of Jimmy's SoulBound and was faced with the wrenching decision to tell Agent Kennedy the truth about Jimmy . . . this coming after Jimmy felt that she had betrayed his trust before, with Vaccaro, but he eventually realized it was for good reasons. Dee's tears had slowed to a crawl and she made the decision she felt was the only one available to her . . . she told the truth.

Agent Kennedy, or just Carol at the moment, waited with baited breath as Dee spoke up.

"You won't believe me, but I'm going to be completely honest with you . . . and it's gonna get strange."

The agent just sat back and tried to appear calm, but she was yearning to hear this "truth."

Dee continued. "These names . . . they are a list that Jimmy gave me to help me better familiarize myself . . . ," she paused, to dramatic effect . . ." . . . with the SoulBound."

"The what?"

"SoulBound. Carol, Jimmy is a Soul-Collector, a Shepherd of Lost Souls, and has been since he was twelve years old. He carries within him . . . ghosts. Real people who died, but their souls never went into The Light. Somehow . . . they talk with him all the time, like they're alive again. I've met with all of them, including the little girl, Carrie Ann."

Dee was speaking rather quickly, but the agent caught all of it. One might think Dee's words would have shocked the agent, but Kennedy had heard many bizarre things as an agent over the years. She was just trying to determine if Dee's tale was partial or complete BS. So, being the pro she was, she listened intently as Dee continued.

"Jimmy has a way of connecting to the SoulBound . . . where he can experience their memories for himself. Naturally he asks first and all . . . but when he attempted to get to understand Carrie Ann better, there was a big problem, and things went terribly wrong. Jimmy lived in the moments of what The Shadow did to Carrie Ann, and he actually died briefly until I brought him back. The ambulance came and they took him to the hospital where he remained overnight, as a precaution. The next morning he went home with me, and rested up. After a quick recovery, Jimmy—who had learned firsthand what that sicko did to Carrie Ann—wanted to do something about it. He wanted to stop the bastard, but knew nothing about who the killer was or where he could be found—a problem you still seem to be having—so Jimmy went to the library to see if he could find out as much about Carrie Ann's disappearance as possible, trying to 'play' detective."

Kennedy's instincts, intuition, sixth sense, or just plain common sense kicked in as she began to realize that Dee's tale, while fanciful, was dripping with far too much detail and conviction to be false. One thing Kennedy concluded with certainty—Dee believed she was telling the truth.

Unabated, Dee went on. "But I noticed he had been having a great deal of difficulty with nightmares and such. It seemed to be tearing him up inside, so I called the one person that I thought could help him, Vaccaro, who I wasn't aware at that time had done those things that upset Jimmy. If I had known . . ."

Dee paused to catch her breath and collect her thoughts before proceeding. "Vaccaro had been aware of Jimmy's special 'gift' for some time now, and she tried to conduct some sort of weird experiment on him about two years ago, so she could learn more about the Souls, but Jimmy didn't like her methods and stopped seeing her outright."

Now deeply intrigued, the agent leaned closer to Dee and asked, "So why did he go to visit with her the other day?"

Dee responded quickly and with verve, "Well, I invited Vaccaro over—God I hate that woman!—anyway, I asked her over, knowing Jimmy would probably not seek her help, and when she arrived at the house, it naturally surprised Jimmy and he wanted her to leave. But noooo . . . she had big news, she said . . . she explained that she could lose her job if anyone found out, but she told him that she was privy to knowledge that Jimmy wasn't the only Soul-Collector around. She showed us a picture of the man she called Randolph, a bald-headed black man, maybe late fifties, who lived in New Mexico and had fifty-eight souls within him. Lies!"

Dee curled up her fists and glared into the distance with that last bit.

Kennedy was somewhat mesmerized. The whole thing *was* bizarre, and frankly not believable, but the big picture gave credence to the fiancée's story.

Dee finished up. "So, you can see why Jimmy would go there . . . and, well, you know the rest better than I do."

The agent needed more time to think things through, and made a decision.

"You and Brando are free to go, but you can't stay at Jimmy's. I'll have someone take you both to wherever it is you want to go. So, let's get back to my office."

The women stood at that moment, and Kennedy went digging for her keys . . . but Dee looked at the agent somewhat disapprovingly. Finding her keys, Kennedy took a few steps . . . walking back to the car, but noticed the younger woman wasn't following her. Indeed, Denise Conway stood firm, glaring back at "Carol."

The agent walked back and asked simply, "What's wrong?"

"This is it? You're sending me away? Nothing more to add? I thought we were going to work together to find Jimmy . . . to figure things out?"

Kennedy responded matter-of-factly, "This is a major federal investigation, Dee, and I have a whole team of people working on it. If either you or Brando, hell—for that matter, anyone you know—can call anytime if you have more information. You are not to leave the state until further notice . . . we'll let you know if we find him. Now please, it's getting late."

Kennedy motioned for Dee to accompany her to the car, the night now in full force.

Dee stood her ground and said, "You don't believe me . . . maybe you think I'm hiding something?"

Kennedy looked into Dee's fiery eyes, but didn't respond, but again started back for her car, when Dee yet again spoke up. "Carol . . . please . . . give me that lie detector test you all use, Tommy too . . . he knows about as much as I do. Please? I swear on the lives of everyone I love that I'm telling you the truth!"

Dee was highly emotional . . . pleading . . . "Give me a truth serum, do whatever you want to me, but don't leave me alone in this! I love him, Carol . . . I love him! Like you loved Tony!"

The impact, the truth of those words, hit Kennedy hard.

Dee kept on. "Let me help you . . . I'm begging you . . ." Dee was nearly broken—liquid silver spilling to the ground beneath her.

Agent Kennedy was touched, her years of expertise on body language and superior instincts screamed to her to consider Dee's plea. Kennedy did need time, but with a very willing detainee offering to take these tests, it made sense to take advantage of it.

"Okay, Dee . . . not tomorrow, but the day after. You can take the tests Saturday . . . Brando too, if he wishes. But tonight, you both go home."

Chapter 49
The Crimson Veil

It was 7:00 a.m. Friday morning, and Jimmy couldn't sleep, waiting in angst of being taken for more "studies," as he had been since his arrival the previous day. He would be removed from his room every few hours and would be gone for an hour at best, hours at worst. He sat in the corner staring at the door . . . lost in his strange existence . . .

The professor was the featured "patient" here at the Department for Para-Psyche Research (DEEPER). Kassakatis was Director Gage's shining star . . . for, according to Vaccaro—who had returned, along with Carl, earlier that morning—Jimmy was a Soul-Collector. Not only was he able to communicate with these captured ghosts, but also maintain their memories and their abilities from when they were alive. The potential benefits in understanding and "bottling" such a unique thing would make him an even more powerful man than his current high standing. Gage craved appreciation, recognition, and more than anything else . . . POWER. His team of doctors, scientists, and psychologists had studied Jimmy intently, conducting a great deal of experiments, not unlike those that Gage had conducted on the Hill boy . . . ahhh yes, the Hill boy—The Shadow That Speaks—the most terrifying being to ever walk the planet.

Gage could take credit for that, or more appropriately, blame. Gage saw his creation as a potential weapon for American military use or to be used for certain government black ops, *if* he could capture and utilize him . . . , and the Director was attempting to do that very thing. He knew that The Shadow had figured out a way to track either Jimmy or himself, and both were here at the secret underground complex in the outskirts of Sterling, Virginia. If Hill was coming, Gage felt prepared, the hunted becoming the hunter.

DEEPER was aptly nicknamed, being an underground operation, hundreds of feet beneath the surface. It was one of an unknown number of sites situated throughout the United States that was created for DARPA—the *Defense Advanced Research Projects Agency*—the Department of Defense's top secret military research outfit, that was founded in 1958.

A new directive came from up high during the tense political stanza that was the early 1980s, as the "leader of the free world," the President himself, disappointed with the lack of results at DARPA, put his stamp on a brand-new ultra-covert research initiative, designated *Project: Crimson Veil*. This multi-pronged venture began in the spring of '82 and fell under the DARPA umbrella, with one major difference—the DEEPER administrator answered only to one of two men . . . The Secretary of Defense and the President himself. No one at DARPA was privy to what was going on.

The new initiative had undertaken the most ambitious government research studies in all of history. The top analysts, physicists, researchers, computer scientists, mathematicians, engineers, geologists, psychologists, biologists, medical doctors, and scientists from many fields were paid a great deal of money to commit to the project. The goal? In the words of President Reagan himself—"Go beyond"—referring to the desire to find answers to the Soviet problem and subsequently other potential anti-US issues and looking the other way—regarding the lack of ethics involved. When Gage was asked to start up the Paranormal & Mind-Phenomena "prong," he was given use of the Sterling complex. DEEPER was in business, and *Project: Crimson Veil* had been an unmitigated—albeit unethical—success ever since.

The Sterling complex had the capacity to "study" as many as sixteen "patients," although they currently had eight . . . with Professor Kassakatis being the latest addition.

Jimmy roamed about his soft-walled room, wearing one of the standard-issue patient's terrycloth attire: pastel blue, pastel yellow, pastel pink, and the latest fashion, pastel green. Jimmy couldn't focus completely to really even recognize which color adorned him, but he was wearing pastel yellow. He was exercising when he'd remember to, but he was mostly just listening within, a ship without a rudder, drifting about his own mind . . . having rare moments of focused thought. He was rubbing his hands together a bit before running his hands through his gel-less dry hair. He was unshaven as well, so he had a disheveled look about him.

He would sporadically yell out or whisper things that sometimes seemed brilliant and at other times insane . . . and at this moment, he was feeling it . . . feeling that urge to let loose the overwhelming creativity that roared through him like a raging river . . . this time he rocked back and forth upon his bed and spilled a musical rap-rock medley . . .

Within his mind, he stood on the stage as a crowd drowned the stadium with adoration and applause. Jimmy was in heaven . . . for but a few fleeting moments . . . as he suddenly sat down and quite pitifully pondered why dogs didn't speak.

He must've napped, as he awakened a bit later to the thought that *they* would be coming soon . . . despite his confused state, Jimmy knew that much.

Chapter 50
A Glimmer in the Din

The SoulBound were at their wits' end, having seemingly extinguished all possible means to help Jimmy. There was a sense of failure, and their collective frustration was boiling over . . .

Marie had each of them attempting to get Jimmy's attention, to break through the malaise afflicting him, and everyone but Carrie Ann rotated in at roughly fifteen-minute intervals. When not the designated attention-getter, they would work on various ideas that were intended to break through the unseen barrier that held them to Jimmy, or would gather in small groups and discuss what to do when Jimmy reconnected with them . . . deciding in advance how to best have Jimmy escape from here or get through the pain he suffered.

There were so many issues at hand, and they all worked nonstop to try to help out—Marie, Koketai, Yi, Dragon, John, Brennan, Millie, Karen, Jean-Paul, and Gina . . . ten beings without true bodies. These ghosts, prisoners in a sense, guests and companions in another, were "alive" within the unique phenomena that was James Kassakatis. Their minds were again their own since merging with Jimmy, as before, as ghosts, they roamed about in a shades-of-gray altered reality. They had been much like Jimmy is now . . . adrift. They didn't eat, they didn't need sleep, but they often did out of habit, trying to follow Jimmy's schedule so as not to inadvertently disturb him. They had learned to dress as they liked, a power derived from talks with Jimmy about how he created places and things through his imagination. They had even created a football-sized "room" with a high cathedral-like ceiling. It came complete with twelve chairs—just in case Jimmy returned—and a few sofas here and there, for good measure. It was Gina Imbragulio's idea . . . so it had a noticeably Italian flavor.

They were more family than community, as best as one could be had here. And as with most families, there were problems . . . and in this case, under these pressured circumstances, arguments.

Millie was agitated and being the oldest (while alive), as well as a mother and grandmother many times over, was saying things in a way that made it seem as if she were speaking to her kids, rather than equal adults. She was discussing the merits, or lack of them, about one of Brennan's ideas. It was an idea on how to break the barrier that separated them from Jimmy.

Yi and John-Paul were listening in as well, still considering his idea . . . but Brennan, not one to let slide even the smallest perceived insult, took exception, and called her a "know-it-all," to which she again spoke "down" to him, rather than reply in a more civil manner. The shouting match didn't go unnoticed as Koketai, Gina, and Karen came over to break up the fighting.

John and Dragon were engrossed in discussion on ways to escape the DEEPER complex, when they overheard the yelling, and went to investigate. They saw their seven companions huddled about the center table, a war of words ongoing, sucking in the lot of them. Naturally, the two men got involved. At the peak of the crescendo, the voices died down quickly, almost all at once, as they noticed the other two souls standing by watching them . . . Marie stood holding the hand of the youngest among them, the recently catatonic Carrie Ann Weaver. Marie said not a word as the little one stared into the eyes of her older companions, of which each felt a bit ashamed.

"I had a dream," she said sweetly, with the voice of an angel . . .

"There was a great light, so bright that it couldn't be looked at . . . and it spoke to me."

The SoulBound were happy to see her up and about, but all eyes were forward as she continued on . . .

"It said that love is strong and love is light . . . that we are special because we have it in our hearts and souls . . . and that Jimmy will be needing us, and our love, very soon. It said to be ready, to answer the call."

Marie smiled at Carrie Ann, nodded slightly, and gently squeezed the child's hand, all in a show of approval.

The other nine slowly walked toward Carrie Ann and Marie, expressing their happiness to see her and their regret for fighting with so much at stake. They all assumed that Carrie Ann just had a nice dream, but what they didn't know was that the child's dream was in fact a "vision" . . . and therein lay the difference.

. . . .

For Jimmy, *they* had indeed come, and eventually returned him to his room. What was done to him was unspeakable . . .

twisted. He was a human wasteland, his tear ducts now dried to dust, his life and very sanity on the fringe . . . but even amidst the horror that was his life, even far off into the misty madness that was a constant in his mind, a sliver of hope found him, found his mind . . . a glimmer in the din.

Chapter 51

The Broken People

"Hello? If you can hear me, don't be frightened, I am real. I am a prisoner here, like you. My name is Cooool. With four O's."

The voice in Jimmy's head was careful to drag out the vowels in his name. The four O's were important to him.

To Jimmy, the voice seemed familiar, somehow, but while Jimmy "heard" the voice, he was not able to focus enough to reply.

Cooool was indeed a prisoner, one of the seven test subjects that some of the more twisted workers at DEEPER referred to as "The Broken People."

Jimmy was joining a small fraternity . . . rather unintentionally.

"I'll get back to you soon, and if you're up for it, I'll fill you in on the others."

Somewhere in the mist, somewhere amid the malaise that washed over him, Jimmy cracked the tiniest smile.

Sure enough, two hours later—Cooool was back. *"Jimmy, it's Cooool. Can you respond?"*

"Howju . . . know me?" came the somewhat slurred response. *"Who . . . a . . . you, where you?"*

"I am a telepath, Jimmy; I read people's minds and can 'talk' to people in their heads. We are in an underground government complex called DEEPER . . . near Sterling, Virginia. You're unique, so they want to examine you, study you, conduct experiments on you . . . as you have already experienced . . . just like the rest of us. So . . . suffer we all. I am in a padded room much like yours, about a hundred or so feet away from you."

"How long you . . . anda udders here?" Jimmy again responded shakily.

"I've been here twelve years, one month, and seventeen days . . . they abducted me from my home in Thailand. I didn't speak a word of English when I got here."

The shock of those comments would've startled him to a great degree had he been his normal self . . . but the professor wasn't quite at that point. His misty swirling world and fuzzy comprehension was clearing a bit, although he was learning this meant that *they* would be back soon. He continued to communicate in hopes that the words he was hearing inside were able to help him focus enough to get some answers about where he was and how he could fight back.

"1996 . . . others are here . . . how many dem?"

"Besides you and I, six others. The assholes here call us The Broken People, and while true for some, it's BS for others. Among the six, only Schae-Schae and Oba are aware . . . able to communicate. The others are too far gone . . . used up . . . broken."

"Tell me about the two . . ."

"*Sure . . . Schae-Schae is fifteen, a California surfer girl, or rather 'surfer dude' . . . although her Goth-chick look mixed with her surfer look must've been a fashion nightmare.*" Cooool laughed a bit before continuing, "*She is a bit wild, that one . . . she has been here for about five months. They think she's psychic because she posted a few predictions on some upcoming events at her MySpace page . . . she got lucky and hit all three. But her luck ran out when they brought her here.*"

Cooool paused. "*She is just a kid . . . not gifted as they suspect. She's has a real strength about her, she's tough . . . but it seems she may be on the verge of a breakdown. She needs to get out soon, or she'll veg, like the others.*"

Cooool paused again. The pain in his "voice" was evident.

"*Oba Ibn Jahi is the most gifted human being I've ever 'met' . . . he's been here about four years. Jimmy, he just knows things . . . it's hard to explain, but the bastards are aware of it somehow. They test him more than anyone else, careful not to push such a valued commodity too hard. He is sixty-five, and an Egyptian, well . . . Egyptian-American now, has been since bringing his family here in the late eighties. Oba is the real-deal professor, if you get a chance to speak with him, it may just change your life.*"

"Well . . . I hope . . . ," Jimmy's reply was cut off as the door to his room was opened. *They* had indeed come.

Cooool knew what was happening and said to Jimmy, "*Find a place within, Jimmy . . . go there and don't break, don't give up.*"

Jimmy did not respond as he was taken away . . . to where The Broken People go.

Chapter 52
Surprise!

Friday, June 13, 2008

Ricky Dinks came strolling through Tommy's front door, which had been locked, as if he owned the place . . . putting his lock picks away as he did and lighting a cigarette after putting a bag of groceries on the kitchen table.

Dee was sitting in the living room and saw him, saying, "Put that out, Dinks. Tommy doesn't allow smoking in the house."

Ricky just looked at her like she was from the Planet of Nine-eyed People, and blew the smoke in her direction, before sitting down and pulling out a sub and soda from the bag. He continued smoking without saying a word.

Tommy came out of the bathroom at that moment, smelling smoke and caught Dee's look, as if she were implying that he should bite his tongue. He did, against every fiber in his being, as he spotted the shorter and skinny *punk* at the table.

Dee and Tommy were both infuriated with his presence, but reluctantly had to go along with Kennedy's decision to have the ex-con take Dee and Tommy home the night before . . . not to Jimmy's home . . . but rather to Tommy's house (Dee preferred to stay with Tommy).

Kennedy said that they were not allowed to go to Jimmy's place until she gave the okay . . . and added that Dinks would accompany them until Saturday's testing at 10:00 a.m.

He did indeed drop them off, but rather than staying as instructed by Kennedy, here he was at 12:30 the following afternoon, returning without word. While more than unhappy, Dee didn't want to upset Kennedy at such an important time. Kennedy was attending her partner's funeral, and had been on edge well before his death.

Dee had slept in one of the two extra bedrooms, while Tommy naturally slept in his bed. Tommy mentioned wanting to punch Dinks in the face on a number of occasions, but knew that he needed to control his temper. Too much was at stake.

Dinks was the sort of guy who oozed something that made everyone around him somewhat uncomfortable and annoyed. The bad smell that most smokers exude didn't help, but it was the way he carried himself . . . like he was up to something . . . all the time. He didn't comprehend the meaning of relaxing.

Dee called her boss, Lou, and explained that a family emergency was ongoing and that she would need to take her two-week vacation now, rather than the scheduled mid-summer one in August. Dee was fortunate to have a great boss, so her job was safe, but after hanging up, and with vacation on her mind, she had a startling thought.

Alex and Kathy!

Jimmy and Dee had planned to go to Australia with his brother and sister-in-law in mid-August, and thinking of them was a reminder that there was a real problem at hand. Alex had called

Dee while she was in the middle of her talk with Kennedy at the harbor, but the younger woman had put the cell on vibrate and didn't notice he had called until she was well on her way back with Tommy and Dinks. Dee decided to discuss the issue with Tommy, but waited until Dinks went back toward the bathroom. The last thing she needed was Dinks listening in, as she didn't want him to know what she had planned. Dee was certain that Ricky wasn't aware of the SoulBound, but figured he was aware that Jimmy was a fugitive and that he was under suspicion for murder.

As Dinks closed the bathroom door, Dee walked into the living room and sat next to Tommy on the couch.

Dee was not one that took well to lying to others, and she realized that Alex and Kathy were both apt to stop by Jimmy's at any time and freak out at the sight of yellow tape around the house and a bunch of people wearing FBI jackets going in and out. So, she quickly discussed the "plan" with Tommy, and they decided to break the truth to Alex and Kathy, knowing it was going to be difficult after they had been through it themselves.

Jimmy's privacy was incredibly important, but things were out of control. One thing going for them was that they both recalled that Jimmy was going to tell his brother soon anyway. So, while the professor wanted to handle that himself, circumstances changed. It needed to be done . . . Alex and Kathy had to know. Jimmy's fiancée told his best friend as quickly as she could about her plan to get word to him.

Tommy was reluctant at first, but after considering it, realized Dee had the right idea. The plan was for Dee to tell Dinks that she was off to the store around 5:45 p.m. to get some feminine products and that she'd return soon. They knew that Dinks couldn't be in two places at once, so he either went along with Dee or stayed with Tommy . . . either way, the other would get over to Alex's immediately. He always got home about 5:30, like clockwork.

Dee and Tommy were still sitting on Brando's new soft-white couch as their decision was finalized, as Dinks could be heard to flush the toilet and reentered the room to sit across from them. Ricky was blissfully aware that he had free reign to ask questions, pry, spy, and whatever else he could think of. He had a talent for it. So, he said with an air of arrogance, "Agent Kennedy . . . she'd be pretty pissed if she knew that you were planning on telling Jimmy's bro and sis-in-law everything . . . really pissed. One might say Kennedy could have you arrested."

Dee and Tommy were dumbfounded . . . how did Dinks know? He couldn't have heard from the bathroom, and even so, they were speaking softly . . .

Dinks pointed at Tommy's shoes and said, "On EBay: well-worn 1998 Air Jordan's, $5." He then pointed to Dee's SpongeBob SquarePants footies and said, "SpongeBob socks . . . maybe $2 . . . BUT . . . ," he laughed as he shook his greasy head sideways, ". . . the look on your faces . . . priceless!"

Tommy had a hunch and looked behind him on the wall where he had a copy of the famous "self-portrait" of his favorite historical figure, Leonardo da Vinci.

Sly devil . . .

Sure enough, Tommy found the "bug" on the back of the painting's lower left corner. Brando smashed the device on the wall and glared at Dinks, but Ricky just shrugged, as if this was commonplace. Dinks then began reciting the things he overheard about Jimmy being a Soul-Collector . . . and Dee and Tommy began to boil. This was not a good thing. Ricky Dinks was good . . . but Denise Conway was better on this day, flipping the script on Dinks before he knew what hit him.

"So you know about Jimmy, no biggie . . . and you overheard that we're going to fill in Alex and Kathy . . . but, no worries though . . . because Kennedy's not gonna know, is she?"

"Really? Hmmmm, I'm pretty sure I'm gonna let her know 'bout this . . . it's kinda why I'm here," Dinks smugly retorted, a nasty "smile" cracking a face that hated using those muscles.

Dee stood up and cocked her head slightly to the right . . . and had that look—Tommy knew Dinks was about to get schooled—that oozed confidence.

"Dinksy . . . now you and I both know that Kennedy specifically instructed you to stay with us here last night, but, hmmmm . . . ."

Dinks dropped the smirk quick as Dee continued, putting a finger to the side of her mouth in that "pretend thinking" pose and looking momentarily up to the ceiling.

". . . you didn't though, if I recall correctly. Tommy, do you recall Dinks staying here last night?"

Before Tommy could respond, Dinks beat him to it. "Hehehe, ohhhh boy, you're good. But . . . how did you know that she told me that?"

Without missing a beat, Dee said, "I didn't."

It was Dinks's turn to boil as he realized the "chick" duped him, and he had anger in his voice when he replied, "You bit . . . ," he was cut off by the sound of a clearing throat behind him.

He whirled about, grabbing the lamp beside him and stood ready to swing when Dee and Tommy both yelled out, "No!"

Standing there, wearing pink pajamas coupled with a scandalous smirk, was Tommy's sister and Dee's best friend . . . Rae. She had wavy brown hair with blonde highlights and wore it just past shoulder length. If she had been a few inches taller, Rae may have considered a modeling career.

Dinks put the lamp back down as the short and quite attractive young woman said, "Surprise?!"

Dee stood, mouth wide open, with an obvious shocked expression, but Tommy stood and asked immediately, "Rae . . . what are you doing here?"

"It's your birthday, stupid."

True enough, Tommy was twenty-six today, three years his sister's senior. Tommy angled his head a bit to one side, still feeling there was more. Before he could utter another word, Dee spoke first.

"Happy birthday, Tommy . . . sorry, but I had forgotten . . . ,"

Dinks interjected, "Wow, what are you, thirty-four, thirty-five?"

Tommy shot Ricky a nasty look, but responded to the women, "Thanks, Dee, and you too, Rae . . . but . . . ," he gathered himself, faced his little sister and said, ". . . did you spend the night here?"

"Yeah . . . in the second guest bedroom, the one I always stay in when I'm here."

Rae Whisprance Brando replied with that "Duh!" look about her. Yes, Whisprance . . . her parents were a bit different.

"You gave me a spare in case I needed to get in . . . and I was worried about you not returning my calls . . . both of you."

She was looking at Dee as well.

Before either could reply, Rae said, "Now I know why."

Those words hammered home like a ton of bricks, as Tommy just stood and stared—dumbfounded.

A stunned Dee thought, *She did **not** just say that.*

Chapter 53
Family Matters

Dee, who noticed Rae was wearing her hair in a very similar fashion as her own (minus the highlights), brushed her locks away from her face, and while fearing the inevitable reply, asked her best friend anyway, "What do you mean 'Now I know why'?"

"I overheard about Jimmy. I've always known something odd was going on with Jimmy, just from hearing Tommy talking with him on the phone over the years. Though I admit to not knowing *all* the details . . . this is unbelievable . . . I feel like I'm in a bad dream or something."

She wasn't the only one.

"Jesus . . . ," muttered Rae's brother as he sat back down on the couch.

"Snap!!," exclaimed a suddenly cheerful Ricky Dinks, his thin, dirty-blond hair was all over the place as he jerked his body for dramatic effect.

"Shut the . . . ," Tommy began, until Dee interrupted him.

"Shut up, Dinks!" She then turned to her best friend Rae, frustration in her voice. "Sweetie, this is a very private matter you've stumbled into . . . you know?"

"Well, I'm sorry . . . I didn't intend to spy or anything, Dee," a defensive Rae volleyed.

"I know, that's not what I meant, I jus . . . ," Tommy cut her off this time.

"This is a serious situation we have here, ladies and germs . . . ." Dinks squished his face at Tommy over the insult, as Tommy continued.

". . . Dee, let's fill Rae in on everything. The cat's out of the bag now."

Dee's facial expression and body language were in tune . . . showing resignation. As Dee sat back down to Tommy's left, Rae came in and sat down on her brother's right. An estrogen sandwich . . .

Dinks ran quickly into the kitchen and grabbed a bag of Doritos he had bought earlier, snagged a Coke from the fridge, and hustled back to sit down upon the recliner, kicking back as the other three prepared to talk. Dinks gave the impression he was in a movie theatre.

"Comfy?" an agitated Ms. Brando asked, rolling her eyes at Dinks as she did so. At least he didn't light up . . . yet.

Nearly two hours later, the "filling in" ended, and Rae headed for a bathroom break, while the unwanted and creepy Dinks had a faraway look in his eyes . . . he was truly stunned by what he had heard. Ricky amazingly kept his mouth shut the entire talk, and just sat by, paying attention to every word, every detail. It was like he was taking mental notes for use later. Ricky always used every bit of info to his benefit. If there was a way to take advantage of the info, he would find it.

Dee went to the fridge to grab a bite as Tommy remained sitting . . . staring at Dinks . . . recognizing that a plot was forming in the punk's skinny head . . . and the two men's eyes collided . . . neither blinked. A test of wills ensued . . .

Brando and Dinks . . .

Richard Dinkins grew up in Washington, DC, raised by his father, Ted, and occasionally Ted's mother, when he was too wasted to look after Ricky. Ricky's mother was a prostitute and heroin addict; she died when he was three, and he had no memory of her. His dad was a welder who worked long hours, making enough money to live in a better neighborhood, but his drinking and lottery—playing afforded them a more modest living in one of the poorer neighborhoods in DC.

His mom named him Richard after the man who pimped her out and supplied her with heroin . . . how sweet. Ricky's dad knew what she was doing, but couldn't care less, as he was just glad she was rarely home. He was a good man who made a bad call thinking he could change her habits and convince her to have the baby after he got her pregnant. Yeah, he was a trick of hers at one time . . . one time only. He loved little Ricky, but not enough to change his ways, not enough to overcome his own demons . . . dying from liver failure when Ricky was twelve. It was easy to see why Dinks turned out the way he did . . . although all people have a choice. Some choices are easier than others. When you're twelve and life utterly sucks, the choice to do bad things comes easier . . . especially with no one looking out for you.

Tommy was not short for Thomas, as one might expect . . . He had been named "Tommy Markus Brando" because his father—Duncan—wanted to honor his Vietnam War buddy, Tommy Markus. The funny thing is that Tommy Markus's real name was Markus Thomas. No one called Markus by his actual name, including Duncan, because there was a mix-up after Markus's transfer to Duncan's unit. No matter his efforts to get it corrected, the switch stuck, and "Tommy" it was.

The two had never met before the war, although they lived just a few miles apart in Salisbury, Maryland, not far from the sun and fun of Ocean City. The boys became fast friends after Tommy's transfer. It was cool while it lasted . . . as no amount of friendship could save Tommy on a hot April day in '69. Their unit was fighting in the jungles east of Tam Ky in South Vietnam, when he took a shot to the throat and died . . . bleeding out, all over Duncan. It was just two weeks before they were to head back home.

Tommy and Richard . . .

Many names have a story behind them. Sometimes they are interesting, sometimes not so much . . . but occasionally, you get more than you figured on . . . you just have to ask.

The men's battle of wills continued as Dee reentered the room and Rae returned from the bathroom. The women sat back down and looked drained after a long and emotional talk. They noticed the quiet in short order . . . and spotted the testosterone-driven contest. The air was thick with "male-ness," for lack of a better word. Still, neither man blinked. And, the daggers in the men's eyes, especially Tommy's, grew sharper by the moment.

Finally, Dee had enough, nudging both men and saying, "Are you gonna do this all day or what?"

The nudge distracted Tommy enough to make him blink, and Dinks broke out the biggest smile his leathery face could muster, having the look of a victorious gladiator. Tommy growled for a moment, but once Dee glared at him in indignation, he decided to voice his disappointment toward the still smiling Dinks, "Ehhhh, I think Dinks won the way he always does . . . shifty-like."

Duncan's boy smiled as widely as Ted's boy ever had, and they came down from their grins . . . simultaneously. Playtime was over.

Dinks then said something out loud, and for all intent and purpose, it seemed to make sense.

"It's 4:30, we have an hour before Jimmy's bro gets home and bombarded with the news . . ."

Rae muttered what the other two were thinking, "We . . . ?"

Dinks continued, ". . . and I don't see the point in telling both of them, when it was Jimmy's expressed decision to tell Alex, and not Kathy as well . . ."

Tommy and Dee both began to speak but Dinks went on.

". . . sooooo, why not call Alex on his cell? Have him come here directly, rather than up and moving all of us to their home and having to deal with Kathy as well, against Jimmy's wishes."

All three of them were prepared to debunk Dinks's idea, but none of them said a word against it. An almost tangible sense of contemplation was in the air, and sure enough, Dee spoke up after a few moments, and conceded.

"You know what, Ricky? That's actually a *good idea*."

She said it without a shred of sarcasm, and Dinks, who could read people with the best of them, was surprised at her sincerity.

"Yeah . . . ," started Tommy, ". . . I'll give you that, Dinks. Good thinking . . . although I'm still trying to work out what your angle is."

Rae spoke up then. "It's not my call obviously, but Dinks makes a fair point."

Ricky stood and had the strangest feeling come over him . . . an actual feeling of being "welcome" . . . a rare occurrence indeed. He kind of liked it.

Alex, after getting Dee's call that made it clear that he needed to get to Brando's right after work, or sooner if he wished, left work early and made a bee-line for Tommy's home. He arrived a few minutes after five and entered the home eagerly in anticipation of something awful. Dee hadn't gone into it, but Alex knew it was bad.

After introductions, including FBI "Associate" Dinks, Alex sat down and asked straight out, "What's wrong with Jimmy?"

It was getting dark outside as Dee and Tommy finished telling Jimmy's brother everything. Alex had reacted more suspiciously than they anticipated, and he paced about almost in a fit as he asked questions and got answers he didn't like. Eventually, he seemed to grasp that this was all real and that Jimmy was as he had feared, in a bad way. Alex, still was not convinced that the Soul-Collector part of it was true, oddly had no trouble believing the parts about the FBI, Serial Killer, and Secret Government kidnappers.

Alex's frustration and shock were evident, and everyone there knew what he was going through, having had to deal with it themselves. Alex shuddered to think about what his brother was going through . . . and despite the craziness, despite the wild stories and sci-fi-like undertones, he came to one singular belief: no matter what, Jimmy needed his brother, and Alex wasn't going to let him down.

Family mattered . . .

now more than ever.

Chapter 54

Voices in the Maelstrom

The stabbing of the needle had to be endured . . . it was crippling pain, the sort of pain that one experiences and instantly wants to die from it. However, he would not be dying this day, not now . . . for there, upon the examination table—under the bright lights and gazes of blue-masked men and women—the darkness within, the fragment of The Shadow's soul, IT, grabbed the opportunity to act and attack Jimmy's mind. IT felt emboldened by Jimmy's painful distraction . . . knowing that an assault at Jimmy's peak awareness would find the takeover of his body and soul harder to achieve. So here and now, Jimmy's mind bent to IT . . . melded with IT, and found himself—*not* himself.

Jimmy's tortuous session was actually more bearable with the deviant being in charge. Jimmy lay restless for a few hours or so once he was back in his room, feeling like a secondary conscious as the "enemy within" spread, its dominance becoming overwhelming.

Cooool again attempted to link with Jimmy, but found only pain instead. The fragment of The Shadow brutally pushed its horrid thoughts back at the Thai man's mind, with the desired result—terrible pain.

Jimmy's senses had been "away" for days, so while the drug effects were wearing off, he was once again feeling that familiar "strangeness" that he knew from his awareness of the SoulBound. He thought he heard other voices somewhere . . . but couldn't quite hear them. He needed help; beginning to understand that he was at war . . . his mind a volatile concoction . . . too many voices in the maelstrom . . . again he twisted memories and reality with dreams and nightmares . . .

An internal rage, a twisted maze of thoughts and memories past . . . An agonizing rift, a scatter-brained shift to recall my sanity last. Where lies the center? My rock? My true inner core? "Melted away . . . ," I hear me say, ". . . insane forevermore . . . more-more-more" cascades through my confused mind . . . IT perpetrates the absence of self. Wherefore art thou I? IT is sinister, I think, or rather, feel, I do believe . . . But what is real, I wonder, am I here or no, deceived?

Random thoughts then trickle in, of violent acts and damning sin . . . A crime inside my very mind, off to where I've never been. Or . . . have I? For vivid flows the blood of those, whose tortuous deaths my memories froze, and fertile grows what IT knows, slowly dominating the me within.

I am what I am, but what am I? Neurotic or psychotic it seems, but why? . . . .

Ahhhhhhhh, I remember . . . as a child, praying for God to help me see . . . For the words that were spoken like gospel to me were just a bit hostile it seemed. They shredded the fabric of truth to start, painting a picture of hatred and pain . . . Warped visions shared in the dark, my objections made in vain.

But enough of that, IT decrees that these memories be faded forever . . . But the past is our history, and these matters of mystery should not be forgotten, not ever.

Oh, my war may rage 'til the end of days, and IT will continue his lies. But I'll quest to find a way, to be whole again someday, I can only hope it's before I die . . .

I am . . . .

in here . . .

can you hear me?

No answer, none that he could hear . . . and at that moment, he let go. And IT, the fragment of The Shadow, reminded Jimmy where Jimmy was; here, in the thorned cradle of his mind, where no light shined . . . only varied shades of darkness.

Chapter 55

Testing

Alex and the others grew quiet in contemplation . . . what to do now? Alex had that very thing on his mind and voiced his concern by saying, "What's next? What's the plan?"

Tommy spoke up in response. "Well, Dee and I have to go to the FBI office tomorrow at noon to take the 'Lie Detector' test. And we've already agreed to allow for any other testing and/or questioning they may want to try on us."

Dee followed up. "We hope that once Kennedy sees that we're telling the truth, that she'll stop looking at Jimmy as a suspect and put out more of an effort to help find him and get him back safely."

Alex nodded and ran with the train of thought. ". . . then if Jimmy is able to, maybe she'll allow him to help her catch the real scumbag."

Rae and Dinks were standing by nodding in agreement, and Dinks then had another idea. "In the meantime, you should be monitoring your e-mails, double-checking your cells and house phones as well, for messages."

Another good idea . . . and the others all agreed.

Rae then said approvingly. "Check out the Dinkster, all with the bright ideas and all."

Everyone mustered smiles . . . including Dinks.

Dee added, "True . . . good idea, Ricky . . . again."

Alex walked over to grab his keys lying on the kitchen table and said, "I'm going home, guys. Call me tomorrow after you finish with the tests . . . I am going to tell Kathy that Jimmy has been kidnapped, but I'll leave out the rest obviously. She's strong and will be okay."

He walked back to Dee and hugged her, whispering, "Thank you," in her ear. Alex then shook Tommy's hand and winked at him approvingly, before waving to the others and heading out the door.

Rae then followed up with, "I guess I'll go too. Call me as soon as you're done . . . promise?"

"Of course, we will," Dee responded immediately.

Warm hugs went all around from Rae, which included a noticeably stunned Richard Dinkins.

The following morning . . . Saturday . . .

Dinks had slept on the couch, Dee slept in the same guest bedroom as the prior evening, and Tommy, who would have normally slept in his bed, decided to sleep on the recliner, just a few feet from Dinks . . . to better keep an eye on him.

When the dawn came, Dee eased into the kitchen and started breakfast. It was just after 8:00 a.m., which was a late morning for her. When she saw the sleeping arrangements that the men had taken, she mumbled something like, ". . . that's stupid." She also did a double-take as she was glancing at them, still sound asleep despite the minor noises of Dee's cooking. Dinks was eerie, even in his sleep, as his eyes were open and he was snoring . . . she figured that a guy like him was bound to weird her out. The bacon, sausage, and eggs wafted throughout the house and she was done making plenty for the three of them. Dee was determined to treat Dinks as well as she could muster after noticing a marked improvement in his behavior since his well-received suggestion to leave Kathy out of the loop. Dee also thought that Rae's hug may have done wonders for Dinks, as she was quite pretty . . . and reasonably sweet.

Dee intentionally made enough noise in the kitchen to wake the heavy-sleeping Tommy, and the awake-but-pretending-to-snore Ricky Dinks, who then brilliantly feigned waking up. The gents took turns hitting the bathroom before making their way into the kitchen, then to the wonderful buffet-style breakfast.

Dinks had said it would be best to leave early, maybe by 10 o'clock, to ensure they arrived in plenty of time, and by doing so, the FBI may even get them started early. So, the three of them finished eating, got ready, and set off at ten.

Dinks drove alone in the FBI-borrowed Dodge Durango, and was followed closely by Tommy and Dee in Tommy's Hummer. They arrived at the FBI office just past 11:00 a.m., after stopping at a gas station along the way. Kennedy wasn't there, but Agent Gottranelli was. He told them that they were early and would have to wait until noon as the "lie detector guy" wasn't available until then.

After nearly an hour-long wait, the time had come. Gottranelli appeared and asked them to follow. They took the elevator up two levels and wound through the offices to come to an open room.

Gotti asked them to enter and be seated in what seemed to be a lounge, but was just set up that way for their comfort. There was another open door in the room, which they noticed, when a man walked out and nodded to the agent. It was the testing room, and a bald gentleman with a serious look on his chubby face was the test giver.

Case Agent Kennedy had arrived as Dee was told to go in first, peeking her head into the "lounge" and nodding to Dee as she stood to go get tested.

Dee came out from her test after about twenty minutes, and Brando was ushered in next. She was brimming with confidence, seeking Kennedy, but noticing the lounge room was empty and the door to exit the room had been shut. All this confidence, and she had no one to share it with. She also noted that Dinks had disappeared, not realizing that Dinks was in Kennedy's office instead.

After Tommy returned, he sat beside Dee, and they talked about what each had been asked. A few minutes later, as Dee and Tommy continued discussing their experiences, the test giver, who had gathered his equipment in arms full, walked out the now-emptied test room and deftly managed to open the lounge room door. Agent Gottranelli was waiting just outside the door and he and the test giver spoke in hushed tones for a moment before the man walked off, still carrying his equipment.

Gottranelli was carrying a printout, which they hadn't noticed, and Tommy spoke confidently as the big man approached them.

"It's like we told ya . . . we're telling the truth."

"Agent Kennedy is getting the results; she'd like to meet with you in her office. I'll take you there now."

The red-haired Case Agent was sitting behind her desk as the knock came. She had just sat back down after double-checking the results . . . and put the jacket to her dark gray pantsuit back on before answering, "Come in."

Gotti entered with Dee and Tommy, and Kennedy invited them to sit, as Gotti took the large leather chair resting a few feet off to Kennedy's left side. Kennedy had been given the results by the test giver just moments before, and she had already worked out how she would respond if they were lying or telling the truth. She had worked with the test giver, named Fenton, to determine the series of questions. They had been well conceived . . . but here she was, sitting across from them, knowing the results . . . the results were conclusive . . . both Brando and Conway were telling the truth. Jimmy's girlfriend and best friend were telling the truth all along, and now that Kennedy knew that, it gave her a sense of direction, as far as how to proceed.

As the pair were seated and anxiously awaiting for her to speak, Kennedy didn't make them wait.

"You passed with flying colors . . . both of you."

Dee and Tommy sat knowingly, but relieved that the machine was accurate . . . and Kennedy continued.

"Under the circumstances, I'm prepared to believe what you've told me about Jimmy. This does not mean that Jimmy is completely absolved of suspicion, but rather that he is no longer being viewed as our Number One suspect."

Agent Kennedy kept her word though, and that was most important.

Dee replied quickly and with great appreciation, "Thank you . . . Carol."

The Case Agent smiled in return . . . then gathered herself before saying, "So . . . I think it's only fair I tell you that my superiors came up empty in determining who may have abducted Kassakatis. We're at a loss at the moment in figuring out how to locate him."

This was not good news . . . not at all.

Chapter 56

The Dark Incarnate

It was late afternoon on Saturday, and it was time for Jack to rise. He was contemplating how he had put things into motion, as he rose from his bed to shower. Jack was so clever . . . so very clever. Dropping the card outside Jimmy's window . . . and removing Kassakatis from the scene of the massacre, leaving his wallet and cell phone behind for the authorities to find . . . *just brilliant!* He truly stirred up a hornet's nest with the killing of yet another FBI agent. He didn't have nearly enough time with this last one. *Ah well.* Jimmy would soon be under arrest and convicted of Jack's crimes, as The Dark Incarnate—The Shadow That Speaks—lived free. And on top of it all, Jack had left Jimmy a little present, a piece of his twisted black soul. Jack had no idea how he did it, but he willed it and it happened . . . that was a new one for him.

My power is increasing for some reason . . . Jack pondered why, but he had business to attend to this night . . . serious business. Randolph Gage would suffer as no one has ever suffered . . . cliché perhaps, but Jack was the only one who could actually pull it off, and he was dead set on it. He knew that Gage would be hiding out in his *high-security hidey-hole,* so Jack would have to be more brilliant than normal, he would have to be perfect.

He shrugged that off with a thought, *No problem* . . .

He entertained himself as he showered, visualizing the deaths of every one of his victims . . . recalling his precision, his brilliance. Tyler "Jack" Hill was a genius, no doubt, but he was definitely "touched in the head." The probing and prodding that was done to him turned into this "gift" of darkness, but it had also warped his little mind forever.

He stepped from the shower to prepare for the evening massacre . . . The Dark Incarnate would be on the move, and soon.

· · · · · · · · · · · · · · · · · · ·

As Tommy and Dee were talking with Case Agent Kennedy, Alex and Rae had each been pacing about their respective abodes. They were awaiting the call from Dee or Tommy to divulge the results of the tests and to update them on Kennedy's response to those results.

Alex's wife, Kathy, had indeed been shocked that her brother-in-law had been abducted, but was a little peeved at Alex because he wouldn't go into as many details as she had wanted. She was holding the baby and pacing back and forth, watching Alex in hope of overhearing something. She couldn't help it . . . she had a need to know. Regardless, she was a good mother and a generally sweet and caring wife. Not to say Alex had no faults, as his quick temper could attest. Speaking of which, his temperature was on the rise . . .

It's been too long, something's wrong, I know it.

He used to get teased as a child, and even a few times as an adult, about having a temper *and* red hair, though it was actually a darker shade, like auburn. *"Fire top,"* or *"Hothead,"* were the most common insults, which just furthered his reputation by inciting him to get angry.

Rrriiinnnggg.

Alex took one deep breath, thought, *"Finally,"* and answered the phone . . .

Tommy's little sister was a ball of kinetic energy, moving about her apartment in a way that an observer would think she were drinking a few gallons of coffee and smoking crack to boot. She wore matching light blue sweatshirt and pants and Reebok tennis shoes. Her pretty highlighted hair was in a ponytail, and she was smoking an "only when I'm really nervous" cigarette. She wasn't drinking coffee either, but Caffeine-Free Diet Pepsi. Rae was jittery when she was this worried, and caffeine made it worse.

She had cleaned her tiny, but fashionable, apartment three times since the entire "Jimmy Drama" came to her attention. She cared a lot for Jimmy, as she had known him for many years as a great friend to her big brother, a great boyfriend to her best friend, and as a sweetheart to her throughout the years. She hoped to meet a guy like him herself, but she now knew that there was only one Jimmy Kassakatis. She put out the cigarette, which she hated smoking, as she had never been a smoker and would only have one in the most strenuous of times. A friend of hers named Stephanie turned her on to it, and Rae found that, for her at least, it did help alleviate the stress.

Rrriiinnnggg.

She bolted to answer the phone, nearly tripping over the vacuum cleaner . . .

An hour later, the frenetic four convened at Tommy's home. Alex and Rae were both annoyed at having to wait to find out the details in person, rather than be told over the phone . . . but nonetheless, here they all were.

Dee and Tommy explained the details of the day as no one sat the entire time . . . they were all too full of angst and energy. As expected, Alex and Rae were angry with the FBI, although neither could see how they could do much more. They were all at their wits' end when everyone heard a cell phone ring . . .

Dee was puzzled, since her personal cell still rested silently on her belt holster, yet the ringing resonated from within her purse. Dee was dumbfounded, but opened the purse and answered the strange red cell . . .

"Hello?"

"Is this Denise Conway?"

"Yes, it is . . ." Dee didn't recognize the voice and assumed it was a telemarketer, ". . . but I'm awfully busy at the moment and I'm registered with the National Do-Not-Call Registry, so . . ."

"Ma'am, this is about Jimmy."

Dee was stunned for a moment and then replied anxiously, "Go on."

The other three began migrating toward Dee as they could tell something was going on. Dee listened intently as the stranger continued. She excitedly motioned for a pen and paper as she listened to the man, and Tommy quickly brought her the items. Dee wrote quickly and then said, "We'll be there. By the way, what's your name?"

She furrowed her brow at his response and then finished the talk with "Okay, bye."

She was shocked, but turned to the others and with her teary eyes wide said, "A man just called and said he knows where Jimmy is."

The others excitedly began to ask questions, but she kept on, ". . . and he wants to meet with all of us at eight o'clock tonight at the Pier Six Pavilion. He says to call him Mr. E."

Chapter 57
Enemy Mind

The worn-down man was quivering in the corner of his soft-walled room, trying to be.

Just *be*.

Imagine . . . within your very mind . . . being taunted, tormented, and teased, scorned and scolded . . . forced to experience the dark side of humanity, lucid in its sickness. Through it all, helpless to do a thing about it; feeling as a tortured puppet upon a set of twisted strings. This was the phantom existence of Jimmy Kassakatis.

The professor, of which being one seemed like an eternity ago, had chewed his nails so low that he was chewing skin. He had just finished "watching" one of the Shadow's murders, in all its gory details. Another in a series from the heartless entity he just called IT. Jimmy had already been bent, but now he was breaking . . .

Between the fragment and the perverse people that ran the facility at DEEPER, Jimmy had little hope, at least hope that was evident.

The SoulBound had been upset virtually nonstop, as they witnessed their tormented friend break before their very eyes. Gina has been crying more often than most, having a hard time dealing with Jimmy's anguish.

Karen and Yi had spent a lot of time together, discussing the dilemma at hand, and recently merged their twosome with the duo of Jean-Paul and Koketai, who had been quietly spending time away from the others, discussing their own ideas and plans of attack that had as yet failed to do anything useful.

The ladies were basically doing the same thing, so after Yi overheard the men talking, she told Karen about it and they decided four heads were better than two. The quartet had tried hard to ignore Jimmy's plight, as they couldn't help him spending their time crying or empathizing . . . though still it *was* a difficult and heart-wrenching task.

John, Brennan, and Dragon had been the most agitated, voicing their frustration with being unable to somehow help Jimmy.

Millie had been spending a lot of time with Marie and Carrie Ann, trying hard to keep her tongue in check and provide a grandmotherly presence for the child. Millie loved children and had grown to love this little one like one of her own grandbabies.

Marie had truly appreciated the assist, as it was not easy trying to handle the delicate psyche and issues that the girl had gone through, and still was coping with. Marie had essentially become Carrie Ann's surrogate mother, and she took to it with the same love, affection, and understanding that any good mother would. Marie was quite aware that Carrie Ann had a mother and would be with her again someday, but the child needed a mothering figure here and now more than ever. It wasn't that long ago that Carrie Ann had been so traumatized that she was on the verge of drifting into a virtual mental chasm, until Marie's efforts brought her back from the edge . . . giving hope to a hopeless child. Giving her the chance to dream again.

Dreams . . . how we take them for granted.

Jimmy would say, "What are we without our dreams? . . . but placated souls without the will to stand and shout that dreams abound and dance within us still."

If only Jimmy could dream again . . .

If only the fragment of the Shadow, the IT that dominated Jimmy, his Enemy Mind, would release him . . .

If only . . .

Chapter 58
The Twilight's Last Gleaming

A rapid-fire question-and-answer session ensued after Dee told them what Mr. E had said.

Dee, Tommy, Alex, and Rae, all four, were to meet later that night with the mysterious stranger, at 8:00 p.m. to be exact, at the Pier Six Pavilion . . . just a short walk from where Dee had her big talk with Agent Kennedy by the harbor. Pier Six was a gorgeous outdoor entertainment facility, hosting musical events as well as many other functions. It was covered by a beautiful eye-catching canopy, which made it seem as if it were a collection of sails, giving it a natural feel and unique ambience. Fortunately for them, it was a Saturday night that had nothing scheduled. But then again, Mr. E must've known that.

Dee raised her hand and said with resignation, "Guys . . . I told you all I know."

They grew quiet for a few moments . . . until Rae broke the silence. "Are you going to inform Agent Kennedy?"

Dee replied matter-of-factly, "Not until after the meeting. Mr. E said to wait to tell her or he wouldn't tell us anything."

"Why don't we all sit down?" Tommy offered.

"Good idea, let's try to relax and discuss this calmly," came the ironic response from the usually testy Alex Kassakatis.

The quartet sat at the kitchen table and Dee filled them all in on exactly what the man had said.

"Okay . . . again, the guy asked me if I was Denise Conway, to which I said, 'Yeah,' and he then said that he knew where Jimmy was and that he knew that the FBI was investigating him. He then went on to say he knew that you three were with me and that he could help me get Jimmy back, and then told me when and where we all were to meet with him. But he said, there was one condition . . . do not tell Agent Kennedy about this meeting until after it was over . . . he said he had his reasons."

"They know we're all here? We're being watched?" came the worried reply from Rae, as she noticed both men had moved to look outside the windows to see if they could spot their observers . . . to no avail. Whoever was watching them had since moved on, or was very well-hidden.

The four of them continued to talk about the call as the afternoon waned. How the cell phone got into her purse and who put it there was a hot topic. They also debated the "point of contention" that Mr. E had—concerning leaving Kennedy in the dark—until after the meeting. They discussed many things, but felt no surer of themselves or the situation.

Alex called his wife and told her that she should take Lissy to her favorite aunt's house and to not ask questions, he would call her later to explain. Alex knew that Kathy would be a bit peeved, and worried even more so, but he also realized she would do as he requested. He felt much better . . . knowing they'd be safe. As it neared 5:00 p.m., Rae and Alex went back to their respective homes to shower and ready themselves, then returned by 6:15 . . . it was near time to go.

They all left at 6:45, giving them more than enough time to get to the pavilion. They took the Hummer, and after a short construction delay, arrived at the harbor at 7:25 and walked briskly toward the meeting place. There was plenty of time to spare, but they were taking no chances. The group made it to the Pier Six Pavilion by 7:40 and stood around waiting for the appearance of the mysterious Mr. E. Although it was a too-warm-for-spring sort of day, they had visions of a man wearing a fedora hat, a beige trench coat, and smoking a cigarette in the shadows . . . what they got was not what they expected. It was 8:00 p.m. sharp when they spotted him.

A man that looked to be about fortyish, with short blond hair approached them quite casually, but his dark blue eyes were all over the place, giving him away. He wore a navy blue short-sleeve tee shirt, beige khaki shorts, and white tennis shoes. Atop his head, he had a pair of yellow-tinted sunglasses, but with the sun setting and a full moon soon rising, he wouldn't need them long. He had a black fanny pack around his waist and a bottled water in his left hand, of which he took one final swig as he took a last few steps up to Dee.

Alex and Tommy maneuvered casually to either side of Dee, and Rae sauntered close behind Dee to be sure to hear the man.

The yellow-haired fellow spoke first, loud enough for them to hear, but no more.

"Dee I assume?"

"Yes," she replied nervously.

The man looked around at the tourists and locals milling about, but none close enough to be of concern.

"I'm Mr. E. I'll get right to it if that's okay?"

"Certainly."

"Your fiancé has been taken by a shadowy government research outfit called DEEPER. He is being tested by them for his special talents. They aren't being gentle."

Dee and the others were noticeably upset by Mr. E's comments, but let him continue.

"My reasons for telling you this are my own. My reasons for avoiding Agent Kennedy and the FBI are also my own and not open for discussion. The information I'm about to give you will help you to get into the facility. Follow these instructions down to the last detail. You need to go tonight."

Mr. E pulled open the black pack at his waist and handed them some papers, of which one was a map.

He finished with "Women, hug me. Guys, shake my hand, like old friends do."

The four did as instructed.

As he stepped back from them, Mr. E looked around casually and yelled out, "It was great seeing you guys again. Tell Mom I said hi!"

The man walked away, becoming but a silhouette, as the setting sun cast an eerie glow upon the cloud-scattered skies.

They would never see him again, and he faded into their collective memories, before disappearing . . . into the twilight's last gleaming.

Chapter 59
Night Moves

Black Jack was a ridiculously powerful being, a "superman" of sorts. And though a billowing black cape would have seemed a natural in his case, he drove where he needed to go, just like everyone else. However, unlike most of us, he got around in a jet-black Dodge Charger RT. He *could* move more quickly through the shadows and darkness in short spurts, switching his form at will into The Shadow That Speaks, but for this venture, he would save his energy for the onrushing feast.

Jack liked fast cars with powerful engines, but was careful not to trick them out too much, so as not to draw too much attention. He was one high-powered machine himself, but not one to take unwarranted chances. He was smart, he was deadly, and he was motivated . . . a woeful combination for those unfortunate persons at DEEPER. If they could see his essence, glean his aura somehow, it would be as if the night itself were moving. And on this night of nights . . . the Hill boy was coming home.

• • • • • • • • • • • • • • • • • •

The four friends moved closer toward one of the tall lamp-posts that dotted the walking areas of the harbor, to be better able to read the instructions that Mr. E had given them. Dee was on her cell phone as they did so . . . calling Agent Kennedy.

"Kennedy."

"Carol, it's Dee. I have something to tell you . . . ."

Agent Kennedy told Dee to come into her office immediately, and Dee did so, with the others joining her. Kennedy was not happy with the revelation that Alex and Rae were now involved . . . not in the least. She called for her team to gather immediately and put together an impromptu "case focus" meeting. Conway, Jimmy's brother, and the Brandos would be arriving in twenty minutes, so she got started immediately.

In the meeting room, there was a large maple table, and Agent Kennedy would soon stand at its head. Her full team would not be required, but the profilers and special agents working closely with her, would be. She asked for those who couldn't make it, to listen in through the Agency's conferencing device.

Agent Gottranelli and others had been ready for a few minutes, awaiting the Case Agent, as Kennedy came into the room, followed closely by "Special Associate" Dinkins. His entrance garnered surprise from her team . . . with more than a few raised eyebrows.

As Dinks sat, Kennedy began . . . "Is everyone here?"

Gotti replied, "Everyone is either in the room or listening in, so yes."

"Good. It appears that a new player has entered the game . . ."

Dee and Tommy had just been here, so getting back was a breeze. They were expected, and after being cleared through security, were escorted by a young female agent to just outside Kennedy's office. There they waited for her and whispered among themselves about their impressions of Mr. E and his plan.

After about a twenty-minute wait, Gotti appeared with Kennedy just behind. She was once again being trailed by Dinks, which raised the foursome's collective worry a bit higher. They went into Kennedy's office and once everyone had been seated, Kennedy began.

"I'd take away the cell phone he gave you, but we may need it. Anyway, I need to see the papers he gave you."

Dee immediately withdrew the papers from her purse and handed them over to Kennedy.

"These are copies, Dee. Where are the originals?"

A nervous Dee had taken Rae's advice to stop and make a copy of each page, as well as the map, and she had done just that a block away from the FBI building.

"Sorry, I made copies becau . . ."

"No copies, Dee, just originals. The copies will need to be destroyed."

Kennedy handed the copies to Gotti and held her hand out to Dee for the originals, at which time Dee had fetched them and gave them to her.

Kennedy read, as everyone remained quiet. She had finished looking over the papers with a concerned look and then reread to be sure she understood. When finished, she looked at them all and said, "This is most unusual . . . but if this Mr. E is on the up and up, then I can't see *not* going through with it. He mentions a connection to The Shadow That Speaks . . . drawing us in. He knew that I would be all over him about that, which is why he explicitly avoided me. Smart man. We suspect he has a person on the inside, but we have no clue who it could be."

"He says that you four must all be involved, or he will make it so the plan will fail, so I have no choice . . . you are all coming. I will need you all to do as you are told and to listen to me no matter what happens. If my watch is correct, and it always is, we'll need to leave right away. We'll talk about this plan on the way. No one but us seven are aware of this. My team knows about Mr. E, but none of these details . . . which means I'm breaking protocol, again. Anyway . . . Sterling is a good hour or so away, and I'm assuming you all still want to do this?"

Dee, Tommy, Alex, and Rae looked at each other and then replied they were in.

It was a few minutes after 9:00 p.m. as the group gathered into the Case Agent's SUV. They needed to move quickly, for The Shadow That Speaks had arrived at DEEPER at the same moment they were leaving the FBI building.

Business was about to pick up.

Chapter 60
The Depths of the Damned

The Department for Para-Psyche Research's headman, Director Randolph Gage, was followed closely down the long hall by Dr. Lena Vaccaro. She was in his ear as he moved.

"I wanted to tell you . . . but thought it best to wait until now . . . that I'm truly sorry about Erin."

Erin Adams was Gage's assistant, but more girlfriend than anything. He never gave her too much responsibility, as she wasn't very bright. Erin felt important though, and she returned his affections many times over. Gage knew that Erin was loyal, that he was sure of . . . but here and now, and for reasons that eluded him, he couldn't say the same about Vaccaro. She *had* done a great job with Kassakatis, as he was in DEEPER hands now, but with her job finished and with his people informing him that the FBI was seeking the good doctor, he determined that she had become expendable. She was a liability that needed to be found dead—with suicide as the evident reason—and sooner rather than later. She was but a ghost in his ear, but an annoyance nonetheless. She did say something amid the drone that caught his attention and he stopped just a few feet from the door he was about to walk through.

There was a tinge of concern in his voice as he asked, "What do you mean Carl is missing?"

"I have not been able to locate him since yesterday morning. He's not at his apartment, nor at the secondary facility. He hasn't picked up either phone, and I checked myself; his car is not parked outside his place. He checks in with me every day like clockwork . . . and I fear something is wrong."

Gage didn't like surprises and told Vaccaro that finding Carl was a priority and to get on it immediately.

She replied that she would certainly, but it was getting late and she would take measures to find him first thing in the morning.

BIG mistake.

Gage grabbed her by the throat, forced her up hard against the hallway wall, and said in no uncertain terms, "You go now! You get him back to me, Lena, or you . . . !!"

He didn't have to say ". . . die!" Vaccaro knew full well his meaning, and after he released her, she rushed away to go find her partner.

• • • • • • • • • • • • • • • • • • •

The Director was oft-times brilliant, and had used his invaluable resources to forge ingenious devices, designed to capture "the one that got away." For lack of a better term, the creators dubbed the devices "Light Traps," which were battery-powered, focused light beams, that created a stream of sun-bright light that, in theory, would knock The Shadow That Speaks unconscious. The idea had merit . . . in theory.

Jack *was* darkness. He was a whisper in the wind and drifted amidst the shadows as he approached the secret facility that had created him many years prior. DEEPER was a super high-security facility. The entrance underground was contained within an electric fenced area that had a coppice of trees to its west, an open field to its south, a long road from which the main gate was nestled up to, and a deep wooded area to the north.

Jack approached from the north after parking on the outskirts of the woods about a half-mile farther north, and easily moved through the trees until getting within range of the powerful lights that surrounded the fenced area. The lights lit up everything, including the areas outside the fence. The woods rested a mere 150 feet or so from the nearest point to the fence.

Jack had noticed that the lights did not go all the way up to the tops of the trees, and knew what he would do.

As DEEPER technically fell under military authority, the facility was guarded by the Army . . . so soldiers patrolled the compound with machine guns at the ready. Director Gage had ordered in an entire company of battle-hardened troops to beef up security, and the dozen or so armored personnel carriers that had arrived and unloaded an hour earlier were parked in an impressive row.

The entrance to the underground complex began in the non-descript building that rested at the heart of the above-ground area. There were twenty guards posted near the doorway to the building. The "base" had been on high alert for the past two nights, but there had been nothing to note since. All was quiet.

Sergeant Morales, one of the guards, moved away from the others, taking his scheduled pass around the building and came around the bend on the north side when he thought he caught movement out of the corner of his eye. He raised his weapon and glared into the distance, along the tree-line outside the fence. He wasn't sure, but it seemed as if the darkness grew darker, if that were possible, but noticed that the full moon had just gone behind some clouds. He figured that must have been it.

Wrong.

The Shadow descended upon the soldier, as if a shredded black sail had materialized from the darkness above.

Sergeant Morales never even pulled the trigger.

Dr. Lena Vaccaro had taken the elevator to the top floor, and had planned to make a beeline to her car parked just outside the building, when she heard the alarm sound. She assumed it was another drill.

Wrong.

She was annoyed at the blaring sound, but continued to ponder where Carl was as the elevator doors opened. She just knew that he had better turn up, or she was dead. The man standing awaiting the elevator shoved her hard, back inside.

She yelled indignantly at him at first, until she saw his eyes . . . jet-black. Dr. Lena Vaccaro, who had been Gage's assistant all those many years ago, knew too late, as the elevator doors closed . . . and her sordid life met with an unfathomable and agonizing end.

After his Head of Security updated him, Gage patched into the intercom system via his headset.

"This is Director Gage. This is not a drill. I repeat . . . this is NOT a drill. There's been a breach. Please give way to the alert teams who are preparing for the intruder. Follow protocol and report to the cafeteria."

As he spoke, Gage's special teams were setting up the "light traps" throughout the facility, as scientists and researchers alike scrambled to the cafeteria as directed.

The Shadow That Speaks felt an even greater sense of empowerment as the intercom filled with preparations of his arrival. As the elevator's doors opened, The Shadow knew it was time to demonstrate a newly discovered ability . . . one with wonderfully deadly consequences.

He pushed his arms forward and sent an unnatural shockwave throughout the facility . . . and dread became DEEPER . . . as every light in the facility went out! And here, in the depths of the damned, the carnage commenced.

Jack was the embodiment of devastation . . .

He was an ebon whirlwind . . .

A razor-clawed wraith . . .

A shadowed riptide . . .

And suddenly . . . a body count of 666 didn't seem so far away . . . .

Chapter 61

In the Shadow's Wake

Jimmy heard the announcement and could sense the anticipation of IT within . . . yes, The Shadow That Speaks had come. The lights had gone out only moments earlier, but he could almost feel the joy of the fragment pulsing through what he imagined as blackened veins. IT's master, IT's creator was turning this once immoral, yet thriving underground facility—into a tomb.

The Shadow knew that Gage would've surmised that *this* Jack was no longer the scared little boy that had fled their clutches those many years ago. At that time, he had been unable to fully harness his cruel gift, and while light was and could be a serious deterrence to Jack in the Shadow form, his power, his understanding of light and darkness had increased a thousand-fold.

Light hurt him, but pain was a friend he was long acquainted with. Their light traps would have hurt like hell, had he given them the chance to use them, but ol' Jack had sent out a shockwave of pure darkness just minutes earlier. The electricity that surged throughout the facility blacked out, and the battery-powered generators were overwhelmed as well. There was only one source of power within DEEPER . . . and for those entombed in the heart of darkness, he was sharing it at will.

Every door had unlocked during the dark surge and subsequent black-out, and the research subjects filtered out of their rooms and into the mayhem. Schae-Schae and Cooool were holding the shoulders of Oba Ibn Jahi, who led them through the corridors to Jimmy's room, as if the lights were on. Oba just knew things.

They opened the door and yelled for Jimmy to follow them, and he snapped out of his haze, feeling more like himself in what seemed an eternity.

Cooool wouldn't try to mind-speak with Jimmy while the fragment was in charge, so Schae-Schae extended her arms into the darkness and felt Jimmy grab them moments later.

Oba then explained to Jimmy that he needed to just keep his hands around Schae-Schae's shoulders and they would find their way out shortly. Oba was indeed special, as he dodged bodies and equipment deftly, and made it past the elevators, which were not running, and to the stairs that led upward.

As they opened the staircase door and began to head up, Jimmy kicked something hard, and reached down to retrieve it. A handgun. He had never held one in his life, but it felt familiar somehow. It was familiar to a couple of his souls, but Jimmy had not remembered them, even as they had been plotting to help him, screaming joyfully as he made his way out of the abyss.

Director Gage was a mess. The phones were down, and there was no power . . . even the generators were out. He had lost contact with his security teams, and hadn't the means to summon more help. So he decided to try to escape, as waiting for death was simply not in his best interest. He and the six others that had been locked within his secured command center grew uneasy, as even the light of cell phones dimmed after a momentary glow.

He told Kalyn Coleman, his current head assistant, who had remained with Gage throughout the siege, to open the door, and to quietly move to the nearest stairway, but she was scared to the point of being immobile.

So when Gage heard that the door hadn't opened, he whispered loudly that she was a coward. The hypocrite then ordered Colonel Clark, a member of his private security team, to open the door.

Clark complied, finding and opening the large steel and concrete door.

"Quickly . . . quietly!" Gage whispered loudly.

There was a momentary rush of shuffling feet and then, the sounds of bodies thudding the floor. A few muffled shrieks and then silence . . . sounds that the Director was familiar with . . . and it meant only one thing: it was dying time.

As Gage awaited the deathblow, he was surprised when his cell phone beeped on, and the glow faintly lit up his immediate area. He slowly moved the phone around to see shapes lying about, and dark fluids staining the floor.

Kalyn was still standing immobile, terror etched, ingrained forever into her shattered psyche and colorless face. Gage wasn't stupid, and knew that Hill was teasing him, playing with his food as a cat does with a mouse.

"After all these years . . . games? You don't have the sack to just kill me?"

An eerie reply—haunting in tone—came from everywhere . . .

"Gage . . . you should know better. You remember what you did to me. Would you expect me to show mercy? Come now, my old friend, pain has elements of pleasure . . . here, let me show you. I'll be sure to take it slow . . ."

As Jimmy and the others were halfway to the top of the stairs, they heard a series of screams that lasted the duration of their ascension. When they reached the top, as they opened the door, all went deathly silent.

The kind of silence that was left . . . in The Shadow's wake.

Chapter 62

Beneath the Midnight Sun

Jimmy and his fellow test subjects made their way out of the facility, yells and screams echoing about as the last of the soldiers were filing into the facility, and scientists and patients alike were fighting past them to get out. Jimmy was still carrying the gun he had found lying beside the guard who had been decapitated.

The researchers and scientists who managed to get out, rushed toward the parking lot; those without keys ran for the front gate.

Jimmy, Oba, Schae-Schae and Cooool were obviously dressed differently, and would have no shot at trying to get out the same way as the DEEPER workers. There were no guards detaining them where they were, but surely there would be some at the gate. So with no evident way out, there were a few moments of defeat that encompassed them, a feeling all too familiar.

That was before Oba (who had gone missing just moments earlier) went zipping past them all in one of the armored personnel carriers. Jimmy and the others watched in amazement as Oba smashed into and through the outer fence that bordered the woods to the north, creating the hole they needed to flee.

Cooool told them all to *"Move!"* and they all began running for the opening.

Jimmy began to run, but his legs suddenly wouldn't move, as IT, which had lost focus with The Shadow so near, had just realized what was going on, and put an end to Jimmy's escape.

Cooool and Schae-Schae grabbed him under both of his arms and moved with him toward the broken fence.

IT became infuriated, and Jimmy's body began to resist his friends. He was trying to fight back against IT, but was outgunned, so to speak. He watched helplessly as he physically began to overpower the friends trying to save him.

Yet, at that very moment, there was a scream inside his head, as Cooool had attacked IT mentally, shocking IT momentarily, allowing Jimmy the freedom to run with them through the opening toward the nearby woods. The full moon illuminated the area, so they were still fairly visible, but the woods and, hopefully, freedom rested just another fifty feet or so . . . when Cooool himself yelled out and stopped running.

"Jimmy, my tangle with IT is over. I will not get to IT again . . . as IT has me blocked from interfering. Jimmy . . . it's up to you now, my friend!"

Jimmy then fell to his knees . . . but Cooool stayed with him, as did Oba and Schae-Schae.

Jimmy began to quiver as the other two men were convincing the young girl to run. Schae-Schae looked at Jimmy, then to her saviors . . . the two people who helped her make it when all hope seemed lost . . .

Again they implored her to go. Schae-Schae was crying fiercely, but did as asked, hugging them tightly and telling them she loved them . . . then scampering off into the woods.

At the moment she reached the first row of trees, Jimmy—still upon his knees—spoke as if in a trance . . . his cracking voice a somber tone, "I cannot hold him off . . . I'm not strong enough."

Cooool bent beside Jimmy and spoke.

"Jimmy, focus on me, on my words . . . fight the darkness that holds you and hear me now! What I am about to tell, is true . . . you have my word on it."

The elder Thai then spoke softly . . . yet with emphasis on all the right words . . . words meant only for Jimmy's ears . . .

What followed touched Jimmy, more than anything he had ever wrote, more than anything he had ever heard, in all of his amazing life . . .

Jimmy turned his head to look into the eyes of his friend, and nodded in eternal gratitude as his tears came in force.

And here,
     upon this field,
          beneath the midnight sun,
               Jimmy found himself . . .
He found the will to overcome . . .
     found the strength to carry on . . .
          and found the courage to fight for his life, and
          those he loved.

Jimmy was still reveling in the aftermath of Cooool's words, when inside him, IT renewed, pounding Jimmy's mind and soul. IT wasn't pleased by the professor's defiance. Jimmy fell forward from the impact and screamed out loud.

Cooool tried to help Jimmy up off the ground, but Jimmy yelled out, "Noooo . . . *I* got this!"

Cooool stood, clapped his left hand upon the troubled soul beneath him, but said nothing and quickly backed away to stand beside Oba.

There were military police vehicles now approaching, as flashing yellow lights painted the trees about them.

Jimmy rose up off the ground, to stand as a man does when he faces his enemy. He was immensely angry, and an overwhelming swell of courage and determination broke the barriers that had separated the SoulBound from him . . . the reconnect sent shockwaves throughout him . . . mind, body and soul. He was nearly whole again, he was nearly back. But . . . the tearful reunion was going to have to wait, as the fragment of The Shadow hammered Jimmy to near unconsciousness, and he again screamed as the onslaught continued.

That is when the SoulBound acted. Carrie Ann stood tall and asked her soul mates to gather around her. The others did so quickly as she yelled out that the time had come, that Jimmy needed them and their light . . . their love. Instinctively, they created a circle around the child and all looked upward as she spoke.

"Jimmy. You are stronger than IT is. You are, because you have us with you, and something IT doesn't have . . . !"

Then and there, a light burst forth from them all, outward into the soul and very essence of James Kassakatis. Jimmy went from nightmare to dream in a split second . . . uplifted, overwhelmed with the most incredible feeling a person can feel . . . unbridled and unconditional **love**.

The fragment, the IT that had haunted him, tortured him, and had nearly broken his spirit, dissolved into nothingness. IT had been eradicated by so strong a thing, so powerful a light that IT could not exist in it.

At that moment, within the underground fortress, there was a scream like a sonic boom. Jack had become The Shadow that Shrieks . . . and he was beyond livid.

Time was of the essence, Jimmy, Oba and Cooool had to go . . . but as they were about to run off, a familiar voice, the sweetest voice Jimmy ever heard, rang out behind him.

"Jimmy!"

It was Dee, followed closely by Tommy, Alex, and Rae; with two people he didn't recognize . . . a skinny man and a middle-aged woman. Dee ran, and leapt into the arms of her lover.

Jimmy was exhausted, and his body hurt in every possible way, but at this moment, nothing seemed to matter. He held her as if for the first time . . . or the last time. His brother and friends gathered around them, but a voice he was not familiar with yelled out quite forcefully, "There's no time! We need to move . . . NOW!"

That had been Case Agent Carol Kennedy, as she directed the group toward her SUV. She held a walkie-talkie in her left hand, listening in as her third partner in this case was descending into the chaos that shook the base to its core.

Steve Gottranelli was terrified, but was doing his job . . . just like Tony Omega, and Kennedy's first partner, Justin Sykes.

Oba and Cooool began to run into the woods, but Jimmy stopped them and asked them humorously if they needed a ride, to which they smiled knowingly and ran back toward the vehicle with everyone else. Jimmy yelled out as they ran back through the broken fence, "I'll introduce you all later!"

Gotti's voice crackled across the walkie-talkie, as the group opened the doors and began rushing into the vehicle.

"Kennedy, there are bodies all over the place . . . shreds . . . this doesn't seem possible . . ."

"Get out of there now, and that's a direct order! I won't lose you!"

Gotti replied nervously, "Dammit! My flashlight's failing . . ."

There were screams in the background as Gotti spoke, and then silence. He was whispering now. "I'm close. I think . . . God in heav . . ."

Dead silence. Agent Kennedy hit the steering wheel full force and screamed, "Gotti!"

She started the SUV up and yelled at Tommy to drive them the hell out of here, she then exited the vehicle . . . an inferno raging in her jade eyes. She pulled her gun and began to rush toward the entrance when a loud rumble was followed a second later by a monstrous explosion. It hit like an H-Bomb, blasting Kennedy back fifteen feet toward where her SUV had been. *Had been . . .* as the SUV was pushed sideways a few feet by the blast wave. Luckily for those inside, the SUV's windows didn't shatter.

Tommy spun the vehicle around, after helping get Kennedy into the back, and maneuvered through the opening in the fence, looking for a main road around the woods.

DEEPER had exploded from within; courtesy of the once-secret self-destruct mechanism discovered in the torture of Randolph Gage.

The subsequent fireball was the last thing Agent Gottranelli saw before he was consumed, along with everything else. The Shadow That Speaks wanted no evidence of Tyler Hill ever being there. No video, no paperwork, nothing linking his name to DEEPER. The facility was now but a blackened husk . . . a shadow of its previous self . . .

How ironic . . .

    how sinister . . .

        . . . how Jack.

Chapter 63
Up on the Roof

Sunday, June 15, 2008

It was 3:30 in the morning . . . The SUV's occupants had arrived at Jimmy's home about a half hour earlier, without Dinks and Kennedy. Dinks had phoned the FBI to tell them that Special Agent Gottranelli was dead and that he was taking Case Agent Kennedy to the nearest hospital . . . mentioning nothing else regarding Jimmy and the others.

Tommy had dropped Dinks and the concussed Agent Kennedy off at the nearest hospital, before continuing back to Jimmy's place. Jimmy earlier had asked Oba if he felt they would be safe going to his home, to which the older man replied after thinking on it, "The Shadow That Speaks is finished *this* night."

As they exited the vehicle, Jimmy was annoyed at the sight of the tape that encircled his home. It was dark, but with a full moon, it was bright enough to see clearly. He proceeded, with help from the others, to tear it all down. After getting inside, he announced to everyone they were welcome to stay, and Dee went about trying to make sleeping arrangements.

Oba was making "an important call," as everyone began to head off to bed.

Jimmy warmly greeted his SoulBound in the moments before he dropped dead asleep.

Marie, Carrie Ann and the others were elated to have him back. But as Jimmy drifted into slumber, the SoulBound were celebrating . . . joyous hugs and shared relief all around. The living settled in to sleep . . . or most of them had. For the two men who had been cooped up in DEEPER, indoors was the last place they wanted to be. Before Dee shuffled off to bed, she gave the men some blankets and said that she and Jimmy sometimes spent time up on the roof, stargazing. It was kind of a small deck that faced the beach and the waters of the Chesapeake Bay to the east, but it had more than enough room for the two men.

Oba and Cooool asked Dee to show them how to get atop the home, and she did so, reminding them to tread lightly with everyone in bed. She then proceeded to join her man in bed, and fell fast asleep.

Oba and Cooool settled in after a moment's pause, drinking in the bay, glimmering in the moonlight. Cooool asked Oba, "The call . . . is it done?"

Oba nodded and Cooool nodded approvingly in return. The pair then lay breathing deeply of the cool fresh air and gazed . . . eyes heavenward. And they saw, as if for the first time, the entirety of the universe . . . as the swirling pattern of stars took stage, immersed in color . . . splashed about by cosmic hands. The enormity of it all gripped them, and amidst this Ocean of Wonderment, they wept in awe, overcome by the visions before them, frozen in glorious gaze. And though it had seemed an eternity since they had last been so blessed, the vision of the night sky was one they would keep with them always . . . a reminder of their newfound freedom, and life renewed.

And as a cool late-spring breeze chilled them, they would not falter . . . and continued to stare off into that starry sea . . . able to dream the beautiful dreams.

• • • • • • • • • • • • • • • • • • •

Awakened at first light, as the dawn's rays kissed their world about them, the two men stood to greet the morning with eyes wide smiling. These "unbroken" had not seen sunlight in so many years that, as with the stars just hours prior, the sight was overwhelming . . . and with the light showering the bay waters, it was a glory to behold.

Cooool had been kept underground, spanning the past dozen years, and though Oba's four years paled in comparison, it was a very long time indeed. The impact of their fortune was not lost upon them and they would revel in it *every day* for the rest of their lives. However, more than anything at that moment, they needed their sleep . . . and quietly returned to their makeshift beds upon the deck, drifting to sleep with the sounds of the bay embracing them.

• • • • • • • • • • • • • • • • • • •

Oba was awakened hours later by Cooool, who sleepily announced, "Jimmy is here."

Sure enough, the deck door opened and Jimmy, roaming alone for the first time since his rescue hours earlier, joked, "You think *you two* had it rough? Try two nights without the sun or stars . . ."

Everyone laughed at Jimmy's play at humor, and he continued.

"The skinny guy, Dinks . . . he just called. Agent Kennedy is still under observation, but besides a concussion, she appears to be okay."

Oba Ibn Jahi replied in a calm and knowing manner, "She'll be just fine . . . Up and about later today."

"I hope so," the professor replied.

"I know so," came the quick response.

"Ah yes, sorry."

Jimmy had just recalled Oba's gift, and felt as if he (Jimmy) were being rude, although unintentionally.

"Not at all, young man . . . You've been through quite an ordeal and have much to think on."

Again, Oba was right on.

Jimmy then said, "I almost forgot . . . breakfast is nearly ready."

The older men were agreeable, and said they would head down right away . . .

Jimmy felt an urge to talk with the older Egyptian man, as Cooool had suggested, but was unsure if it was appropriate, given the circumstances.

But naturally, Oba knew that Jimmy wanted to talk, so he said to Cooool, "We'll be right behind you."

Cooool understood, grabbed his pillow and blankets, and moved back through the door.

Jimmy was anxious and concerned, sensing that something profound was unfolding . . . as though his life hung on the words of the older man.

Oba understood, breathed deeply . . . and said, "Soon . . . you'll sense it coming, moving toward you in secrecy . . . a bloodlust quivering the lips of this enemy grim. So strong its hatred, that ebon sweat drips to line its trail of darkness. A creature so vile, it haunts demon's dreams. For it is The Un-Soul, Mercy's Bane, The Collector of Screams . . ."

Jimmy stood mesmerized, looking into the man's distant eyes as Oba carried on . . . , ". . . but there is more to be seen and known, more than what the mirror shows. For when it catches you, seeks your end . . . it will learn with certainty that you are more than Jimmy Kassakatis . . . you are Souldier! . . . Guardian of the Lost! . . . Wielder of The Light!"

The man's raised voice had hit a crescendo, and then paused to let his words hit home, before he finished confidently, "And this Shadow . . . will find you ready."

Chapter 64

Far, Far Away

Oba turned away from Jimmy, to rest his arms upon the deck railing, and stared off into a deep blue sky.

Jimmy stood still, too stunned by what Oba had just said, that he, well . . . said nothing for the next minute or so. Finally, the professor spoke up, inquiring, "What did you mean . . . when you said I was a soldier . . . wielder of the light?"

"Souldier . . . s o u l . . . anyway, I don't really know," came the truthful, yet unpopular, reply.

"I thought you knew everything . . ."

"I know things, Jimmy . . . many things, but not *every* thing. Two last things . . . your friends . . . you cannot protect them, but you'll need them before it's over. And finally . . . your deed will be done, but only when you wield The Light . . . by making a leap of faith."

Jimmy furrowed his brow and moved a few feet to stand beside the older man, and came to the conclusion that Oba knew nothing more or he would have said so.

"Thank you," Jimmy said sincerely, as he joined his wise colleague in staring out . . . into the blue beyond.

The solace was interrupted when Oba said aloud, "Yes, we're finished. It's time."

"Huh?" came the confused response from the younger gentleman beside him, as the door to the roof opened.

Cooool had returned and joined them, striding to stand on the opposite side of Jimmy.

Jimmy figured correctly that the Thai man must have spoken to Oba telepathically. He was right. It was a familiar exercise for the gifted pair.

Jimmy then asked the obvious. "It's time . . . for what?"

Cooool replied somewhat somberly, "To *go*, Jimmy. To find our place in the world again. We will eat and then drift away, as if you had never known us."

"Aren't you going home?"

"No, my friend," Cooool began. "We cannot risk putting our families through another nightmare. Oba is uncertain of our fate. DEEPER was destroyed, yes, but it may be rebuilt. And *if* so . . . they could come looking for the three of us."

Before Jimmy could ask, Cooool said, "I communicated with Schae-Schae and thankfully convinced her to join us."

"If I may ask . . . where will the wind take you?" the concerned professor asked, borrowing a favorite line of Karen Two Storms.

Oba answered, "Jimmy, you remember the original Star Wars movie, in the very beginning where it said 'A long time ago in a galaxy far, far away . . .'?"

The youngest among them nodded . . . as Oba finished with . . . "We're going even farther than that."

The unexpected and beautifully timed humor set the men to roaring with laughter. Any neighbors that were still in bed were likely awakened . . . and sure enough, Jimmy's least favorite responded . . .

"Will you please keep it down?! It's 8:30 in the morning. For God's sake, how's a good Christian woman to get a decent sleep . . . ?"

Vernice Lumbutter was throwing a fit and could be heard within her home 80 feet away. The normally respectful Mr. Kassakatis then laughed as loud as he had ever laughed in his life, and the other men couldn't help but join him.

Meanwhile, the kitchen was bristling with activity, as Alex and Rae had arisen early and were preparing breakfast for everyone. Alex was putting the finishing touches on some killer Belgian waffles, using the very waffle maker that he had given Jimmy this past Christmas, while Rae was arranging a sliced-fruit platter.

Alex and Rae had already showered and had begun breakfast when they spotted Jimmy and Dee up and about, followed soon after by Mr. Grumpy, Tommy Brando. Tommy hated getting up in the morning, dreading even the thought of moving a muscle while still lying in bed, much less showering. He wasn't rude to the others, but kept to himself and tended to get back to normal within an hour of rising.

Dee wasn't feeling well, and after spending more time than usual in the bathroom, finally came out.

Dee, Tommy, Alex, and Rae were sitting quietly at the kitchen table when Jimmy and his newfound friends returned from the roof, looking to eat. There was plenty to eat and Cooool and Oba kept beaming, overjoyed by a home-cooked meal . . . it had been so long . . .

Dee and Tommy had already finished eating and made their way to the sink to wash their dishes, before proceeding to sit in the living room. Rae and Alex gobbled down their remaining food and followed Dee and Tommy's example by washing their own dishes.

Rae then said politely, "Please, have a seat, we're all done."

She was motioning for Jimmy, Oba, and Cooool to sit, and after filling their plates, they did so, nodding to Rae and the others. Alex and Rae then joined Dee and Tommy in the living room.

No one spoke the entire time the three men ate, and Alex decided to check the Weather Channel to see what was called for. He turned the volume down, and they all noticed that thunderstorms were expected the next two nights. After getting what he was looking for, Alex turned the TV off as the doorbell rang.

Dee hustled off the love-seat to answer, while everyone stood, alarmed.

Cooool then announced, "It's all right, it's a friend."

Dee opened the door to see an "interesting looking" short girl. Dee thought she was probably about eleven or so. It was Schae-Schae, who began to speak when Oba and Cooool moved out to greet her, hugging her tightly.

Cooool said, "Schae-Schae! So glad you got here okay."

Schae-Schae was happy to see the older "dudes," but wouldn't show it too much.

Dee then invited her in, to which Oba mentioned, "We'll be leaving in a few minutes, the three of us. But if I may be presumptuous, would it be okay to offer the girl some breakfast?"

Dee immediately responded that she was more than welcome and ushered everyone inside, noticing as she did so that there wasn't a car or anything waiting. Dee wondered if the girl had walked.

Schae-Schae had been born prematurely and had never grown as tall as other girls, and most were fooled into thinking she was weak, vulnerable. Nothing was farther from the truth. She was a fighter, and while generally very cool, she could turn from tulip to tiger if provoked.

Schae-Schae was escorted directly to the kitchen to eat as Cooool introduced her to everyone. She was used to being stared at, but she didn't care enough about what others thought to let it get to her. She was a rebel of sorts, and liked it that way. Beyond the makeup, she was a very cute girl, with wildly braided jet-black hair, black lipstick, heavy mascara, and two thick finger-made marks below her left eye . . . a black one with a matching white one underneath it. She wore black tennis shoes, surfer shorts, and a long-sleeved, see-through, black blouse over a white sleeveless-T.

Dee's first impression was right on, Schae-Schae was indeed "interesting."

The young girl was finishing her food alone, as Oba and Cooool had moved into the living room to chat with everyone for a few minutes.

Cooool had let Jimmy know that it was all right to tell his friends the truth about he and Oba, so Jimmy took the time to explain how he had come to know Cooool and Oba, as well as the still-eating Schae-Schae . . . and the truth about them all. Questions abounded and were answered openly, and everyone present seemed satisfied that they were "caught up" on the important matters.

The sadness and totality of the situation that had occurred to these three at DEEPER became evident, and Dee was particularly overcome with emotion.

Cooool spoke to her telepathically and attempted to express that it was okay . . . it was over. The surprise at having someone speak to you without words was enough to distract one from their thoughts, but the way he said things gave her a sense of comfort. She could see why Jimmy had come to care so much for him. It was as if they had known each other forever, though not at all.

Oba then asked Jimmy to join him and Cooool topside . . . just once more. Jimmy agreed and followed them up to the small deck.

The men stood as they had earlier, leaning on the wooden railing . . . overlooking the calming waters of the bay . . . enjoying the beautiful silence. The wind began to pick up, and the sky, which had been so blue, had begun to fill with gray.

Oba then said aloud, "It's time."

Cooool nodded knowingly and pointed into the distance for Jimmy to see.

There was a big plane sinking as it got closer. For a moment, Jimmy thought it would crash into the water, but it was a seaplane and touched down, gliding across the bay, leaving a long trail of disturbed water in its wake. It was headed in their direction.

"Perfect timing," Cooool said.

Jimmy wanted to ask, but decided against it. Instead, he smiled and followed the men back downstairs. Oba and Cooool gathered Schae-Schae from the kitchen and waved to the others before heading out the back door to make their way down to the beach.

Jimmy moved his head to indicate that Dee, Tommy, Rae, and Alex should come see this. Sure enough, Jimmy and the others walked out the back door and down the stairs to see the large seaplane resting a few hundred feet off shore. The powered rubber raft sounded like a muffled dragonfly as it skipped away from the plane to come ashore, where the three escapees waited.

After the passengers were settled within the plane, Jimmy and the others went back inside the house as the plane lifted off and sped into the gray. Jimmy went to stand again on the roof and watched as the plane faded away into the distance. Dee had come up through the deck door and brought him the phone, telling him it was Oba, before returning back through the door. Jimmy answered.

"Oba?"

"Yes. My friend . . . take care . . . and beware the reluctant dragon." Oba then hung up.

Jimmy was surprised. It was something his father had always said to him and Alex. He then stared off into the gathering dark clouds and finally, for the first time, understood its meaning. He shifted his gaze heavenward, winked, and said, "Thanks, Dad."

His thoughts moved once again to the plane's occupants. Jimmy had just met these good people, but had felt as if he were losing good friends. He was. He would never see them again, but somehow knew that they would be okay . . .

no matter what they faced . . .

no matter where they were going . . .

and no matter how far, far away.

Chapter 65

. . . Off to See the Soul Man

It was nearly 10:00 a.m. as the doctor left the room. His patient's headache was one for the ages, and the cut across her left cheek had been deep, but an otherwise-healthy and fortunate. Carol Kennedy had just been told she would soon be released from the hospital. Dinks was with her in her room the entire time, leaving only briefly for a bathroom break. He had just—minutes earlier—filled Kennedy in on what had occurred after the blast. She lay in bed, focusing through the pain, considering a great many things, including the loss of her latest partner, as well as Jimmy Kassakatis. But at the moment, she was deciding whether or not Ricky Dinks had fulfilled his obligation to her and the FBI. Her conclusion came quickly . . . and she said to him in a professional tone, "You're free to go, Dinks. You owe neither the FBI nor society a debt. Under your circumstances, I can arrange for you to enter the Witness Protection Program if you wish it."

Dinks averted her eyes for a moment . . . thinking about the significance of her words. One thing for sure, he wasn't the WPP-type. And though every instinct and shred of good sense screamed at him to just go into hiding in some other big city, to leave this place and never look back, he looked back at her and shocked himself with what he uttered.

"I'd like to finish this thing first . . . help you end it."

The Case Agent was just as surprised by his response as he was, but could tell he was being sincere. She then cracked a smile through her pain and kept the "unforeseen response" theme going.

"Thank you, Ricky. I'd like that."

Dinks nodded, pleased that she was agreeable on one hand (even calling him Ricky) . . . but on the other hand, he was wondering what the hell he was doing.

Kennedy continued, "Now that you're sticking around, you need to know something. Last night, before the explosion . . . I saw something . . . I saw *him*."

She had a faraway look in her eyes and continued as Dinks was all ears.

"There was a *rush* of *darkness* that shot out from the doors just before the blast. It was him, The Shadow That Speaks."

Dinks's eyes were wide enough to drive a tractor through, and he was taking it all in as the agent added, "That means Kassakatis is off the hook, although whoever The Shadow is, it's unlikely that he knows that. There's little doubt that he was too busy getting out to realize who I was. This is my first real break on this case."

Kennedy then sat up fully, threw her feet to one side of the bed, and finished with, "So . . . we have work to do. I'll call the team together, brief them all, and then we're off to see the Soul Man."

· · · · · · · · · · · · · · · · · · ·

Jimmy spent roughly twenty minutes on the deck, catching up with the SoulBound, aware that Dee and the others were waiting on him. He didn't mean to be rude, but this was "only going to take a minute," he thought. Everyone had gathered into the cathedral room created for the professor's return. He shook the men's hands, hugging Marie and the other women, including a very jubilant Gina Imbragulio. She was becoming noticeably more open with her emotions. He then came around to Carrie Ann and gave her a hug she'd not soon forget. Jimmy was delighted to see that the child was not only okay, but very well indeed.

They all sat down at the table and discussed the events since his disconnect with them a couple days prior. After the quick exchange, he explained that he needed to go do the same with Dee and the others, and thanked everyone for everything they'd done for him. He apologized for being so quick, but they all understood completely.

Jimmy entered the living room to another round of hands and hugs. Although they spent the ride home with him the night before and had a brief discussion on the way, somehow seeing him here moving about his own home was confirmation that Jimmy was really back. He sat next to Dee and they held hands as Jimmy said, "Sorry, guys, I know you've been waiting, but I had to go over things with the Sou . . ."

Jimmy had paused, as he was still not used to being open about his gift in front of Alex and Rae. He continued. ". . . with the SoulBound. Look, we all understand the seriousness of what's happening. And you need to understand that this is something that I will need to handle alone. I can't risk any of you."

Jimmy expected and got a backlash . . . Alex beat the rest with an animated reply. "Strength in numbers, bro! You need a plan, and we can help you with that. Look . . . I know you have a lot of help with all those people inside you, but we're your family. You'd want to do the same for any of us if things were switched around . . . you know it's true."

Dee added quite emotionally, "Baby, please don't expect us to just go away while you fight this . . . this monster! No human being can do what it does . . . look at how many soldiers it killed all by itself!"

Rae remained quiet, although she nodded agreement with Alex and Dee.

Jimmy tried to respond, but his best friend beat him to the punch.

"Dude, are you serious?"

Though he hadn't raised his voice, Tommy was noticeably angry as he rose from his chair and continued.

"I may not know much, but I do know that a great many people have lost their lives in recent days, and we've all been affected by the twisted prick! Look at what just a small piece of him did to you. And it's not over. And you figure that we—who have gone through a bit of Hell ourselves—are going to let you have at it alone? Not a chance, Jimbo . . . you're my best friend . . . I'm sticking with you, dude . . . no matter what."

Jimmy sat rubbing his hands together, looking down at his feet, contemplating how to respond. He didn't want their involvement . . . *that* he was sure of . . . but he remembered Oba's message. This was that moment Oba spoke of . . . Jimmy would need them, no matter how he felt . . . he would need them. He was conflicted, shaking his head, trying to make this fateful decision, when Marie spoke to him and settled him.

"Jimmy, remember Nan's message . . . remember . . ."

Jimmy was confused momentarily when he caught Marie's meaning . . . She was referring to Nan's message given to her family, while on her deathbed. Jimmy could still feel Nan's essence within him and recalled her deep-rooted thoughts on abandonment. Dee, Alex, Tommy, and Rae . . . they wouldn't abandon Jimmy, and though it was against his better judgment, he wouldn't abandon them.

"Okay . . . I understand . . . and appreciate it. But things are going to get worse before they get better . . . you need to know that."

A figurative sigh of relief permeated in the room, but Jimmy then said quite seriously, "There's something I haven't told you . . . something you should know . . ."

Chapter 66

Brazen Hatred

Agent Kennedy had just finished meeting with her team, wherein she had explained what had happened since their last meeting. This included explaining the death of Special Agent Gottranelli, as well as her actually seeing the serial killer the night before. She reminded them to stay on alert and to be ready to move on a moment's notice. As the team broke up, one might have expected that hands would be patted upon her shoulder, and condolences uttered, but no . . . nothing but "yes, ma'am" and cold emotion.

Kennedy knew that in law enforcement, whether it be a local Sheriff's department, a big city police force, or the FBI, losing a partner, especially more than one, was frowned upon . . . in a deeply profound way. She was becoming a pariah . . . an outcast, losing her hard-earned respect and credibility. But she had a job to do . . . and she never wavered from her goal.

It wasn't traditional for an agent to inform a dead partner's family of their loss, but Kennedy felt responsible and took these matters to heart. As she had with Sykes and Omega before, she began preparations . . . and would soon be off to see Gotti's wife. Kennedy was severely shaken . . . emotionally drained and slowly breaking down after dealing with the devastation of losing another partner. Dealing with the families was just so hard, as there were no words to comfort them . . . only helplessness, emptiness.

As she gathered her things, her superior—Field Office Supervisor Aiden Dashiell—entered the room and asked her to join him in his office. He was tall and thin, about six feet five, with thick white hair that had remnants of the blond from his younger years. He had served as the senior agent before Kennedy and knew the job as well as anyone. Dashiell was a good man, but since taking the job five years prior, had become more and more "management" and less and less "one of them."

She followed him to the office and sat, thinking this was not going to go well.

Dashiell shut the door behind him and proceeded to his chair, where slowly he sat down, tapping his fingers upon his desk as he did.

Kennedy knew that tap.

"Carol, it's great to see that you're okay. Your well-being is important to this office, as the senior active agent, everyone looks up to you as a . . ."

"You have something to say?" replied a knowing and agitated woman.

He smiled sarcastically and replied, "Certainly. You're putting both this office and me on the hook for a shot at personal glory . . . the big catch . . . at any cost. I understand the thing with Dinkins, to a point, but for God's sake, you're going rogue on us, Kennedy. It stops . . . NOW!"

The veteran agent sat taking the barrage while preparing a counter that was so well-orchestrated she should have had a baton in her hand. She stood and walked through his office and stared out the window and began her deft reply.

"You may be expecting a strong rebuttal, but I admit that my lack of judgment has to be cause for concern. I would be upset too, if I were you."

Carol paused a moment and then found her seat again, looking Dashiell in the eye.

"Sir, I'm this close to catching him and in understanding your position, the right position, I'll be vigilant in my duties. I've worked too hard and too long to embarrass myself or this office. I realize that I've been a bit loose with things, but losing three partners can do that to a person. I owe it to the agency and to the memories of those men to finish it the right way . . . you have my word on it."

"Glad to hear it, Kennedy . . . ," Dashiell replied as he leaned forward, his large hands became demonstrative, as he continued.

"And let me make sure that I'm clear . . . If you keep vital case information to yourself, or openly break protocol again . . . you're not only off the case, you're history here. Period! I'm bringing you a new partner . . . out of New York. His name is Kevin Goldring, and he's come highly recommended. He'll arrive here tomorrow."

Kennedy then rose from her chair and replied convincingly, "Thank you."

Kennedy shook his hand, nodded agreeably as she did, and then walked out of his office and back toward hers. As she went, she thought proudly, *He doesn't even know what hit him.*

• • • • • • • • • • • • • • • • • •

Torture resonated throughout the dank, hot air of the basement, and fear was a constant until the eighty-seven-year-old man's heart could stand no more . . . the agony, the sin-laden session, ran on for nearly half an hour . . . twenty-nine minutes longer than Jack expected. This was how Hill "stretched" . . . how he "worked things out." He had been livid right from the moment his eyes opened . . . there was hell to pay, and he was the collector.

The victim's name was not "old man," but rather Albert Showers, and he was one of the good people in the world. He was a WWII veteran who served his country, fighting valiantly on the beaches of Normandy. He had seven children, and so many grandchildren and great-grandchildren that he had lost count. Albert fiercely loved his wife, Anne, letting her know it every day of their beautiful existence together. He was in mourning, since she passed from cancer only a few weeks prior. She fought the good fight and would not go gently into that good night . . . no, she wanted to live . . . despite the odds, despite the pain. Like Albert had just done.

Albert had always been known as a kind and gentle soul, and a real sweet fellow his whole life. The man had just finished visiting with some of his great-grandchildren when The Shadow That Speaks struck. Albert didn't deserve to go out this way . . . he had earned respect and admiration from all who had known him . . . loved him. But Jack couldn't care less. He hurt Albert in ways that would make a normal mind want to shut down from the horror. Thirty minutes of anguish and Jack had bloody loved it.

At this moment, the exhilaration of the kill was wearing off and the anger over Kassakatis was on his mind. Gage had suffered

The Shadow's wrath, but Jimmy was going to experience the full gambit of misery.

Brazen hatred pumped through his cold black veins, and even Jack cringed . . . as the sick wheels began to turn.

Chapter 67

Heartbeats

Everyone was paying close attention to Jimmy, as he had something important to tell them, and the room was dead silent as he began.

"Just a bit ago, Oba told me something quite . . . profound. As I explained earlier, Oba is gifted, he just knows things . . . and he says that the Shadow is going to be coming for me soon. He says that I am Souldier; Guardian of the Lost . . . and Wielder of The Light. I guess, he means that I'm not just a Soul-Collector . . . that I am something more. And that 'something' will overcome The Shadow."

Dee and the others were astounded . . . and not one said a word, as if they were hoping Jimmy would continue with answers to questions still forming in the wake of that bombshell.

While he offered nothing concrete, he did add, "I feel as if I can sense him . . . and I expect he's coming for me . . . tonight . . . here."

That raised their eyebrows and their blood pressure . . . their hearts beating a mile a minute. Here? Tonight?

Dee, who had still been holding her man's hand, squeezed it and asked, "Did Oba tell you how . . ." she paused uncomfortably, "Do you know how . . . to kill him?"

"Not exactly, no.

"Carrie Ann and the rest of the SoulBound created a sort of a wave of light, and destroyed that thing within me . . . but it was where they could get to it. I'm not sure how that would work, if at all, on The Shadow."

Dee stood, and though she wasn't feeling especially well, squeezed Jimmy's hand, kissed him on the cheek, and then whispered in his ear, "You're my warrior/poet . . . I believe in you."

Something warm enveloped him, as he soaked in her words, soaked in the smell of her, and looked into her proud doe eyes. He squeezed her hand back, smiled, and felt a surge of confidence wash over him.

The phone rang just then, and Alex answered. It was Agent Kennedy. Alex motioned Jimmy to the phone, and after Jimmy answered and had a brief exchange, he hung up and announced, "Agent Kennedy is coming over to meet with me. She'll be here in about two hours."

Dee then responded that she was going to take Rae with her to the pharmacy to pick up some medicine and that they'd return shortly.

Tommy felt like a caged animal . . . having a great deal of energy, but nowhere to focus it . . . not yet at least. He picked up the phone and placed a delivery order from Momma Asonte's. He ordered four pizzas, figuring he could woof one down himself.

Alex was in a similar state of mind and paced about the house, waiting for the food, for the girls to return, and for the agent. He figured this was his best chance to talk with his brother.

"Jimmy . . . bro, things are getting a bit crazy. I feel useless. What can I do?"

Jimmy responded that he understood and that it would be great if Alex could stop at the store and get the highest possible watt bulbs for every lamp, light fixture, and security light around the perimeter of the house. This was an important job, Jimmy explained. And Alex responded, "I'm on it . . . consider it done."

Alex grabbed a pen and a sheet of paper from the printer and went about noting the lights in and around the house, before heading out to get the upgrades.

Jimmy took this "down time" to discuss his ideas with the SoulBound. Everyone was abuzz as they were once again seated in the cathedral room. Koketai came right out and asked Jimmy how he planned to defeat this enemy, to which Jimmy truthfully retorted that he didn't know.

Jean-Paul spoke up then, *"Oba said you were Souldier . . . not 'a soldier,' but rather 'Souldier,' as if that meant something special."*

Brennan added, *"Yeah, no one has mentioned it, but I took it as if it were spelled S O U L . . . perhaps it means that your souls . . . us . . . have to help you, like we did with IT?"*

The discussion continued as everyone, including Carrie Ann, chipped in with thoughts on how to survive and defeat the Dreaded One.

As Jimmy was engrossed in the meeting, the doorbell rang and Tommy was pleased to see a young delivery girl at the door, who then handed over the pizzas. After paying and leaving a generous tip, Tommy laid the four pizzas out on the table, yelled aloud that they were in the house and ready to eat, and then grabbed a thick paper plate and indulged.

Jimmy heard him and finished up with the SoulBound, agreeing to check back with them later. He headed for the kitchen and grabbed a few slices of sausage and pepperoni pan, his favorite. It was so good . . . the two were eating like there was no tomorrow when Tommy, being Tommy, said, "Dude, this is so good . . . so heavenly, perhaps you can throw it at the dark bastard and send him back to Hell?"

Jimmy choked briefly on a slice and coughed up a storm, trying to laugh at that pathetic, but funny, comment.

Tommy, seeing Jimmy in this state, snickered even more, but was patting the professor upon his back as he did.

Jimmy was fine and threw a slice at Tommy, which, as Tommy proudly pointed out, "Missed me!"

Some things never change . . .

Dee and Rae had come unnoticed through the front door with a couple of plastic pharmacy bags in tow, and upon spotting the men's juvenile antics, Rae remarked, "Excuse me, children . . . Did we miss anything?"

Tommy and Jimmy weren't insulted in the least, and Tommy intentionally and playfully stood in front of the kitchen table and responded, "No, nothing to report . . . no pizza being delivered today or anything."

"You're such an idiot," came Rae's partially playful response, as she and Dee both rolled their eyes and headed into the bathroom.

Tommy and Jimmy eased down from their messing around, and finished up with their pizza. They knew the time for play was done with . . . like they were in the eye of the hurricane . . . the gathering darkness encircling them. And they were right.

At that moment, a scream resonated from the bathroom, and the men leapt to the shut door in a few heartbeats, when Jimmy knocked and asked, "Is everything okay?'

Rae cracked opened the door with a weird look on her face, and squeezed past Jimmy to grab Tommy by his arm and lead him away down the hall.

Jimmy then looked back to Dee, who slowly opened the door all the way open, walked up to him with a nervous smile upon her face . . . and said, "Two tests, both with the same result. Sweetheart, I'm pregnant."

Chapter 68

. . . Something Wicked

Jimmy beamed like a supernova, aglow in a moment he had been looking forward to for quite some time. He immediately hugged his love, squeezing her, before backing off a bit, and apologizing for being too rough with her.

Dee laughed it off and said, "I'm not suddenly fragile."

Jimmy smiled in return, and was bombarded by the SoulBound's congratulations. His happiness was undeniable, but he suddenly felt compelled to take Dee outside to the flower garden; and after asking, she joined him. They were holding hands as lovers do, although their normal giddiness was pale in comparison to the joy they felt.

Jimmy had told Dee about the garden, and why it was so special to him. There was a cool-looking gnarled wooden sign that was hung upon a lattice that proclaimed warmly: Nan's Garden.

Dee really loved it and had planned to help out with it when time permitted, but was new to flowers, besides knowing about the common ones everyone seems to know. Her mother had a garden similar to this one; with dozens of varieties sprinkled generously about in a floral rainbow. Dee looked back and wondered where her head was during those days, but she saw now that she had missed out on something special.

Jimmy asked Dee to pick one that she liked . . . he had an idea. He said she needed to be sure, to sense the right one.

She was a bit confused, but knowing her man, she figured he was up to something interesting. She did as was asked, looking at so many lovely flowers, and most all in full bloom. She came to one that just felt like the right one, a gorgeous white rose.

"This one, sweetheart . . . I love it."

Jimmy was elated with her choice, and replied, "Call it fate or destiny . . . but it was the one I hoped for most! It's the flower I'd always thought would make a great name for a baby girl . . . it's an Anastasia Rose."

"Awwwwww . . . How beautiful. I love it, Jimmy. Although if it's a boy, we're staying away from the floral arrangements."

Jimmy laughed with her and said he agreed on that. He picked the soft-petaled white rose for her and told her that he wanted her to keep it safe forever . . . as a reminder of this moment, of their happiness.

Dee became somber as he handed her the rose . . . and Jimmy sensed what this was about.

"I'm going to be all right; we all are, sweetie. The Reverend reminded me of an old passage that referred to not being given more of a burden than you can bear . . . or something to that effect."

"Losing you on this day . . . of all days . . ." she replied and began to tear up, wrapping her arms around herself.

"I am stronger than I knew, recently coming to that conclusion through the help of some good friends . . . and whether or not this gift that I have is divine or not, *whatever* the reason is, it seems destined that this would happen. I dunno . . ."

Jimmy looked away at the ever-darkening skies, and then said, "I sense him . . . he'll come late . . . like a thief in the night. And as Oba said, I'll be ready. I don't yet know how . . . but I won't fail. I'll find a way to end him."

Jimmy then turned to Dee and said, "Sweetheart . . . the baby . . . please see that you need to lea . . ."

Dee had cut him off, "I'm staying, Jimmy . . . period."

Jimmy knew this was going to be difficult, but backed away from it . . . for now.

Alex pulled into the driveway to their right, around the front of the home, and he was loaded down with bags.

Jimmy told Dee to go back inside where it was safer and that he'd help his brother.

She did . . . too concerned about the oncoming collision to haggle over his over-protectiveness.

The brothers went around the home with Tommy pitching in, and fitted the new high-watt bulbs. Alex then said he had a cool idea, and began to show them, when Dee cleared her throat and widened her eyes at Jimmy, as she deftly brushed her hand across her mid-section. Jimmy caught her meaning and announced, "Thanks, Alex, just a sec . . . Rae knows already . . . but Dee and I have news; we're pregnant."

Tommy said to a round of laughter, "Both of you?"

John Jaden said to the other SoulBound, who were gathered together, *"I like this guy; he took the words right outta my mouth."*

As was happening around Jimmy, within him followed suit. There were laughs all around . . .

Alex immediately shook Jimmy's hand, all the while congratulating them both, then hugged Dee gently. Tommy shook Jimmy's hand and smiled, before following Alex in line to hug Ms. Fragile.

Despite the congratulations and apparent happiness, the men had an air of awareness about them. They were certainly happy about the baby. But under the circumstances . . . and on this day, of all days . . . it was hard to get too excited.

Alex then went back to his "cool idea." He pulled five utility vests from the bags Jimmy helped bring in a bit ago, and explained that it would take some time, but these may just be lifesavers. He went on to show them that by cutting holes in various locations throughout the vest, it would allow for them to rig some ultra-bright spotlights to the vests, to bombard The Shadow with light if he attacked. They would have the ability to turn the vest lights on and off at will with a switch, although he explained that the plastic vest would melt in short order, so to use it sparingly, if possible.

Neither Alex, nor the others, knew that Gage's minions had attempted a similar light barrage the night prior . . . with deadly consequences. So everyone agreed that it was a good idea, and told Alex how smart he was to cook up the idea. He said there was more . . . and pulled out some battery-powered portable spotlights . . . one million candlepower.

Jimmy and Tommy nodded appreciatively. Something to wear and something to hold . . . Again, they thanked him for everything and Alex nodded his head in acknowledgement, then got started right away on the vests.

The doorbell rang and there was a knock at the door, simultaneously. Everyone tensed up as Jimmy answered the door. As expected, he got his first good look at the woman he had heard so much about . . . Agent Kennedy. She was dressed, as usual, in a professional pant-suit, dark blue this day, and was accompanied by her pet project, ex-con and ex-many things, Ricky Dinks. Standing out at the end of his driveway were two agents, the blue jackets with the large yellow letters "FBI" giving them away.

Agent Kennedy saw Jimmy's gaze and said, "Friends . . . ."

Jimmy nodded and introduced himself (even though they had briefly spotted one another the night before) and then welcomed them inside. He added that an introduction seemed proper under the circumstances, to which Kennedy responded, "I agree, Jimmy . . . may I call you Jimmy?"

"Yes, of course . . ."

"Good. This is my associate, Mr. Dinkins."

She tilted her still-hurting head toward Dinks and the men shook hands . . . with Ricky appearing a bit wary of the taller man.

Jimmy then asked the agent where she wished to discuss matters, and she said that she'd like it if he would accompany her back outside. Jimmy was agreeable and turned to tell everyone that he was going to be outside with Kennedy for a bit.

Dinks sauntered inside, and Rae smiled at him . . . he was starting to dig her.

Jimmy trailed the case agent, as they walked around the south side of the home. Kennedy wound up in almost the identical spot that she had been shown the black jackal card and footprints. The agent turned to the professor and just looked at him, into his deep blue eyes.

She wasn't speaking, but Jimmy got the sense that she was testing him somehow, sizing him up. In what amounted to merely an eight-second delay, the agent finally broke the uncomfortable silence.

"Something tells me there is not much time . . . you get that sense?"

"Yeah . . . I believe he's coming here, tonight."

"I figured that he might . . . Jimmy, before last night, you had become our prime suspect . . . I was certain at one point that you were the killer."

Jimmy would've been shocked if not already aware of this through Dee, and he shifted a bit as he was taking it all in . . . standing here having a chat with the woman who headed an FBI Task Force that was just hunting him down.

Kennedy continued. "I still have questions for you though . . . there are things I need to understand if I'm going to be able to catch him."

"Well . . . as I said, he's coming here tonight, I know he is."

"How can you be so sure?"

"When I was last with him, he left me a little present . . . it's hard to explain, but it was a small part of his essence, his soul . . . . It tortured me throughout It's stay, and had virtually taken over my mind . . . controlled me. That is until last night when my friends helped me fight back, and It was destroyed . . ."

Kennedy stood transfixed as Jimmy continued.

"Since last night, and even a little bit before, I seem to have a connection to him . . . I can sense him . . . his eagerness, thrill to kill."

Jimmy had drifted off a bit at the end as he looked away . . . and the rains began to fall lightly in the wake of the first rolls of thunder.

Kennedy replied, "We're standing just outside your bedroom window . . . did you know he stood where we are standing now?"

Jimmy shook his head no, and was upset at the thought that The Shadow had already been here. Just a few feet from Dee!

The case agent continued. "He dropped a card, this . . ."

She pulled a copy of one of the business cards that The Shadow often left behind, the one with the black jackal imprinted, and Jimmy became even more agitated as he glared at the figure . . . just like the one from his nightmares.

The rain began to increase and the agent said that they should get inside, and while he heard her, he was too busy focusing every fiber of his being into his thoughts. The old Jimmy, the one untainted, never got this angry. But this Jimmy, this scowling man who had been through a living Hell, was somewhat changed . . . as he could feel the hatred coursing through his cold veins. It was undeniable; he was beginning to like it.

· · · · · · · · · · · · · · · · · · ·

There was a cool and ill wind that blew through Jimmy's soul, and the SoulBound cringed at what was happening. They were not at all happy with the development.

Karen Two Storms, who had loved going to her local playhouse in D.C. to watch the various Shakespearean plays, walked past the others, still huddled within the cathedral room, and muttered the quote from *Macbeth* in Spanish, *"Algo diabólico viene."* *(Something wicked this way comes.)*

Chapter 69

And the Night Crept Upon Them

The tempest picked up strength and the rains fell hard as Jimmy and Agent Kennedy spent the next few hours talking in the kitchen, spilling everything they could think of to help one another understand as much as possible about both the killer, and Jimmy's gifts.

When Jimmy explained the incredible information received through Oba, without divulging his name, the agent ran her hands through her hair before removing her jacket. She had an odd look about her . . . as if she was having a hard time digesting his words. She was. This . . . all of this . . . was too much. She was trained in science, in forensics, in cold-harsh reality . . . and even though she saw The Shadow with her own eyes, she felt as if this train was jumping off the tracks.

Kennedy stood and thanked Jimmy for being honest with her, but explained she needed a few minutes alone . . . she needed time to think.

Jimmy moved away from her to go check on his now pregnant fiancée.

Rae and Dee were lying down in Jimmy and Dee's bedroom, and Dee had fallen asleep while Rae was watching the TV.

Elsewhere, Alex had gone home shortly after Kennedy and Dinks arrived, but said he would be back before long.

Tommy was online, while Dinks had stayed in the living room, switching between The Learning Channel and the Sci-Fi channel, because he figured he might just find something useful for later that night.

Kennedy remained alone in the kitchen, but decided to go to the bathroom instead. She'd had wanted to go for a bit anyway . . . at least here she'd have a few minutes to herself without Dinks pretending not to listen. Her mind was assailed with innumerous issues and thoughts. But she was used to that as an agent. She focused and organized the most important thoughts as if she were at a computer and had set up a spreadsheet.

Prioritize.

She was caught between a rock and FBI protocol. Protocol and common sense dictated to have these people taken away from the home under knowledge that a serial killer was coming later that night . . . but she felt that this was her one best shot to end it, with Kassakatis's help. If he could sense The Shadow That Speaks, it stood to reason that the monster could sense Jimmy. So pulling them out wouldn't work . . . only delay the inevitable showdown.

Kennedy calmly dialed a special number on her cell phone and was connected to her team within moments.

"I need everyone, and I mean the entire team, here at Kassakatis's home . . . ASAP! We have a date with destiny, and we don't want to be late."

Jimmy stood in the doorframe, leaned on one side, and stared at the future Mrs. James Carson Kassakatis . . . lying fast asleep in bed. Rae was looking at him, smiling. Jimmy returned her slight smile with one of his own, as he looked back at Dee for a split second, then back to Rae again. He then winked at her, nodding his head a bit to indicate his appreciation for her friendship with Dee.

It's funny how body language can say what takes verbalizing much, much longer. It's a language that everyone can understand, no matter what country they are from or what time. Jimmy spoke six languages, but always told his students and others that it was the seventh that was his favorite.

Alex had returned, just after five o'clock, and just ahead of the swarm of agents that descended upon the home. They had all been here before, but there was a real sense of urgency in their movements . . . was it their resolve or just their need to get out of the rain? It didn't really matter.

Kennedy came out to the large truck that had parked close to the driveway . . . it had a ramp into the temporary office inside. It was a mobile command center of sorts, where she then met with her team leaders, who started issuing orders per her instructions. First order of business . . . they had to clear the neighbors from their homes and then block off access to the large cul-de-sac.

Outside was filled with yelling, movement and purpose, while inside Jimmy's home there was an eerie calm. As the minutes turned into hours, their calm became nervous anticipation. Alex had just finished with all five of his so-called Onslaught Vests.

He said he liked the name because they were only potentially devastating while "on."

Rae and Dee didn't say a word, though they both thought that naming the vests was pointless . . . but knew guys loved to come up with cool names for their gadgets. After a few tests, and subsequent adjustments, it seemed that the vests would work on some level. Again, Jimmy thanked his brother for the effort.

Ricky Dinks was watching Alex work all along, and had remained unusually quiet. He seemed to blend in, be forgotten . . . and it was most often by design, but not really in this case. He was paying attention . . . trying to understand the plan. He was a smart guy and figured that once he understood exactly what Alex was going for, then he could tweak it perhaps, improving it somehow . . . and impress everyone, including Rae. But Dinks felt useless . . . he had come up with nothing. He was used to figuring out something once he put his mind to it. However, he resigned himself to the fact that he may have bitten off more than he could chew, and went back into the living room.

The rain had stopped moments earlier, but every station called for an escalation of the ongoing storms throughout the night. The sun, which hadn't been seen most of the day, was setting, and with that as the backdrop, Kennedy finally returned. The case agent asked that everyone gather around, and they did, in the large open kitchen.

"The neighbors have been removed from the general area as a precaution, and we've insisted that they keep this quiet. The last thing we need is word getting out that we are here. A few of my best people are in various locations around your property, and the rest of my team is hanging well back, but close enough to get here in a hurry. As you have obviously seen, there are agents inside the house as well, a few posted in the bedrooms, in places that cannot be seen, and Agent Faust is on the roof, equipped with a sniper rifle and infrared scope. We've cleared out all the vehicles so as not to attract attention. Jimmy's explained that not many cars come through here, especially on a stormy night . . . so we should manage all right."

Everyone nodded and she continued.

"Normally, you would all have been cleared out along with the other neighbors, but I feel that I need Jimmy to make this work. That leads me to the rest of you. I see no reason to endanger your lives, regardless of your involvement up 'til now. We have this under control."

Dee was livid and pulled no punches. "Omega had it under control. Gotti as well, right?"

Kennedy's temperature was rising as Dee went on.

"The police had it under control when Jimmy was taken a second time! A real-life monster wants to kill the man I love . . . the father of my unborn child! This is after he's thrown hundreds of deaths in your FBI face, and you . . . who have been trying *in vain* to catch him . . . **for years** . . . have it all under control?!"

Jimmy tried to cool the tension with, "I think what Dee is tryi . . ."

He was cut off by Kennedy, who having already been on the edge, responded with, "*Dee* isn't trying to say anything other than calling me a failure. But let me tell *you* something." Kennedy moved forward a few steps to get in the face of the younger and shorter woman. "They call me something at my job . . . behind my back, but I hear them . . . they call me the 'Alpha-bitch'! It's because I busted my ass to get where I am, seeing more horror in a typical week than you have in a lifetime. I fought against male bias and the odds, to rise to the senior-most agent at my Field Office, doing a job I do better than anyone else. You're right though, Dee . . . this bastard has torn apart men I cared a great deal for, killed hundreds and laughed in my face as he did, and slaughtered men, women, and even small children along the way . . . adding to his "black and crimson caravan" . . . but if you think that . . ."

"Enough!" Jimmy shouted and sat back down at the table, as everyone's eyes were on him. "The Shadow enjoys our fear . . . weakens our minds and spirit, and promotes hatred throughout. You can feel it inside you, perhaps not as I have though, and let me tell you, he hates all of us. He wants us all to die, and in the most horrific ways. He shows no mercy, no compassion . . . and he *will not* stop. How can we overcome such a thing when we fight among ourselves? Your anger comes from the pain and anguish caused by him . . . not each other. Agent Kennedy . . . we all stay, or we all go . . . your call."

You could hear a pin drop as Kennedy contemplated a response. Her answer seemed inevitable. "I was only looking out for . . . well, anyway . . . they can stay."

Dee was feeling a bit ashamed at her outburst. She then apologized to Kennedy, who simply said, "It's over . . . it's done."

With those words, the unseen sun went down . . . and like a hungry predator, the night crept upon them.

Chapter 70

Dead Sure

The thunderstorm seemed alive . . . sinister, but Jimmy's thoughts went beyond the lightning and past the thunder that shook his home. He felt nothing at the moment, no sense, no connection, as if The Shadow didn't exist. But Jimmy knew he was somewhere out there, somewhere in the night.

Agent Kennedy walked up to him as he looked out the living room window . . . the one facing the bay. She asked him if he felt anything, if there was anything else she could use.

"No . . . but he's out there . . ."

Jimmy continued to look outside as Kennedy moved away from him and spoke aloud. "When he comes, my people and I will do what we can to catch him . . . it's our job."

Those last few words were true, but rang hollow. No one believed that the agents stood a chance, and while Kennedy wouldn't admit to it aloud, she had her doubts as well.

Jimmy responded coolly after a few moments, "You'll die . . . you and your agents. It's not coming for you though, it's coming for *me*, and I'm the only one who can stop him. You're trained, an expert . . . you know truth when you see it, when you hear it. But no, you'll go down swinging futilely when you could've just backed away and let me find a way to put him down permanently."

Jimmy stood and stared deep into the agent's eyes, then proceeded to the bathroom . . . leaving silence in his wake.

Dinks could feel the impending doom, like a pair of cold dark hands squeezing the air from his chest . . . and he was terrified. When Rae asked him if he was okay, Dinks spoke in hushed tones, loud enough for Rae alone to hear . . . fear layered thick on every word . . .

"I dunno, I feel like I'm climbing a mountain that doesn't want to be climbed. I have an uncanny sense of knowing when to get out of wherever I am, when it just feels wrong. It's how I've survived all these years. That sense, that feeling . . . *that's* what I'm getting right now . . . that turn-back-before-it's-too-late shit."

Rae leaned in as Dinks continued.

"This is different because I know it's coming, and the feeling rises up inside me and sticks in my throat. Everything moves in slow motion, while whatever it is that's coming for you moves fast . . . like a nightmare from my childhood, except this time I'm awake . . ."

Rae understood exactly what Dinks was saying . . . as she was feeling a lot like that herself. But she leaned closer to him and gently put her forehead upon his, looked deep into his eyes and said, "Fear doesn't make you a coward, Ricky . . . all of us fear. It's what we do *despite it* that defines courage. We're going to get through this . . . all of us."

Rae's words were just what he needed to hear. And as she smiled at him, rose and walked away, Ricky felt something he had never known before. And he wondered in that moment if maybe, just maybe . . . he was falling in love.

Hours passed, and Jimmy looked intently at his watch. It was accurate to the second, and it showed 11:36 p.m . . . . exactly. Jimmy noticed . . . he always noticed. He had been debating most of the night whether to approach Dee again, trying to convince her, again, to leave for both her and the baby's safety . . . but knew time had grown short. He needed to act quickly. Jimmy went over to Dee just then, pulling her aside for privacy . . . and in a very serious tone said, "Dee, please . . . I want you," he looked at her belly, ". . . *and the baby*, to get away from here."

Dee had expected this, and calmly replied, "Jimmy . . . I would never forgive myself if I were not here with you. That's a guilt . . . a negative energy, that I'd rather not carry with me the rest of my life. Would you abandon me if places were switched?"

"Dee, nothing is more important than the baby . . . nothing."

Jimmy had replied with a strong emphasis on that last word. He stared into the eyes of the woman he loved, pleading for her to see reason, but as she began to consider his words carefully, it was too late. Jimmy's face went pale as he felt that awful feeling . . . he pulled away and said aloud, "It's time . . . he's here!"

Goose bumps raised throughout as everyone had huddled in the living room.

Kennedy who had just reentered the room after making her rounds about the home, stopped in her tracks, and said quietly, "Are you sure, Jimmy?"

"Dead sure."

There was a darkening ongoing . . . and it had nothing to do with the storm, nor the night. But Dee noticed . . . and so did the others. The SoulBound still felt the chill that ran rampant throughout Jimmy, and it had not let up a bit. They were too scared to interrupt him at the moment, but Carrie Ann said aloud, without care if Jimmy got angry or not, *"He needs to find The Light within . . . it's the only way."*

Marie, who was standing beside her, had come to believe that the child's visions were real messages . . . but from whom? So she asked, *"Sweetheart, who is telling you these things?"*

The six-year-old shrugged her shoulders and replied as if it was only for her to know, *"A friend."*

Meanwhile, Alex had passed out the Onslaught Vests to Jimmy and Tommy, and put one on himself. He handed them each a portable spotlight and then thought aloud, "Uhhh, Dee and Rae, maybe you two should put a vest on . . . I made them for you."

Dee responded that she thought it was sweet of him, but she felt that perhaps Kennedy or one of the agents could use them.

Rae agreed, although the vests were somewhat appealing, despite the guys looking a bit like Ghostbusters.

At that moment, Dinks had a proverbial bolt of lightning strike him, and he leapt up excitedly and said, "I think I know how to kill him!"

That caught everyone's attention except Agent Kennedy, who had moved away to break radio silence, telling the other agents that Jimmy believed the killer had arrived.

Dinks continued, "Lightning!"

He ran to the window that looked to the beach and went on.

"Look at how bright it gets . . . everyone tells me that this thing is darkness personified, well, if we could somehow have it struck by just one bolt of lightning, it could fry his ass!"

• • • • • • • • • • • • • • • • • • •

Great idea if they had more time . . . they didn't.

Chapter 71
Fade to Black

The rain was almost blinding, it fell so hard, but Jack didn't need to see so well outside the Kassakatis home, as his killing would take place indoors. He had a plan . . . and Jimmy would suffer. Ohhhh would he ever. Jack was wary, knowing full well that they could be expecting him. So he came from the south side of the home, as he had before, with a thick wooded area to hide him on this stormy night. He was not walking through the woods as his human form might, but rather as The Shadow That Speaks, a pitch form, as if a thousand long and thick black ribbons were released collectively into the wind around a darkened center. He moved with grace and speed, and came to rest just twenty feet or so into the woods, and just another fifteen to the bedroom window.

Jack noticed that security lights were much brighter, and could see that the lights of the home were on as well. Someone was home . . . and he just knew that special someone was inside. He could snuff the lights out with ease, but that would give him away. However, they would make him easier to spot, so he once again used the trees to his advantage and crept to the top of one, then moved about the treetops as the rain crashed down. If a photographer had been in position to take a shot at just the right moment, and from just the right angle, the split second that the lightning flashed as The Shadow eased upon high would have been unforgettable, and an image that only those about to die had seen.

Jack positioned himself on the tree nearest to the home and floated down above the lights, to land silently on the roof. He then moved to the small deck to the east and right atop a well-hidden Agent Faust.

The sniper rifle went off far too quietly to be heard, but the guttural screams coming across Kennedy's walkie-talkie sent a terrifying shockwave through the home and scattered Kennedy and the other agents, who moved quickly with guns drawn toward Faust's position.

Kennedy yelled into the walkie-talkie for the rest of her team to come immediately and to get ambulances to the home ASAP! She had been the second agent to rush to the roof, and she moved through the garage and began to climb the stairs. The door to the small deck above stood wide open, blowing back and forth in the heavy winds, and blood poured down the stairway. Flashes of lightning afforded her a grisly sight, bearing witness as Agent Jones, who had been posted in the garage, was being mangled in midair by the night itself!

Fear struck hard, but she fired her .40 caliber Glock pistol, and the remaining body parts fell toward the earth. Kennedy rushed to the deck and saw The Shadow moving like a shredded black sail, blowing wildly toward the beach and bay beyond. She was right, he wasn't expecting the FBI.

Meanwhile, Jimmy and the others remained lodged in the living room as directed by Kennedy earlier, until they heard her gunfire and Tommy spotted The Shadow through the window, moving off toward the beach. He could barely speak at the sight of him. But he was stomped his feet and pointed, and the others rushed to see . . . barely catching a glimpse of the demon before he vanished out of sight. Agents fired their weapons at him as he disappeared over the ridge that led to the beach, but they either missed him or hit him without slowing him down.

Dee and the others hadn't noticed that Jimmy was not with them, until seeing him outside and rushing past the surprised agents. Jimmy's portable spotlight bounced hard as he ran down the path toward the beach. He threw his vest to the ground as he did, as it only slowed him down. Tommy and Alex immediately ran to catch him.

For Jimmy, this was it. The Shadow was here, and it was the moment his life seemed destined for . . . designed for. Not far behind him, four agents, including Kennedy, hustled through the downpour after him, and were immediately followed by Tommy and Alex, wearing the weighed-down vests and carrying the spotlights. Dinks, Rae and Dee remained behind, watching in fear as the scene unfolded. Agent Dorsey, a big man and nine-year veteran, remained to guard the home.

Jack was furious that his big night had been interrupted by the trap. He couldn't understand how the FBI would know he was coming, and apparently no longer considering the fool that was chasing him, a suspect. His rage became determination, for as he reached the down slope to the beach, he feigned left and circled back to the right, just out of view, and just in time, as Jimmy went hustling down the slope and moved off in the wrong direction.

Jack merged naturally into the shadows as the agents and other foolish friends soon followed Kassakatis north down the beach.

Jack was even more motivated to carry out his plan, and he circled back around toward the wooded area he had come from just minutes earlier. As the rains slowed noticeably and the storm seemed to be moving away, Jack sensed time was of the essence. So, with no time for subtleties, he crashed through Jimmy and Dee's window.

Though the big agent surprised him by getting two shots off after kicking the bedroom door open, The Shadow was far too quick and gutted him in a split second.

Rae, Dinks, and Dee were in the living room, fearing the worst. And—as if on cue—their worst fears spilled outward from the bedroom, into the hall and toward them with uncanny speed . . . right at the women who were too busy screaming to move.

Ricky Dinks reacted without thinking. Had he had time to think, he would have fled as far away as his slow-motion legs would have taken him. But within him emerged a hero, and he leapt in front of Rae, who was closest to the monster, grabbed the extra portable spotlight, hit the switch, and threw it at the onrushing abyss as it reached out. Ricky's death was so quick that he was already dead before he had time to cry out. The

Shadow dispatched his head and tossed his limp corpse to the side, knocking Rae unconscious to the floor beneath him.

Dee tried to run, to save herself and her baby . . . but The Shadow cut off her escape route, lifting her flailing off the ground. The deepest pitch enveloped her as The Shadow pulled her in close . . . to stare into the eyes of his prey. Dee stopped screaming and gathered an unknown courage to stare back defiantly at The Dark Incarnate.

Jack smiled, as his plan had come to fruition . . . his target acquired . . . and he did what he does best.

Alex and Tommy had stopped following Jimmy and the agents down the beach, and instead climbed over the ridge and searched farther west toward some homes in the distance.

Jimmy had stopped running . . . something just seemed wrong. Had the coward slipped past him or was he just too fast to catch? One thing he seemed resigned to, he wasn't here. Kennedy and the other agents came upon him as he treaded along the beach toward them. He explained that he saw nothing, and Kennedy immediately lifted her walkie-talkie and asked Agent Dorsey if everything was okay. Silence.

Jimmy and the agents then ran hard back toward the house. Jimmy ran as quickly as his legs could take him in the wet sand, and as he came around and up the walkway that lead from his home to the beach, he saw a great many people moving about the home and three ambulances pulling up out front. Kennedy's walkie-talkie crackled to life just then.

"Ma'am . . . he was here but has gone . . . it's not good."

His lungs were burning, but Jimmy kept right on, with the agents right behind him. He never heard the message that came across, he was too far away. Three agents outside the home had their weapons raised and yelled out for Jimmy to identify himself as he came upon the home, but he didn't hear them. Luckily Kennedy yelled back that it was okay as the professor reached the back door and moved into the home, yelling for Dee.

The house was swarming with FBI and a still-unconscious Rae was being taken away on a stretcher. A couple of agents moved to stop him as he came toward the living room. Kennedy entered right behind him, and as the agents were holding Jimmy at bay, she came to see what had happened . . . saw the pitiful sight . . . and said simply, "Let him go."

Jimmy brushed the arms off of him and moved forward.

Noooo.

The living room had become a bloodbath . . . Dee's mutilated body lay in too many pieces to count. Her head, however, was left perfectly intact, without a scratch, but for the horror permanently etched into her contorted face . . . a reminder of her last moments.

Jimmy kept looking at her . . . and it was as if his bloodshot eyes were turning to ash. He then spotted the rose that he had given to the mother-to-be . . . it lay crushed upon the floor. He bent and picked it up and then collapsed into the nearby recliner, without tears . . . without emotion. He was empty, deep into shock. The light within him faded to black. The Shadow had killed him without putting a hand on him. To say he "wallowed in anguish" was too weak a thing to say. He was a shell, a lifeless husk. Within him, The SoulBound were devastated . . . yet they had no problem screaming, weeping openly, and getting visibly upset . . .

But for Jimmy . . .

for Jimmy . . .

the world had stopped turning.

Chapter 72
Unleashed!

The light bars upon the law-enforcement vehicles showered the area in colored light as Case Agent Kennedy's angered superior—Aiden Dashiell—arrived at the Kassakatis home. A couple of ambulances had just turned their sirens on and were moving past him . . . Jimmy in one and Rae in the other. Kennedy's fateful decisions this night had been a career killer. Three more agents and two civilians were dead, including a pregnant woman. She had blown it, and as the tall man ominously ambled toward her with his trench coat flapping in the winds, it was reminiscent of the very killer she had seen up close and had been hunting for three years. Regardless . . . mentally, and emotionally, she was already clearing out her desk.

• • • • • • • • • • • • • • • • • • • •

The ambulances arrived at the local hospital within ten minutes or so. Rae, who was just coming to, and a still motionless and irresponsive Jimmy, were carted inside. Rae would be all right physically, yet the fear of those last few waking moments would take its toll. The loss of Dinks would be difficult to cope with, as he had lost his life defending hers . . . but discovering that her pregnant best friend had been literally slaughtered, would haunt her for the rest of her days.

Jimmy was being pushed down the emergency room hallway toward an examination room on the first floor. He was in shock . . . as bad as it gets. As the nurses and doctor converged on him, the SoulBound were trying to get Jimmy to say something, to respond in some way, but were having trouble focusing, as their world within Jimmy had been turned upside down. The cathedral room had vanished, and the warmth they had always known throughout their stay within Jimmy had begun to change . . . with the cold and dark "wind" becoming more prominent, stronger as the night wore on. It was as if a tempest was rising within him . . . a far stronger force than the dark fragment that had occupied him just the day before.

Jimmy *was* in shock, but not catatonic, not quite as dead inside as he seemed. Deep within, he began to regain his strength, regain his senses and focus . . . and as the "lights came on," his primal instincts took over. His body reacted, as his legs and arms began to twitch, and he began to utter guttural noises . . . ones emitted from the animal in all men.

The nurses and the doctor, who had finished looking him over seconds before, tried to calm him down to no avail, as his twitching became powerful flailing. He was quickly overcome and fastened down with the thick leather straps that were used for these situations. His eyes had not opened as yet, but his veins were bulging as he exerted a great amount of energy fighting his bonds.

The doctor moved to calm him medicinally, preparing the needle in a hurry. But then it happened. Jimmy wasn't strong enough, but somehow he tapped into the source he usually did when he needed it . . . his SoulBound. Jimmy relaxed completely, breathed deeply one time, opened his scarred eyes and . . . in one cataclysmic full-bodied motion, broke free of the leather straps holding him, sending the doctor and nurses scattering to the floor from the impact.

He flipped the still-shaking bed on its side and stood shirtless, as it had been cut from him moments earlier. His anguish had built to impossible levels, his ravaging thirst for revenge encased him, and as the scene settled, and with all eyes upon him, he unleashed an epic scream. It shattered the glass windows in the room, spilling the shards outward to the parking lot outside. Never has anyone screamed as intensely, for none had faced the horrors he had, nor had the collective power of twelve souls to back them. Ahhh, but Jimmy did. The sound resonated throughout the hospital and outside it as well.

When a mind and soul are pushed beyond their human limitations, that person breaks . . . and Jimmy was no exception. He couldn't hear the now-weakened SoulBound, nor the hospital staff, as he rushed through the broken first-floor window to the ground outside.

Marie and the other souls were facing a proverbial nightmare as Jimmy not only was not responding to them, but also had somehow used their combined spirits to physically summon the strength of twelve people. He had never tried anything like this before, and they had felt violated by his unforeseen gambit. They were shocked by what happened, each wondering . . . How did he do that? Will he try it again? Will he return to his normal self? They had no answers, just more questions as they watched in vain—this meltdown of a once-beautiful man.

The Shadow asked for it . . . this awakening of the beast. And Jimmy would come for him . . .

untamed . . .

    unforgiving . . .

        unleashed!

Chapter 73
Leap of Faith

Tommy and Alex, who had both been detained answering Supervisor Dashiell's questions, arrived at the hospital just as Jimmy was running through the parking lot. Neither spotted him at that moment. Alex let Tommy out of the car at the ER entrance so that Tommy could get in more quickly to see his sister, while Alex proceeded to look for a parking spot. Tommy rushed inside, but Alex caught sight of his crazed brother. For everyone, on a night none would ever forget, the insanity seemed never ending.

He sped up to chase Jimmy, who was headed out toward the main road, shirtless, on foot, and running at a high rate of speed. Alex beeped the horn repeatedly, and after powering down his windows, he began yelling excitedly at Jimmy. The stop sign that led out to the main road was approaching fast and Alex had no choice but to slow down and stop. Unexpectedly, Jimmy also came to a stop and cocked his head to the left at Alex. Alex put the car in park, left it running, and leapt from the vehicle to approach his obviously distraught big bro. There was enough light to see him by in the area, but not well enough to see the dark tint in Jimmy's eyes.

As Alex was telling him everything was okay, Jimmy looked upon the man with the wheels as an opportunity. As Alex walked cautiously up to him, Jimmy grabbed him with tremendous force and lifted him high off the ground.

Marie, along with the other SoulBound, screamed at Jimmy as loudly as they could.

"Jimmy, nooooooo!!!" . . . *"Jimmy, that's your brother, Alex!"*

Alex then said something that was barely a whisper. "I loved her too, Jimmy."

Somewhere in the torn psyche of the professor, it registered, and he put Alex back onto the ground, virtually unharmed. Then, two hospital security vehicles rushed toward them. Jimmy moved quickly to Alex's car, jumped inside, and sped off into the night.

Alex was stunned, despite the madness in Jimmy's actions, he knew that if someone had killed his wife and child, he would've lost it as well. Security arrived then and asked him if he was all right, and he said he was fine. They then asked Alex to give them the make and model of the stolen vehicle so that the police could be informed . . . but Alex, in a moment that defined who he was, calmly told them lies. This was Jimmy's fight, right or wrong, and he'd get his chance at vengeance.

The SoulBound tried everything to get Jimmy's attention as he headed north along the highway, but he wasn't listening. And the world that they "lived" in within Jimmy had settled into a swirling deep, gray void. Dreams became nightmares. All they could do was watch. Jimmy drew upon the brief connections with The Shadow and just knew which direction to go to get at the bastard. He kept his speed normal, so as not to draw attention to himself. He needed to get to The Shadow, he needed to end him . . . it was all that mattered.

The nondescript home rested at the end of a small, but lengthy dead-end road. It resided in an area that was mere minutes from where Carrie Ann disappeared after school and was surrounded on three sides by a copse of thick trees . . . and no neighbors within 200 feet. There were many areas in and around Baltimore that made you feel as if you were way out in the country, when in fact you were on the edge of a bustling big city. There was charm in that, in many respects, but this home held no such charm, only darkness, only misery.

Jimmy parked the car right out in front of the home, got out, and amid the white noise that he heard inside him, ran forward toward the front door and kicked it in, splintering the door and sending it flying inside. Jimmy was seething and yelled out, "You wanted me . . . come get me!"

The house was nearly pitch-black, as the dead-end street had no streetlights. Jimmy couldn't see a thing, but Jack was in his element. He needed to end this quickly, as Jimmy's yelling could draw attention . . . and Jack wanted no visitors.

He slithered along the floor of his home, crawling toward the man that had sought to end him . . . and as dark as Jack's home was, The Shadow That Speaks was darker. Jimmy was not only tapping into the physical power of the SoulBound, but he also was unconsciously taking memories, skills, training . . . every ability they had ever had, and the SoulBound went "unconscious." For they all, twelve lives intertwined by fate, had became one.

Jimmy was shaken to the core by the events unfolding, as the dark side of his mind and soul took charge, and this made the takeover by the fragment look pathetic in comparison. He felt things no human being in recorded history had ever felt, nor ever would. His awareness was myriad. Jimmy went too far, he was not superhuman, his mind was not able to do what he commanded . . . the overload would kill him if he didn't let go.

The mind has many secrets, but self-preservation is at the core of it. It took over, and Jimmy fell to the ground just as The Shadow rose to strike, and the professor drifted into unconsciousness.

Jimmy awakened hours later with the sunrise, although in the dank and dark basement of the Hill home, he had no idea what time it was. He was exhausted, but slowly began to remember his actions of the night before and began to realize where he was and why. He then felt a strong sense of trepidation come over him, and it wasn't the steel cuffs and chains that bound him, but rather the SoulBound. Jimmy, knowing his time was short, called out to them, going within himself as he had so many times before. The deep gray and ill wind that blew had vanished, and everything seemed normal.

The SoulBound had huddled together as Jimmy found them, back in the reformed cathedral room . . . staring at him with great concern. He was devastated, overwhelmed with grief,

for Dee and the baby . . .

for what he had done,
> for what he became.

Marie and the others walked quietly to him, moving to hold him and comfort him. They forgave him, for they knew him, and needed him to become whole again. They all gathered around him, with Carrie Ann snuggling up close to whisper in his ear . . .

"Nan told me to tell you . . . The time draws near Souldier . . . trust in The Light . . ."

Jack had returned from stashing Alex's car far away from his home and had worked to repair the front door enough to get through the day. He turned a small lamp on in the corner, giving off enough light for Jimmy to see him fairly well. Jack introduced himself arrogantly, after punching Jimmy right in the face.

"Jack Hill. You know, you fascinate me, Jimmy . . . I mean a man like you is, well, kind of like me . . . a freak. So, while I'd love to get to spend my day torturing you in the worst ways, I'm too close to finishing my mission . . . just 123 more to 666 and then, well, I may just start all over again."

As the madman went on, Jimmy held Carrie Ann in his arms and held her tightly, and whispered back to her, *"I'm so proud of you . . . Thank you, and tell Nan I love her."*

He then stood up within himself and stepped away from these warm spirits, these close friends, and told them all he loved them, and would see them all soon . . . and to not be afraid. He then waved good-bye and said before vanishing, *"There's no time for questions . . . trust me . . . go into the light."*

Jimmy opened his eyes wide to look upon Jack as the killer continued.

"I always kill as The Shadow That Speaks . . . you know . . . like with Dee . . ."

Jimmy did not grow angry, but was preparing himself for what was coming, and Jack finished up.

"But for you . . . you're special, you get just Jack . . . no demonic entity, no dark embrace, just my hands around your throat, enjoying every horrific moment as you die!"

Jack wrapped his hands to encircle Jimmy's windpipe and squeezed, as he did when he killed Carrie Ann . . . but these were hands, not dark clawed tentacles. Jack smiled as Jimmy struggled beneath him . . . Jimmy's eyes were bulging, as he had no air and the world about him dimmed.

Jack venomously uttered into Jimmy's ear, "May Mother Dark embrace your soul!"

Marie and the others were screaming for Jimmy to use them again, offering their will to be taken again in an effort to save their hero, their friend. But he would not do that again, and his body began to quiver uncontrollably as he withered away. Amidst the innumerable thoughts and emotions that raged within him, Jimmy stayed as focused as he could . . . he had to believe that The Light would lead him. He had to trust . . . believe . . . take this leap of faith.

Then, in an extraordinary and fleeting moment, every memory of his life and the lives of the SoulBound crashed into him at once . . . all the pain, all the laughter, all the tears, all the love . . . every beautiful thing they had ever seen . . . an explosion of life! His eyes shone brilliant, and then it was over . . . Jimmy Kassakatis . . . was dead.

Within moments, the lamp's bulb shattered and the basement grew as dark as Jack's soul. Jack stood and watched in awe, as one by one, flashes of misty light rose out of Jimmy's corpse, blinding him in their ascent . . . disappearing into the ceiling . . . then nothing.

All grew quiet as Jack contemplated what had happened, and then suddenly, there was one final sensational surge of radiance that didn't rise like the others, but rather seemed to collide with him. Into him.

What the hell? he thought, and laughed a bit as he did. He didn't laugh for long . . .

Chapter 74
The End

Suspended indefinitely pending a review, Carol Kennedy was walking out the front of the FBI building toward her SUV, parked along the curb with the back opened. She carried the last of the boxes from her office. The review was just a formality . . . her career was over. Agent Goldring had arrived an hour prior; the white knight of New York, come to save them. Nothing could change that now . . . or so she thought.

The man who approached her as she took a few steps from the door toward her SUV had an odd look about him. Her instincts had her gently putting her hand where her gun would have normally been . . . but on suspension, she had been relieved of it earlier. She backed up a step toward the building entrance as he continued to walk quickly. Was she imagining things? He wasn't an agent, and something in the look of him just sunk her soul. He moved straight to her as she lay the box down and moved back into the building, the man coming even quicker as she did.

The guards on duty could see there was a problem and drew their weapons as the man rushed through the entrance with a gun pointed to his own head and stood eyes wild and focused on Kennedy.

The guards were yelling at the man to drop his weapon, but he remained focused on her and said loudly, "Agent Kennedy, the time for running has ended . . . I've come to give myself up."

The look on her face was one for the ages . . .

Was this him? Is this happening?

He continued, as more agents rushed to the scene, their weapons trained on the demented soul.

"My name is Tyler Hill, but I go by Jack. Jack Hill." He said it in the way to tell her he was the Jackal.

"In my back pocket, you'll find my wallet and ID, and inside my home, you'll find all the evidence you'll need . . . including a freshly killed Jimmy Kassakatis."

Everyone was stunned as he went on.

"Yessss . . . I'm The Shadow That Speaks."

He flashed the billowing dark form of The Shadow, a foul and ghastly visage . . . his eyes first, then remaining body and otherworldly extensions became pitch. Then as quickly as it had begun, he reined it in.

Kennedy and the others were too shocked to speak . . . the guards' hands shook as they held their weapons on him.

Jack then lowered his voice, shifted the gun even tighter against his head, and said directly to Carol Kennedy, "For all those lives I've destroyed . . . and those who sacrificed it all to stop me . . ."

He winked at her, and then lifted his eyes heavenward, and as he pulled the trigger, Jimmy, yes *Jimmy*—SoulBound with, and in control of, a desperate Jack Hill—spoke their final words,

"Dee . . . I'm coming home."

The End

LaVergne, TN USA
20 January 2010
170657LV00004B/58/P